HIM

OTHER WORKS BY ERNIE LEE

PROFESSIONAL TEXTS AND WORKBOOKS

Contracting for Control and Disposal of Hazardous Materials, 1993, Southwest Logistics Institute (out of print)

Public Procurement Professions, 6 vol. Published by: University of Texas, Extended Learning program, 1997, 1998 (reprint) (out of print)

Risk Management for Buyers e-Group & Associates, Extended Learning program, Training Module, 2012 (reprint) (out of print)

Analysis Techniques for Buyers, e-Group & Associates, Extended Learning program, Training Module, 2013 (reprint) (out of print)

Economics for Buyers, e-Group & Associates, Extended Learning program, Training Module, 2013 (reprint) (out of print)

The Ring of Gyges, Ethics When No One is Watching, e-Group & Associates, Extended Learning program, Training Module, 2013 (reprint) (out of print)

NOVELS

AQUASAURUS, Aim-Hi Publishing
Canyon Lake, Texas 2016 ISBN; 978-0-9971284-0-6
Canyon Lake, Texas 2016 ISBN; 978-0-9971284-2-0
Canyon Lake, Texas 2016 ISBN; 978-0-9971284-1-3

Poetry

Where the Wild Rice Grows, Aim-Hi Publishing Canyon Lake, Texas 2017   ISBN: 978-0-9971284-3-7

HIM

by

ERNIE LEE

AIM-HI PUBLISHING

© 2016, Ernie Lee

Aim-Hi Publishing
1542 Lakeside Dr. West
Canyon Lake, Texas 78133

Publisher's Catalog-in-Publication Data
Names: Lee, Ernest (Ernie), 1946 - ; cover photograph by Donna Lee: design by Ivan Cakić Cacamura and Vesna Tisma, Cacamura Art Studio, Belgrade, Serbia
Title: HIM / by Ernie Lee
Description: Aim-Hi Publishing LLC, 2017. | Summary: In 1885, a serial killer known as the Servant Girl Annihilator skulked the streets of Austin, Texas. One of the suspects was a Malay cook who went by the name of Maurice. Three years later, the Jack the Ripper murders began. One of the suspects in those murders was a Malay cook named Maurice. This is a fictionalized account of Maurice's story.
Identifiers:
Library of Congress Control Number: **2017912002**

ISBN: 978-0-9971284-5-1 (Mass Market paperback)
Subjects: Serial murder – Historical Fiction. | Jack the Ripper – Historical Fiction. | Servant Girl Annihilator – Historical Fiction | Texas – History

For my brothers,

TROY W. HENSON
SCOTT LEE

Acknowledgements:

There is much more to writing a book than a good story, and putting sentences and paragraphs down on paper. This book is the product of several people who helped me put it together in a readable form. I would especially like to thank the following:

Susan Eisenbrey and Maria Elena Alvarado, who suffered through extremely rough concept ideas and drafts for this story, **Billy James Wall**, who gave me encouragement to finish this story and taught me how to use a hard return.

Robert Carpenter and the inmates of the James Crabtree Correctional MSU, who read the first rushes,

Carrie Fredericks, who proofed and gave valuable feedback on middle drafts.   Finally,

especially to **Sandra Gayle Young**, without whose editing, encouragement and support this volume would have many, <u>many</u> more commas.

Without all of your help, support, and assistance, I could not have completed this book. My heartfelt thanks to each of you.

WRIT**ING** **IS GIV**ING   The author's goal is to give away <u>2,016</u> copies of *the novel AQUASAURUS* to **Cancer Fighters**. If you or someone you know is currently fighting cancer, or has survived a cancer fight, please go to <u>www.Aim-HiBooks.com</u> and sign up on the website. Then send a personal message to Ernie Lee (contact button at top of webpage) with the <u>name, details, type of device (e-Pub, Kindle, .pdf, or other) and contact information of your nominee</u>. A copy of the award winning novel AQUASAURUS will be provided to the nominee in your name, free of charge. For details on the number of books distributed to date, please check the **Writing+is+Giving** page on the website. Your purchase of a book on Amazon, Barnes & Noble, or your favorite outlet helps pay for this campaign.

HIM

He is with me always, even from the beginning. He is with me yet. I am not sure when I first became aware of him, but it was long ago when I was still a boy.

I was born in the small fishing village of Kadan Kyun on King's Island across the channel from Mergui on the archipelago in Burma. I am called Maurice. You will forgive me if I use only that name. You will understand why by and by. I am Moken, although people who do not know better say I am Malay. The Burmese of my homeland call my people Selung or Selone. After I traveled a bit, I grew tired of correcting people and simply identified myself as Malay. For some reason it seems to satisfy most people. I have far fewer questions now. I do not like questions. Maybe what offends me most are the answers.

I was born on the island sometime around or just before 1865. My people are sea gypsies. They traditionally roam from place to place, without a true homeland. We speak a common language but I have not used it for so long I can no longer remember. My father grew rich in the spice trade, and settled on King's Island before I was born. His wealth afforded me all of the luxuries of life. I was an only child. My parents were loving, but they were busy business, which allowed me much freedom to roam. I spent my early years running free on my island and exploring the area around my home including the heavily jungled forest. When I was old enough for school, my parents hired a teacher – an Englishwoman who taught me English, reading, and basic arithmetic. It has been so long since I spoke my native tongue; I converse, think, and dream in the English language. I have a British accent, which amazes most people. A brown man with an English accent is a novelty in some places it seems.

At the age of ten, the local authorities despite my background and race allowed me to attend their local school. I am sure my father's money prompted the decision. It was around then I first met … "him." Perhaps I have not used the right expression; it was then I first became aware of him.

This is the story of myself – and of him; of how we met and became close; and how I took care of him all these years. It is a tale of how he became obsessed with me, and how I tried to get away from him so many times. A story of how he always wedged his way back into my life somehow, and how I protected him when I believed he was innocent. Mostly, it is the reason I sit tonight in a darkened room, waiting for … him to come home, so I can kill him in cold blood.

As a boy, I had a certain place in the forest where I liked to sit and dream. It was a peaceful place, shady and well enough out of the way that I could play undisturbed.

I practiced my English on the trees, pretending them to be various people I knew. I would make speeches to them. They never taunted, or corrected, or made me write the same sentence fifty times. They were perfectly happy with anything I said, and their often applauded my witty offerings with their leaves.

My father hired a teacher for me named Mrs. Prichard. I liked her very much. She was a prim and proper Englishwoman who taught me many things. Often, she could be so condescending and critical. My English was actually good despite how little formal schooling I had. Mrs. Prichard gave me a distinct English accent. I never noticed it at all. To me I did not sound any different from everyone else. After three years with Mrs. Prichard, I rarely spoke in my native tongue. Having few interactions with anyone other than my family, I gradually learned to speak mainly in English. My father made sure all of the books in our home library were in English. If any others lined the shelves, I never saw them. My parents insisted on speaking English to me but sometimes late at night, when the house was quiet, I could hear them conversing in Moken. Few people speak Moken these days, and I barely recall it at all.

On one certain day, alone in my place in the forest, my mind was troubled. The coming Monday I was to report to the English School in the village. My parents, with Mrs. Prichard's blessings, made the arrangements. I was ten years old and Mrs. Prichard taught me all she could. She assured everyone I would be able to keep up with the other students. As for Mrs. Prichard, she planned to return home to England. She was finished with King's Island, she said. I would miss her terribly, which increased my nervousness about going off to a real school.

On several previous days, after coming to my spot in the forest, I sensed someone was watching me. The first few times it happened I quickly gathered my things and returned to the safety of our compound. I feared a tiger might be stalking me. However, after a while, I grew my courage, since I never saw a tiger anywhere near my home. Yet the feeling persisted, and I felt something, or someone, watched me. I was sure of it.

On this particular day I mentioned, our cook, a kindly man named David, taught me to cook one of Mrs. Prichard's favorite meals – a stuffed pita bread. She loved the little pockets filled with ground meat and spices. Mrs. Prichard was to leave on the train the next morning, so David prepared this special dinner. He even made a little extra to carry with her on the trip. The meal would not be served until seven, so in the afternoon, I took some of the freshly baked pita bread with me to the forest.

As I said, I was troubled over what would happen to me with Mrs. Prichard gone. I would be going to a new and unfamiliar school. As was my habit, I placed my bread on a nearby rock and taught the trees to speak English.

In the middle of conjugating the verb "was", I thought I heard a twig snap. I looked around to discover my bread missing! Something had taken it! I walked toward the rock as something loudly crashed through the lush forest beyond my sight. I believed I saw the figure of a boy running. He looked near my size, but before I got a good look, he disappeared.

Since he ran from me, I reasoned this native boy was no threat. He probably feared me more than I feared the tigers. Thereafter, whenever I taught my wooden class in the glade, I always carried something for him. Gradually, he became bolder; I occasionally got a peek at him. Sometimes he seemed to be waiting for my arrival. He became more comfortable in my presence and soon stopped running away each time I looked or moved in his direction. After a few weeks, he would sit and listen to me instruct the trees.

One day, after several months, I decided to take a chance and speak to him directly. I had never spoken directly to him before, and I was sure he was ignorant of English. I was not sure, yet, of his race or what language he spoke. He was a grubby little skinny thing.

4

Filthy dirty. He looked as if he had never taken a bath. I judged him to be my age or younger. He was my height, but much thinner, and a much faster runner you can be sure.

So, I turned to him one day and said, with a smile on my face, and in the gentlest voice I could muster, "Hello."

"Hello."

I was astounded! Not only did he stood his ground, he spoke to me! Encouraged by the unexpected, though pleasing result, I spoke to him again. "What is your name?"

"What is your name?" he repeated with exactly the same inflection.

This was as confusing to me as it must have been to him. What kind of native boy speaks English? Did he speak English, or was he just repeating everything I said like a kind of parrot? I decided to find out. I rose from my spot, extended my hand in friendship toward him, and said,

"What is your name?"

He leapt through the jungle as rapidly as a deer. He did not go far; and once I sat on the ground again, he slowly returned. He sat and looked at me, watching my every move. Soon, he gestured toward the trees lined up in my classroom and I understood I was to resume teaching. Not knowing what else to do, I taught. Over the next few months, it became clear to me what he was doing. He was learning English. He learned much quicker than the trees, but not much. So gradually, I changed my focus from the dumb trees toward him. He was intelligent, and he soon learned rudimentary words. I often left my English book in the forest for him to use in my absence.

School was a disaster for me. Having lived among adults all of my life, I had no idea how to relate to my classmates. In addition, being of a race different from their own, I did not feel completely accepted by them in many ways. Whenever I was included in their games, they always chose me last, and reluctantly. Someone had to

5

take me. I was taken, rather than chosen. They rarely spoke to me or addressed me directly. The teacher seemed fair enough and gave me ample attention and instruction. However, it was plain I read and spoke at a much higher level than most. Through jealousy or because of my race, I was alone, even among my classmates. So having someone like the strange boy in the forest excited and encouraged me. I longed to teach him enough English so we could converse. But sadly, after several months, he had not formed a single thought of his own; or if he did, he did not express it. He simply repeated everything I said. I was beginning to get bored with him; but since I was so needful of a friend and confidant, I kept going back to the forest to see him. I was not going to surrender my favorite spot to him. A dumb friend was better than no friend was at all.

One day, I taught him and the trees the difference between lie and lay. "You lay a book down. You lie on a bed."

"You lie," he repeated.

"Yes. You lie on a bed," I wearily assured him.

"No. You lie," he retorted in an accusing tone.

I was confused. Why did he say "no"? Was he calling me a liar? I looked at him blankly.

He spoke in halting, unsure words. "You ..." pointing at me, "... said ... before today ... lie ... was ... not true."

I realized his confusion. I explained the word "lie" had different uses. "Lie" could mean to recline or lie could mean to tell a falsehood. He nodded his head as if he understood. I congratulated him on paying attention. Suddenly, I realized we were conversing. He actually formed a thought and expressed it to me. I was overjoyed but still too cautious to leap for joy or to approach him directly, for fear he would run off again. It was a good sign finally.

Still, it was many months before we could conduct a normal conversation. By then he trusted me not to harm him, and he allowed me to get closer and closer. He was a quick learner. However, he stank to high heaven!

One day, I brought a bar of soap and motioned him to follow me. I took him to a green, shady pool nearby. I stripped off my clothes and entered the water. He crouched on the rocky shore and would not enter no matter how hard I coaxd. He watched as I rubbed soap all over my body and saw how the soap bubbles floated on the water. He stared at those little bubbles intently. It was clear he wanted to touch them. He reached out one skinny leg and felt the water, but he would go no further. We made bathing a daily ritual for the next few weeks until one day he simply stood and walked into the water with me. I handed him the soap, which he happily rubbed on his body. Oh, how he loved those little bubbles, chasing them around the pool and trying to hold them in his hand, pouting as they disappeared. From then on, we bathed together often.

And, so it went, from month to month, as time passed into years. I knew nothing about him other than he was always around. He was always willing to sit and listen to me talk about my life, and my hardships at school, and all of the things I endured each day. He progressed from simple sentences to the point where we could converse together quite well. He did not have the use of English as I had, but he could make himself understood, and I knew he understood me perfectly. If I asked him anything personal about his life, he would always change the subject. His favorite pretense was to act as though he noticed something new and needed me to give him the English noun.

After five years in the English school, my relationship with my classmates only slightly improved. I was still last in everything. I still had not formed any close relationships. Although I was accepted, I still did not feel I belonged. I felt … tolerated. It did not help that the teacher singled me out for excellence on occasion.

I noticed whenever someone did an unkindness to me, something unpleasant would often happen to them soon after. I thought it was karma, which I understood to be a sort of justice; the way the world balanced itself naturally. Once, someone pushed me down the steps, and badly bruised my knee. I am not sure if it was intentional, negligence, or simply a boy's eagerness to get past me. Three days later, the same boy fell from those same steps and broke his leg. He claimed someone pushed him; he did not know who had. Another time, a boy struck me accidentally with a cricket bat while playing. Several days later, the schoolmaster found boy who hit me beaten nearly senseless. The schoolmaster found a fragment of a broken cricket bat near him. He did not see his attacker.

These coincidences happened more frequently and became predictable. Soon, word spread that bad things happened to those who molest me, even accidentally. Although I was completely innocent of wrongdoing, nearly everyone thought I was vengeful and vindictive. I became even more of an outcast to my classmates.

On the day they found the boy who was beaten, I was not at school. I was relieved no one could accused me of the attack on the boy. Later in the day, I was in the forest with him – my forest friend. As I recited a poem from Longfellow, he tapped on a rock, keeping time to the rhythm of the poem. I looked at the stick he used, and I was shocked. I stopped reciting, as I could not take my eyes from it. It was the broken handle of a cricket bat.

As the years passed, his command of English grew; and he came to trust me a little more as time went by. We had many meaningful conversations over the years. I told him of my life and he marveled at my lifestyle, which was so different from his own in nearly every way. My parents were rarely around, having to earn a living to maintain our standing. When they were present, they were doting, loving parents. They lavished gifts upon me, and I never knew hunger or want. There was a steady stream of house servants to protect and nurture me. I went to school and became educated. While my schoolmates were still standoffish and distant toward me, my teachers delighted in my ability to learn and express myself. Though successful in school, I had no friends but him.

His life was much different from mine. His mother and father were cruel and uncaring. He fended entirely for himself. When they were around, they would beat and punish him for the most trivial offenses. He learned to stay out of their way, which they preferred. His father was a fisherman and was gone for days at a time. His mother was a drunk and earned her drinking money by working at a local tavern. The rumor was that drinks were not the only thing she served. When his father came home from the sea, the pair would disappear into a drunken cloud for a week. If either of them noticed him, they would beat him for something. Anything. For being. Then, when the money ran out and the liquor was gone, his father would blow out to sea again. It was a pattern repeated often. I saw the scars and bruises myself each time we bathed, but he rarely would tell me any details.

Most nights, he slept in the jungle. He showed me where once. It was a sort of hutch where he stayed. It was made of leaves and vines over a dirt floor. There was a reed mat, like a nest inside where he slept. There were bits and pieces of broken candles he collected from discarded trash and melted down into bowls of wax, which he burned for heat and light. He seemed proud of the spot, claiming that it was much better than the house where he lived. Since no one knew where his camp was, except for me, he felt safe there. To me, it seemed hideous and filthy. I could not imagine having to live that way. I pitied him and his circumstances. His life was my first knowledge of how mean and cruel life can be for some. I felt guilty that I had everything and he had nothing – nothing worth having.

After he showed me the hut where he lived, he opened up to me a little more. Finally, he confided to me that his name was Mawken. This I took as a joke or another dodge of his since surely he was aware that I knew this was what our people called ourselves. He may as well have told me his name was Selung for all the good it did me. It would be like saying 'My name is American,' or 'My name is British'.

He made me promise that I would never use his name with others. Of course, I wanted to know why. He told me his father recently sold him to a ship captain who would take him away as his slave. He was afraid that if I spoke his name in public, bounty hunters would follow me. I might unintentionally lead them to him. I asked what I was to call him.

"What do you call me now?" he asked suspiciously.

"He, or him," I responded. He decided that those designations would suffice, but he would rather I never spoke of him at all to anyone else, under any circumstances.

I believed his story that he was in great danger, so I agreed. He made me promise. From that time on, when speaking to others, I made a habit not to mention him at all if it were possible.

He was incredibly secretive, and sometimes I had trouble believing some of his stories. Of course, nothing in my protected and privileged life could to relate to them. He told me that he had older brothers and sisters who disappeared and were never seen or heard from again. He told me a story that haunted me for years. I can actually see it in my dreams some nights as if I were there; it haunts me still. One dark night, he said, while scavenging for food in an alley, a tavern door flew open and a woman flew headlong into the dirt and filth. She was haggard, and her hair hung down covering her face. Her clothes were dirty and ripped, and her breasts were partially exposed. She pulled herself to her hands and knees and raised her head, pulling stringy hair away from her face. He immediately recognized her as his sister. She looked at Mawken with terror in her eyes and cried out.

"Run! Run away! Don't let them catch you!"

She was about to say more when the door flew open again, and a rough man grabbed her by a foot and dragged her, screaming, back inside the dark room. The door slammed behind them. He ran as far and as long as he could, until he collapsed in the jungle from fatigue.

I could not imagine that sort of life. I know better now, having lived the life I have these past few years. I have seen tragedy and meanness as I traveled from place to place, but these stories and others he related to me over the years were more horrible than anything I ever experienced in my own life up until that time. I could not understand why people should suffer such mistreatment. I did not know, at the time, that I would see much more suffering and pain before it was over. So very much more.

In those days, though, I was still naive and ignorant about the abuse some people tolerate daily. At night, alone in my room, I would often think of Mawken sleeping out in the dark jungle. I imagined him jumping at every sound in the night, not knowing if it were some animal about to attack or if someone were coming to claim the bounty. Anyone could easily overcome him and tie his hands and feet. I imagined they would throw him roughly into the back of a wagon and haul him away into the darkness. I shuddered to think of what would become of Mawken if they captured him and bound him into slavery. I imagined it would be horrible, but little did I know how horrible it would have been. At my tender age, protected as I was, I had no idea such worlds existed. I had no concept of the depths of human cruelty. I was soon to learn otherwise.

Once during the rainy season, a particularly bad storm battered our island for three days and nights. The wind howled, and the cold rain blew against my partially opened window. The breeze from my window made my lamp flicker and dance, casting eerie shadows on the walls of my room. Beneath the eaves, the wind sang a siren's song – eerie and forlorn. I lay tucked neatly in my bed. The lightning flickered, causing the ghostly shadows on the wall to take hideous shapes. The thunder boomed from far away. It awakened me from a deep sleep. I had been reading before I slept, as was my habit, and I drifted off without blowing the lamp out.

The wind had shifted, causing the rain to come in through the window, wetting the floor. I crossed the room to close the window. The dark shadows cavorted and twisted in the dim light and disappeared in the sudden bright flashes of lightning.

I could see my reflection in the glass pane of the window as I reached out to pull it closed. I looked at my reflection, growing larger as I neared the window when suddenly it changed into another face – Mawken! I quickly jumped back in total fright and horror. I tripped on my sleeping shirt and tumbled backward, hitting my head against the end of the bed, and nearly toppling the lamp table.

Was he actually there, or was it my imagination running wild? I neared the window again, and cupped my hands to my face, the better to see outside; and there he stood. He was soaking wet in the downpour. A brief flash of lightning illuminated his face, and I gawked as water ran down his cheeks and his bare arms. He looked like a skeleton of a man with the bright streaks shining on his cheeks. His eyes receded into dark hollowed sockets with black shadows when the lightning faded. If I did not know better, I would have thought him a ghoul or a robber in the night.

Immediately, I pushed the window open and extended my arm to pull him inside. He was soaking wet and as cold as a fish. I gave him something to dry his head and offered him one of my spare sleeping shirts. He seemed thin and small, and he trembled and shivered in the wet cold.

"What are you doing out there?" I asked.

"I have no place to go. My hut blew away in the storm, and I was in the rain and cold. I did not know what else to do; so I came here, hoping I could find shelter beneath your window. I don't mean to trouble you."

"Trouble me? My good man! How could I possibly go back to sleep knowing you were huddled beneath my window on such a cold, rainy night? Here!" I tossed him a pillow and a blanket and indicated he could sleep on the floor near my bed. He thanked me profusely. When I awoke in the morning, he was gone. I suppose he left through the window.

So commenced a nightly ritual. I would retire to my bed; and he would appear, tapping at my window; and I would let him in. It happened practically every night. I even missed him on nights when, for one reason or another, he did not appear. After several months of this arrangement, the weather took another turn for the worse; and our island received a rare cold spell. I felt so sorry for Mawken, that I moved over in the bed during the night and threw back the covers. I allowed him to get into the bed with me. The pattern would repeat itself over the course of my life. I unknowingly set a precedence that would become difficult to break, even when we became grown men. Only, I did not know it then.

When I turned seventeen, I was nearing the end of my formal schooling. In preparation for being on my own, I discussed with my father the possibility of opening an office in another port. My father booked cargo on ships leaving our ports toward the western lands. He dealt mostly in spices and silks. He was continually having difficulty with lost or misrouted goods at various ports where the ships docked and discharged cargo. The worst port of all losses was Yangon, which the British called Rangoon.

I devised a plan to open an office there to supervise the off-loading of our goods for transfer to larger, more reliable ships that would deliver them farther west. Many of the local freighters were not adequately equipped to round the cape of Africa. My father could not depend upon accurate recordkeeping as the goods moved to different ships. He repeatedly traveled to Rangoon to investigate losses. This put the burden of operating the local office on my mother, who was not happy with his absences and with having to operate the business on her own. Putting me in Rangoon would be a perfect solution to the problem. I was looking forward to the new adventure and to finally being on my own in the world.

By this time, I had grown tired and bored with Mawken. It would be a burden off my back to be away from him finally. He was not easy to befriend. He was continually in an unpleasant mood, and he seemed to like no one in the world except for me. He continually found fault with me, telling me I was naive and too trusting of others. He felt that I let my parents direct my life too much and that I listened to them too much. He wanted me to leave, to run away and strike out on my own without any prospects or any assistance from anyone.

There was nothing from which to run away. My life was not like his. His idea was for us to go out together into the world and find our own way – to make our own fortune. Oh, the tales he would spin of the great fortunes we would make and the adventures we would have. I did not have the heart to tell the poor fellow that dragging him along with me was the last thing I intended to do.

I did not tell Mawken of the plans I made with my father, nor did I intend for him to accompany me when I left. We would make a clean break. I had helped Mawken all I could in this life; and when our paths crossed again in the future, if they ever did, we would greet each other as long separated and fond friends.

In the late summer of 1883, my father and I traveled to Rangoon to search for a likely new office. I told Mawken only that my father wanted me to assist with some problem there. I was afraid to even to hint that I might eventually be moving to Rangoon permanently. I preferred to save that revelation for a later time once irrevocable and unchangeable plans were in place. I was not sure how I would tell him or what his reaction might be. I briefly considered misdirecting him by telling him that I was relocating to Singapore. However, I decided that would be unnecessary; he had no more means to get to Rangoon greater than to get to Singapore. He was a penniless little beggar. Besides, he might figure out that Singapore was east, ahead of our ownership of the goods, and he might discover my deceit. However, I dreaded the parting and I hoped that he would understand. After all, what choice would he have? I was moving, and that would be that.

My relationship with my father grew closer during our trip, and I believe he was proud of me. I felt I gained his full confidence at last. I was happy to be alone with my father as a man. I understood his distance from me, and his preoccupation with his work. I comprehended his insight and sense of responsibility, and I was proud and honored that his labor eased my introduction into the business world. I seriously doubted that I could have built such a business on my own.

While in Rangoon, we located a suitable office on the wharf, advertised for employees, and registered the business with the government and the port master. We returned home with the expectation that I would return to Rangoon in the new year to open the office. I planned to go alone.

By the time the winds shifted from the south, announcing the end of the monsoons, I was preparing to leave. I had postponed the one final preparation until now. How was I going to tell Mawken? He made himself scarce for most of the winter, only coming to my window when the weather was particularly cold or wet. I thought that maybe he found lodging somewhere else. I fervently hoped he had grown weary of trying to convince me to run off, and was making plans to leave on his own. He did not show up in the glade or at my window for a week. I thought he was gone finally. However, one midnight in the middle of a storm, he came again to my window. Of course, I let the poor thing inside to share my bed, warmth, and comfort. Was I ever going to be free of him?

A few days later, I left a note for Mawken in our glade shortly before my scheduled departure. The note said that I needed to see him, and I set out a date and time.

I intended to break it off clean by telling Mawken I was leaving to live in Rangoon. I arrived in our place before him and sat looking at my former wooden students, standing just where I left them. They were aged some of course, and they were taller and thicker than I remembered them. For some reason, they did not seem as attentive as they once were. I taught them all I could. In fact, they did not seem to notice that I was even there at all. I decided not to examine their proficiency.

Suddenly, he burst into the clearing excited and out of breath. Between gasps, all he could get out was to repeat my name while trying to catch his breath. I had no idea what could have caused his great excitement. Finally, he related an amazing and unbelievable story.

Pirates invaded on our island! They came ashore on his father's fishing dock in their cove. Amid tears and confusing narrative, I understood that they had attacked his father and mother and had burned their hut to the ground. They also scuttled and sank his father's boat on the reef offshore. Both of his parents were dead! He lost everything.

I could not understand why they would do such a thing. Why bother with a poor fisherman with nothing of value except a boat, which they sank offshore? He explained to me that his father was just in the wrong place at the wrong time and that other, richer victims were their real goal. The pirates killed his parents to keep them from spreading the alarm.

He described in great length the gruesome details of their murders. The pirates nearly beheaded them with an ax and laid their entrails out on the rocks in the sun as a warning to those who might interfere with their plans. I knew the pirates of the South Seas were brutal and merciless. There was a long history of their atrocities but generally, they left us alone, as we had so little to attract their attention. Mawken told me that he only escaped because he observed the attack unseen from the edge of the forest.

When the pirates left his family dead, he followed unseen, hoping to learn what they truly wanted on the island. He said he followed them overland toward their final objective.

When he said this, he became remarkably sad and looked at me with dark liquid eyes. He paused as if he did not know how to continue the story.

Finally, he spoke, "I discovered what they wanted."

'What?"

"Word of your family's success and great wealth has spread throughout the islands, and they intended to rob your parents."

"No!" I screamed. I immediately jumped to my feet and ran back toward our compound as fast as I could run. He followed close behind, trying to stop me. I ran as hard as I could, and had I not tripped upon a vine, I would have burst headlong into our clearing. Before I could regain my feet, Mawken was upon me.

"It is too late!" He whispered roughly in my ear. "Stay here on the ground with me and watch. You will see!"

Great clouds of smoke rose from our house and outbuildings. Flames still flickered from and licked around the wooden building my father used for a warehouse. The wall around our compound was in shambles, kicked down in several places. Authorities from the village moved from place to place within our compound. There was no sign of my father or mother or any of our house servants. It seemed the pirates fled back to the sea.

"I must go!" I told him. "I have to go to my mother and father."

He kept his grip on my arm.

"Keep low and follow me," he demanded.

Under cover of the forest, we moved around the edge of the glade to the side of my house. As we neared the southern edge, I saw it! My mother's body hung from a rope affixed to the eaves of our house. It was too horrible to see; I closed my eyes. I immediately tried to regain my footing, intending to go to my mother; but he would not let me rise. He covered my mouth with his hands.

"Quiet! They will hear you!"

"What if they do?" I moaned as I flung his hand from my mouth. "Let me go! I must go to my dead mother. I must find my father!" I felt like I would vomit.

"Shut up, you fool!" He hissed. "You cannot! Your father is dead too. There is no use to go now."

I struggled to escape from his powerful grasp, but he held me down.

"You cannot go," he said. "You cannot go. It would do no good! The worst is over, and you cannot help them now. They are dead, just as my mother and father are dead. No one can help them now. You cannot show yourself. You cannot be seen."

I did not understand. "Why? Why can't I be seen? Surely I must go to claim the bodies of my dead parents!"

He looked me squarely in the eyes. I could see the great pain and concern he held for me at that moment as he tried to comfort me.

"My people were killed so that no one would know about the pirates. They have done their evil deeds and escaped back to the sea. The pirates are gone and are beyond any pursuit or capture, taking their plunder with them. I am the only one who knows that they were even on this island."

"We can tell them! They must know!"

He hooted a cold and bitter laugh. "They would not believe us. They would not understand!"

"Why? We can tell them."

"No." He sadly shook his head. "We must get away and go far from here! We must leave right away and disappear into the jungle."

"Why? Why would they not believe us?"

His dark, piercing, unreadable eyes bored deep into me. "Because they think you are the killer!"

It was beyond my understanding that someone might think I murdered my own parents. It was unbelievable to me. Yet, the more he talked, the more I believed him. It was true that no one knew the pirates landed on our island. My body was missing and not among the dead. His parents were dead and their boat was missing. It all added up. They would think we killed our parents to escape the island. I was an outlaw, a wanted murderer of my own people.

Gradually he persuaded me to move back into the forest, back to the safety of our old clearing. Once there, we planned our next move. He begged me to stay hidden in our hideout while he went around gathering supplies we would need for our escape. In my condition, it was easy to persuade me to stay. I was numb with shock. I wanted to be alone to go over everything I could remember about my beloved parents. I sat, unmoving – unfeeling, for what must have been hours before he returned.

He brought two large bags containing food and supplies. He sat before me and told me the plan. We would escape over French Bay Peak, the highest point on King's Island. On the other side of the mountain, we would come to a sheltered cove across the narrow channel from the port of Mergui. He told me his sister worked in a tavern there; she would put us up, and give us work.

Maybe I could be a cook, or work in the kitchen. Once the trouble passed, we might be able to come back to our home one day. If we returned now, he was certain they would hang us at sunrise. I believed him. As darkness fell, we walked toward the great mountain in the distance.

Despondent, and in grief, I followed along as if in a daze. It was still not real to me that my parents were dead. Surely, this was a bad dream and I would awake soon. My life and all that I had known before was gone, and I was a fugitive. It was more than I could understand. This could not be real. If I had not seen mother's poor body with my own eyes, I could not have believed it. I never had a chance to say goodbye; and now, I would never see her, or my dear father, ever again. When we stopped at daybreak, I dropped from near exhaustion.

We slept through the day; and in the early evening, he rose and fixed us some food. I had not eaten since I saw my dear mother swinging from the eaves of our home. That scene comes back to me often in my dreams and in my mind's eye. I did not seen my father's body, and so I do not have images of him in my mind.

I took my food he gave me and placed it aside. I was not hungry. How could I eat? Mawken encouraged me to eat but all I could manage was a few sips of water. He begged me to eat and drink. He said if I did not, I would not be able to climb the mountain. If I could not travel, they would catch us and haul us back to Kadan Kyun for hanging. I managed to choke down a few bites, though it seemed it would not stay down. I felt the food lie in my stomach like a rock.

He squatted in front of me, his dark eyes piercing into mine. He was clearly concerned about me.

"Get ahold of yourself!" he demanded roughly. "If you don't, we will surely be caught!"

"I don't care!" I flung at him. "What have I to live for now? My mother and father are dead. The pirates have stolen everything of value we owned. My house is in ruins. I am alone. What do I care if I hang?"

He said slowly, "If they catch you," his voice softened, "they catch me also. We both hang."

"Why would they bother with you?"

"They will not believe you did this on your own. They will think I am your helper." He nodded his head trying to get through to me. "I will be judged harsher than you! They will think that I beguiled you and killed my own parents as well. They will hang us both!"

"But we are innocent," I protested.

"They may believe you, but they will never believe me. If we go back, or if they catch us, then I am a dead man. Even if they believe you, they will never believe me."

I knew he spoke the truth. How unfair it was. While I did not care if I lived or died, I did not want to see any harm come to my friend – my friend who had been by my side for all these years – my friend who saved me from the hangman's noose.

Surely, he must be in as much grief as I. Yet he did not show his pain. Why? I believed it was because he was more of a man than I was. Despite his kindness, his patience, and his concern, he made me feel like a sniveling child. Something inside me said that I must be a man and move on with my life. Nothing could bring my parents back to life, not even if they hanged us. Mawken worked hard to keep us alive, and it was time for me to put aside my heartache and my pain and help him. If not, we would both die.

I nodded my head as I realized our desperate situation and that of our irrevocably linked fates. I looked at him and promised that I would be able to keep up. I took a bite of the food and a sip of the water he gave me. It stayed down. I felt a little better.

As the sun went down, we resumed our trek up the mountainside. In the dark, the forest pressed in on us from all sides. The night took on a more frightening scene. Things moved in the trees and under the branches – things we could not see but could clearly hear. As we climbed higher on the mountain, the forest gradually changed. The canopy opened above us, and we could see stars. By morning, it was much cooler. So far, the weather held fair and there seemed to be no threat of storms. If a storm caught us on the mountain, I am certain we would have become hopelessly lost.

I wondered how far we traveled. We were still climbing, so I knew we had not reached the summit yet. I hoped when we did we would be able to see where we were going a little better. The sky slowly turned seashell pink, like beautiful coral. I realized we had traveled the entire night. In my grief, I was unaware of the rigors of our walk or of the passage of time.

I realized how tired I was, and I welcomed the chance to stop and sleep. I had slept only fitfully the last two days. I sank to my knees grateful for the halt. As he prepared food, I lay back on the grass gazing at the quickly fading morning stars.

"Do you suppose they formed a search party to hunt for me? I asked.

He has such a cruel laugh sometimes.

"Oh, yes! I'm sure they have! They are probably searching the forest for you right now – with rope in hand," he added menacingly.

"They must have buried my poor parents by now. And they have found your parents dead as well."

"Maybe," he agreed emotionlessly as he handed me my share of the meal.

As I ate, I could not help but wonder again of the fate that threw us into this desperate flight.

"Maybe they think I was taken or killed in the forest somewhere…"

"Listen to me!" He looked at me with hard eyes and squeezed my hand hard in his fist, "Listen to me. They think you are a killer! They think we killed our parents and escaped by sea in my father's boat. I told you they scuttled his boat off the reef. They are looking for us even now – as escaped killers. You must understand this. You must stop seeing yourself as a victim they will try to rescue. You are a criminal they will try to arrest, Maurice."

"I know," I admitted. "I was just hoping for a better outcome –for a way out of this … nightmare…" my voice trailed off into the cool breezes flowing down the mountainside in the growing dawn. The sounds of the forest awakening to the new day surrounded us.

"You are a dreamer!" he accused me. "There is no better outcome for us except escape."

There was a sudden loud barking in the trees just beyond our camp. I immediately jumped and hid behind a large tree. I thought the dogs had found us! He sat still and mocked me in my fright. It seems he was always laughing at me these days; making me feel like a foolish child.

"Come back and sit down," he said hiding his snide grin behind his hand. "It is nothing but the deer," he assured me.

I never heard a deer bark like a dog! Muntjacs he called them – barking deer. I never heard of them before, but he assured me that they were certainly real and exceedingly plentiful on this side of the mountain. If we could catch one, we might have some fresh meat.

I did not feel his enthusiasm and fell back into my mournful grief. Nothing seemed to cheer me, not even the thought of food. However sad I was though, I realized I had not cried in my grief. I found that strange. Why had I not cried? I just felt numb, and had no feelings at all.

"Still," I whined, "I never had a chance to say goodbye to my dear mother and father…"

"Nor did I!" he interrupted. His patience was wearing thin. "Of course, my loss could not be as great as yours," he taunted. I knew he mocked me – derided me. He seemed to enjoy humiliating me for some reason. I guess he thought that if he made me angry enough, I might become more helpful. He reached into his bag, "Perhaps this will give you some comfort. I obtained this with great risk to my liberty and my life. It is yours."

I took the dirty rag he offered and slowly opened the bundle. I caught my breath! Tears finally fell as I touched the glittering necklace of fine filigreed silver – her locket that she never removed from her neck. The locket contained a snip of my grandfather's hair. Somehow, the necklace still seemed warm from her touch. I looked at Mawken with grateful tears in my eyes.

"There's more," he gestured. "I thought you might want that as well."

I opened the cloth further and raised the next item by its silver chain. I looked at him through tears in wonder and confusion. How did he get this? I tenderly caressed my Papa's pocket watch and chain, still caked with my father's blood.

I awoke the next day sometime around mid-afternoon. I was tired and hungry, and my feet were sore. I was unaccustomed to walking such great distances. I rolled over on my side, expecting to see Mawken still sleeping, but he was not anywhere in our camp. I immediately got to my feet and searched the surrounding area. It was as if he vanished into the mountain air. I saw no sign of where he slept. I had no idea where he was. I was alone in the forest.

My first thought was has he abandoned me and left me alone on the mountain to die? With me out of the way, I would no longer be a burden or a danger to him. No one would be left to know what happened in Kadan Kyun. With me out of the way, he could more easily escape. He could even blame the murders on me.

Once again, I fingered my father's watch, and I opened my mother's locket to see my grandfather's hair. I drew the locket to my nose to see if I could catch my mother's scent. No, there was no longer any trace of her on it, also from my father's watch. Only the black bloodstains remained. I scraped some of my father's dried blood into my mother's locket. I felt grateful he prevented me from seeing my father's dead body. The sight of my mother swinging and twisting from the eaves of the house will haunt me forever. Yet, not going to them, not being able to kiss them or caress them one last time, made the specter of the unknown seem even more frightful in my mind. It seemed as if it was not real – I imagined them alive still – but I knew they were dead. Blood lay crusted on my father's watch.

Time passed slowly, and I was still alone in our camp. I decided Mawken was out searching for food; and if he did not return in a few hours, I planned to travel on without him. I did not know where to go, except up. Was it still necessary to travel by night? The nights were colder, and we were not even on the summit yet. I yearned for the downhill side and the warmer temperature. We must reach the lofty summit soon. The forest thinned, and the wind moaned through the leafless trees.

A nearby creek flowed into a still and silent pool of water. I decided I would wash the blood from my keepsakes so I might be able to forget the details of their horrible deaths. Even so, I knew it would be impossible for me to forget. I took the watch and locket and knelt by the brook to wash the chain, taking care to make sure the watch itself did not get wet. Flakes of my father's blood came off and floated in the slow moving water. Swirls of blood curled from the flecks as the dried blood became liquid again. The swirls quickly vanished, disappearing into the cold clear water.

The washed the necklace next. I examined it closely, but I saw no blood on either the chain or the locket. I sat by the pool and thought in my mind how these things must have come into his possession. I shivered again at the memory of seeing mother hung. I remembered the angle of her head tilted off to one side, her neck obviously broken. I suddenly got the image in my mind of my mother with her unblinking eyes open. I collapsed into tearful grief once again at the thought of my dead mother's body.

The pirates must have attacked my father near the house and murdered him in cold blood. I longed to know how they killed my father. I hoped to remember to ask Mawken once he returned. Was he shot or stabbed with a sword? I did not know. I tried to imagine for myself how it must have happened. I would think the pirates circled our home and came in from the back of the property. Heavy woods grew behind our compound, providing ample cover. My father was probably coming back from the barn after having harnessed the carriage for their trip to the office in town. David – what became of David? – must have seen Father walking toward the house that morning. H may have seen the dark shape leap from behind the barn and attack my father. Maybe he tried to warn Mother. Probably, he was bludgeoned to death as they dragged my screaming mother from the house by her hair. Who else was in the house? Tiny Katherine, the upstairs maid would have been thrown down the stairs to her death, if she did not hide. They would have hastily secured a rope around my dear mother's neck before they hoisted her twitching body to the eaves. I felt sick to my stomach.

Someone must have climbed on the roof and cut the rope around Mother's neck to lower her gently to the ground. Once on the ground, they would have covered her with a sheet or some coverlet to protect the body. With two fingers, they would have closed her eyes. The authorities would have carried my father's bloody body and placed it near my mother's lifeless form. They would have covered him with a sheet also. They would have brought other members of the household and, if they were dead, would have lined them up beneath sheets in the yard. If any were alive, they would have asked them to identify the bodies. The authorities would have interviewed the survivors. They would need to gather evidence. They would have noticed I was not with the dead or among the living. They would have tried to understand why. Was I kidnapped and taken away? Was I dead and hidden somewhere on the property? They would make a search, no doubt, at least of the nearby area. Not finding my body, would they have expanded the search? They would surely be looking for me. Were they looking for a victim or a murderer? I shivered at the thought.

Then, I imagined Mawken silently creeping into the yard, unseen by the guards. He would have come from the forest, quietly slipping in while the authorities were not looking. Pulling the cover back from my father, he would have unhooked the chain from the vest button and pulled the watch forth. Then, he would have moved to my mother and taken the locket. He would have had to raise her head or roll her onto her side to reach the clasp. How much quicker it would have been for him simply to break the chain, especially if he was in a hurry. It would have taken him longer to unhook the clasp, exposing him to detection and possible arrest. It was a great risk he took. Had Mawken been caught, they would have thought he plundered the dead and would have hung him immediately. I could imagine no other way for Mawken to get the locket unless my mother took it off and gave it to him. I rejected the thought as impossible – my mother would never surrender her locket if she were alive. She was surely dead before they cut her down. I wondered how Mawken managed to recover these things and get away in broad daylight. Surely, the police were guarding the bodies.

I gathered my things and returned to the camp. I found Mawken kneeling by the fire, cooking something to eat. I summoned all the courage I could muster and held the necklace out toward him. "How did you get this?" I asked. "And the watch?"

"While I was out gathering supplies for our escape, I crept into your compound and took them from the bodies."

"You were not seen?"

"I am not seen if I don't want to be seen," he assured me. He quickly changed the subject. "We will stay here tonight and strike out again in the morning. We are far enough away we can safely travel by day now. Let's eat and rest tonight. We can get an early start in the morning." He pulled a stick with meat from the coals and handed it to me. It sizzled and steamed in the cool air. "Here. I trapped one of those barking deer. It's good – eat."

I took the food he offered. I was grateful for additional time to rest. I was not sleeping well, and additional rest would allow me to regain my strength. Nourished, I slept through the night and woke as the sun bathed our campsite with yellow light.

After a few hours, the path gradually went downhill. I imagined we would come out on the summit of the mountain, but I did not notice any kind of pinnacle or high point. I was disappointed I was not able to stand on top of the mountain and look out over the ocean. We walked until the sun dropped from the sky and we stopped for the night.

On the afternoon of the next day, the land leveled out as we neared the coastline. Even though it was not yet dark, we found a secluded place to make camp. As he roasted the last of the meat over the glowing embers of the fire, he looked at me through the curling smoke. He thought long before he spoke.

"We are at the end of the first part of our escape. Tomorrow morning, you will take the ferry across to the town of Mergui."

"You will not be coming?"

"I will come later. It is best we do not stay together in case they are already looking for us in Mergui. Once you arrive on the other side of the bay, you will go to a tavern on the mill highway. Ask for a man named Haji. He is the owner of the tavern. Tell him your name is Maurice. Tell him you are Yana's brother. He will know Yana. She is my sister. Tell him you know how to cook, and he will give you a job. They always need a cook. Do not mention me to him at any time."

"What about Yana? Won't she expose me as a liar?"

"She will not be there. She left more than a year ago."

"Where is she now?"

"I do not know. It does not matter. Tell Haji you came up from the south, from the islands. Do not mention Kadan Kyun. If he asks, tell him you never heard of that place. Tell Haji you have no money and no place to stay, and he will let you sleep in the tavern after it closes at night – for a price. Everything Haji does will come with a price. Do not trust him with anything. And remember to not mention me at all!"

"If I say I am Yana's brother, won't he know I am lying?"

"How will he know? I told you she is gone from there. She is probably dead by now. At one time, Yana was his favorite, but no more. She is gone. He will put you up for her sake. But keep your head about you, and do not be fooled." He stared at me with serious eyes. "Haji is not your friend. I am your only friend. Trust no one else. Leave your window unlocked at night, and I will join you soon."

"Where will you be?"

"I will be making plans for our second escape."

"A second escape? Escape from what?"

He looked at me with cold dark eyes, "The escape from Haji!"

30

Late in the day, I arrived at the loading dock to find the ferryboat gone. Small groups of travelers sat nearby. I found a spot near a family with several small children. The ferry would not return until the morning, so everyone camped overnight to be first in line. When they saw I was hungry, they were kind to me and offered me part of their meal. They asked many questions but I was afraid to say much about myself, so I busied myself playing and running with their children as a diversion. Afterwards, I claimed to be tired and went to sleep early.

I realized I was in need of a story explaining who I was and where I came from. As I pretended to sleep, I devised a story I hoped would conceal my true identity. Mawken was not been much help, except to have me claim I was from the south and had a sister named Yana. I decided I was from Malacca, where I learned English while serving as a houseboy for a British envoy. I decided I should only speak English while in Mergui, in case anyone was already looking for me. I would say when my sponsor returned to London, I decided to journey to England on my own. I worked my way north on a cargo freighter. I was thankful I knew something of the shipping trade to make my story seem true. I would say I left the boat on King Island, and I traveled across to Mergui to see if I could find a job on another vessel sailing north. I would claim to be a cook, since David taught me how. I thought if any of my fellow travelers saw me later as a cook in Mergui, my story would hold up. It would also serve as a story for Haji and others I met along the way.

By morning, I memorized my story and I could answer questions if necessary. However, the family I befriended were too busy rounding up their children and their belongings to pay much attention to me. The ferryboat inched to the dock as men leaned heavily on their push poles. Still, I was glad to have a history and I was sure I would need one eventually.

Off shore, I could see the ferrymen take down the canvas as the crew steered the boxy boat toward the dock. Several of the boatmen in the stern dipped long poles into the water. The wind whipped strong waves across the channel, and the boatmen struggled with difficulty guiding the boat into its slip. Finally, they rammed the boat onto the bank and secured it to tall posts with thick twisted hemp ropes. The passengers waiting to cross the channel stood in lines more or less in the order in which they arrived, as passengers arriving from the other side prepared to disembark.

It took some time to unload the boat. The ferrymen served double duty as porters and off-loaded many bundles as well as wagons, carts and livestock. The ferry landing was a busy and confusing place as waiting passengers stood in the path of the arriving passengers. A few minor disagreements and loud arguments broke out, but nothing violent. Eventually it all sorted out, as the arriving passengers pushed their way through the group and assembled off to one side. If the anxious passengers wanting to get on the boat only waited for the boat to empty instead of grouping up in the way of people coming off the boat, it would have been much more efficient. Finally, the boat was empty and we boarded.

When the ferryman came around to collect his fee, I suddenly realized I had no money to pay. I did not anticipate paying a fee; my father always arranged for that. I was unfamiliar with ferry travel. At first, I was afraid he would throw me off the boat and not allow me to cross. He sized me up and down; and then told me once we reached the other side, I could pay for my passage by helping his crew unload the boat. I agreed, relieved to know I would be allowed to cross.

Once away from shore, we pitched and yawed as waves and currents tossed our boat. Once the captain ordered the sails hoisted, we picked up speed and were able to guide the boat toward the other shore using the rudder. Because of sea conditions, it was still a bumpy ride, but at least we were going forward. I did not know what my duties would be on the other side. I assumed I would be engaged in unloading passengers and their belongings.

I could see across the channel to the far shore, still shrouded in morning clouds. I learned from my friends the night before the passage would take more than an hour; but at the speed we were moving, I thought it might be sooner. The bright sun warmed the air around us, and it was quite pleasant. As the sun rose, the wind seemed to die down and our speed diminished. I revised my expectations. Unless a favorable wind rose soon, it could take even longer than predicted.

No matter, with nowhere else to go and nothing else to do but wait, I watched my fellow passengers. None of them seemed interested in engaging me in conversation, so I contented myself with watching the sea birds flit and swoop around our ferry. Most of my fellow passengers were nodding off in the warm sunny morning. I looked into the water, hoping to catch sight of a fish or something, but did not see anything interesting. I could not see the bottom of the sea past the pale green foam curling around out bow. I peered deep into the water, but gradually the depth faded into a blueish green.

After a time, I looked up to see the far shore was much closer. I was amazed we traveled so far in so short a time. It seemed the boat was barely moving forward. The low clouds lifted, and I could clearly see trees and buildings in the distance. When I looked back into the water, I could see the bottom, heavily carpeted with waving green vegetation. In and among the sea plants, little fish darted and flashed their silvery sides as they flitted around.

I saw several of the crew rise and move to the stern of the boat. The captain stood, pointed toward me, and yelled for me to lend a hand. I took a wooden staff at least fifteen feet long from the bottom of the boat and moved to the rear with the other men. I watched as one of the men gauged the depth of the bottom with his pole. Finally, one of them shouted something to the captain who ordered the sails lowered. Once again, we were in the clutches of the currents and choppy waves. All of the pole men leaned into their rods and pushed the boat slowly toward the shore. I did the same. As we neared the shore, the captain beckoned me forward. I moved toward the front of the boat. The captain handed me the looped end of one of the large ropes and pointed to the thick posts on shore. I understood I was to loop my rope around one of those posts to secure the boat. As soon as the ferry struck land, I leaped from the bow and pulled as hard as I could toward one of the posts. Once we were close enough, I looped my rope over the top.

I still held my pole. I took one end of the pole and shoved the wet end through the crowd near the center of the landing. I waggled it back and forth to motion the crowd on one side to move to the left and the other side to move to the right. Gradually, the crowd parted as they stood waiting on either side of the landing dock. I returned to the ferry helped people step out of the boat onto dry land. I kept everyone moving up the cobbled street to allow more passengers to disembark.

After the boat stood empty, the captain waved the waiting passengers on one side onto the boat; then he gestured to the others. The boat emptied and loaded much faster this time than before. The captain beckoned for me.

"Good job," he said. "We emptied this boat and reloaded it in less than an hour. If we can do that every trip we will be able to make at least two more crossings a day!" He slapped me on the back. "Come on. Let's push off!"

"But I cannot go. I just got here."

"I'll offer you the job of first mate! I will pay you well. You can be in charge of the crew and the loading and unloading. With two additional trips a day, we'll both make money!"

"I cannot. I am sorry. I must be on my way. Surely, others can do as I did and you can still make your additional trips."

"But, I like you, boy," he said. He gave me a sad look, as I slowly shook my head no. It would have been a wonderful opportunity for me, but I must remember I am a wanted man. It would not take long for them to find me if I were in such a visible job.

I sadly turned away as the boat left the shore. I turned and watched as the boat once more bounced on the choppy waves. Then I walked up the cobble street toward my future. I did not know it at the time, but I had left King's Island behind me forever.

After asking around the town, I found the mill road. There, just outside the village sat a rundown shanty with vines growing up the side of the front. A rock wall enclosed the rear, and I could see trees growing in a sort of garden behind the wall. The old rocks in the wall were dirty and molded. The entire place looked uncared for and shabby. Great piles of greasy rubbish lay on the corner near the end of the wall, and two children were rummaging through the refuse. Heavy iron bars covered every window. It looked more like a prison than a tavern.

Someone washed the walkway in front of the door, and the landing was still wet as little pools of water reflected the rough exterior of the door. A brown horse and a wagon stood nearby, hitched to a rail running along the front of the building. As I watched, the horse suddenly hunched and dropped a load of black dung beneath the wagon. The horse shivered as its skin crawled down its haunches in ripples. He swished his tail across his flanks as he patiently waited. I moved to the side of the horse and rubbed his neck and his round, tangled mane. He snorted and looked at me with brown, wet eyes as he nosed my clothes. I suppose he thought I had an apple. I wished I did. I would have eaten it myself and given him the core.

I stepped up onto the short porch and looked at the rough wooden door. I knocked. No one answered so I knocked again. This time louder. No one came. I saw an empty pewter cup lying on the floor, and I used it to knock even louder. The door suddenly jerked open and I stood face to face with a heavy dark-haired man. He was bleary-eyed, with red streaks in the whites of his eyeballs. He wore a dirty white shirt, and a dirty cloth towel hung from the front of his pants below his bulging belly. A small loop of beads dangled from his hand.

"Who the hell is pounding on my door?" he screamed. "Who the hell knocks on a tavern door anyway? Who the hell are you and what do you want?"

"I beg your pardon," I said calmly. "I am looking for a man named Haji."

He looked at me with surprise on his face. "Haji?" he repeated. "I am Haji. What do you want?"

I took a deep breath and muttered, "I am Yana's brother."

A look of bewildered amusement crossed his face.

"Yana?" I could see he was confused. I was afraid for a moment I said the name wrong.

"Yana's brother?" he stupidly repeated. He looked me up and down, laughed a hearty laugh, and then stood aside so I could enter.

"Oh, yes, her brother. Yes. Yes, of course. Come in, I am sorry I did not recognize you," he laughed again. "Come inside and have something to drink."

He jerked his thumb at a man sitting at the bar who then picked up his tankard and moved into a dim corner of the room. Haji pointed at the empty stool indicating where I was to sit. Haji stood behind the bar and fingered his brown wooden beads. I sat and watched the heavy door close and block out the outside world. I did not know it at the time, but I would never see that door swing open again.

Haji went behind the counter bar and looked at me with great interest. It seemed like he tried to be serious and not laugh, but lost the battle. Later, I would know Haji always seemed about to laugh. He laughed the most wonderful, contagious laugh. Many things struck him as extremely funny. I soon learned, just because he seemed jolly did not mean he was happy. His laugh was a diversion. It was a laugh designed to fool the unwary.

"Yana is not here," he informed me. I decided to pretend I did not know.

"She is not?" I shook my head in wonder.

"No. She left several months ago. You did not know that?" He tilted his head sideways and flashed his big white teeth in a smile.

"No. I have not heard from her. Where did she go?"

"I wish I knew," Haji laughed. "What is your name?"

"I am Maurice," I told him, trying to look as innocent as possible.

Haji pursed his lips and looked at the ceiling. "Maurice." He looked back at me, stuck his tongue in his cheek, and then repeated, "Maurice." He laughed as if it were funny.

"Yes. Maurice." His giant teeth flashed again in the dim tavern. "She spoke of you often," he said. My heart stopped beating.

"She did?" I muttered, unsure of what to say next.

"Yes. She missed you very much. She often said how you were her favorite. Would you like some chi?" The man who moved from the bar into a dark corner coughed. I could not see his face, but from his frequent hacking, I knew he was there.

"Yes, thank you, I would like chi. It was very kind of her to say." My mind raced for some way to conceal my confusion. "I ... uh, I was a young boy when she left. I am sorry, but I am afraid I

37

barely remember her at all. It is such a shame. She is my sister, but she has been gone from our family for such long time." I paused and looked at his face, trying to judge his reaction. I felt like I would fall through a crack in the floor. I was afraid he could hear my heart pounding in my chest. "You don't know where she went?" I made my eyes as wide as possible.

"Not really," he smiled. "I think she went to Kadan Kyun on King Island – you know the place?" he asked quickly.

I did not react outwardly, but inside I felt trapped. "No. I don't." I looked him straight in the eye without blinking.

He turned his face toward the ceiling and laughed again as a man brought a tray which held two small glass demitasse cups of steaming tea. The tea was in small clear cups decorated with leaves around the sides and a gold-like trim.

"Sugar?" he asked. When I nodded, he spooned in raw brown sugar into the tea and offered me a cup. He looked me straight in the eye and said in a laughing voice, "I find it hard to believe you are unfamiliar with Kadan Kyun. Didn't you just come over on the ferry from King Island this morning?"

"Yes. How did you know?"

"I am Haji! I know everything," he laughed. His continual laughing disturbed me greatly. It made me feel he knew everything I said was a lie. However, the fact he laughed was a good sign, was it not? I felt the confidence ebb out of me like the departing tide.

"My boy, the entire town is talking about you – how you managed to empty the ferry with such efficiency and speed. Therefore, I find it curious you do not know Kadan Kyun since you came only this morning from King Island."

I remembered the warning to claim I did not know the place and to remember Haji was not my friend.

"Please excuse me. I am not from here. Yes, it is true I was on King Island this morning, but I never heard of Kadan Kyun," I lied. "Why is it important?"

"I believe Kadan Kyun was where Yana lived before she came here. Don't you know?"

I shook my head and tried to be as convincing as possible. "Perhaps she was in Kadan Kyun for a time. I do not know. I came here from the south, from Malacca on a cargo boat. I am working my way to England. I only stopped to see if I could find my sister, Yana, to tell her goodbye. A friend told me he saw her here with you. I am sorry. I don't mean to cause any trouble."

"Nonsense!" he laughed. "You are not causing trouble. I was only curious. Do not be offended at my questions. Yana and I are great friends. I also would like to find her." Something about his words seemed ominous to me.

"If she returned to Kadan Kyun, I would like to know. That is all. How did you end up on King Island instead of here on Mergui?" His head tilted at an odd angle once more.

"My boat was not going to port here in Mergui because we were bound for Rangoon. I asked them to put me ashore; and since we were sailing on the port side of the channel, they rowed me ashore on King Island in a small dinghy. They told me the ferry would bring me across to Mergui. Only after the boat sailed did I realize I forgot to get my pay. I have no money. I worked my way across the channel on the ferry. That is how I got here – to find my sister."

"Only to find she is not here," Haji laughed. "And you have no money."

"That is true," I sadly admitted.

"If you barely remember your sister, why is it so important for you to find her?" Haji asked as he tilted his head again in his curious manner.

39

I had not anticipated that question. My mind raced for an answer. Why would I need to find my sister? "I … uh, I n-n-needed to tell her some important news."

"What did you need to tell her?" Head to the side.

I said the first thing that popped into my mind. "I needed to tell her our mother is dead." I could not believe I said that!

Haji immediately seized on this information. His eyes became soft and sad, yet he grinned as if he had caught a big fish, and he looked at me as if I had fins.

"Her mother, your mother?" He stood up and came around the counter. He placed a meaty hand on my shoulder. All I could think was Mawken's dead mother. He squeezed my shoulder with his powerful fingers and looked at me with a sad face.

"Your mother? I am so sorry for your loss. Yana will be devastated. She loved her mother very much, as I am sure you did." Then he said something in a strange language I did not understand, except I caught the word Allah. Was it a prayer, or was he talking to the coughing man in the dark corner of the tavern? I did not know, but it made me nervous.

I ducked my head and mumbled, "Thank you, sir. It was a great loss."

"How did she die?" Haji asked, tilting his head as he sat on the stool next to me. I believed that Haji was unconscious of his mannerisms. It occurred to me that when he tilted his head, he probably already knew the answer and wanted to trap me in a lie. I felt sick. I had not lied as much in my entire life as I lied the last few minutes. He knew I was lying. I was sure of it.

I caught myself in time before I could say she was murdered. "She died quite peacefully in her sleep."

"In Singapore?" he said quickly.

"No. In Malacca," I corrected. "She lived in Malacca." The trap snapped closed empty.

"Oh, yes. Malacca. I am sorry; I forgot you said that." I knew he was lying. He was testing me.

"What are your plans now, if you cannot find your sister, and you have no money?"

"I will try to find work on the next northbound ship leaving Mergui."

"Maurice, ... it is Maurice? ... Yes, Maurice, there will not be another boat through Mergui for three days. What do you plan to do until then?"

I knew this to be a lie, as I learned at the wharf the *Glendora* would be sailing the next day. "I will wait. What else can I do?" I tried to look disappointed. I could not leave on the *Glendora* because I must wait for Mawken.

"What did you do on the boat?"

"I was a galley boy – I worked in the galley."

"Excellent!" Haji jumped to his feet excitedly. "You will work here for me. I need a kitchen boy, and you will do nicely. You have no place to go for three days, and you can live here at the inn and work in the kitchen. I will give you room and meals until you decide to leave to catch another ship going north. Is that fair?"

"Yes," I acted relieved. Let Haji think it was his idea. Maybe he will be less suspicious. "Thank you kindly, sir. I will work hard. But, as soon as I can get a new ship, I must leave."

"Understood!" Haji stuck out a meaty palm, and we shook on the deal. He called out in a loud voice, "Sofi!" Then to me, "You can start in the morning. We start early here, before daylight. You can have the day to rest from your journey, and you can begin in the morning."

A pretty girl came from a room behind the counter. She looked to be a few years younger than I was. I guessed she was fourteen years old. She looked young and innocent. She was beautiful with soft black hair sweeping across her shoulders, pouty red lips, and dark blue eyes darting from Haji to me and back to Haji.

"Sofi, this is Maurice. He is the new kitchen boy. Show him to a room and tell him his duties. Attend to his needs," he added with a wink. Then to me, "Maurice, this is Sofi. She will tell you everything you need to know. Get some rest, and she will come and fetch you in the morning. Have a good sleep. If you need anything," he winked again. I wondered if something was in his eye. He repeated, "Anything – let Sofi know. She will give you whatever you need." He laughed as if at some great joke. "On the house," he laughed as he slapped Sofi's behind hard as she passed.

As I followed Sofi down a dark hallway, the coughing man moved back to the bar. He and Haji conferred with their heads close together, as we went out of a door, down some short steps, and across the square walled garden. On the opposite side of the garden, Sofi took a key hanging from her neck and unlocked a heavy wooden door. I entered a small room containing a small lumpy bed, a wooden chair, and a table with a bowl and lamp. "You can sleep here," Sofi said. I looked around the dim room. The room offered only one small window, which barred from the outside. "Will you need anything else?" Sofi asked in a soft timid voice.

"Can you leave something to light the lamp?"

"In the drawer," she gestured toward the table.

"Thank you. Is there a clean towel?"

"Also in the drawer." Sofi looked at me softly as her tongue briefly ran across her upper lip. "Shall I fetch some water for the bowl?"

"Yes, thank you."

She left the room and returned right away with water and a rough bar of soap. She poured the water into the basin and laid the soap on the tabletop. She opened the drawer, and took out a folded towel and placed it next to the basin. She turned toward me and shrugged a bare shoulder from one sleeve of her dress.

"Shall I get undressed?" she asked.

I suddenly realized the purpose of the towel, the water bowl, and the bare shoulder. Sofi was prepared to give me – anything. As Haji instructed, she was prepared to do anything to make me happy. However, she caught me completely by surprise. I was not expecting that kind of service. 'No," I stammered. "N-n-not today, I think." She seemed disappointed. "I am tired. I think I need some sleep. I slept on the ground last night in the cold. Wh-wh-why don't you come later this afternoon, and we will see?"

Sofi shrugged her pretty shoulder back into her dress and turned back toward the door. Did she know I had not been with a woman before? I felt ashamed. Was she secretly laughing at my inexperience? She halfway turned and pointed toward the bed,

"Yes, get some rest. I will come back in a few hours with your meal. Will there be anything else?" she asked with her voice as soft as the wind. I wondered if she was only teasing me.

"Yes!" I said firmly. "When you return I will need something – you can be sure," I said boldly with all the confidence I could muster, although, I could feel my face turn red.

She laughed a tiny laugh, like running water, and smiled at me. "It will be my pleasure," she smiled and blew me a kiss. She glided into the garden, closing the door behind her. I heard the unmistakable sound of the metal key turning in the lock. I waited until I was sure she was gone before I tried the handle. Sofi locked me in the room, leaving me no way to escape.

I felt uneasy locked in a room. Yet, I lay on the cot and soon fell fast asleep. I awoke later to the sound of the metal key turning in the locked door. I sat up on the bed as Sofi entered the room bearing a tray with bread and food. "I cannot stay," she said hastily as she placed the tray on the table and turned to go.

"Why am I locked in?" I demanded.

Sofi handed me a cup filled with white yogurt. "This is a dangerous place," she said. "There are thieves about and much worse. Do not be alarmed. You will come to no harm … here." I wondered why she paused before she said 'here'.

I gratefully drank the warm sweet yogurt. I realized how thirsty I was. I held out my cup for more, and Sofi refilled it from the pitcher on the tray. I wiped the tasty yogurt from my lips with the back of my arm and asked, "I am allowed to leave the room then?"

"Of course. I only locked the door while you were sleeping so no one would disturb you. Haji wants you to get your rest – to be ready for your work tomorrow. I will come for you early, before light. You are free to leave the room – you should stay within the garden, though. It is not safe beyond the walls." She went to the door and paused,

"I must go. I have other duties needing my attention. I will come for you later at dinner. You should rest." She gave me a teasing look over her shoulder as she turned to go.

"But…"

She placed two fingers to her pursed lips as if to silence me, "Soon," she said as she went through the door and closed it behind her. I listened but did not hear the door lock. After I was certain she was gone, I tried the door and it opened easily. The sun felt warm and a nice breeze blew over the wall, so I took the remainder of my meal into the garden. Several benches stood around the wall. It did not appear anyone used them often, as they were full of leaves and small twigs. I cleared a space on one of them and sat down.

44

I looked around the enclosed space. Several trees, some of them bearing fruit, shaded the yard. Birds sang as they flitted from limb to limb and pecked at the fruit. Vines with beautiful fragrant purple flowers trailed along the wall. A well made of stone with a rope and pulley hanging from a tripod over it stood in the center of the garden.

A curious square table sat in the center of the enclosure. At first, it appeared to be a table with no legs. It was black, made from some kind of dark wood. I went over to the square and inspected it. It was not painted or oiled. It seemed the wood itself was black. It was level and smooth along the top and around the four sides. I could find no opening in it. I could see no scratches or indentations on any of the surfaces of the monument. I knocked upon the top with my knuckles and it sounded solid. It appeared to be one solid cube of some kind of black wood. I attempted to lift one side, but it was so heavy I could not move it at all. I could not determine its purpose or meaning. It looked like an altar of some sort. It seemed designed for some religious purpose.

I returned to my bench and finished my meal. I stood on the bench and was able to see over the top of the wall. The horse and wagon I saw out front were gone, and two different wagons stood hitched to swish-tailed horses. Nothing moved up or down the road. Even the pleasant breeze had died. I judged it was late in the afternoon. The heat of the sun became a little unpleasant, so I looked for shade beneath the trees. Across the garden on the outside wall of the tavern was a gate. Next to the gate was a woodpile with an ax embedded into a chopping block. It reminded me of our woodpile at home. Father always kept the ax embedded in the chopping block – just like this one. Near the woodpile was a shady spot, so I left my tray on the bench and sat down with my back against the cool stone wall of the tavern.

I heard muffled sounds from inside the inn, but I could not make out the words. Suddenly, I heard a door close from inside and voices became louder. I knew Haji's voice from his laugh. I did not recognize the other voice. It was a man who spoke in a hoarse voice and who coughed several times. I did not want to interfere in Haji's business, so I was preparing to return to my bench when I heard them speak of me.

"The boy is a fool." I decided to stay quiet and listen.

They laughed and Haji added, "He is no doubt the one."

"What makes you think so?"

"For one thing, he came across on the ferry this morning from King's Island. He said his former master rowed him ashore. I know of no ship's captain who would waste valuable time rowing a rapscallion like him ashore!" Haji laughed. "He would be more likely to throw him overboard. No. He did not get to King's Island the way he claimed. I know that for sure."

"Yes, no doubt," the other voice said through several coughs. "You think he is the boy who murdered his family, then?"

"I am sure of it! He claims not to know anything of Kadan Kyun, but what would *you* say if you murdered your own mother and father?"

"What do you plan to do?"

"He concocted a story of his coming up from Malacca. I do not know, but I do know he is not Anya's brother. I will have Sofi quiz him further. If he is from Malacca, does he know of the Friday market in the square, or of the fruit vendor Salim? We shall see."

"Everyone knows Salim." Cough, cough.

"The boy does not want to be found. I plan to make sure he is not found, and to profit from the arrangement, of course," Haji laughed. "He will bring a good price in the trade. He is young and able, and he has a good mind about him. You heard how he managed the ferry landing? Raheem will arrive in two days – he will pay well for this boy, you can be sure."

"How do you plan on convincing the boy to go?"

"That, my friend, is the easy part. Sofi will seduce him. She will ask him to help her escape from me, and he will help her. She will tell him he is also in danger. Sofi is very convincing – believe me. She will tell him he must help her escape to an uncle who will take them to a safe place."

"And the uncle?"

"Raheem, of course." Haji laughed.

"And if he does not believe her?"

"Sofi will convince him his secret has been discovered, and he will soon be arrested and hung for the murder of his parents."

"Yes, Sofi can be very convincing."

"Raheem can have Sofi as well; I am through with her. Raheem will get two for one. Besides, Sofi's father has already sold me her younger sister, who is much prettier. Wait until you see her. She is magnificent!" The men laughed loudly. Their pewter mugs made a dull clanking sound as they hit them together. Then Haji's voice lowered as he confided, "Sofi does not know. Soon I will be rid of them both. They will escape, but neither of them will be coming back."

The other man asked, "Can I have her until then?"

"What? I gave you Anya, and now you want Sofi also?" Haji laughed.

"I only had her a short time before you sold her to Raheem! You owe me a replacement!"

"Ahhh! I rented her to you. Besides, you could not pay the price. As for Sofi, take her for as long as she is here. As long as you pay the fee, she is yours."

"Done! What will you do without her?"

"I told you, I am done with her. Besides, as soon as she is gone, Pasha will deliver her sister. That one, you cannot have for a very long time. She will be kept busy – you can be sure." They laughed loudly and clanked their mugs again.

I could not believe what I heard. It was just as Mawken said; Haji was no friend. Haji intended to sell me into slavery.

Despite my alarm, I suddenly felt heavy and unable to raise my arms. It was difficult to keep my eyes open. Everything whirled around my head – the mysterious black box – even the trees would not stay still. I did not know what was happening to me. I managed to crawl across the garden back to my bench where I collapsed on the ground as blackness overtook me.

In what seemed like a minute, I awoke on my cot. No light came through the dingy window. I could not remember coming back to my room. My head ached and felt large and heavy. The lamp flickered and the feeble light danced across the stone floor. As my eyes focused, I wondered who lit the lamp.

"Ah, you are awake," a soft voice said. "You must have been tired. You fell asleep in the sun after your lunch." Sofi sat on the side of the bed and rubbed my shoulders. "I was hoping you would wake sooner before I had to leave. Now, it is too late. I cannot stay longer."

"Why didn't you wake me?"

"I tried, but you were sleeping so soundly."

I moved my feet past her and sat on the side of the bed. My vision blurred as I tried to look at her, but I could see her face. Her eyes were alluring as she looked at me. My mind was so dull it was hard to think. She bent her head forward and kissed me softly. Her lips were warm and wet. It was my first romantic kiss; it seemed so strange. I wanted to kiss her more, but she quickly stood and walked to the door.

48

"I am sorry. I should not have kissed you when I must leave so soon. I will come back later, and there will be a little time for us then. I will take good care of you. You will be very happy, you will see."

I was still a little groggy and unsure if I could even stand. I could not understand why I was so sleepy. I rubbed my face and looked at her standing by the door with her hand on the handle. I became more awake and remembered things. The memory of the conversation I overheard was fresh in my mind again.

"I brought you something to eat," she pointed at the table. "Fresh fruit off the boat from the Monday Malacca market." The trap was set. I knew then she was not truthful with me. She watched for my reactions. I knew she would report everything she saw to Haji.

I pretended to be confused. "Monday? The market is on Friday. Did the fruit come from Salim? He has the finest fruits in the Malaccan market."

"I do not know," she admitted. "I retrieved it from the boat on Monday."

"I see. I thought you were saying Malacca changed the market day during my absence."

"I would know nothing of

. I must go now. I have work to do."

"You work both day and night?" I asked.

"If I am awake, I am working. It is very hard here, Maurice" she nodded. "Very hard. You do not know." I did not know. Nor did I know how I should respond.

She looked at me kindly from the doorway, "Maurice?" she asked softly.

"Yes?"

"Do you trust me?" Her eyes were damp as if she would cry.

I decided I should not tell her all I knew yet. "Yes." I lied. "Why do you ask?"

"Maurice, I have become fond of you. I confess I am attracted to you. I will come to you later. Please sleep for now and wait for my return. I have many things I must tell you, but I am so afraid."

"Afraid of what?" I asked.

Her eyes moistened, "I am afraid if you know me, you will not love me." Tears ran down her cheeks. She held her arms out to me. She took a step forward only to drop her arms and return to the door as though she were unsure what to do. She turned back to face me, "I have much to tell you. I will return before morning, and you will know everything. Please do not hate me. I have done nothing of my own choice – until this moment."

She cried so pitifully; I stood and moved toward her. She held out her hand and placed her other arm over her face. "Wait. Please. I will return soon. Eat your dinner, and I will be with you later. Please." She dabbed her eyes with her apron, "I must go."

She opened the door and walked quickly across the garden toward the inn. I watched her go inside the tavern. She left my door standing open. I sat in the chair at the table and looked at the food she brought. Bread, eggs, cheese, and rice, and another tankard of yogurt along with a pitcher of water. I decided I would not eat the yogurt – it did not sit well with me.

Not knowing what to expect or who to trust, I decided I should stay awake and alert for as long as possible. I blew out the light and sat waiting in the dark, wondering why the door was unlocked. If this was such a dangerous place, as Sofi explained, why leave the door unlocked after dark? A locked door can keep someone out as well as someone in. The only purpose for a locked door is to deny entry or exit. If the threat of thievery is no less because the door is unlocked and open, then denial of entry could not have been the reason to lock it in the first place. An open door makes no noise and one can enter silently. The threat of my leaving is no less likely unless someone is watching to make sure I do not. Through this reasoning, I determined the door was unlocked for only one purpose – to allow someone quick and silent entry into my room. They did not fear my exit.

I decided to test my theory. I went to the door and peered outside from the shadows of my room. Nothing moved in the garden. I could hear loud music and laughter coming from the tavern. In the darkness, I edged alongside the wall outside my door to an area where bushes grew near the wall. I quietly walked beneath the trees and vines and sat on the bench near the wall. I waited. Everything was quiet except for the wind in the trees.

I heard something move in the dark nearby. Ah ha! I thought. I was right! Someone is watching me. Someone is guarding the garden to prevent my escape. Suddenly something heavy came over the top of the wall and fell onto my bench, nearly causing me to faint! I nearly cried out but stopped myself in time. A large black cat jumped from the top of the wall to join me on the bench. The cat looked at me hungrily and licked its whiskers with a long pink tongue. I could see its yellow eyes and its nostrils flare as it tried to determine if I would give it anything to eat. I did not. I tried to remain as silent as possible, and did not address the cat, as I normally would. I sat for a time and finally the cat lost interest in me and wandered away into the darkness. I did not mind to see it go.

The sound of the cat prowling through the garden would mask my own movements, so I decided this was as good a t any to escape. I could easily jump the wall or go out the garden gate and make my escape. Where would I go? It was best to stay and wait for Mawken to return. I remembered Sofi was in danger as much as I was, except she was unaware of her danger. While the cat was pawing in the leaves, I returned to my room by the same route I left it.

I was nearly back to my door before a cough came from out of the darkness – the same ragged, throaty cough I heard from the man Haji talked with earlier. Yes, there was no doubt. I was sure Haji had someone watching me. I realized if I left the garden, the guard would sound the alarm or follow me. They could easily overpower and capture me. Besides, I where I would go in the dark? I could think of no escape. I knew now why my door was unlocked.

I slipped back into the room under cover of the darkness. I slowly eased the door partially closed and placed the table chair in its path. If anyone opened the door, the chair would topple. I would have a few seconds warning before anyone could seize me. I looked around for a weapon and could find nothing useful. I remembered the ax in the garden. I moved the chair and left the room again by the same route as before. I sat on the same bench again for a moment and listened. I did not see or hear the cat. On the other side of the wall, near the gate, I heard the same raspy cough, muffled behind a sleeve or an arm. I knew from his position behind the wall, he could not see me. However, if I went to the woodpile, he might be near enough to hear me moving around. It was too risky to attempt to retrieve the ax. I looked at the well.

The well had a wench with an iron crank attached, used to raise or lower the bucket. I judged the well was too far from the gate for my guard to hear. I slowly moved to the well in the darkness and pried the iron crank from its mounting. I returned to my room as quickly as possible past the bushes along the wall.

I replaced the chair in the path of the door once more and lay on my cot. I fingered the iron crank next to me on the bed. It was substantial and would do some damage if I hit anyone with it. I felt safer.

I wondered what time it was, and how long it would be before they came to take me. How long would it be before Mawken would return for me? He would not come too soon as far as I was concerned. Sofi would try to lead me into the trap the next night. If Mawken did not show up by then, I would have no choice. I would need to try to convince Sofi she was in as much danger as I was. If he came in time, Mawken could help us both escape. After all these months of wishing he would go away, I was glad to have an ally on the outside who would come and help me. But, would he come in time?

Long before morning, I heard the door hit against the wooden chair. It did not topple over but scraped against the floor as the door pushed it out of position. In the dark, I gripped my crank handle. A ragged moon rose slowly behind the wall, sending slivers of light through the doorway, and illuminating Sofi's soft form. I carefully slid the crank handle beneath the cot out of sight. "Maurice," she whispered. "Maurice, are you awake?"

I pretended to be caught unaware, "Sofi? Sofi is it you?"

"Yes, I am here. Are you awake?"

"I am now."

She moved the chair near my bed and sat. "Maurice, we need to talk. Something terrible has happened. I am so frightened for you!"

"What has happened?"

"Haji knows," she said.

My heart stopped. Not knowing what to say, I stalled. I sat on the edge of the bed rubbing my eyes with the back of my arm. "What does Haji know?"

"He knows everything. He has spies everywhere. He knows about you. He knows you killed your mother and father. Maurice, is it true?"

I decided to pretend to be outraged. "What?" I said loudly. "He says I …" She stopped my protests by placing her fingers across my mouth.

"Shush. Quiet!" she whispered in my ear. "They will hear you. You are being watched."

"But, I did not…" Her tightened across my lips as she shushed me.

"Do not speak. Just listen," she admonished in a hoarse whisper. "He knows. He has sent one of his servants to King Island to bring the police. Haji wants the reward on your head. In two days' time, they will arrest you. They will probably take you back to Kadan Kyun to hang. You must believe me."

"I did not kill my mother and father," I said quietly.

"It does not matter. Haji will say you did. Who will believe you? Your mother and father are dead just the same."

I knew she was setting the trap. I knew what she would say next to try to get me to leave the next night. I decided I could no longer wait for Mawken – something must be done right away. I must leave tonight. Tomorrow would be too late.

"I believe you. You have too kind a heart to be a murderer. But they will believe Haji, and they will hang you anyway."

I stood up. "I must go now!"

She grabbed my arm to hold me back. "No, wait. I want to help you. Sit back down. They will not come for two days. We have time to plan. We will escape together – you from the hangman and me from a horrible life of slavery and … and … and worse," she looked pitifully into my eyes.

"How can you help me? I must leave before they come! I can be over the wall and away from here in a few minutes?"

"No! They are watching you. If you leave the garden, they will seize you and lock you in chains until the police arrive. Haji wants to collect the reward. I have a plan."

The jaws of the trap spread wide. "I will send for my uncle. He will come tomorrow night. He has a supply caravan going back east in a few days. He will help us escape. We can be together, free from this horrible place."

I decided to spring the trap. "I know, Sofi."

She looked so confused. "You know what?" she softly asked as she shook her head. Her eyes were wide with innocence. If I did not know better, I would have been totally deceived.

"I know everything, Sofi. I know about the man you call your uncle. I know where he will take us. And I know something you do not know." Her eyes were wide with alarm.

"What do you know?"

"I know you are in danger also. Haji intends to sell us to this man you say is your uncle."

"No! That is not true! You lie!" she jumped from her chair. She did not deny what I said. She merely became angry and defensive.

"It is true, Sofi. I even know his name."

"How could you? That cannot be true!"

"His name is Raheem. True?"

The anger left her eyes as she wept. She circled the room in confused circles, not knowing what to believe. Then she became angry again. She pointed a sharp finger at my face. "How you know his name, I do not know! I know you are lying. Haji will not sell me away. Never!"

I moved to hold her in my arms but she moved away. "Sofi. I can help you, just as you said you wanted to help me. We can escape together, but we must go tonight. Now! If you take me to Raheem, you will not be coming back to Haji. You must believe me. I do not know what will become of either of us."

"No!" she said in a loud whisper. "It is a trick. Haji would never sell me away! He loves me!" Her eyes flashed in anger, before melting into large tears that fell in drops from her face.

"Sofi," I said calmly. "He already has. He has already arranged to replace you."

Sofi stopped breathing. Her face turned white. I placed my arm around her shoulder. A loud sob escaped from her mouth. She did not know what to believe. "How do you know this?"

"I overhead Haji talking to the man who coughs – the man who stands watch on the other side of the wall. As soon as you are with Raheem, your father is bringing your sister here. It is already arranged."

She flung my arm from her shoulder, pushed me onto the bed, and ran to the door. "You are lying! It cannot be true! You are trying to trick me. If you are lying, I will let them hang you!"

Before I could stop her, she pulled the door closed and quickly locked it. "Sofi! Sofi! Let me out!" I called through the door.

"No! I will go to Haji and learn the truth. If you are lying, you will hang like a dog. They will come and take you away by force. If what you say is true, I will return and we will run away together. I cannot let you go until I know the truth!"

I listened as she moved away from the door and slipped through the garden. It sounded as though she stopped near the black box and wept. Suddenly the crying stopped, and I thought I heard the back door of the tavern close loudly with a bang. Now what? Surely, she would tell them I was aware of their plan. At any moment, they would simply burst into the room, seize me, and lock me in chains. Then, it would not matter if I ended up with Raheem or the hangman.

How long would it take? Maybe only a minute or two, and they would storm my room. I tried the door in vain. I tried the small barred window. It would not move. The sky in the east was barely turning a pale pink. I retrieved my crank handle from beneath the bed and planned my defense. I decided to stand behind the door and wait to attack the first person to come through.

I do not know how much time passed as I stood sweating in the dark. Every sound was an alarm for me. The light outside the dirty, barred window was dim and tinged with damp fog. I heard footsteps. I listened closely. Only one person walked. I heard the metal key slide into the lock, and the tumbler force the bolt open. Gradually the door opened into my dark room.

I stayed behind the door, waiting to see who would enter. Was it Sofi or someone else? Carefully and quietly, the door swung into the room, concealing me behind it as it swung into the room. Quietly and slowly, someone stepped into the room. It was not Sofi! I swung the crank handle with all my might toward the dark form. The handle hit the edge of the door and vibrated violently in my hand. The handle flew from my aching throbbing hand and it crashed onto the floor with a loud ring. I fell violently against the wall, my breath knocked from my body. A dark form loomed menacingly over me. It was Mawken.

I was never so happy to see anyone. Mawken reached down and pulled me to my feet. I immediately went to the door and peered into the garden. Nothing moved in the silence of the night. "We must go! Sofi is going to warn Haji. We have to leave now!"

He looked at me with those dark hateful eyes. "What did you tell her?"

"Nothing! She told me Haji thinks I am the murderer! Any minute he will be here! Come on, we have to run for it before it is too late."

He held me back from leaving the room. "Wait! Sofi will not tell Haji anything," Mawken said.

"How do you know?" I asked desperately. "And ... and, how did you get in here? Where did you get the key?" I was entirely confused.

"From Sofi," he calmly answered. "I took it from her. She can be trusted not to say anything to Haji, believe me. She is on our side. Just wait a moment. I must tell you our plan."

"We don't have time! Haji has already turned us in. Let's go somewhere else to make our plan."

"No. Be patient. We have a little time. Sit down. The sun will be up soon, and we will be gone by then; I promise you. Just sit and listen."

I sat and wondered how he could be so calm. The room might fill any moment with men with chains, and our journey would be at the end. He stared at me with those dark, unreadable eyes. He waited until I sat.

"Good. Now listen. A ship is at dock in Mergui – the *Glendora*. She is leaving on the morning tide, just before sunrise. When we leave this place, you must immediately make your way to the docks and announce yourself as a cook to the captain. He will take you onboard immediately."

I was astonished. I knew the ship sailed this morning, and I intended to try to be on it; but how could he know the captain would take me on? "How do you know this?" I asked astonished.

"Simple," he smugly answered. "The ship must leave on time to meet his schedule, and the captain is in desperate need of a cook. He will take you on immediately."

"How do you know these things?"

"While you have been here romancing Sofi, I have been out arranging our escape. Have no fear. We will escape."

"What about you? Where will you go?"

"Also on the ship. I have made the arrangements. It is settled. Just do as I say. You must stay close by me. I cannot protect you if you lag behind. If we lose sight of each other for any reason, you must get to the ship as quickly as possible. Take your position as cook and I will come as quickly as I can. Once on board, do not indicate you know me; and do not mention me at all. I can be of more use to you if they do not know we are together."

"What about Sofi?"

"We must leave her behind. We have no choice. The captain would never take a woman on board – even for himself. The crew would not tolerate it. Sofi is not your concern. Remember, she tried to lure you into slavery for Haji."

"We cannot help her?"

"All that can be done has been done. Once Haji discovers I have the key nothing you or I can do will save her. Believe me silly boy; Sofi does not love you," he laughed cruelly. "Of that, you can be sure. Forget her. We must save ourselves."

I realized he was right. How could Sofi love me? She hardly knew me. She believed me to be a murderer. She tried to deceive me and lead me into a trap. How could I have been such a fool? Another thought suddenly occurred to me. "The garden is being watched! One of Haji's friends has been keeping watch. He is on the side of the wall near the gate. I do not know if the other walls are being guarded."

"Yes, the man with the cough," he said thoughtfully.

"Yes! What will we do?"

"He is no longer watching," he said calmly. Once again he adopted that haughty attitude I detested in him so much. How could he be so sure? He must have seen my puzzlement. "You know these people. They tire easily. He has grown weary of his vigil. Haji should have paid him more. Sofi was not enough reward, I suppose. He has quit his post."

"He was not replaced?"

"Not with anyone I could see."

"Then we must leave now. Before it gets light."

He sat on the edge of the cot and looked at me darkly. "Maurice, you must learn patience. If we go now, it will be too soon. It will give too much time for the captain and the mate to ask questions. You must arrive just before they lift the anchor, and they have resolved to sail without a cook. The prospect of sailing on dry rations will be weighing heavily on the entire crew. They will take you on board out of desperation – with no questions asked."

"Where is the ship heading?"

"It matters not. Away from here. North. To Rangoon probably."

"What happens after we get to Rangoon?"

"Who knows? The ship will not stay in port long. It will reload and head for another port. Wherever it takes us is where we will go. So long as it is not back to Kadan Kyun."

I am not sure how long we waited. Mawken did not seem to want to talk any longer, so I waited for him to decide to leave. It would not come soon enough for me. I was afraid Haji might discover our plan and prevent our escape. Meanwhile dawn was coming and it was lighter and lighter outside. The sun was not up, but I could definitely see more pink in the sky.

I tried to think of all the things that happened over the past day. At this same time yesterday, I waited on King's Island for the ferry to take me across to Mergui. It seemed as if I lived several days since then. Was anyone who they seemed to be? I thought of the family who befriended me and fed me, and lost interest in me as soon as the ferry came into sight. The ferry captain, who I feared would throw me overboard, turned out to be a kind and fair man. Haji, who smiled, laughed, and acted friendly, was actually a bad man who took advantage of everyone. Sofi was a temptress, and no doubt a whore. I felt a great disgust for the fraud Sofi. Were all women like her? She made me believe she cared for me and made me want to save her. The only one who did not try to fool me was Mawken. He came back to save me as he said he would with a plan for our escape. He would protect me. He was the only one I could trust. I realized I could not rely on anyone else. I must put my trust in Mawken only.

After what seemed like much too long, he rose and went to the window. The barred dirty opening did not show much of the outside, but it was enough to see nothing was moving outside. He said, "Follow me and stay close behind. Remember the plan." He went through the door and I followed. He said in my ear, "We will go through the gate. Do not fall behind." He strode quickly and purposefully toward the gate.

I thought it would be light enough to see by now, but darkness still shrouded the garden. The trees and vines blocked any light filtering through the foggy skies. I could see nothing. The limbs seemed to clutch at me from the darkness, and the vines caught against my legs slowing me and seeming to pull me toward the ground. No lights or sounds came from the tavern, and even the birds were silent in the trees. I moved toward the gate as a dark form leaped from a bush in front of me and jumped onto the strange black box in the center of the garden. Once I realized it was the black cat again, I did not give it much attention. I tried to reach the gate with as little delay as possible. The cat suddenly cried out loudly and then leapt from the box to the ground. The sudden movement and noise drew my attention. Although I saw the cat jump from the box, it appeared it was still sitting on top. I could see the breeze ruffle the black fur on its back. The cat did not move. Another cat? On my way to the gate, I intended to look closer at what it might be.

Suddenly my legs entangled in something, and I fell forcefully forward. I only avoided landing on my face by catching my fall with my hands. I was not hurt, but I realized I needed to hurry to catch up with Mawken. I felt around the ground, trying to find something to help me regain my feet. My hand came across a solid pole-like object I thought was a limb covered in morning dew. It was slick and wet, and as I lifted it, I discovered it was the ax from the woodpile. Someone must have thrown it aside and not replaced it in the chopping block. I could not help to think Father would not be pleased. "You must take care of your tools," he always said, "because they take care of you." I decided I would replace it in the woodpile on my way out of the gate. The handle of the ax was slippery with dew but also strangely sticky. The dew colored the handle dark black, as though it had laid on the ground a long time. I used it as a sort of crutch and balanced myself against the black box as I rose from the ground. I placed my hand on top of the black box to pull myself up and found the same wet, slippery, sticky stuff on the edge of the box. As I rose, my eyes slowly came even with the top of the box. I found myself staring into the unseeing eyes of Sofi's severed head.

62

In absolute shock and revulsion, I ran as fast as possible toward the garden gate. I blindly burst through into the darkness on the other side. My mind filled with the vision of Sofi's open unseeing eyes, and I could see nothing else. I paused just outside the gate to get my bearings. The horrible image of poor Sofi flooded my mind making it difficult to think. I looked around but saw no sight or sound of Mawken. Had he left me behind!

Several feet away in the darkness, I saw a curious red glow. It was a tiny pinpoint of light, but it was surely real. I rubbed my eyes and looked again to be sure. I moved closer to see what it was. After three steps, I froze in my tracks. Standing still and staring directly at me an old whiskered sea dog calmly smoked his pipe. He watched me without any undue concern, nor did he try to stop me in any way. Smoke curled up around the briar as he lounged lazily with his arms looped over a branch of an apple tree just under his arms. His hat was on the ground by his feet. I expected at any moment he would sound the alarm, and everything would be finished for me. I did not know what to do. He did not speak or challenge me. He just stood, watching me. His gaze came from inside a cloud of gray smoke curling up from his pipe as it twisted and wrapped around his white beard and hair. The pipe was a white Turkish meerschaum carved with a huge turbaned Turk's head on the bowl. A red coal glowed in the opening of the bowl.

Since the old sailor did not challenge me, I slowly got my senses about me. I moved slowly to my left to see what he would say. He said nothing. He did not even turn his head to follow me with his eyes. He serenely watched the gate behind me. Was he asleep with his eyes open? Since he did not contest my moving, I circled him as quietly as possible. He must be asleep because he did not stir as I walked past on my toes. Beyond the range of his sight, I turned to look back at my silent sleeping guard. I was horrified to see there was no back to his head. His brains and blood oozed slowly in thick clotted clumps down his back and left leg. Black blood formed a puddle behind his left boot. My guard was not asleep – he was dead! Someone sliced the back of his head open like a melon. He died so suddenly, he remained hung upright on the branch of the tree. It happened so recently his pipe still glowed red.

No alarm would sound from this watchman. He had coughed his last. Doubly horrified, I fled down the road as quickly as my legs would take me. I ran through the dark on the smooth wagon road leading away from the tavern, just as Mawken instructed. I ran from Haji. I ran from the dead guard. I ran from Sofi. I ran from the pirates. I ran from Mawken. I ran until I could run no longer. There was a pain in my side from running. I stopped and dropped to the road to rest. I looked around to get my bearings, and discovered in my haste and shock I was no nearer the town. I traveled uphill away from the sea – not towards it! We ran in the wrong direction! We would have to return and pass Haji's tavern again to make our way to the ship. I looked for Mawken ahead of me, but could not see him. There was no time to waste. Dawn broke fast as the sky turned light gray. I was thankful I realized the error in time.

I did not want to go past Haji's place again, but I did not know any other way. If the ship left without me, I would have no escape. Everyone would be looking for me – a killer. They would probably blame me for killing Sofi and the guard also. I ignored my extreme exhaustion and ran holding my side back toward Mergui and the ship docks. As I passed the tavern, I was relieved to not to see any movement or commotion. The party was over. No lights came from the tavern or from the garden. Ignoring the pain, I ran on until I could see the town in the gathering light of dawn. I was relieved to see the ship still sitting at her berth at the wharf. They were pulling in the gangway as I arrived. "Stop! Please let me come aboard!" I cried out of breath.

"Sorry, mate! This ship has sailed!" someone called from the deck.

"But please! I must come aboard. Please lower the gangplank again."

A gruff man with a white beard came slamming out of the wheelhouse and stared down at me.

64

"Who are you and whatdaya want?" He sounded angry. He must be the captain. I wondered if he broke the door to the wheelhouse, he flung it open so violently.

I did not know what to say, so I just blurted out, "I am a cook – looking for passage north."

He shielded his eyes with his hand as if he were looking into a nonexistent sun. He peered at me over the rail. "A cook?" he said doubtfully. "You are a cook?"

"Yes, Captain. Please take me aboard. I am a cook."

The captain looked at the mate by the gangway. "Well, damn you! Let 'im aboard, or do ya want dry rations this time out? Get 'im aboard, and show 'im 'is duty! Let's be off! Tide's goin' out fast! Get ta cookin', Mr. Cook!"

The captain laughed loudly and returned to his wheelhouse, as the mate reached a meaty arm over and hoisted me into the boat. "Don't need no 'anging gangway to get this pup aboard!" As soon as I got to my feet, he pointed to a seaman. "Show this pup to the galley, and get some tea going. Bile up some Turkish coffee, and get it up to the capt'n right away." He turned to the crew shouting orders as the boat moved slowly away from the dock.

The seaman led me down a narrow deck slanting rearward on the port side of the ship. His name was Sticks. I marveled at the fine knife attached to his belt. The handle was white and looked to be bone or ivory or pearl carved in the shape of a mermaid. The mermaids protect the Selung from drowning. I longed for such a knife. Sticks turned suddenly into a small doorway. Inside the small galley was a stove and piles of stores. Bags, sacks, and barrels stood haphazard around the walls of the room. Implements hung from the ceiling. The seaman lit a small lantern and a yellow flickering light lit the remainder of the room. I looked around the jumbled and disorganized galley. It looked as if the sailors just dropped things wherever they wanted.

65

"Don't ja be keepin' this lit if ya ain't here," the seaman said, pointing at the lantern. "Stove's thare. Don't ja be leavin' while that's lit neither! You'll be findin' what you need in the stores or in tha cab'nets. Tea fer the crew, Turkish coffee fer the officers. Capt'n likes it thick – like mud. Don't ja go waterin' it down none neither!" I looked around at the mess and wondered where they kept the coffee. Meanwhile, the seaman kept giving me my orders. "Meal time's at shift change, thirty minutes afore 'n' after. You hear the bell yer too late! We got fourteen crew not countin' you 'n' three officers. You eat last. We don't come in to port for three more days; figger out how ta make it last. Cook what you got; there ain't no more." He pointed to a set of doors. "Through that portside door's the crew mess where they eat. Keep it clean. Officers eat in the wheelhouse. Capt'n eats in 'is quarters, the next door down on the port side. Capt'n eats when Capt'n wants it. You be ready. You'll know when. Capt'n gets rations the crew don't get. "

"What is the door on the starboard side?" I asked.

"That's the cubby 'ole. Stores go in thare, and that's where ya sleep. Yer lucky – ya got more room than most. Keep the galley door unlocked at all times, 'n' keep the cubby locked when yer not in the galley. Bastards'll steal ya blind, they will. Key's on a string by tha door. Don't wrap it around ja. If ya go overboard, we'll have to break the door in. Capt'n don't tolerate fools, so yer likely to go over any time. If ya only get slapped around, ya got lucky!"

He looked at me with an incredulous look, as if he were looking at a bug. He shook his head as if he could not understand something. I was confused. He held out his hands toward me palms up. "Whut the bloody 'ell are you waitin' for? Ya ain't even got the stove flamin' yet! I give ya a hour afore yer swimmin', I will." He turned and left the room. "Calls 'imself a cook'n ain't got the stove 'ot! Blimey!"

I lit the stove, found a couple of pots, and filled them with water – one for tea and one for coffee. I poked around through the cabinets and bags until I found the coffee and tea. I heard the kettle

66

whistle when the water boiled. I made coffee and tea. No sooner was it ready than a sailor appeared at the door and demanded three cups of coffee for the officers. I gave him coffee and he left. I dug around the bags and barrels and found some vegetables, which I peeled to start a huge pot of soup. It would simmer all day and be ready for the evening meal. There was no way to judge how much stores there were, so I put whatever I could find in the soup. I decided I needed to make a sort of inventory so we would not run out of food. I was sure if we ran out of food I would not have to worry the captain would throw me overboard – the crew would. Inventory kept me busy for most of the morning. Every so often, a crewman would show up at the door. They stood at the door and waited until I acknowledged them. Then, they would serve themselves – usually tea – sometimes a hard cracker or two. I was too green to know if they were supposed to have the crackers, but we seemed to have plenty.

I kept so busy I did not have time to think of the horrors I saw earlier in the day. As I gradually got everything in order, I was able to sit and sip my tea. The boat was slowly making its way up the coast. I sat in a chair in the galley door watching the countryside slide past. With nothing to keep me occupied, the thoughts flooded through my mind. Mawken killed Sofi – and probably the guard also. It was too horrible to think someone was dead because of me. Was it necessary to kill them? We escaped, why kill Sofi? Couldn't we have just slipped past without harming anyone? I felt so sorry for Sofi. She only did what she needed to do to survive. There was no reason for her to trust me any more than anyone else. I wanted to save her. Why was it been necessary for Mawken to kill her is such a savage way? I shuddered at the image in my mind of me staring into Sofi's vacant eyes in the dark.

Where was Mawken? Was he below on the crew somewhere? I ran the direction he told me to run. Did he keep going the wrong direction as I doubled back toward town? Surely, he would have seen the lights across the cove just as I did. Was he captured? Was he on board some other vessel moving up the coast? I did not wish him ill, but I hoped never to see him again. Something was wrong with him, and I hoped I was done with him forever. I did not feel I needed his protection now that I was underway. I planned to travel to Rangoon and open that office like my father and I planned.

I kept checking on my soup. I did not intend for the captain to slap me around or throw me overboard. Late afternoon, I drank cup of tea myself and ate a cracker or two. I found some flour, rolled out some dough for biscuits, and set it aside to cure. I decided to see what was in the cubbyhole. It struck me as oddly funny to keep a door locked with a key hanging right beside the jamb. I tried the handle and the door swung open easily. It was dark inside the windowless cubbyhole. I lit a lamp and found even more bags and barrels stacked around. I added these to my inventory. I wondered where I was to sleep. Bags of rice stacked as high as my shoulders crossed the front of the room. I climbed on top, looked over through the gloom, and saw a bunk on the floor. Since I did not want to climb over rice every time I went to bed, I rearranged the stacks leaving a passageway in the middle. I sat the lantern on the top sack of rice and looked at my bunk. Someone was in it! I was never so disheartened to see Mawken.

I could not believe my eyes. "Mawken! What are you doing here? How did you get on this ship?" I was astonished. I thought I was done with him at last. Secretly, I hoped I was, although I felt guilty at the thought, I did not want anything bad to happen to Mawken. I was just ready to be on my own. I was away from Mergui on a ship heading north, and I felt safe. In my mind, I looked forward to the next steps in my great adventure. I feared now he would be making all the decisions again. He peered at me quietly from the darkness.

"The same as you," he responded. "They took me on to be a deckhand on the night watch. Since this bunk is empty in the day, I shall sleep here. No need to tell anyone. It'll be best for you and me if they do not know we are together."

"Why did you kill Sofi?" I said without intending to say it. My anger overcame my fear of him. If he could murder Sofi and the watchman, I was sure he would not hesitate to get rid of me when the time came.

"What?" he asked. His eyes grew large and I could see the white around his pupils. "Sofi is dead?"

"Yes! Someone cut off her head! Didn't you see her in the garden when we left?"

"No. Is that why you were late arriving at the boat? I was afraid you would miss the ship."

"Yes. The guard was dead too. Someone bashed in the back of his head. Did you kill them?"

"Maurice. I did not kill anyone. You must believe me. I am sure she went to Haji and told him of your escape plan. She was of no use to Haji any longer, so he must have killed her. Haji planned to get rid of her anyway. When he found out she gave up the key, he probably became outraged. I do not know who killed the guard. No one guarded the gate when I left."

I looked closely at him. He seemed sincere, and it was possible Haji killed Sofi. However, the guard was Haji's friend. Then, I remembered the warning about Haji –not to trust him; Haji only cared for Haji. I knew Haji was fully capable of killing Sofi because he wanted her sister more than he wanted Sofi. What of the guard? Was it believable Haji also killed his friend, the coughing watchman? "No one was guarding when you left?" I asked.

"No one," he assured me. "The watchman must have already been dead. I did not see a guard as we left. When we ran from the garden, I did not slow down to look around. I told you to stay close. Not until I was in town did I realize you were not behind me. I went aboard the ship and signed on as a deckhand. I thought if you did not show up by the time we sailed, I would jump overboard and come back to help you."

I saw no indication Mawken lied. If he was, he certainly showed no remorse. I lit a lamp and secretly looked at his pants and shoes in the dim light. I did not notice any blood on his clothing.

"Besides," Mawken said as I looked up, "you need me."

I shook my head not understanding. "Why do I need you?"

"Because I am on the night shift, I can make sure you are awakened in time to prepare the shift meal. Also, you can wake me before my shift each day. I can guard you and the galley while you sleep. We can help each other. You do not know this captain. He is a brutal, cruel man. He once locked his entire crew in quarters for three weeks with nothing but bread and water. No telling how many men he has thrown overboard at his whim. He is a master of the lash. The entire crew hates him. He goes about day and night armed to the teeth. He is a cold, dangerous man. Without me, no telling what might become of you. We are safer if we stick together, and if no one knows we are allies."

What Mawken said made sense. It was true I would not be using the cubby during the day; I barely had time to sit, much less get into the bunk. Having Mawken to watch out for me during the night would be a great benefit. "What makes the captain so mean?"

"He is one of those who loves to cause pain and torture. I hear he keeps a boy locked in his cabin day and night. No one ever sees this boy. The night watch reports the most horrible sounds coming from the captain's cabin at night. It is the only way they know the boy is still alive."

"Why doesn't the boy stop him?"

Mawken cruelly laughed, "Just as there are those who like to cause pain, there are those who like to receive pain. Besides, he has no choice. The captain owns him."

I hated it when Mawken laughed that way. It always seemed he was laughing at me – belittling me.

I shuddered at the thought of what might be going on the captain's quarters. "Where does your crew think you are sleeping during the day?"

"No one asks questions on a ship. Did you know, Maurice, you are in a unique position on this ship. Did you know that?"

"How so?" I asked.

"Other than the captain and the first mate, you are the only one who is armed day and night."

"Armed? How am I armed?"

He laughed at this as if it were a great joke. *Damn him! Why does he make me feel foolish always?*

Mawken spread his arms wide indicating the entire galley. "Look around you. You have knives, meat hooks, hatchets, heavy pots, and fire! The only other weapon onboard is a fire ax hanging in the wheelhouse. All of the others are under lock and key in the captain's cabin. Other than the captain, no other crewman on any ship is as well armed as the cook!"

I never thought of it before, but Mawken was right. So began our three-day run to Rangoon. He would wake me up two hours before the morning shift change, and I would have the meal ready in time. After I fed the day watch in the morning, he and the rest of the night watch would eat and retire. Mawken slept in the back of the cubby, and I would work cooking and cleaning all day.

Finally, in the evening, I would wake Mawken an hour before his shift, when he would eat and report with the night watch. Then, after feeding the day watch and cleaning up the galley and mess, I would retire. Everything went smoothly, and the meals were always on time. I received many compliments for the meals I prepared.

Each night I heard the most horrible sounds coming from the captain's quarters, which was located just on the other side of my cubby wall. I could clearly hear chains rattling and the captain's voice cursing and screaming the vilest words imaginable. I could barely make out all of the words, but the ones I could hear were profane and revolting. I heard a nightly string of slaps, pops, grunts, and moans coming from the other side of the wall, which utterly horrified me. I lay in the dark imagining what must be happening just feet from where I lay. What tortures the poor boy must endure. Occasionally, I would hear him crash into the wall as if the captain flung him with great force. I could hear him whimpering and crying. Sometimes he would scream in pain. The captain would laugh cruelly when the boy would beg for relief. Then a rhythmic bumping against the wall, accompanied by heavy breathing and finally ending with a loud moan-like shout from the captain. Then silence would return, and eventually, I would hear heavy snoring. I could not imagine the horrors the boy endured. At least I knew the boy was still alive because the next night it would start all over again. I had no idea what the boy ate, as the captain never asked for additional rations. Of course, the captain always got provisions the others did not get.

The next morning, as we pulled into Rangoon, I discovered the large butcher knife missing from the galley. I looked for it everywhere. I feared someone took it. I decided I must remember to ask Mawken if maybe he put it in the wrong place. Everything in my galley had a proper place. Early in the third morning, Sticks, the first mate, came to the galley and instructed me to make a list of stores I would need for the next run. I asked how many days, and he said to prepare for sixty days. We would be making a run to the Americas. I volunteered to go ashore to select what we needed but Sticks ordered to stay aboard the ship. I was to stay in the galley and watch the stores. I was not to leave at any time or let down my guard. The captain did not trust anyone with the money but the mate. Sticks would take a couple of the crew ashore to gather the supplies on my list and cart them back to the ship. I took inventory, calculated the goods I would need, and wrote them on a list. By the time we were pulling into Rangoon, my inventory list was ready. I turned the list over to the second mate, a man named McGinty, who was called Hognose by the crew behind his back, who told me we would be in port for two days, and I only needed cook for the five men left on watch. The others would go ashore and fend for themselves.

I watched from the rail as men came toward the boat and secured the ship to the dock with huge hawser ropes. After they tied down the boat, several members of the crew turned giant capstans to tighten the ship to the wharf. Others prepared to lower the gangplank. They seemed elated to have a couple of days in dock. Suddenly behind me, I heard a scuffle and loud voices. I could not understand the words, but the crying and screaming were unmistakable – I heard them the last two nights. The captain pulled a half-naked boy by his hair. He yanked the boy from his cabin door and dragged him toward the bow of the ship. The boy screamed and grabbing onto everything he could grasp. The boy wore a dingy white shirt and nothing else. He was naked from the waist down. The captain hauled the boy to the side and heaved him over the rail. The boy landed on the small of his back upon the rough planks of the dock. He lay crumpled and cried out in his pain; I feared his back was broken. The seamen and the men on the deck laughed and applauded, rather enjoying the indecent show. Sticks laughed and asked the captain, "Aye, sir! Throwin' yer boy away, are ya?"

The captain looked at the mate with a wild hateful look. Sticks was not intimidated in the least and fearlessly stared right back at the captain. "Bloody bugger got to where 'e was likin' it, 'e was," captain said. "Didn't have nae fight or spunk in 'em anymore."

I watched as the boy picked himself up from the rough planks and slowly limped down the wooden dock toward shore. The mate smothered a laugh behind his hand and said, "Ya might 'ave waited for us to lower the gangplank, Captain."

"I could'a throwed him off t'other side, I could. And let the fishes have 'em. The pup could nae swim!"

Sticks dared to provoke the captain who was in such an obvious foul mood by saying, "Mebbe, ya could'a given' 'em 'is breeches, though."

The captain scowled and spit over the rail. " 'E didna' 'ave any! Never ya mind, Mister. I'll 'ave another 'for I sail. This town's crawlin' with 'em."

The captain brushed his hands as if he had taken out the garbage, then turned and went back down the deck to his cabin, leaving the entire crew, but me, laughing and pointing at the poor soul dragging himself ashore. I did not see anything humorous in the incident – especially since the police immediately seized the boy and dragged him away from the end of the dock.

For two days and nights, the *Glendora* was unburdened of her old cargo and loaded with the new. A steady stream of wagons and carts traveled up and down the dock carrying away goods or bringing new goods to be loaded. Carts of many shapes and sizes, some pulled by animals and some by men crowded the dock. The waterfront was an active and noisy place. I did not know or much care, what they loaded onto the ship. That was none of my concern, as the second mate pointed out to me loudly and plainly. I did observe, however, the ship sat a little lower in the water than when we docked.

There was no difficulty feeding the five crew who remained onboard to watch. I saw no sign of Mawken, so I supposed he went ashore with the others. On the last day before we sailed, Sticks returned with two sailors who brought aboard the stores I listed. These men did not assist in stowing away these goods but left the barrels and sacks scattered around the galley in a jumbled pile. The galley looked much the same as I first saw it. It was up to me to get things in order and prepare to sail. I much preferred it this way, since I would then know where everything was stowed. The putting away took me most of the final day. Sticks told me the crew would come aboard at midnight; we would sail at dawn. This would require me to prepare morning mess earlier than usual.

At the appointed time, I was ready and I served the meal, first to the day watch as was normal, then to the night watch. I still did not see Mawken anywhere about the ship. Neither was he among the famished sailors. I wondered if maybe he would stay behind in Rangoon. I was curious, but I was strangely unconcerned about this. I was off for America, and I planned never to return to this part of the world. If he stayed behind, I would likely never see Mawken again. I was grateful for all he did for me, but I was sure I could make do on my own. When the *Glendora* reached America, I would go ashore and make a new life in a wonderful place, never looking back. I knew something of the shipping business; and I was sure I could make a go of it in the place called New Orleans, the place they said we would come to port.

After I finished my duties in the galley, I went out on deck to watch the Port of Rangoon fade away into the distance. I was eager to go back to sea and leave this place. Rangoon brought to my mind a kind of sadness of what may have been had my father lived. From the ship, I could see the building we intended for my office. The thought occurred to me to go ashore and see if I might be able to recover my intended position and the family business. Then, I remembered the authorities might be looking for me as a murderer. Was there any way to clear my name? Besides, my orders were to stay aboard. I felt no desire to disobey this captain. I was not sure what the punishment would be if I disobeyed. Besides, the ship leaving port and it was already too late by the time I thought of it.

Rangoon sits on a kind of peninsula at the point where two rivers joined. The Yangon River meets the Bago River flowing out to sea together. Yangon is the traditional name of the place the British call Rangoon. The ocean tide in the harbor is not strong enough to take us out to sea. We must catch the river current and drift until we could set the sails and plow into the sea on the wind, the river flow, and the tide. I watched the crew load the kedging anchor onto the skiff and row to the end of the anchor line. They dumped the anchor into the bay and signaled the ship to begin the warping out. The entire deck crew rewound the anchor line around the capstan, pulling us toward the kedging anchor and away from the dock. At the end of the rope, the rowers retrieved the anchor, only to row it even further out into the bay. We repeated the process three times until we reached the river current and began to make progress with further warping.

As Rangoon receded in the distance, I suddenly realized someone stood next to me at the rail. It was Mawken. He did not speak to me, nor I to him. I was not sure what to say, or even sure how I felt about him still being aboard. I was ready to turn and go inside. Mawken stopped me and pointed, "Wait. Look yonder."

I looked out as we were drawing abreast of Pirate's Pointe, so named as the place the government hanged pirates. The local authorities would hang them from an old yardarm and leave them for days as a warning against piracy to sailors arriving or leaving

Rangoon. The pirates hung until they rotted. Seabirds would pluck out their eyes, and the corrupt flesh would slough from the putrefied bones. After a time, the corpse would turn black, and the stomach would bloat and sag below the hips. The body would eventually burst open in the hot sun, and bile and juices would flow down their legs to drip into the green seawater below. I had seen it on a previous trip. It was not something I cared to see again, but he insisted and held me back.

As we neared the point, I could see a body swinging from the gallows. I told him I had no desire to see a decomposing pirate, even though this one still looked fresh. "Wait," he said again as I edged away. So I watched, as the gruesome sight grew closer and larger in my sight. As we drew alongside, I was appalled to see the body on the yardarm was none other than the captain's boy, who the captain callously threw from the ship when we arrived. I remembered the police seized the boy as soon as he crawled to the head of the dock. I thought they took him in to give him aid. Now, here he hung on Pirate Pointe, still without pants. I did not understand why; this boy was no pirate. He was a harmless waif who fell into the brutal hands of a pitiless ship's captain.

I looked at Mawken with questioning eyes. "Why did they hang the boy?" I asked.

"He was a dangerous lot, he was." He looked at me with those dark eyes. "A killer some said."

"That boy? A killer?"

"Yes. They say in a fit of rage and spite he murdered his own mum and dad in cold blood – on Kadan Kyun." Those cold eyes bored into me, daring me to refute it.

I was aghast! "Where would they get that idea?" I asked although I feared in my heart to hear the answer. Mawken explained Haji sent word ahead to be on the lookout for a boy leaving the *Glendora* in Rangoon. Haji turned him in as a murderer. Of course, it was possible it happened that way. Nevertheless, something made me think the real informant was Mawken. I could not contradict his story. I was glad I stayed onboard ship while we were in port. It could be me hanging from the old yardarm on Pirate's Pointe.

He disappeared into the galley before I recovered enough to ask him about the missing galley knife. I turned to follow him into the galley. A sailor arrived and informed me the captain "wanted fed."

Once on the high seas, things returned to a more normal routine. While sailing among the islands of the archipelago off Malaysia, the ship worked only two shifts daily. The sailors hated it. However, once we left Rangoon and entered the Bay of Bengal, the captain allowed alternating four-hour watches. On this new voyage, there was no longer a day watch and a night watch, but six watches each day, divided between the first and second crew. I found it confusing until I took a paper and drew up a schedule like this:

> 8:00 in the evening until Midnight
> First Crew – First Watch
> Midnight to 4:00 in the morning
> Second Crew – Middle Watch
> 4:00 in the morning to 8:00 o'clock
> First Crew – Morning Watch
> 7:30 Second Crew – Breakfast Mess
> 8:00 in the morning to Noon
> Second Crew – Forenoon Watch
> 8:30 First Crew – Breakfast Mess
> Noon until 4:00 in the afternoon
> First Crew – Afternoon Watch
> 7:30 Second Crew Supper Mess
> 4:00 in the afternoon to 8:00
> Second Crew –Dog Watch
> 8:30 First Crew Supper Mess

Since common sailors rarely own a timepiece, the wheelhouse would ring the ship's bell every half hour. Someone would report to the helm all was well with the shift on duty. At eight bells, the shift would change. Then the bell ringing would commence again with one ring. After a while, you could tell the time from the quarter of the day and the number of bells. I became so accustomed to this routine, I would rise in the morning at five bells without even realizing I heard them. This gave me ample time to prepare breakfast for the crew going on watch.

A world of water from horizon to horizon produced boredom day after day. It may have been a fortnight into the sail when the captain summoned me to his quarters late one afternoon before the evening meal. I did not know what the captain wanted of me. A seaman already took the captain his dinner – stew, biscuits, and strong, hot Ceylonese tea.

As soon as I arrived at the captain's door, he lunged at me and pinned me against the gunwale. He grabbed my hair and forced me to my knees. He twisted my arm behind my back and screamed into my face, his spittle soaking my cheeks and neck.

"Bloody 'ell! What'us that bilge ya sent me for ma vittles?"

He cruelly ground my arm behind my back as I struggled to answer without whining.

"Stew and tea, sir. Same as the mess." I felt an excruciating fire in my arm and shoulder.

"That was no bloody tea, you lit'l shit. It was a cup o' piss, it was! I know piss when I see it." He thrust his cup toward me with his free hand. "Here! Drink this tea, then!" he ordered.

I looked into his cup and was horrified to see it was not tea. It was piss! I could smell it. I quickly realized what happened. The treacherous seaman either drank or poured out the captain's tea and replaced it with his own brew, knowing the captain would blame me. I tried to think. "It was tea when it left the galley, sir."

"Then go'wan and drink it then!" The captain pushed the cup to my lips and forced it hard against my teeth. I gagged as the still-warm liquid ran down my chin. Then he jerked me to my feet and slapped me hard against my cheek. I fell back onto the deck on my back.

The captain stood over me, grinning at my helplessness. I remembered the captain loved inflicting pain on others. Now, he got his pleasure from me. Something about the struggle excited the captain, and his eyes took on a joyful look of pleasure. The captain grabbed me again and went back to work on my poor aching arm. I remembered with fear how he treated his cabin boy. Suddenly he pushed me back onto the deck and shouted, "You'll do!" He grabbed me by my ankle and dragged me across the deck toward his cabin. I knew where he wanted to take me, and I imagined why. I thought the captain intended to chain me in his cabin like his other boy and beat me every day. I did not know at the time what his real intentions were. Oh, I know now what he intended; but then, I thought a beating was the worst of it.

Suddenly, rough hands snatched me from his grip and pushed me away down the deck as a sailor stepped between the captain and me. As I overcame my shock, I realized it was Mawken.

"Captain! Leave the boy alone!" Sticks shouted his hand on the haft of a knife in his belt. It was a beautiful knife with mermaid handle.

The captain looked Sticks up and down with a despicable look. "You? And why would I be

listenin' of you? Stand aside er be thrown over, ya lout!"

"Captain, this boy is no measure for you. Leave him be!" Sticks stepped toward the captain.

"Whut's 'e ta you? 'Sides, I'll take who I want!" The captain's red-streaked eyes were wild, and drool dribbled down his whiskers onto the deck. The captain was like a wild animal, ready to attack anything in his path. He pulled a pistol from his pants and cocked the hammer back, and pointed it directly at Sticks.

80

"Stand aside, I tell yer! Or, yer'll be feedin' the fishes a'ter I blow ya open!"

"Captain, the boy's our only cook! You take him, and we've got nothing but hard rations the rest of the sail."

The captain moved forward menacingly until the gun pressed deep into the mate's chest.

"Take me," Mawken said from behind the two sailors.

The captain moved from one man to the other and placed his gun against Mawken's chest.

"You don't want no weakling runt like that boy." Mawken thumped his chest with his fist next to the gun barrel without attempting to brush it away. It appeared he was daring the captain to fire.

The captain grinned an evil toothy smile that sent shivers up my back. He looked past Mawken and gave me a wicked wink. Then he laughed loudly, slowly uncocked the gun, and laid the hammer back down.

"Back to tha galley, you scum," he yelled at me. "Ya pass me piss again, and I swear by God I will shoot you dead."

I hurried back toward the galley as the captain tried to stare Mawken down. I could not hear what they said, but I did not see Mawken again for many days afterwards. Mawken sacrificed himself for me. I shudder to think what would have become of me had the captain taken into his cabin. I would have become his boy! A beating would have been tolerable if that were the end of it. There was no way of knowing it would have been the end of it.

I returned to the galley so frightened, I looked around for something to use for my own defense. I found a marlinspike and put it in my pocket, but I was not sure that would be good enough. I grabbed the largest blade in the kitchen. It was then I remembered the missing knife. Somehow, I knew who had it.

We sailed the Bay of Bengal for some days and were nearing the western edge of that great sea. At one time sailors thought it was the end of the world. The island of British Ceylon was our next stop. We were to port in Colombo, re-provision, off-load some cargo, and take on a huge load of tea for our run to the Americas.

For days, I expected trouble. I saw no sign of Mawken. The suspense kept me awake at night as once again I listened to the sounds coming from the other side of the wall. The noises were different this time. Unlike earlier, with the wretched boy, I could hear little of anything at all, just some bumps and the sound of things knocked about. However, I heard no sudden screams or moaning. I had no idea what occurred on the other side of the wall. Sometimes it sounded more like a fistfight. I could not make out what they were saying. I could only hear the banging against the wall. Whatever, it was certainly quieter than before.

Once the Captain did not appear for two days, and during the entire period, he had not demanded any food or drink. Once he finally came on deck the third day, he had a black eye, which he tried to conceal beneath the brim of his dark hat. When Sticks asked, the captain laughed his raucous laugh revealing a newly missing tooth but gave no real answer. It seemed things were a little more difficult with Mawken than with his former boy. However, since I did not see or hear him, I had no idea how Mawken fared. Since the captain was still alive, I feared the worse. Knowing the butcher knife was still at large, I looked as closely as I could at the Captain's forearms and face, but I could not see any cuts.

Our stay in Ceylon was brief; the captain ordered all hands to remain aboard the *Glendora*. No one was to go ashore as we would depart as soon as we were laden with new cargo. Sticks posted guards to prevent anyone from jumping ship while it was in port. The Captain took no chances of losing crew.

"Ya signed on for tha job and yere not finished 'til the sail is completed, yere discharged, or yere dead!"

We decided to sail around to the western side of the island to reach the port of Colombo. A decrepit, seemingly abandoned fort stood sentry over the wide deep-water port. Portions of the ramparts were in ruins. I wondered if it was defeated in some battle. The British no longer needed the defenses and decommissioned the old fort. The locals used the salvage materials to build much of the rest of the city. The locals sold, stole, or gave away the rocks and blocks from the old walls. The old fort headquarters served as a tax office and other government functions. A large, beautiful clock tower stood in the center of the town.

After weeks at sea, I longed to go into town but I thought the Sticks might shoot me if I tried. The crew lowered the gangway to allow townsmen to come aboard with supplies and then stowed it away under guard after visitors left the ship. Again, they left my galley in a jumbled mess. I spent my day trying to put everything back in order. Before I knew it, we were sailing away from the dock, bound for New Orleans. I wondered what it would be like in the new land. I heard so many wonderful things. I made secret plans to leave the *Glendora* in America.

Late in the afternoon, a week out of Colombo, I saw an amazing sight. I stood on deck just outside the galley, looking out to sea when I first saw it. I could hardly believe my eyes! I saw a fish swim along with the boat, then suddenly launch itself skyward and soar over the waves on what looked like wings. Several more appeared and took to the skies. They could travel aloft a far distance, but gradually splashed down back into the sea. Their wings looked like overgrown fins. I later learned flying fish live in most of the world's warm tropical waters, but I never saw or heard of them before. I never tired of watching them. Sticks said at dinner they often fly onto the deck. If one come aboard, I was to gut and fillet it immediately. Then I was to bring it to him uncooked, because they were delicious raw. All of the flying fish I saw flew away from the boat, so I was not able to catch one. I wondered what it would taste like. I decided to keep watch in case I might be able to catch one with an improvised net. I attempted a couple of times, but I could not get close enough to get one in my net. I laughed to myself my "sky fishing" was no better than my other fishing attempts.

Our voyage found excellent weather and favorable winds. The northeast trade winds push us along. I overhead Sticks instruct the crew to push for as much speed as we could manage, since we must round the cape and enter the Atlantic before June. As it was early April, the captain calculated we would make it in time. Even so, he wished for a favorable storm might push us in the right direction. His wish soon came true.

At first, we could see the dark clouds billowing behind us grow closer each day. The winds ahead of the storm picked up, and we made good daily runs. The captain was pleased and ordered more meat and beans for the crew in the coming days. Most of the experienced sailors knew we were in for a run before the storm. The captain was not being kind; he simply wanted everyone to be at maximum strength in case we could not cook for a couple of days. Once the seas grew to a certain level of intensity, the captain would order all fires on board extinguished, and we would only have cold provisions. No one looked forward to that.

I watched the clouds draw closer each day, and the seas grow heavy under our ship. Gone were the smooth waters of the days since we left Rangoon. The angry sea was rough and choppy. The sky grew dark, and we burned the navigation lamps even during the day. The temperature dropped noticeably. The crew brought piles of rain gear from below decks and distributed to the men. Sticks wished we would reach Madagascar before the storm hit. If we were to gain the island, we could find safe harbor on the western side. Stick's wish would not come true.

The third morning after we first saw the ominous clouds coming from behind, it was impossible to tell if the sun was up or not. It was dark as night. The wind grew steadily throughout the morning and howled in a ceaseless moan. It was clear we would not gain landfall before the storm overtook us. The order went out to extinguish all fires, and secure all goods. My orders were to stay in the galley and protect the food stores as best as I could. The captain would hold personally accountable for any losses. I locked the cubby where most of the stores were and decided to sleep in the galley. I was not sure what I was to protect the stores from – the weather or the crew. Either way I decided it would be safer to lock the goods inside the cubby than for me to be inside with them. I would sleep on the hard floor of the galley. I pulled out my blankets and bedding and made a pallet in the corner of the room. Remembering Stick's advice not to hang the key around my neck, I draped the key on a hook behind the stove.

I never rode out a serious storm on the ocean. I sailed several squalls near the shore, and they were frightening enough. Never was I this far out to sea. I was unprepared for what would come. Without lights, it was dreadfully dark in my galley. The little window was not large enough for me to get a good idea of the storms fury. I could hear the storm even if I could not see it. Black wisps of clouds streamed past the little porthole. I did not know it was possible for clouds to be so low.

Once I opened the galley door to the deck, and the wind jerked it from my hand and nearly ripped it from the hinges. The wind howled across the decks, and screamed in the rigging. The sound of the sea crashing into our ship was a roar such as I never heard before. I tried to get the door closed but the wind was too strong. The salty spray soaked me, and I swallowed some seawater when a wave lapped over the side of the ship. I choked on the salty water, and spat over the side of the ship. I looked up to see the masts were naked. The crew took down and stowed all of the sheets. We were at the mercy of the wind, the waves, and the current.

I struggled trying to close the door, but the wind was too strong. The blast was so strong, it physically blew me down the deck several feet before I could hold on to something and struggle my way back to my door. The heaving green sea turned black and rose up against the wallowing boat. The wind screamed through the masts and across the deck. The awesome ferocious force of nature was against us. I put my feet against the bulwark and tried to force the door closed against the wind. I was afraid I would not be able to get the door shut again. If I lost control of it again, it might rip from the jamb, and blow into the buckling sea carrying me away with it. I let the door rest against the wall, and groped my way back inside the galley hand-over-hand. I found a length of rope and tied one end to the leg of the iron stove. I carried the other end back out on the pitching deck.

The seas were even larger now. Huge waves piled up taller than the ship, and the valleys were deathly deep. It was like climbing a steep hill, then slipping down the other side. If the waves caught the ship sideways, we would have surely swamped. I could see the crew in the wheelhouse above struggle to turn the great wheel to turn the boat to face the wailing wind. Our survival depended upon keeping prow into the waves. It was safer, though each new wave pushed us farther out to sea and away from our destination.

I finally managed to secure the end of the rope to the door and worked my way back inside where I assembled a makeshift capstan out of a small cask and a pulley. I saw sailors pull a great weight by this method when we left the port of Rangoon. If I used the weight of the barrel, and wrapped the rope around it, I might be able to pull the door shut. Gradually the door moved. Once I pulled the door far enough, a favorable swirl of wind slammed the door shut and I hastily secured it. I decided not to open the door again unless I was prepared to leave the ship.

Gradually the lurching of the ship diminished. I spotted a little blue sky in the dim light through the porthole. I carefully inched open the door and looked down the deck. The wind died down and the clouds blew past. The captain was in the wheelhouse, and I heard his order to turn the boat back to our western course. The captain and Sticks walked the deck to inspect the damage. By nightfall, we learned we lost less than a day, which the captain took as good news. "Could 'ave been worse!" was all the captain said as he returned to his cabin. He gave me a fierce look as he passed and ordered the fires and dinner started.

After the storm, we sailed out of the Bay of Bengal into the great and vast Indian Ocean towards the east coast of Africa. A few days later, we crossed the great invisible dividing line between the seas. New stars appeared in the sky.

Things on the ship settled down into a daily routine, which seldom varied in even the slightest degree. The storm caused some damage, but we charted a course for some small island port to make repairs. We were only there a few hours without incident. We needed sail mostly.

There was not much to see except a vast sea stretching from horizon to horizon. There were few islands and no distractions except at daybreak and sunset; at those times, the sky took on the most beautiful colors. The beauty frequently left me breathless. I never saw such skies, streaked with color each night from horizon to horizon. The sight of a huge red sun slowly bursting from the water was wonderful. In the evening, the golden sun slipping slowly below the horizon in the gathering darkness as the stars popped out one by one was even more beautiful. At those times, I fully understood the lure of the seas, and I realized few people on land had ever seen such sights as these.

The old sailors told me sometimes when the sun sank beneath the water level, a bright green flash would occur. I looked often but never saw it myself. Other stories were shared as we moved through the endless ocean of water. During slow times, the old sailors never tired of telling of the great sea battles and victories of the British Empire. I especially loved the tales of the horrible sea monsters. I looked for endless days in the sea for the sight of mermaids, but saw none. The stories of ships sinking in the calmest of weather and seas frightened and thrilled me at the same time.

I discovered sailors were the most superstitious people I ever knew. The superstitions were many and varied. For example, sailors considered it unlucky to begin a voyage on Friday. This superstition was so widespread, the British Navy attempted to stamp it out by scheduling some naval ships to depart on a Friday. The reason I was able to catch the *Glendora* on time back in Mergui was it waited until Saturday to depart. Otherwise, I would have been left behind. They claimed the British Navy named a ship the *HMS Friday* and launched it on a Friday. On her maiden voyage, after she sailed over the horizon of the great Atlantic, she disappeared and was never seen or heard from again.

Sailors had names for everything. A Jonah was a ship, or a sailor, or anything thought to bring bad luck, because a great whale swallowed Jonah of the Bible. Anything lost overboard was relegated to "Davy Jones' Locker", a sort of nautical hell from which there was no escape or rescue. Not much attempt was made to recover anything overboard; and I often heard the saying, "What the sea wants, the sea shall have." I wondered if that included a person who might fall into the waves. At any rate, whatever was lost to the waves was regarded as not worth spending the time it might take to bring it back aboard. We had cargo to deliver. Sailors also had a heaven beneath the waves, which held many wonderful things, but not much was ever said about that place. Despite its glorious description, I noticed no one wanted to go there.

Red skies were lucky at some times of the day and very unlucky in the mornings; I never understood why except it had something to do with storms or threat of storms. I noted often we would have a red sky morning, but nothing much ever came of it. Most of the storms I sailed through on the sea were dark and black with greenish-yellow clouds, not red ones.

We would sit out of sight of the bridge each day and I would hear the most interesting stories. If the captain came on deck or one of the mates came down from the wheel, everyone scattered and got to work – doing something. Once they discovered I was an eager and willing audience, they lingered over their meals and spun their tales to my great delight. I heard stories of survival at sea and of castaways on deserted islands. I heard tales of pirate gold and piles of jewels as high as my head stashed away on some mystery island, especially in the Caribbean where we were headed. There was no end to the stories. They spoke of seeing strange lights on the water or up in the sky. They told of overtaking ghost ships sailing the seas with no crew on board at all. I heard of catching and hauling aboard strange fish and creatures no one could identify.

We spent long idle days in the shade of the sails telling these tales and many others. At night, with the yellow oil lantern casting shadows on the bulkhead, the tales turned dark and mysterious.

I learned most of what I knew of the sea in those days. Of course, I was the butt of most of their jokes – being sent on more than one occasion on some impossible mission or searching for some tool that did not exist. I took it in good humor, realizing it was their way of accepting me into their society. Most of them had fallen for the same timeless ruses in their day.

I learned the ways of the sea. I thought ships moved only by the massive white sails endlessly flapping and popping high above. This is mostly true, especially since it gives the ship greater speed. But I learned the oceans of the world have currents in them, like great rivers. If a current is going the direction you wish to travel, then you have easy sailing so long as the wind is also favorable. However, going against the current, even with a favorable wind, is always difficult. Sailing against the current and against the wind is often impossible. Ships often have to sail several degrees of the compass off the oncoming wind to keep the sails filled enough for forward movement. Then, to stay on course the ship would have to sail off the other side. The sailors call it tacking, and it results in the ship sailing many more miles than a straight course would take. Ships would move through those waters by sailing off the starboard side, then to the port in large back and forth paths. You can imagine how the current would complicate such a plan. To know if the ship was on the correct course took numerous sightings through use of a complicated instrument and countless course changes.

On this trek, we were fortunate indeed. Once we reached the area of the African continent, we would have a favorable wind and a strong current to carry us swiftly in our desired direction. However, there was urgency about it. We must reach it in time. At some time, which was generally in the month of June, the current shifted. If we were late, we would be fighting the current to make the great sweep around the Cape of Africa. A different current swept down from equator through the Atlantic Ocean, and sheered eastward across the west flowing Indian current as it turned back in on itself. This great clash of currents causes great turbulence in the seas, which results in waves and swells impossible to imagine. Countless ships, much larger and better fit than the *Glendora* have been lost beneath these massive waves. Considering myself seaworthy after having weathered the great storm of a few weeks past, I tried to join in their conversation. They laughed at me in my ignorance, assuring me I had yet to see a truly huge wave. They told tales of waves towering three times the height of the *Glendora*. The thought thrilled and frightened me, and I hoped I would never see such a sight.

If we could reach the great cape of Africa before the currents and winds shifted, the sea would sweep us around and sling us into the north flowing Atlantic current flowing swiftly up the western African coast. The massive current would carry us along with it until it reached the equator and then would sweep us westward taking us across the Atlantic to the continent of South America. The longer it took to reach the favorable current the more tense and nervous the captain and officers became. The more agitated they became, the meaner and stricter they were on the crew. The crew reacted as an abused dog would. Daily, they became more surly, resentful, and angry. The more sullen they became, the meaner the officers became. It was a vicious circle and grew worse daily. Punishments and lashing became common for the most serious offenders.

One day, I was late bringing the Captain his dinner because no one came to the galley to pick up his meal. No one wanted to approach the captain during this time, so I was to deliver his meal myself. I timidly knocked as the captain snatched open the door and grabbed me my throat, screaming about how late I was and how I should have come earlier. Fear immediately filled me with dread he might order the crew to give me lashes, despite the immediate threat he might choke the life out of me where I stood. I believed in that moment, I would rather he choked me to death than to be whipped.

Suddenly, he released my throat, swung his arm in a great arc, and slapped me across the face with a meaty open hand. I fell to the floor, senseless with the pain. I imagined those in the wheelhouse must have heard the slap. My mind raced with the thought maybe Sticks would come and rescue me again. That thought evaporated as the Captain's boot caught me full in the stomach, causing me to retch black bile across the deck. I braced for another kick, hoping it would not be to my head or face. Suddenly, the captain stopped and stood with legs widespread and ordered me to clean up my mess and get back to the galley. Grateful not to receive any more punishment, I looked between the captain's legs into the darkened cabin behind him. In the gloom, two eyes stared from the darkness, fixed in a hateful glare at the Captain's back. I thought I saw the yellow glint of a knife blade as the Captain turned and slammed the door closed.

And so it went from day to day as we sailed toward and down the east coast of Africa and inside the large island of Madagascar where the current was strongest. Doing so exposed us to greater risk of being detected by pirates, but the advantages of greater speed overcame our need for safety. The Captain ordered the watch doubled to detect any followers. We could outrun any potential threat, if we got a big enough lead.

Again, I saw no sight or sign of Mawken. The Captain still walked the deck each day unescorted. The cruelty and depravity toward the crew continued unabated and unchallenged.

Generally, the Captain was the only armed person aboard the ship. For a few days, until the threat of piracy passed, the officers wore pistols. An ax hung on the wall outside the wheelhouse, for use in case of fire, but no other arms were available in case of emergency. Of course, the galley held a wide selection of heavy objects, cleavers, and knives – minus one.

The crew was in high spirits, and even the Captain forced a smile. The current and weather still held, and it appeared we would be able to round the Cape in time to take advantage of the famous Benguela current, which would sweep us up the west coast of Africa. The current we were on also had a name but I no longer remember. If the winds were favorable and the clash of the opposing currents was calm, we would have smooth sailing. If we arrived late, not only would we suffer the wrath of the Captain, but the wrath of the sea as well. The fear of an angry sea was so strong many preferred to suffer the Captain. The tales of eddies and suck holes that could pull any ship to the depths, frightened me.

All of our fears, worries, and precautions came to nothing. We did not see a single ship in the swift channel, and we swept around the cape without incident. The dreaded equatorial southward wind did not find us, and we easily sailed toward the junction of two of the great oceans of the world, the Indian and the colder Atlantic. As we neared the transition point, all hands assembled on deck. At first, I thought it was a bad sign, but I soon discovered the real reason why every sailor wanted to be present as we entered the famous Atlantic.

Far ahead on the horizon, I could see a strange dark line stretching from one side to the other across our bow. It appeared to be a shoreline far ahead; but as we neared, the faint line grew more distinct and thicker. This was no shoreline. It looked as if an artist painted a line right on the surface of the sea ahead. The sea beneath us remained the sea-green foamy water we sailed upon since we left port. As we drew nearer to the strange line, it grew darker and thicker. It did not appear to be moving toward us at all. As we came nearer, we saw the division was not perfectly straight had a scalloped edge, like a cloud. It appeared as if the shadow of a huge dark cloud smothered the surface of the sea. I had seen clouds on the water many times. Cloud shadows would make the water appear to be dark. But, those shadows moved, sometimes ran along with us, and sometimes away. I never saw such a cloud extending from horizon to horizon. It seemed strange and peculiar.

My duties in the galley forced me from the deck, so I abandoned my position on the forward rail. Soon, I heard cheering and a lot of commotion coming from the sailors grouped on the deck. I decided to take a chance and return to my observation point on deck. I was amazed at what I saw. It was obvious now this shadow was no cloud. We were sailing from our familiar green sea into a fearsome ocean of dark blue water. I wondered what it meant and if it would still float our ship. Those nearby roundly laughed at me for my stupidity, but it seemed odd and threatening to me. As we got closer and closer, the massive expansion of this new ocean became obvious. The change was dramatic. I could see why the sailors gave up sleep to come on deck to see the sight. After months at sea, any new occurrence was a welcome distraction.

When I asked what it was, the sailors said we were moving from the Indian Ocean to the Atlantic and the waters did not easily mix. We made our transfer in time, and I was relieved to hear the sight of this immense dark blue pool meant we would not be caught in the clash of the two oceans. This discussion brought forth opportunities to tell the tales of less fortunate voyages and the fearsome fabled clash of water on water. It was clear the waters did not readily mix. As our prow plowed through the dividing line, the water parted, and we slid into the dark, deep, blue expanse. Still, the seas did not blend. It was if we sailed from green tea into thick dark blue water the consistency of wine. As a lark, the sailors pulled aboard a bucket of this new seawater, and I was amazed it was not thick, and it was not blue. It was clear, just like the familiar sea we left behind.

Far to our starboard, I could see the faint hills of the African continent. It was as close as we would come to the great land mass. I wanted so much to see it, but faint faraway mountains would be all I would see.

Meanwhile, behind us the green Indian Ocean I knew all my life receded until it became a faint gray line and eventually we could not discerned it any longer. It faded and disappeared quickly until all we could see was the deep blue of the sea. Even before the blue was all we could see, the sailors returned to their bunks and normal routines. It was late and I worked like a madman to catch up and prepare the evening meal on time. The stories this night moved into the strange and unusual happenings of the Atlantic. The farther north one sailed, the colder the water became until eventually the entire sea turned to ice. Along the way, huge pieces of ice, many times larger than the ship, floated on the ocean. I knew the ends of the earth were icebound, but I never knew anyone who had seen it.

I longed to know of the other oceans of the world and set a goal for myself to one day sail them all somehow. While I was eager to leave this cruel captain, I loved the sea and wanted to live my life on the water. I was happy and content as a ship's cook. The adventure and lure of traveling to different countries and seeing new ports suited me fine. I could not wait to see what we would find in the strange port of New Orleans. The old hands told me it was just like sailing into France, and the people even spoke a French dialect, which I found odd. I could not find a single sailor who had been there, much less any of the Caribbean ports. All of them knew of such places, but none had ever been ashore. I wondered how true the stories were and if these places were as exciting as they sounded.

Meanwhile, the great misty continent of Africa passed slowly off our starboard side. I longed to go ashore and walk in the jungle. The sailors knew much about the African jungles. They told fantastic tales of the sights they saw. Ebony goddesses went out with their breasts fully exposed with no shame or timidity. It was natural and normal in their culture. I heard of fearsome beasts that could devour a man whole. Snakes and poisonous plants abounded in the jungles, which were so thick in places only a native could pass. Life began there, they say. In the ancient past, humans lived deep in the earth and finally emerged to rule the land and all of the animals. The extreme range of humans now lived in these jungles, from impossibly tall giants to tiny small little people. Some of these strange people ate humans, and no man could escape their capture. They exalted in collecting the human heads of their victims, which they shrunk and wore around their necks. The natives used poisons from plants on their darts and arrows, which could instantly stun or paralyze the strongest man; after which they would boil and consume the man alive! Even the frogs in the trees were lethal. Meat eating beasts with huge teeth and impossibly large snakes lived in the forest and consumed any living thing. I heard of snakes as long as the *Glendora* was wide, whose major weapon was the ability to wrap around a body and crush it to death before swallowing it whole. Even smaller snakes were more dangerous than most others were.

The rivers and lakes were teeming with dangerous animals like flesh eating fish and huge reptiles with jaws filled with huge teeth. The massive hippopotamus also bathed in the rivers and could kill a human with ease. The jungles held two types of swimming reptiles that could kill a normal man. Cats of all types hunted in the darkness. Massive beasts flocked in herds so massive they stretched from horizon to horizon, and trampled and crushed everything in their path. Strange animals that could change their shape and appear differently each time they appeared, allowing them to get closer to their prey, were common. A massive four-legged beast with a horn on its snout could outrun the fastest human.

95

If that were not enough, dangerous spiders and insects were in the trees and vines. Great, hairy poisonous spiders lived in the trees and rocks and were so potent a person stung would die within minutes if bitten. Only their sea snakes were less dangerous than ours were but they were still deadly. A scorpion lived in the jungle that could kill a grown man. Once bitten, a man would suffer the most unbearable pain and sickness, eventually begging his companions to kill him swiftly rather than suffer the bite and its unavoidable consequences. Flying, nearly invisible, biting insects so vicious they could draw blood swarmed the sky in such massive clouds they blocked the sun.

Even the waters of the sea were treacherous, hosting giant man-eating fish, poisonous snakes, and even tiny shells that if stepped upon would kill in less time than it took to drink a cup of tea.

I decided, after hearing such tales, if even half of them were true, I had no more desire to see the great dark mystic continent of Africa. I would stay on ship where the worst danger I would face was a vicious and insanely cruel captain.

As accurately predicted by the old sailors of our group we swept around the Cape of Africa without incident. Except for the dramatic change of color, one would not have noticed we had passed from one great ocean to another. Now we were carried northward on favorable winds and sea currents. We did not regret not being caught within the fearsome clash of oceans.

We kept within sight of land but not so near we would be bothered, or so close a crewman might be tempted to jump into the sea and swim ashore. As I listened to them talk, I was astounded that many of them could not swim anyway. Why would a man make his life on the water and not be able to swim? It was a puzzle to me. As we slid up the western side of Africa, some would point off into the distance at the fabled old slave ports of older days some twenty years past. I tried to imagine what it must have been like to sail those waters with 300 chained men below decks. I could not. The tales and memories of the cruelty and hardships related by the older seamen were impossible for me to imagine. For me, those stories were just stories. But for the men who had lived them, you could see the regret and remorse in their eyes. Nothing – not a single thing we lived through on the *Glendora* that these men would not compare to the horrors of those older times in these waters. I noticed the tales were only told by the younger men; men too young to have witnessed them. The older sailors kept to themselves and did not speak, except in sly glances toward their partners when some things were mentioned. If pressed, they would simply say, "Them was dark times indeed, mate!" Nothing more.

Each day the light lasted longer and the air grew warmer. The weather was clear and the night skies sparkled like never before. The drag net overflowed daily with the most pleasing fish, so we hardly had to go into our stores. In the Indian Ocean, we often only had fresh fish enough for the officers. Now we were in the Atlantic, we had more than enough to feed everyone. After a week though, the sailors tired of fish. But it was good while it lasted.

The warm, northward flowing current and favorable winds were taking us nearer to the equator. I was born on the equator, and the farthest north I had ever been was Rangoon. Once we rounded the Cape, I had never been so far south. As we sailed north, we were nearing familiar latitudes, even though we now sailed up the western side of Africa. It seemed to me to have been a year since I stepped on dry land; but in reality, it was only a couple of months and a few days. Time passed so slowly; and the days drifted past with such regularity, I no longer knew the day of the week or the time of the month – nor did I care.

The captain stayed mostly out of sight. I did not see Mawken at all. Talk on the ship was the captain spent most of the time in a drunken stupor in his cabin. I wondered, at times, if either still lived. I wondered if Mawken killed the captain, and hid inside the Captain's quarters. It would be an easy thing to do, and from the hate I saw in Mawken's eyes when the captain slapped me down, I feared for both of their lives. It was also possible Mawken tried and failed to kill the captain and his body was tossed into the sea during the night. I had no means to find out. The ration of food bound for the captain's door did not vary from day to day, so it seemed reasonable two were eating.

We ran low on water and some minor food stuffs. The captain blamed me but was distracted before he could mete out any punishment. The captain allowed a two-hour stop at some port along the African coast. I am not even sure it had a name. The captain allowed some crew to take the barrels ashore to refill. I was not allowed that privilege, although I wanted so badly to feel solid ground beneath my feet. I watched as the selected crew rowed ashore, loaded the huge empty water barrels onto a rickety ox cart, and trundled off with a few African men into the lush green forest. The cart creaked and rumbled as it rolled. I wondered how it would possibly carry the full barrels. The surrounding forest was covered with vines and the most amazing wildlife, including loudly screaming monkeys. Monkeys were everywhere. I even saw some as pets, riding on the heads of some of the naked children. I saw the tales of nakedness were true, as the women did not even attempt to cover themselves. They walked around as if it were the most natural thing in the world to be naked. Those women must have no pride at all. They were shameless. The sailors left on board the *Glendora* attempted to lure some of them onto the ship until Sticks threatened to shoot them and any natives they brought on the ship. That stopped the invitations but not the leering gestures and crude remarks shouted at the poor women from the ship's rail. Sticks did not seem to care about the loud and rude shouts. As for me, these were not particularly attractive women. Most of their breasts were misshapen and baggy. Most, except the youngest, carried babies.

They all had skinny but muscular legs, but a pouch at their waist. While their breasts were exposed, they kept the lower part of their body covered with a sort of flap of hide or soft leather, circled by a belt. Feathers and beads adorned their hair, and rings and objects were inserted into holes in their noses, ears, lips, and even their nipples. It was easy to see which of these women had children, and most of them did, except the very young girls. A few of them were obviously with child, despite the fact they were still quite young and barely developed breasts at all. Some of the sailors commented that the baby would surely starve to death with a mother so poorly endowed. The women all gathered in groups and were constantly working at something, either milling dry seeds into flour, or pounding something inside a rounded hollow rock with a huge mortar, or kneading some doughy substance. I wished for some of the flour, but Sticks would not hear of any unauthorized trades.

While these women worked, they constantly chewed. Their jaws rarely rested. After a while, they would take whatever was in their mouth, throw it into a large boiling pot, and begin chewing another cube of what looked like some fat rubbery meat substance. When I asked a sailor what it might be, he looked me dead in the eye and laughed, "Mate, that's tha last sailor that went abroad alone in tha night." I thought he was teasing, but I could not be sure.

The men of the village did not work and preferred to lay sleeping in the shade. They were nearby and occasionally roused to swat away a fly or other insect daring to interrupt their nap. I wondered why they were so tired all day and if they roamed the jungle all night. Each of them owned spears and shields, which leaned against every vertical surface, ready for instant deployment. Bows and arrows abounded; and long decorated tubes, which I was told were used to blow poison darts at game … or enemies as the situation demanded, stood ready for use. Long sharp knives of every shape and description lay about, including huge steel blades used to clear the jungle trails – and kill snakes. I wanted one of those blades, but I had no way to obtain one. I heard so many wild tales I did not know what to believe, so I believed it all. It was a strange place.

After an hour, the ox cart returned with the barrels. The head of the expedition cupped his hands to his mouth and called for the captain, so Sticks went to fetch him. Soon the captain appeared on deck. I realized it was the first time I saw the captain in two weeks. He walked regally toward the deck rail and stood, legs wide spread, surveying his kingdom. He stared down at the sailor on shore a short distance away. The captain waited, saying nothing.

"Captain!" the leader shouted. "Water here is not fit! We must go deeper in the jungle! Two miles. Two more hours!"

The captain looked at Sticks and shook his head. "We'll wait!" He grumbled and returned to his cabin while Sticks gave them a go-ahead sign. I watched as the crew turned the wagon and rumbled off into the jungle again. I followed the captain back to his door, hoping to catch sight of Mawken. The captain turned on me just before he went inside. "And, what would you be wantin'?" he sneered.

"Nothing, sir! I was checking to see what you might need."

He turned his head aside and looked at me from the corner of his eye. "Well enough. Fetch me one of them fat apples from below. Make it a big one."

One. "Aye, sir. An apple it is!"

I turned away before he barked. "No! Fetch me two of them apples."

After I brought his apples, I returned to the galley to prepare the evening meal. By evening, the new water was loaded and stowed below. Two apples was a good sign I thought.

I missed the loading of the water, and before I knew it, we were moving out to sea. It was the last chance to go on land until we reached the Americas. I heard a rumor we would make another short stop at a place called Port Royale. But for now, we sailed well off the coast of Africa. We could see the peaks in the distance on occasion, but the captain took no chance one of the crew might jump ship and swim ashore. Day after day, the coast slipped slowly past our starboard side, when we could see it at all. Finally, one day, I noticed we were following the sun, which meant we had already turned west. We had reached the west flowing equatorial current that would sweep us to the great continent of South America.

We made our westward progress day after day across the boundless ocean; one day led into another with merciless routine. The only change in the vast world of water was that our craft headed directly into the setting sun each evening. There was no need to take readings because we were on a course due west; we followed the path of the sun.

After several days, I lost track of how many, lookouts climbed high upon the mast to search for land. I imagined how cool the sea breeze must feel so high in the air, while down below we were sweating in the cruel stifling heat. I longed for land. I longed to feel the solid ground beneath my feet again, to roam aimlessly through green grass. And, I longed for trees: tall, beautiful trees with rough lined bark and soft green leaves; trees with branches filled with colorful singing birds! And fruit! Oh, how I longed for fruit. All we had onboard were tiny little knobby apples as hard as a rock. I envisioned trees that cast dim cooling shade across the expanse of soft green grass. For the first time, I realized how much I missed life on land. I wondered if I would ever see my home again, and then I remembered why I could not – would not. I tried to think of something else.

Even when we reached land, I was sure that the captain would never let me go ashore. Even if he did, I had not received my wages and I had no money. None of the crew was paid. I knew the reason he withheld our money was so that we would not be tempted to leave the ship at the first port. The captain always posted guards to make sure we did not jump ship. If I were to escape the *Glendora*, I would have to escape. It seemed to me that I always had to escape from something or someone. If I were going to escape, it would have to be before we reached a port. But, what of Mawken; what would become of him? Could I just leave him here on this ship with such a mean and brutal captain? He, who saved me from hanging, slavery, and unimaginable torture from the captain, would be left alone to face whatever came – if he were still alive.

I felt guilty abandoning the only friend I knew. Mawken helped me so many times. But, I felt my survival depended upon my escaping. I thought through various ways I could escape from the *Glendora*. If we tied up at a port, escape would only be possible through trickery or bribery. I owned nothing I could offer to bribe anyone. Trickery left open the possibility of detection and punishment, even death. If there was some way to trick them into sending me ashore, I could think of none. If I were caught escaping, I was not sure I could stand the lashing I saw others endure. I watched seamen tied to the mast, and whipped so badly the blood ran in streams down sweaty flinching back muscles, flayed open like a fish. It was unthinkable. I searched my mind, but I could think of no way to leave the ship once it arrived at the port.

That left the sea. Here my thoughts were more productive. I reminded myself I was Selung. 'You cannot drown a Selung.' I knew this to be true because I have known of many people who have drowned, not one of which was Selung. The mermaids protect us from the sea. It would be much easier to escape from the ship if I entered the sea just before it came to port. That way the currents would help sweep me to landfall. Since most sailors could not swim, not much care was taken to prevent someone from going overboard when we were far from shore. I leaned over the rail, pretending to be spitting into the ocean. It was fully two body lengths down to the surface of the water. If I could catch one of the large swells, it would be a much shorter drop. I thought I found my perfect plan. When we sighted land, I would simply wait until the early hours of a dark morning and then quietly slip over the rail into the sea. In just a short while, the boat would be out of sight in the dark, and I would be free to swim ashore. Even if someone noticed me missing, the boat would not, turn back for me. 'What the sea wants the sea shall have.'

So, I put together my escape plan. I would need something to help keep me afloat in the deep water. I found a partially empty wooden drum and poured its contents into another container. I filled several watertight flasks with water and stashed them in the cask along with the marlinspike and a few lengths of hairy sisal rope. I collected hard bread, wrapped it in heavy oilpaper, and added it to the secret hoard. I would use the container to store anything I might need while floating in the sea. Even the keg would help keep me afloat until I could paddle my way ashore.

My plan complete, I hid my tub in the galley and waited for a good chance. I went out on deck the next night, and my stomach sank. The moon was near full. The sky was so clear; I could look out on the sparkling water and see for miles. Any disturbance in the water was immediately obvious. I might as well jump into the ocean during the day. I was disappointed that it would be at least two weeks before it would be dark enough to make an attempt without being detected. Besides, we were too far at sea anyway. Maybe, by the time the lookouts sighted land ahead, the night sky might be dark enough.

Before even five days passed, the shout "Land!" came drifting down from the tall masts. We reached the shore of the South American continent. I would need at least another week to have any hope of escaping in the dark. I longed for a cloudy or foggy night that would hide the moon.

We no longer followed the sun, and within a few days, the sun sat across the coast off our port side. The captain kept us well off the coastline, especially at night. We could see the lights twinkling sometimes on the great southern land mass, but we never got near a port. The sea turned choppy and irregular. It seemed that we were fighting the current, but I could not be sure. The cross currents slapped against the side of the ship. The winds were favorable enough and kept us moving northwest. I had no map or any way of knowing, but if my memory was correct, we would enter the Caribbean with its hundreds of islands. Once we passed Cuba, we would enter the Gulf of Mexico. That was where New Orleans was; where the famous Mississippi River emptied into the ocean.

As we slipped past South American coastline, the unthinkable happened. The ax that hung on the wall of the wheelhouse went missing. No one knew how; the wheelhouse was manned every minute of every day. Every man was questioned and threatened within a hair of his life. Several were whipped to no avail. The whippings were awful enough but somewhat less painful than the lashings. The whippings did not draw blood. No one would admit to having the ax. Every public area was searched. When the searching did not recover the ax, then every sailor's personal effects laid out and viewed. More whippings followed as contraband was found in sea bags and trunks. They even searched the galley. I was afraid they would find my hidden keg, but they passed over it, thinking it was part of the food stores. I realized that the ax would not have fit inside anyway, so it was of no interest to them. They did probe the tall barrel of flour and plundered through every cabinet in the galley and the cubby.

At last, Sticks announced to the Captain that the ax was not on the ship. Sticks' reward for his futile search was a slap across the face for his incompetence. For a moment, I thought Sticks might fight back, but he simply stood aside, head lowered, and rubbed his jaw. As the captain turned away, I saw the hatred in Stick's eyes and watched his hand clench into a hard fist, as his other hand brushed the handle of the knife in his belt.

The captain turned and saw Stick's defiant look and laughed a cruel mocking laugh. "Go on, matey! Do it, Sticks!" Sticks dropped his hands to his sides as the captain drew his pistol and aimed it at Stick's head. "If ya ain't goin' to use it, gimme that little pig sticker," he demanded.

"Cap'n, if I pull my knife you'll shoot me dead." Sticks raised his arms above his head in a wide arc, keeping them well away from his body. "Take it yerself!" The captain looked at Sticks, sneered, and then walked to where Sticks stood. The captain slid the knife from the first mate's belt and eyed the mermaid carving. "Such a pretty little thing it is," he mused wickedly as his thumb caressed the smooth breasts of the carving. I was sure the captain would murder Sticks at any moment.

The captain stood smirking at the first mate who kept his hands raised in a sign of submission. The captain's lips curled over his yellow teeth, "I don't need yer bloody knife, mate. Ya ain't got the spunk ta use it anyhow!" With that, the captain quickly raked his pistol roughly across the first mate's face, causing blood to flow down Stick's cheek onto his white shirt. Sticks fell back against the bulwark as the captain threw the knife onto the deck between his feet. I stuck into the deck and wobbled between Stick's thighs. "If ya give me tha evil eye again, I'll kill ya," the Captain promised in a sincere, calm voice. "I want that ax back, ya hear?"

Stick's eyes focused on the rough wooden deck as he mumbled, "Aye, Captain. I'll double the search!" My heart sank; surely, they would find my barrel this time. I decided I would make my escape that night despite the moonlight.

I retired early, thinking I would need my strength to survive in the ocean for I knew not how many days and nights. Long before sunrise, I heard steps and a great commotion on deck. I rose from my bed, went onto the deck, and discovered we were moving into the bay of Port Royal. My chance of escape had evaporated.

I stood on the deck of the *Glendora*, heartbroken and frustrated to see we were preparing to tie up at a dock in this strange island city. It was once a pirate haven and all of the famous Caribbean pirates had harbored there at one time or another. Port Royal was once the largest town in the Caribbean, but an earthquake and tsunami destroyed much of the five forts that once guarded the harbor. The capital moved to Spanish Town, farther inland. The harbor was still used as a safe harbor for ships crossing the Caribbean into the Gulf of Mexico and as a safe haven from the hurricanes that frequently lashed the small, scattered islands.

It was still a dangerous place, even though many of the most terrible pirates were long dead. Their offspring, now civilized and accepted into the community, controlled the area; many of them turned to acceptable trades – but not all. It was home to all of the distractions and perversions which drew men like flies to butter; especially men who had been at sea for several months.

The crew literally howled like dogs to be allowed to go ashore. Dogs, mind you! Their howls came from all parts of the ship. They would stop and pretend innocence whenever Sticks approached them. But the moment his back was turned, they would bark and howl again. Animals! They refused to stop until permitted to go ashore.

Sticks gathered the men and declared only the most trusted would to leave the boat. This seemed to satisfy the most vocal of the howlers. Of course, I was not allowed to go, although I desperately wanted to leave. It would have solved a huge problem for me. Sticks announced half the crew would be able to depart the ship at first light, with instructions to be back on board by noon. Sticks promised to hunt down and severely punish those who did not return voluntarily. Suddenly, ashore did not seem such a grand idea. Stick's announcement set off a most joyous celebration among those lucky enough to be included, and a fathomless depression for those who were not, including me.

No one seemed to know why we came to this port so unexpectedly. We did not offload or load cargo. No one appeared to do any maintenance on the hull or any part of the ship. We still had ample supplies and water. I could see no reason at all for the stop. At least, the delay would increase the chance I would receive a dark moonless night, under which I could easily escape into the sea before we reached New Orleans.

After breakfast, I stood on the deck and watched the finest coach I had ever seen pull out onto the dock and stop near the *Glendora*. The horses were spotless white with long flowing manes. Gold fittings gleamed in the morning sun, and uniformed coachmen looked regal and dignified in their ornate uniforms. The coachmen had black skin but did not appear to be African, like the natives we saw before. They wore short waist length jackets with golden-fringed shoulder boards, which blazed and sparkled as they moved in the sunlight. Their white, tight pants disappeared into knee-length boots shining like mirrors. They looked stunning. They opened the door of the coach and out stepped the occupant. He was even more polished. Across his chest stretched a sash of white silk emblazoned with four large gold stars worked into the material. A long sword, with a handle glittering like silver, hung at his side.

Oh, how I wished for a sword so fine. The coachmen saluted and stepped aside as the officer stood waiting silently by the carriage. His head was smooth and bare and glittered in the morning sun as he stood waiting. One of the coachmen brought out a colorful umbrella and held it over the officer so he would have some shade. He did not hail us or acknowledge our boat in any way. He stood, perfectly still and at peace, beneath the umbrella shade.

The reason for our unscheduled stop appeared on deck shortly thereafter. Our captain was dressed in his finest English naval uniform, with medals and shiny buttons sparkling in the sunlight. I had never seen the captain so attired, and even I was impressed. He sauntered down the deck toward the gangway. The officers stood at attention and saluted as he went down the gangplank, and entered the beautiful coach with the officer. It became obvious to me this stop was not as unscheduled as I had believed. The captain intended to stop here all along; he had simply not announced his intentions to the crew for whatever reason.

I knew from Stick's announcement the crew would be back at noon, so we had at least four hours to wait before they would return. Lunch would be unnecessary. We left aboard, would have a cold lunch, but I need not prepare anything for the land party. I asked why, and Sticks laughingly informed me once the crew returned, more would be coming out of their mouths than going in. I did not understand at the time, but I certainly do now. So, with no lunch meal to prepare, other than lay out some fruit, hard bread, and salted fish, I took the time to explore a little on my own.

My first thought was to try to discover what became of Mawken; to find out if he were still alive or not. But the deck was too crowded just then, so I decided to wait awhile. Sticks was ashore also, although not as royally escorted as the captain was. No glittering coach drove the mate from the dock.

The second mate was in charge. His name was McGinty but everyone called him Hognose for obvious reasons. Since Hognose was the night officer, I had not as much contact with him as with Sticks. However, we all knew McGinty was lax and was easiest on the crew when in charge. All thoughts of the missing ax were set aside I guessed until we went back to sea. They would obtain a new one in town. Once everyone left, most of the men were drowsing off in the morning sun. I crept about the ship trying to find anything I might use in my escape.

Since the captain was not on board and most of the crew were asleep, I had access to every area of the ship not locked down, including the wheelhouse. I looked at the wall where the ax once hung and noticed the shape of the ax still appeared on the wall. The ax had shaded the wall of the wheelhouse for so long, the paint underneath was not bleached like the rest of the ship. It looked like the shadow of an ax hanging on the wall. I slowly entered the forbidden compartment to see if I would draw a challenge. When I was not, I quietly opened every door and compartment to see what was inside. I found all sorts of tools and instruments, but nothing I thought would help me survive alone in the ocean. While in the wheelhouse, I looked closely at the map spread wide on the chart table. The map, which the officers called a chart, was littered with words and numbers hastily scribbled or jotted down in the margins. I easily found our present location on the chart, and then found New Orleans. I saw we would sail between the island of Cuba and a large landmass labeled 'Yucatan' to enter the Gulf of Mexico. Cuba and Yucatan were like the doorposts of a huge doorway leading into the circular gulf. I hoped the sea waves would be somewhat calmer down inside those waters. But, once inside the Gulf itself, there were no islands or ports before we reached the mainland at the mouth of the famous Mississippi River. I looked at this map for several minutes, trying to decide where I should enter the water. The Gulf was huge and had no landmarks to guide me. I realized I could drift for weeks and starve to death before I reached any kind of land. I judged my best chance was to escape as we passed between the gateposts and then try to swim ashore to one side or the other.

The difficulty would be to know when we were at the precise location where land was close on either side and to hope the darkness would cover me until the ship was out of view. I decided we would be closer to the mainland than the Cuban island, so I planned to swim eastward. I tried to calculate the date we might pass that point on the map. I knew of no way to measure the progress of the ship, but I knew from where we had come. I counted back the days to when we first sighted land in South America until today. I measured out the days on the map and got a rough idea of how far the ship could travel each day. I calculated how long it would take to place us

110

exactly between the gateposts of the two landmasses. I did not want to enter too late and find myself adrift in the Gulf of Mexico, so I decided I would jump into the sea four days from tonight. Satisfied I had found the best solution to my escape plan, I left the cabin; but not before I toyed with the huge polished wooden wheel.

My nosey ways nearly cost me dearly. Somehow, turning the wheel did something that made a noise and alerted Hognose. He roused from his sleep, and called above, "Ooose thar? Oose that meddlin' with tha 'elm?

I knew if he caught me, I would be punished severely. My first thought was to stay silent and hide, but Hognose got to his feet as if to come upstairs to investigate, I decided to play innocent and came to the rail and reported. "No one up here, Sir."

"Whut are **yer** doin' up thar?" he asked.

"I thought I heard a noise and came to see, Sir. I didn't want to disturb you, sleeping as you were."

"Sleepin'? Oose sleepin'? Not me. Get down from up thar an' go on about yer business!" he barked.

Glad it was Hognose on duty and not Sticks, I climbed back down to the main deck that circled the ship. I waited for McGinty to settle back down, and then went aft and tried the captain's door. For some reason, I timidly knocked as if the captain were still inside, which I knew he was not. No one answered. I went back to check if McGinty had roused, and found him snoring soundly on the foredeck. So, I returned to the captain's door and knocked again, this time harder and louder. Still no answer. I looked up and down the deck and tried the captain's door. It was locked. Finally, I knocked as hard as I could, but no sound came from inside. I fully believed at that moment my friend and life-long companion was dead. The captain probably threw his lifeless body over the rail during the night some time ago.

111

While I grieved for the loss of my friend, I no longer felt any reluctance to leave the ship, believing he was beyond help anyway.

As the sun rose high in the sky, the day heated up, and naptime was over. My time for snooping was over. Preparations were made to receive the crew back on board. Hognose ordered several buckets of seawater lined up on the deck. The early arrivals were just a little groggy, but the ones that boarded near noon were nearly mad with drink. I understood what Hognose meant by his earlier remark, as most of them vomited as soon as they stood on the deck. The buckets of water were sloshed across the deck to wash the putrid vomit back into the sea. Several sailors did not even make it back on board before they spewed their alcohol-laced puke into the stale sea alongside the ship.

One group of sailors were in company of a rather heavy black woman, and they begged Hognose to let them come aboard with her. McGinty laughed and taunted them, "Is she tha best yer could get, Mates?"

They claimed she had important information for Sticks and the captain. Hognose watched her closely as she came aboard. Neither Sticks nor the captain was back from town, so Hognose was still in charge. He was not going to miss on opportunity to get some information that might put him in favor with the captain. We gathered around to see what this strange woman might tell us. She spoke a heavy accented English, but we could understand her words clear enough. She called herself Aida Wedo, which one of the sailors said meant "Coming Soon" in her language.

Aida was dressed in a white flowing blouse worn over a dress, which showed at least ten colors. The blouse had a low neck exposing much of her bosoms and all of her shoulders. I never saw anyone dressed as she was. She wore long dangling earrings that brushed the bones of her upper chest. A spotless white cloth, like a turban, was tied around her head, with a large knot or bow that rested on her forehead. Her face and lips were unusually large, and her cheekbones were high on her face. Her face was fully twice the size of mine, but it did not look overly large on her oversized body. Her eyes were pitch black, and the whites were more of an ivory cream color than white. Her cheeks were bright red, and something protruded from her nostril, which looked like a sliver of bone. She wore a necklace of bone beads that dangled down the front of her open-necked dress. Her breasts were huge and swung from side to side, as she waddled up the gangplank. One side of her head, her hair was braided and interlaced with the same beads as was in her necklace, and a huge orange flower laced into her hair ornamented the other side. There was an evil look about her, and I shivered beneath her gaze as she looked directly at me.

I immediately recognized her as a *Penanggalan*; I fearfully waited for her head to separate from her body and fly around the ship, casting a curse on the *Glendora* and everyone aboard. I wished they had never brought her to us. After one look at her, and I was ready to go hide in my bunk until she left the ship, but I was fixed in place, too fearful to move.

She slowly looked around the ship, and then looked directly into the eyes of each one of us. She seemed to focus directly on me for a time, knowing I recognized her. I shivered under her gaze. Soon, her eyes moved on, and she slowly drew herself up as tall as she possibly could, and then she melted back onto the deck in a sighing heap of brown flesh and white cotton dress. She breathed deeply for several minutes then opened her eyes, looked around, and spoke.

"Big storm a'comin'." She looked off into the distance seeing something we could not see, although every one of us looked in that direction. "Big blow." She shook her head back and forth as if she saw something awful.

The sailors laughed at her warning, and Hognose told the men to get her off the boat. One man reached out to touch her; he was frozen in place by an icy stare, like daggers to his heart. He froze with his hand extended toward her until he suddenly sat back flat on the deck on his butt as if he was pushed. He sat throughout her visit with his arm still extended and a glassy look in his eyes. No one else dared try to touch her. Not wanting the *Penanggalan* to freeze me on the spot, I moved to hide behind the capstan.

"Who big man here? Who captain?" she asked.

Hognose had to show he was not afraid, but I saw his hands shaking as he stepped toward her, "Tha captain's on shore," he said as gruffly as he could manage. "I'm the one whuts in charge here," he said with authority.

Aida Wedo looked Hognose up and down, puffed out her cheeks, and made a sound like "humpf." She repeated, "Big storm a'comin'. Comin' soon."

Hognose looked at her closely, "When?"

"Four, mebbe five day. You keep ship here Port Royal; you be safe." As an afterthought, she added, "Mebbe." She looked up at the clear blue sky above, fully showing the creamy whites of her eyes. It was spooky; her eyes were milky white with none of the black showing at all. She trembled, her eyelids fluttering over the bulging globes, which appeared to move in large circles. Just before her head flew off, I was relieved to see her round black round eyes came back down from inside her head.

"Yes. You be safe here. Ship don't go 'til after storm. Stay here; you be safe."

The *Penanggalan* looked directly at me, as I peeked out from behind the capstan. She pointed a long, knobby finger in my direction but did not speak to me. Her fingers trembled as she pointed my way. The crew, except the man frozen, followed her finger until everyone stared at me.

Hognose loomed over her in contempt, his hands on his hips. "We been through storms a'fore. Had one a while back. Big 'un. Big'er any in these waters I wager! Captain ain't gonna sit in this greasy port a week waitin' for some storm that might never come!" He turned to the sailor who still sat in a daze with his hand stretched out toward her. "Get 'er out a'here!"

When the sailor, still in a trance, did not move, Hognose kicked him in the side and sent him sprawling across the deck. The spell broken, the sailor rose and helped Aida Wedo to her feet. As she walked to the gangway, she paused and looked deep into McGinty's squinty eyes. In the sweetest, kindest voice, I heard her say, "You not go to sea. You stay here; Port Royal; be safe."

Hognose wiped his wrist across his bulbous namesake and snarled, "An' whut if we don't? Whut o' that, Missey? Whut then?"

Aida Wedo looked Hognose deeply in the eyes. I feared she would levitate and whip him around the deck like a rag doll, but the *Penanggalan* just glared at him and in a calm voice as if it were the most obvious thing in the world.

"Den, you die."

Two days passed before Sticks and the captain learned of the strange visitor and the storm warning. It happened by accident. Sticks and Hognose shared opposite ends of the watch; Hognose was on nights. Each morning, after Sticks finished breakfast, Hognose would come into the mess and report what had happened overnight. I wondered why they went through this daily routine since each officer had to mark his log at the end of each shift. Sticks never reported to Hognose, and I later learned this was Stick's way of impressing seniority over the second mate. As I served Hognose his portion of the watery rice breakfast, one of the sailors entered and sat down to eat. As the sailor poured tea, he stuck a hard cracker in his mouth and mumbled as flecks of cracker flew.

"Wind's up, joost like 'at old 'ag said it'd be."

Sticks eyes narrowed as he slowly turned from the cracker-crumb spraying sailor toward Hognose.

"Whut the devil's 'e talkin' about, McGinty?" he demanded.

The look of panic in the eyes of the second mate was pure horror. Hognose gulped for air as he looked toward the pitiful sailor who stopped chewing, his mouth hanging open. I am sure Hognose contemplated telling a lie, but he managed to choke up the truth mostly.

"Tha men brought'a witchy lookin' hag on board th'other day. That's all. I kicked 'er arse off soon's I found out, I did." Only the last part was a lie.

"Are ya tellin' me ya brought a woman on this ship?" Sticks voice rose.

"Aye, sir!" Hognose rose from the table clearly frightened. He braced himself with the edge of the table, expecting to be attacked at any moment. "She'us a crazy old hag, Sticks. I'us below when they

116

brought her on; got rid o'her soon's I seen 'er, I did," he pled his case.

Sticks pointed to the sailor who was still standing with the cracker hanging from his gap-toothed mouth, sensing this was not going to end well.

"Whut's this about a blow?" Sticks asked him, crooked finger extended.

McGinty jumped in before the sailor could answer, "She'us crazy, Sticks. She 'ad a wild look about 'er, she did. Crazy on that weed they chew all a'time. She was ravin' and rantin' about a big storm comin'. I got rid of 'er soon enough. She was 'teched, she wuz."

Sticks was beside himself in anger. Bringing a woman onto the ship was forbidden, I knew, but I did not understand the real reason for his anger until later. Sticks stood and loomed menacingly over Hognose, who walked backward until he was trapped, cowering in a corner.

"Damn yer eyes! These people been in these islands over two hundred years! They knows things. What else did she say, you fool?" Sticks cocked his fist and drew back his arm.

Hognose was terrified at the beating he knew was coming. "Whut?" he asked, confused.

Sticks said it louder, "Whut else did she say, you bloody bag o'scum!"

"Nothin', Sticks. She wuz crazy; she wuz. I got 'er off the boat..."

"When?" Sticks screamed into Hognose's face, spittle sprinkling his cheeks. "Tell me when a'fore I rip yer guts out right here in the galley!"

117

Not understanding the question, Hognose stuttered and repeated he got her off the boat right away, which was not what Sticks wanted to know. Sticks slapped Hognose leaving white finger marks on bright red cheeks.

"When!" Sticks kept screaming. "When did she say the storm was comin'? You ass!"

Hognose blocked his face with his forearm and spoke beneath his elbow. "She said four or five days, Sir."

Sticks whirled and threw his teacup against the galley wall, smashing it into countless glittering pieces. Then, with a murderous glare, he slowly turned back to Hognose. Without taking his eyes from the second mate, he said to me over his shoulder,

"Cook! Go get tha' captain."

"Now!" he barked when I did not move fast enough. I arrived at the captain's door as he closed it behind him. The captain brushed past me on the deck as he made his way onto the deck.

"Out'a my way ya pup! Big storms comin'. Can't you smell it?"

"Sticks wants you in the galley," I shrieked into the wind, but he did not acknowledge he heard. Behind us the wind and the sea were rising in frothy swells; I saw dark billowing clouds over the heaving sea so thick you could not tell where the horizon was. I had seen clouds like these before, and I knew what they meant. The captain went directly to the mess room, so I considered my task done and went back to the galley to tend the stove. I stowed everything away and prepared to douse the fire when ordered. I knew by now, in a storm all fires were extinguished. I could hear the loud shouting coming from the mess. Soon after, Hognose came running out holding his hand to his left eye and barked orders, including one for me. The captain wanted coffee. I anticipated that also and took it to him in the galley.

As I entered the mess, the Captain and Sticks loomed over the large map from the wheelhouse, which lay across the table, and they were discussing what to do.

"No turnin' back now," the captain observed. "If we do, we'll head right into it, if it's four days. We've got ta' run it!"

Sticks agreed, "Yes, we've lost two days a'ready. She's comin' on us fast. If we can get to the lee side of this point, we might reach safe water. We can cut the gap between here and Cuba and see which side she's fallin' on. If the storm goes north of the island, we have a chance. If she comes from the south, we've got to run."

"Agreed. Get all the sheets up! Every last one of 'em. Make all speed. Post a good man in the riggin' to brave the wind; one whut knows whut a gale is and can tell us of the wind. All hands not workin' get below, repairin' every sheet we got that ain't been sewed yet. Test all the ropes and halyards. Dig out the storm sail, and make sure it ain't weak. If it is, make a new 'un. Make sure the crew knows how ta use it if we need it, and we are goin' to need it! Douse all the fires!" This last order was to me to put out the cook fire, which I did immediately.

Barely four hours lapsed before the captain came back on duty and took the helm. It was obvious we were going to be pummeled by the fast approaching storm. Not wanting to be trapped inside like last time, I decided to stay on deck as long as I could. I was afraid if we foundered while I was inside, I might not get out in time to avoid drowning. The wind howled like an animal in the throes of death. The monstrous swirling black clouds were getting nearer and nearer the ship. The water turned black like ink, and the sky showed only a pale spot where the sun was supposed to go. The captain and Sticks would take turns at the helm in four-hour shifts.

Hognose would remain on deck without relief. Soon after the captain took the wheel, the man in the rigging bawled something I could not understand. The captain turned the wheel over to a steersman and came out of the wheelhouse, shouting to the man above.

Suddenly with a loud ripping sound, the mainsail broke loose from its mast and flapped wildly in the screaming wind. The captain shouted to McGinty, "Get tha crew up from below!"

Once everyone was on deck, the captain screamed orders.

"Clear the jibs and bare the mizzens! Drop that main'sl and get 'er down! Leave tha top'sls up to give me some control 'til you can get tha main sewed and back flyin'. Furrow the topgallants and the royals. Keep 'em furrowed, but loose! Bring up the storm sheets and lay 'em out."

By the end of the next murky day, all preparations were finished as the rain pounded the deck. The rain blew so hard it slanted nearly flat across the deck and stung like tiny ice crystals against my cheek. Even the wind tasted salty. It became so dark you could not tell if it was day or night. Only the ship's bell ringing out the hours marked the time. When Sticks came on to man the wheel for his shift, we were on the leading edge of a huge storm. We were running ahead, but the storm built fast and was quickly catching us from behind. Waves were crashing over the stern, swamping the deck.

"Flush them decks!" Sticks screamed. "She'll push the bow up and upend us!" Some men were attaching lanyards to the masts in case they were washed overboard, as they worked to push the seawater off the stern decks. If they were washed away, no one would have noticed, so confusing were things on deck. Men were shouting orders and running back and forth, pulling ropes and tying them off in a maddening, unending stream of orders screamed into the wind. It was clear the storm had the upper hand. The captain was in his cabin resting before his next four-hour shift, and Sticks was torn between shouting orders and wrestling the huge oaken wheel.

The angry sea turned against us and threatened to kill us all. Afraid of being washed overboard; I changed my plan and took my old refuge in the galley. I found my keg of supplies and tied it to my waist. I abandoned all thought of voluntarily going into the ocean to escape. Now, I feared I would have no choice. The sea slammed against the ship in a merciless and unending series of loud thumps and splashes. The noise was unearthly; the wind shrieked as the sea pounded against the wooden hull, and the rain came down in huge globules rattling on the roof and across the deck.

Alone in the dark galley, I rode out the storm. I could not see; but I could certainly hear the fearsome power and feel the ship lurch, bob, and sway in the waves. Sometimes it seemed as if we were traveling sideways, and sometimes in a whirl. It seemed to me to be worse than the storm before. We would rise upwards in a stomach- churning ride to the top and then fall through space as if we were falling from a steep cliff. Then we would slam down into the bottom of a deep valley, as though we were been dropped forty feet onto a brick street. I felt like I was going to vomit. The ship hit the bottom of the troughs so hard I feared it would bash in our keel and crash through the bottom. The old ship groaned and creaked with awful noises as we rose then violently fell in ceaseless repetition.

I wondered how much more the boat could withstand. I believed without a doubt that one more drop into the watery chasm would be the end of the *Glendora*. Yet somehow, she held together and took us on yet another wild ride up the steep waves to a precipice and into the deep canyon with a horrendous slam as she hit bottom once again. I imagined the ship breaking up under me, and I wondered if I would survive. I crouched in fear on my pallet wondering how I would know when it was time to go overboard to escape the sinking ship. *"What the sea wants the sea shall have!"*

A loud pounding sounded on my door that was not from the storm. I barely cracked open the door. Were they allowing us to abandon the ship at last? My keg was ready. The wailing wind immediately caught the door and tore it from my grasp. The upper hinge gave way, and the door nearly struck Hognose broadside. He stood outside my galley, grasping a safety rope attached somewhere forward.

"Get the Cap'n!" he screamed through the wind that sucked your breath away, as water streamed down his face. I could see McGinty was frightened near the point of death and I was just as scared.

"I canna' leave the deck! Fetch tha captain straight away! Sticks needs 'em! Be quick about it!"

He hoisted himself back toward the bow hand-over-hand on the rope as I struggled not to be sucked from the galley and blown into the sea. Step by step, and handhold by handhold, I groped my way down the deck toward the captain's door. I discovered if I kept low to the deck, and used the railing to pull myself along, I could make progress. I pounded on the captain's door but got no answer. The captain must be inside; there was no other place for him to be. I pounded harder. The door opened, and the captain stood naked to the waist.

"Captain! You are needed in the wheelhouse!" I shouted as loud as I could.

The captain, having just been awakened, stood groggily in the doorway. It was the first time I ever saw him without a pistol in his waistband or at his side. He listened to me report my message, but he did not hear or see what happened next. But, I did! I would never forget the sight.

The head of the missing ax struck the back of the captain's head and cut deep into his skull, splitting the skull in half. The captain dropped like a brick. The next blow to his neck nearly clove the Captain's head from his body.

Emerging from the darkness, Mawken rolled the dead captain over onto his back. I saw the missing kitchen knife disappear into the captain's chest, and rip downward toward the captain's navel. Then he slashed sideways across the upper stomach making a bloody cross. I stood horrified against the rail as Mawken butchered the captain in front of my eyes!

Mawken was on the captain like an insane man, his eyes flashing wildly; insanely. Mawken reached into the body cavity and pulled forth whatever he could grab. He slung fistfuls of bloody meat over the rail into the heaving sea. Blood slung from his hands as Mawken stood and stared directly at me. I was afraid in his madness he would kill me next.

"I thought you were dead," I said.

He looked at me but did not respond, as he threw the knife onto the deck. I picked it up intending to throw it over the side, but mainly so he could not use it on me. The storm strangely calmed in a lull, as if it were over. I could see clear sky above, but heavy dark clouds hovered all around the *Glendora*. It was as if we were in an island of clear air, inside a bubble, except all around the edge, the sea was sucked into the twisting, churning, angry clouds engulfing us. You could hear the whooshing sound as the sea was heaved skyward into the dark mists.

I turned and saw Mawken withdraw the ax from the wooden deck and throw it into the sea. I stood with the bloody missing kitchen knife and wondered if I should throw it overboard or use it to protect myself. Mawken obviously was out of his mind. Suddenly, Mawken was nowhere in sight. I thought he went back into the captain's cabin probably to retrieve the Captain's gun. I decided to throw it into the sea, but as I turned back, I saw Sticks and Hognose running down the deck toward me. They saw me holding a bloody knife, standing over the dead captain lying at my feet! They came to a dead stop as Hognose grabbed Stick's arm.

"Maurice has killed the Captain!"

Despite the urgency of the storm, the crew of the *Glendora* swarmed the deck alongside the captain's cabin. I stood holding a bloody galley knife over the dead captain. When Hognose advanced to take me, I brandished it at them, and ordered them back. Hognose stopped cold, looking from the bloody knife still dripping with the captain's blood, to Sticks, and then back to the knife again. Soon sailors surrounded on all sides, gawking at the dead body lying on the deck. I heard comments from the growling crowd.

"He's gone mad!"

"He's killed the captain, he did!"

"He'll kill us all!"

The mob surged toward me; I was trapped in our ship inside a bubble of danger. Murderous shouts sounded across the bucking deck; and the ship, unmanned and skittering wildly across the heaving ocean. I was heartbroken because, among the accusing faces in the crowd, I saw Mawken!

There was only one escape for me. I took refuge in the captain's cabin. With a warning for everyone to stay back, I ducked into the darkened cabin and barred the door. Immediately someone pounded on the door and ordered me to open it. I shouted through the door, "Stay back! Anyone comes through that door, I will shoot!"

"Shoot? With what?" I heard Sticks mock me.

"I've got the captain's gun," I bluffed. "First man through this door will be shot dead!"

"He's lyin'," I heard one man say.

Sticks replied, "Then knock down tha' door!" Then I heard laughter as the sailor backed away and changed his mind.

"Captain's gun is not in 'is pants!" Hognose reported. "He's got it for sure!"

Sticks thought for a moment and then ordered everyone back to their posts. "We can't get in and he can't get out! Ever'one back to ya places! We've gotta get through this storm or we all die. We will deal with 'im later. He ain't goin' nowhere!"

"Whut about the captain?" I heard someone ask.

"Throw 'em over!" was all Sticks replied. "Check 'is pockets first and dump 'im over!"

Soon, it was quiet outside the door. I knew better than to peek, knowing surely Sticks quietly posted a guard outside. Meanwhile, the storm picked up again where it left off. Once more, the ship was tossed like a leaf around on the ocean, on the very verge of breaking up. I imagined we were being sucked into the angry clouds on the edge of our bubble. I lit a lantern and checked every nook and cranny. I found the captain's gun but little else that could help me. The other guns were chained to the bulwark, and no doubt, Sticks had the keys. I realized he had the key to the cabin also. The crew probably found them before they dumped the captain over. The door was reinforced with metal and barred from inside, so I had no fear they could enter unless I opened the door. I was safe for now – as safe as one could be, locked inside a room on a sinking ship.

I anguished over the memory of Mawken standing in the accusing crowd. Mawken, who killed the captain, shifted the blame to me! My friend. I was heartbroken and felt betrayed beyond words. Why was he against me? He saved me from every disaster up until tonight. Why had he forsaken me? I could not understand, and I cried at the thought I would be blamed for a murder I had not committed. I wept at the loss of a friend. I vowed never to trust Mawken again. Not that it mattered I realized; we were going to die on this ship! Either way, I was done with him for good. What treachery! Once again, I wished never to see Mawken again.

How could I prove my innocence? How could I convince the crew I had not murdered the captain? It was impossible. There were no means to convince them of my innocence. None, at all. I realized the image of me standing over the dead captain with a bloody knife in my hand would have far greater weight than anything I might say. I was doomed. I tried to think of all the things that might happen next. The ship could sink and we could all be lost in the sea, in the middle of a great storm, miles from shore. I might survive because 'you cannot drown a Selung', but it was certainly not the best choice. The ship might pass through the storm, and I might escape into the water before we arrived in port. I thought that was my best chance for survival. I decided to wait out the storm in the Captain's cabin.

After a while, Sticks came to my door to try to convince me to surrender. He tried all possible ways to get me to come out. They did not care about the captain anyway he claimed, and they would have killed him themselves if they could. Sticks tried to make me believe I had done everyone a favor. He said no harm would come to me. The boat was in trouble, and they were starving and needed food. He even tried to convince me the ship was sinking, and I needed to get out to save myself. Sticks tried everything he could think of to get me out of the cabin, but I knew it was a trick.

I tried to tell him I did not kill the captain. It was not me; it was Mawken. Sticks even tried to convince me he believed I was innocent. He promised to put Mawken in irons if I would only come out. He said as captain now, he would pardon me and put in the log the captain had gone mad. I acted in self-defense. When trickery or cajolery did not work, Sticks next became angry and threatening. He threatened to nail the door shut so I would drown when the ship went down. He threatened to set the ship on fire to get me out. He said they would breach the door and rush me since I could kill only one of them. At the end, he screamed in frustration and banged on the door with such force I thought he might break his fist. Nothing worked. I remained inside the well-secured cabin.

Meanwhile, I continued to look around for anything that might help me stay afloat in the water. I knew, at some point, my only option would be to go over the side. In my haste, I left my escape barrel in the galley. I hoped maybe if Sticks went away from my door, I might be able to retrieve it. Soon, Sticks exhausted his frustration against the door and stopped his bellowing. It was quiet, except for the wailing wind. I could no longer hear him outside the door. I knew Sticks would need to return to the wheel, so I believed he was gone.

All the while, the storm continued unabated – if anything it grew worse. It grew so dark inside the cabin, my only option was to light a lantern. I found the matches on the desk and struck one against the rough plank wall. In the sputtering light, I found and lit the lamp. The ship continued to twist and turn in the storm; and in the faint light, I was more aware of the wildly tilting room. It made me dizzy and confused. The thought of needing my barrel became the foremost on my mind; and regardless of the danger, I felt I must retrieve it to survive in this lurching sea. I could not find anything else in the cabin to sustain me.

I carefully edged the door open, taking care not to have it ripped from my hand by the wind. I kept the gun ready, in case a guard waited outside. I peeked out and saw no one. But what I saw was horrible and my entire body went cold. Surely, we would all die! The wind shrieked insanely and blew so hard the masts on the ship bowed in giant arcs. At any moment, they would snap like matchsticks. Most of the sails were shredded and fluttering wildly in the wind. The flapping sounded like guns firing. The seas were heavy, frothy, and much higher than the ship. Hand over hand on the rail I made my way to the galley. The door still hung from one hinge.

Inside, hanging from a hook beside the door, was my little drum of supplies. I did not remember hanging it there, but I lashed it to my waist and went back on deck to return to the captain's cabin when someone grabbed me roughly from behind.

"I've got 'im!" screamed Hognose into the howling wind.

Hognose grabbed the gun away and spun me around. He pointed the gun directly at my head and pulled the trigger. Thankfully, the wet powder refused to ignite and the gun did not fire. Sticks appeared behind and snatched the gun from Hognose before he could hit me with it, and stuffed it into his belt. "Thar's the littl' bugger," Hognose chortled.

"Finally come out, did ya?" Sticks pushed past the two, and grabbed me by the collar of my shirt. He held his mermaid knife against my stomach.

"Come with me, littl' man," he said as he pulled me backwards into the captain's cabin – my little cask dragging along behind. Once in the cabin, he threw me on the cot.

"I ain't got time fer ya, ya littl' runt," he ranted. "Whut am I gonna do with ya?"

"Sticks, I didn't kill the captain – I swear!"

"Tha captain?" he shouted. "Tha captain? We are sinkin' you stupid arse! We'll be lucky if we ain't all dead in an hour! I don't give a hang for the captain – or you!" He eyed my wooden keg on the floor. "Whuts that?

"Nothing. Just powder for the gun," I lied.

"Well, ya won't be needin' that now, will ya?"

Suddenly the room spun and lurched wildly, as loud shouts erupted from the deck. Sticks threw the bar from the door over the railing into the ocean. "Ya can't lock us out now! But we can lock you in!" Hognose stuck his head inside the door and roared, "Sticks, tha storms'ls 'ave come loose; she's breached in the trough!"

Sticks screamed, "Turn 'er into tha wind, damn ya!" as he pushed past Hognose and ran for the wheel. "If'n we don't get 'er into tha wind, we're sunk!"

Hognose followed Sticks down the deck toward the wheel, leaving me locked in the cabin. I knew my time had come. I realized I was going into the ocean, one way or the other – either locked in the Captain's cabin or cast adrift. My eyes flittered around the cabin, searching for anything I could use to survive the sea. The captain's huge wooden desk stood in the middle of the room. I looked outside one more time to get my bearings as the ship twisted in the waves. I decided to leave the ship as we rose to the top of the next wave – if we made it to the top.

Inside the cabin, I pushed the desk over to the curved windows that formed the rear of the ship. I watched through the door as the mountainous wave overtook us, and the ship slowly climbed the monstrous wave toward the summit – sideways. The ship slowly turned into the storm. The wind and waves were coming from our bow, as I could imagine Sticks madly twisting the great wheel. Had this wave struck us broadside, it would have carried us to the bottom in minutes. The ship would have broken into a thousand splinters.

We stalled for a moment at the top edge of the wave as the ship struggled to gain the summit. I knew if I went out and the ship failed to top the wave, it would come crashing back down on me. We hung on the lip of the wave for what seemed an eternity. As soon as we leveled, and just before the stern rose level, I pushed the huge desk through the rear windows and plunged headlong into the violent yawning sea.

As soon as I hit the water, I regretted my decision to leave the ship. The water was much colder than I expected. The first crashing wave slammed me headlong into the side of the *Glendora*. My head swam in dizzy circles as I fought to remain conscious. If I thought the motion on the ship was bad, I was unprepared for the way the sea was violently tossing me. Were it not been for my drum lashed to my waist, I would have surely drowned. I felt like I was sliding down a steep hill. Once I reached the bottom, I looked up and trembled in fear. A huge wave loomed darkly over me, and quickly closed over me. If the enormous wall of water collapsed on top of me, there was no way I could survive. Somewhere in that massive wall of water was a ship. My only hope was to remain afloat near the surface and try to ride the wave to the crest as it passed under me, like a cork. The captain's desk floated near me in the trough, but I judged it too heavy to ride up the side of the oncoming wave. My barrel was light and full of air, and as I was very thin myself, I did my best to clutch the drum to my chest and hope for the best.

Like a fishing float, I rode wave after wave, as they pushed me farther and farther out to sea. At the crest of the waves, I looked to see if the ship was nearby. It was nowhere in sight. A mass of dark clouds still covered the sky, and rain was pounding in huge globs of water. No sooner would I crest a huge wave than I would begin the downward slide again. Up, up, up to the ragged crest, then down, down, down into the deep watery trough. No sooner was one ride up and down completed than we rose on the waves again. I made sure my barrel stayed closed, and I hugged it as close as possible trying to become one with the cask. I wanted to be one with the surface of the sea.

I swallowed a fair amount of salty seawater when I tumbled from the boat. My chest felt tight and I had trouble catching my breath. Every time I coughed, wet sticky fluid came up in my throat. Back on top of the wave, I searched as far as I could see, finding nothing at all but an angry sea and an endless line of tumbling waves coming toward me. Back down in the trench, I saw nothing at all but cold dark water. I never saw the ship or the desk again. I was hoping the desk might stay afloat, and I might be able to use it as a sort of raft after the seas calmed. I had no idea where it went. I suppose it broke up and sank like the *Glendora*. I was glad I had not held on to the desk. It would have dragged me to the bottom as it sank.

And so it went through the long night. Up, up, up, up – then down, down, down, down in a ceaseless cycle on a maddening seesaw. Gradually, the sky grew lighter as the waves became shallower. At the top though, the wind whipped through the whitecaps spraying the surface of the sea; and the rain fell in a wet curtain all around me. I saw some blue through the clouds in the far distance, so I believed the worst of the storm was over. I still could not see the ship – any ship – or any sign of land. I had no idea where I was, or how long I might be adrift. Once the waves became more regular, though still heavy, I carefully opened my keg and brought out some fresh water. Everything inside was still dry, and I estimated I could survive out of my barrel for at least three days if needed. Eventually, I could see the sun break through the low clouds in the distance, which I knew to be west because of the slant of the sun in the sky. It was becoming evening.

The waves were hardly as high as a standing man was and they were coming in at a much more regular rhythm. I realized the worst was behind me. I wrapped the rope from the barrel around my shoulders and laid my head on the wet wood. I felt safe enough finally to try to sleep. I dozed off immediately.

I awoke in the middle of the night; I could see stars in the sky and a crescent moon rising in the east. The seas had calmed somewhat, but they were still choppy. I estimated the swells to be a meter or so high. I ate some of my supplies and drank some more water. I expected the waves would sweep in toward some landmass soon, but I had no idea how long it might take. I did not even know which direction to swim. I conserved my energy and floated with the waves and the current. I had nothing to do but wait to see where the wind and the tides would carry me. I ate some crackers and took some more fresh water.

Sometime during the second night, early in the dawn, I believed I could see land ahead. At first, I thought it dreaming. There were no ships or boats around and no lights were visible in any direction. Just the dark, lonely, empty ocean with one little cork bobbing on the surface.

As dawn grew near, though, I believed I could make out the faint outline of a shoal directly ahead of me. As the light grew, I became more certain I some sort of land lay ahead. I hoped people lived on the island or that it at least had fresh water.

Just as the sun broke the horizon, I smelled land and could see great white birds soaring over a rocky beach. In another few moments, I could hear their calls as they swooped and soared in great circular clouds. Birds meant eggs, and I was so hungry I eagerly anticipated raiding their nests for some breakfast. I bobbed and swung on the waves as the land grew nearer and nearer; and after a while, I discovered I could touch bottom. Up to my chest in the water, I stood on firm ground for the first time in months. I rejoiced at my survival and plodded my way ashore against the current, a step at a time, keeping a sharp lookout for where those birds might have their nest.

By the time I stood on the beach, the sun was up; in the growing light, I could see a wooden shed not far from the beach. It sat on the edge of a green meadow, which was the prettiest sight I had seen in months. I made my way to the shed. There were benches outside around the two sides of the shed, and two ends were completely open. Inside was a large shelf-like table stretching along each side. A large wooden pen surrounded the shed all around. What the shed was for, I did not know; but there were signs of recent activity, so I decided to lie down on one of the benches in the shade and sleep. I thought someone might come soon, and I might find out where I was before I planned my next steps.

I awoke with a sharp pain in my side. A man in a huge hat stood in the bright light holding a stick. I could not see his face.

"You're a day early," he grumbled and spat a stream of brown juice on the grass. "Shearin' don't start ta mornin'."

I sat upright and shaded my eyes with my hand so I could see who spoke. He was dressed in canvas britches with a white shirt many sizes too large for him; like a nightshirt. His sleeves were rolled to his elbows, and he wore suspenders. His hat had a tall crown and a wide curved brim. He wore his white beard long and shaggy. A pipe drooped from his mouth. He did not seem upset I was there, so I repeated dumbly, "Shearin'?"

He looked at me like I was the stupidest person in the world. "Shearin'! Ain't that why you're here? Won't start 'til mornin'," he said without feeling. "You're a day early. Where you from, boy?"

I was not too eager to answer. I thought the less he knew about me, the better. "No place; every place, Sir," I answered cryptically.

He laughed a deep laugh. "Well, you sure ain't from any place around here. You sound like some Englander or something, but you are dark like an Injun. Are you an Injun? What's your name?"

"Maurice," I said from habit before I could remember to change my name.

"Maurice?" he hooted. "Maurice?" he said louder and belted out a hearty laugh again. "That sounds like some Frenchman name. You a Frenchman?"

"No, sir. I've never been to France."

"Well, you don't have ta go to France to be a Frenchy. Hell!" he snorted. He sounded exasperated, but I later came to realize it was just the way of him. He was actually amused. "We got about a million of 'em just a couple hundred miles that a'way," he pointed with his stick. "Are you one of them coon asses?" he squinted at me?

"I don't even know what that is," I responded and sat straight as I could. "Certainly not!"

He had a good laugh at that. "Well, Mawreece," he drug out the name in a strange way, "as I said, you're a day early. Shearin' don't start to tomorra."

I realized he thought I was here for the "shearin'", whatever it was. At least I did not have to come up with a story. "Might I wait here until morning, then?" I asked.

He laughed so hard he doubled over.

"Here? You want to stay *here* 'til mornin'? What in hell would you do that for? Come on up to the bunkhouse and stash your gear. You can sleep in there, dang gummit! You can help me drive the sheep into the pens this afternoon. I ain't had my breakfast yet, so I'll rustle some up for both of us."

I picked up my wooden keg and followed him out of the pen onto a dirt trail leading up a small rise. He stopped after a few steps and looked back at me tagging along, my barrel in my arms.

"Carry your stuff in a wooden keg, do ya? I've seen some odd thangs in my time, but I never seen nobody carry their truck around in a cask."

"It keeps everything dry," I said.

He laughed his deep, cheerful laugh again, and resumed walking.

134

"Yeah. I suppose it does. Keeps everything dry," he laughed to himself several times, as we topped the hill. A farmhouse and several outbuildings stretched before us, nestled in a beautiful grassy field. Across the way, dozens of white short, wooly animals were grazing the green grass. Sheep. Shearing. Gradually, I understood his strange way of talking. The next day would be shearing day and he expected several workers to show up to shave the sheep. He thought I was one of them. Perfect. I felt a little more comfortable now I understood and decided I would go along with his assumption. I had no place else to go anyway, and besides, he said something about breakfast.

I followed him to the house where he pointed with his stick toward a low building with a wide porch across the front. "Stash your gear over yonder. Pick any bunk you want – first come; first served around here. You got first pickin's. Once you get washed up and changed, you can come up to the house for some bacon and eggs." I understood most of what he said, though I wondered what "yonder" and "pickin's" were.

He looked down at my clothes. "Why you dressed like that?" he asked.

I was still dressed in my white canvas britches, which were cut sailor style below the knees, and my cotton seaman's shirt. "I don't have any other clothes," I said. "Maybe I can just wash these out."

He belly laughed. "You do, and they'll fall apart in your hands. You'll find some britches and shirts left behind back in there. Ya might have to wash 'em out in the pump out back. Take what you want; ain't nobody comin' back to get 'em, I suppose. Shoes too, if you can find some to fit. Hell, I don't know how you got this far from Lousianne without no shoes!" He kept walking toward the house talking over his shoulder. "When you're done, come on up around back. We'll eat on the back porch."

135

I was not sure where "Lousianne" was, but I was sure it was far better for him to think me from there than anywhere else. I worried if the *Glendora* made it to port after all, I might be in a tough spot.

I entered the dim bunkhouse. A dozen cots lined one wall with their mattresses folded double at the head of the beds. Bedding and pillows were stacked at the head of each bunk. The room was dim but seemed clean enough. The roof was good; the floor was dry from the recent storm. One large table stretched across one entire end of the room, and a dozen wooden chairs stood spaced along it. The other end of the room contained wooden shelves; some of them stuffed full, and some of them empty. I opened the back door and saw a wide porch and an outhouse in the yard. A basin and stand stood on the porch, and I filled it from the pump between the porch and the outhouse. I stripped, washed, and cleaned the salty rime from my arms and legs. Then, I went out and held my head under the spout as I pumped the handle. Cold, clear water covered my head and neck. It was cold, but it was heaven. It was my first bath in months.

I went back into the bunkhouse naked and searched through the shelves until I found some pants and a shirt, which fit reasonably well. They seemed clean enough. I wondered who left them and if they would come back to claim them tomorrow. I hoped they would not mind I wore their clothes. I saw some boots and low ankle shoes in the bin too, and I quickly found a pair of short boots that fit perfectly. I wondered who would leave behind a perfectly good pair of shoes. They felt tight and odd on my feet, as I had not worn shoes for the past few months.

I found a brush on the table near the basin, ran it through my hair, and looked in the mirror nailed to the wall. I had aged since I last saw myself. I tried to think of how long, and then remembered it was back in the mountains as I washed the blood from my father's pocket watch. I noticed I still did not have any facial hair. I wondered if I would ever grow a beard. I longed to have a beard like the old man, who I suddenly remembered was cooking our breakfast back at the house. I also remembered to take the watch and my mother's locket from the wrapped packet in the barrel, and carefully placed them in the pocket of my new pants before I walked up the path toward the house. I also took my marlinspike in case it might come in handy.

I went around to the back as instructed. I stood with my hands behind my back outside the back door, not sure what to do next. He came through the door onto a screened porch with a steaming iron skillet in his hand. He placed the sizzling pan on the table, reached out and opened the screen, and spat a wad of tobacco into the grass.

"Well, come on in!" he said in a rough but friendly way, as he motioned me to the table. I knew he did not mean anything by his tone of voice – it was just the way he talked. I guess living alone he did not realize how gruff he sounded.

"You can eat here with me today. Woman won't be here to cook for the hands 'til tomorra. You'll have to settle for me. Can't mess up bacon and eggs too bad, I guess. No biscuits, but I got some corn bread left over from last night if you want it. It'll have to do. I got some beans if you want 'em."

I sat down as he dished out four eggs and several strips of crisp bacon. He poured two cups of coffee and we ate our breakfast.

I did not realize how hungry I was until I smelled the food. I ate my breakfast as quickly as I could. I looked up embarrassed and found my host kept up with me.

"Don't waste much time eatin', do ya?" he snorted. "Me neither. Shouldn't take longer to eat it than it does to cook it, I always say. Want some more?"

He was a most friendly and accommodating man. I liked him immediately, and the longer I was with him I liked him even more. His name was Ben. He did not pry or ask too many questions, and he usually settled on the answer himself I could answer. Ben seemed to come to his own conclusions about who I was and what I was doing. I did not correct him. His own ideas about me were a lot safer than the truth!

He laughed a lot. He liked to talk and did not expect much in return from me. Through his steady stream of talk, I learned a dozen men were coming the next morning to shear his sheep. He thought I was one of those. It must have landed in the most opportune place I could have picked. I had a new life and a new job for however long it lasted.

After breakfast, we cleaned the dishes. I did some odd chores like filling the water buckets from the well and feeding the chickens. Around noon, Ben told me I could go rest in the bunkhouse and he would call me for supper. I slept until late in the afternoon until I heard Ben calling my name. Ben called up the dogs, and together we rounded up the sheep and herded them into the wooden pen surrounding the shearing shed. In all, we pinned nearly a hundred sheep.

Once we penned up inside the 'corral', as he called it, Ben slapped me on the back and thanked me for the help. "Let's go ta town!" he said his eyes dancing. "We'll have some dinner and some beer, and sit and talk. It'll be our last chance to get out for near a week!"

"I don't have any money," I offered sadly.

"Well, I owe you a day's wages, I reckon. So don't worry. Come on! We'll go on to town. I'll take it out of what I owe you." I followed along, wondering what a 'reckon' was.

138

Ben and I struck off across country toward a village a couple of miles away he called "Old Town." I still saw no reason to share my true story with Ben, so I kept such information to myself. He did not seem interested anyway. It was clear sheep shearers came and went all the time and it did not matter much where they were from or where they went so long as they would work. It was well enough he not know any more about me than necessary.

I learned we were on an island named Goat Island. Goat Island was a long, skinny island with a lighthouse on the Western shore, protecting a wide channel. Old Town was a small fishing village near the lighthouse. I learned the island got its name from wild goats that once roamed the island at will before the settlers came. Few trees grew on the island because of the salty air, but grass grew well because of the frequent coastal rains that seemed to fall in the area, watering the island. The island was practically useless for anything but sheep and fishing. I found out without asking the mainland was not far away, and the best way to get there was to get across to the narrow channel to Galveston Island, then take a ferry to the mainland. No one had much reason to go to the mainland, because everything anyone ever needed could be had right here, or in Galveston. Galveston was a large town with a major port where large ships came in and out every day.

The Old Town Tavern had a low ceiling under a tin roof. It was similar to Ben's bunkhouse. A long wooden covered porch stretched across the front. The building had no door to open or close, just an open hole in the front to enter. Inside, it was dark because there were only a few windows along the side. Short wall divided the tavern into two sections. A wide ragged gap in the wall served as a pass through. Tables and chairs filled the tavern. It was darker in the rear half of the room because there were no windows at all in the back. The only true door was in the middle of the back wall that stood open leading to a sort of alleyway between the outhouse and several other buildings.

It was cooler inside the darkened pub, and I was glad to be out of the heat. Ben and I drew heavy wooden chairs up to a rough wooden table scarred with burn marks in various places. Several men at the other tables, who obviously knew Ben because they joked with him as we made our way to the back half of the tavern, were playing strange square wooden blocks with pits on one side – Ben called the game dominoes. The players took great delight in slamming down a domino to great laughter among the others. In the middle of the larger room was a strange oblong table with rails went all around, and several colored balls that rolled on the surface. Some of the men were having fun knocking these little balls around with a long wooden stick. They would mark their "count" with chalk on a slate nailed to the wall nearby. I did not know how they played the game, but I soon learned no one wanted to be "snookered!" The players would become excited whenever one of them got snookered.

The innkeeper brought a large pitcher of warm beer and a couple of glasses. Ben ordered chicken, and soon a platter of baked hen appeared. We sat eating chicken and sucking the bones while Ben kept up a running dialog with his neighbors. Much of the banter I did not understand, but I was quickly learning the local expressions. "Hands" were workers. I figured out "reckon" meant something along the lines of "I believe" based on how it was so frequently used. It seemed to be a favorite word. "Yonder" was any place away from wherever you were standing, usually in the direction speaker pointed.

"Who's yer friend," a grizzled old man asked Ben eventually.

"This here's Maurice," Ben said, and patted me on the shoulder. "He's come over from Lousianne to help with the shearin' tomorra." I believed Lousianne to be the next city or place to the east since it was the direction he indicated every time he said it. "He ain't no coon ass though, so don't go callin' him that. He don't like it much," Ben laughed. I still was not sure what a coon ass was but I still did not like the sound of it.

After that short introduction, no one seemed to take much notice of me at all. By this time, darkness was gathering and the bartender lit the lamps. I noticed no women were in the tavern. Most of the men drank beer, but a few ordered whiskey. I wanted to get a good look at what their money looked like, but I was not close enough to examine the coins. I decided I could wait until Ben paid me, and then try to figure out the local coinage. Up in the front room, some of the drinkers were playing darts. I knew that game, though the local rules seemed odd. I noticed some of the dart-throwers sounded like Englishmen. I asked Ben about it.

"Aw, about thirty years ago a ship wrecked off the coast here. There's been a bunch of wrecks over the years. That's why they built the light over yonder (pointing west), 'cause of all the shipwrecks. Anyway, this one ship run aground here, and it was full of the Brits. Most of 'em stayed and are still around hereabouts. Some of 'em ain't been off this island in thirty years. This tavern we're sittin' in here was made from the wood from that very ship." He paused and looked at me closely. I was becoming more uncomfortable – I did not want to talk about shipwrecks or pirates.

"Come to think of it, you sound more like them than a coon ass! Oops – sorry," he laughed. I laughed along with him, pleased that the subject changed. I would rather be a coon ass than a pirate, I thought.

Soon two of Ben's friends, Joe and Frank, joined us. The subject quickly slipped back to pirates when they heard us talking about shipwrecks. Frank swore treasure was been buried all over the island. They told tales of pirates named Black Beard, Lafayette, and spoke of them with great admiration and child-like wonder. Their eyes sparkled with excitement as they told about pirate ships that visited the island. It was obvious to me these men had never met a

141

real pirate. Real pirates were plundering, murdering wretches offering nothing to be admired, let alone buried treasure. I could not help but wonder, if the pirates had money why did they bury it? The pirates I knew would have spent it on rum and women as quickly as possible. They certainly would not have dug a hole and buried it on some deserted beach somewhere; then go off and leave it. The thought was laughable. I said nothing aloud, but inside I laughed at their ignorance. If pirates had walked in the door right this moment, they probably would have killed half the people in the tavern, while the rest would have fled in terror for their lives.

After Joe and Frank educated me on pirates, they moved away to argue over who was the most fearsome pirate of the bunch. Ben laughed and told me not to bother with them because they were "pirate crazy. "Besides, there is something I want to talk to you about."

I shivered at his words. Had he thought of something that made him suspect I was a fraud? Did he think I might be a pirate myself? While he ordered some more beer, I tried to come up with a better story. My fears unfounded when he finally got around to telling me his thoughts,

"So, Mawreece, what do you plan to do after the shearin' is over?"

I had no idea; I was not thinking that far ahead yet. I was just happy to be on dry land and to have a roof over my head for the immediate future.

"You goin' back to Lousianne?" he pressed.

I did reveal any particular plans, so Ben made a generous offer.

"Well, you don't have to make up your mind right now, I reckon. You could even stay around here with me if you was a mind to. I can use a hand to help with the sheep; if'n you don't have nothin' better to do, that is. Stay here. I've come to takin' a likin' to you, by gum. You can stay as long as you like." He slapped me on the shoulder again.

I thanked him and said I would keep his kind offer in mind. Ben related he had no family around. All of his daughters were married off, his wife died, and his sons wandered to the mainland to find jobs. There was a cook woman who came out to cook for the hands twice a year during the shearing season; but for the most part, he was alone with the sheep. The more he talked; the more I wanted to stay. It was safe and quiet here, and I liked him very much.

Suddenly, something exciting stirred out front of the tavern. A large crowd, brandishing flaming torches, gathered in a group outside in the dirt street. Many of the customers left their tables and crowded onto the long front porch. Ben stopped talking, and although we did not leave our seats, it was clear whatever happened out front was drawing his attention away from me. One by one, the groups of men came back inside the bar and order more drinks, as shouting and loud talking filtered into the tavern.

"What's goin' on out there?" Ben asked one of the men nearby. My heart sank at the response.

"Shipwreck! A body's been washed up on the shore! Poor devil is half-dead. They are bringing him up here now on a wagon."

My first instinct was to run out the back door, but I made myself sit and wait. A huge storm was not unusual at sea; maybe this sailor was not from the *Glendora*! Maybe some other ship had wrecked – he was some other sailor. What if it was Mawken? I gripped the edge of the wooden table to keep my hands from shaking. Why had I told Ben my name? I excused myself to go to the privy out back while I plotted my escape just in case I needed one.

A short distance down the island, a lighthouse cast its light across the sandy spit of land. The lighthouse must stand on the edge of the channel. I wondered if that was where they hung the local pirates. I was sure if this castaway exposed me, being accused of piracy would be the least of my problems. They hung murderers too. If I could get across the channel, I would be on the next island – Galveston, I think they said – and then I could escape to the mainland. As much as I wanted to stay with Ben, I could not help but fear my past, making it impossible for me to stay. Why did I always have to run away? Would this bad dream ever be over? I just wanted to stay in one place and rest without being in danger. I thought of running for the lighthouse immediately, but I was able to calm myself and go back into the darkened bar. I made sure to sit at the table where shadows covered my face.

In the main part of the bar, more lamps were lit, and space was made to receive the shipwrecked sailor. One entire table was set aside for him. The crowd grew huge, eagerly anticipating the arrival of the castaway as much as I feared it. A great uproar went up in the tavern as everyone expressed a personal theory. Soon, a great whoop rose up as a wagon pulled up to the huge porch. A gang of men poured out onto the porch, and other men shouted at them to get out of the way and let them pass. Two men appeared, supporting a man who slumped between them. He was on his feet but apparently was too weak to walk. A blanket was thrown over his head so I could not see his face. Gradually, the wall of men parted as they sat the man in a wooden chair in the center of the room and called for whiskey. I could see beneath the blanket that the wind and tide ripped away most of his ragged clothing. As the men jostled the poor survivor into a chair, the cover shifted and I caught sight of a long knife with a handle carved in the shape of a mermaid. I could not take my eyes from the knife as the men called for more whiskey and hot tea. I shrank farther back into the deep shadows as the blanket pulled from his face. Even before I saw him, I knew Sticks was beneath that blanket.

In the front of the bar, dozens of men arrived and crowded around to see what the half-drowned sailor would say. The bartender, standing on a chair and shouting for silence, brought the loud talking and speculation to an abrupt close. I moved further into the darkened rear room, trying to stay out of sight. I took care no came between the back door and me. It was not difficult as everyone crowded into the front room surrounding Sticks.

Whiskey-laced hot tea was delivered to Sticks in great quantities. As quickly as he would empty his cup, he would demand a refill. As soon as the barman would quieten the room, someone would shout out a question. Before Sticks could even answer one question, he was interrupted with dozens of more questions, and the room would erupt into disorganized chaos again. The barkeeper stood atop the bar and banged on a pot with a metal spoon.

"Quiet! Hush! Let the man speak!" he demanded the crowd. Once more, the room became quiet as all eyes focused on Sticks.

"Three days," Sticks' voice cracked as if he had not spoken in days. "I was afloat three days with no food or fresh water."

"Get him something to eat!" someone shouted! A pile of biscuits and a plate of meat was placed before Sticks, but he seemed more interested in the whiskey tea.

"*Glendora*." he croaked in a hoarse voice I could hardly recognize. "She'us named the *Glendora*. She wuz a triple-masted schooner we sailed out o' Rangoon the first of March, under the cruelest captain ever sailed the seas. We wuz laden with tea and silks, bound for New Orleans to take on cotton. We got overtook by a storm that roared inside Cuba, and pushed us past the Yucatan into the Gulf of Mexico."

Sticks was just warming up. He relished being the center of attention. He rose from his chair and went around the circle of men

145

telling the horrors of serving aboard the *Glendora*. He described the captain and his ugly, foul moods. He told of the boy they dropped off in Rangoon, to the gasps and amazement of the crowd. He moved from one man to another as he mimicked a close reproduction of the captain's mannerisms and his voice. He acted out nearly every incident that occurred in our voyage from the Indian Ocean to the Atlantic and into the Caribbean.

He built up steam as he went along, and I dreaded the moment he would come to my part of the story. When he did, no doubt he would expose me as a killer. I edged closer to the back door. The mob would probably hang me at once. There were no trees to speak of on Goat Island, so they would probably hang me from the roof. The thought occurred to me I might die exactly as my mother had – hung from the eaves of a house. I moved a little closer to the door in the rear of the darkened room. I eased it open and left it standing agape in case I needed to run.

I looked out onto the back alley and planned my escape. If I needed, I would run as quickly as I could to the lighthouse, which stood near the rocky shore. Once away from the tavern, I would hide among the rocks until I could decide what to do. Maybe it was close enough to swim. Maybe I could hail a passing fishing boat to take me across the channel. I would find some way to gain the mainland and somehow lose myself in the wilds of Texas. I could leave now, but there was a chance Sticks would not expose me. He already told them how cruel the captain was. Maybe he might skip over my part and say the captain was murdered and deserved what he got! I decided not to leave unless I was in immediate danger of being exposed.

Sticks was not skipping much of the story, however. He seemed to get stronger as he went along, bolstered by the whiskey. He got to the part of the missing ax from the wheelhouse wall. He described the search of the ship, and how the cruel the captain whipped his sailors. Sticks brought a lantern close to his face to show the still raw, jagged wound running down his left cheek. He told how much he hated the captain and even bragged that he knocked the captain flat for his cruelty to the crew. It was a lie, but enraptured crowd accepted it as fact. They could see it happen for themselves, as Sticks acted the scenes out, nearly striking one of the men in the crowd who he had appointed as the evil Captain.

He told of the mysterious woman from Port Royal, who warned of the coming storm. He even placed a cloth over his head and mimed her every act. He replaced Hognose with himself in the story as he interrogated the woman, switching roles by removing the veil when he was Sticks. Since Sticks was not present, his rendition was not close at all. His false high-pitched voice was much more shrill and squeaky than the real woman's voice. But who was to know but me? Sticks never saw the woman in person. He had not known about her until we were three days out to sea. Sticks was never one to let the truth get in the way of a good story. In Stick's version, he believed the warnings, and he urged the captain to stay in port. The evil captain put the ship and crew in danger by trying to outrun the approaching storm.

Then Sticks did more than tell of the terrible storm – he acted it out. He pulled a chair close and placed a man on each end of the heavy wooden table. Sticks instructed them to alternatively raise and lower their end of the table, simulating the motion of the boat on the seas. It was clear he had acted out sea stories many times, in taverns in ports around the world. At first, he had the men wave the table gently and regularly, which he stated was the normal motion of the ocean. As the story went on, he would instruct the men to raise and lower the table higher and faster. Bottles and cups went rolling, as someone grabbed the lantern, and all else they could from the pitching table. Glass broke and scattered across the hard wooden floor enhancing the drama. All the while, Sticks drained his cup and motion for a refill. Near the end, he told the men to increase the vigor

147

of their motion and to try to wrest the table from the other. The violent pitching of the table simulated how the storm lashed the ship.

"Imagine buckets and buckets of water 'uz washing across the decks, and the wind 'uz howling like a wild animal pushing you across the pitching deck."

Sticks turned his eyes toward the ceiling of the rough building as though he could see right through it.

"See?" He pointed upwards. Everyone looked up.

"See tha sheets ripped from the masts as they flap helplessly in the ragin' wind? See tha masts bent 'most double? Hear the howls, as the wind rips through the ragged, fluttering sheets? Hear the crack of wood, as tha spars come near ta' splittin' in two? Feel the shudder as the thunderous waves pound the ship?"

Finally, Sticks spread his arms over the pitching table and calmed the heaving seas as he motioned the table to settle back on its legs. The seas sufficiently calmed, he sat in the chair again and placed his elbows on the table.

"Suddenly, the storm calmed," he related. He looked around the crowd with bleary eyes.

"Whut? No whiskey?" he grunted.

Immediately his cup was refilled. He drank it dry and shook it at the man with the jug to replenish once again. He looked around the room of silent men, who stood waiting to hear what would come next.

"In the midst of the calm, that's when it 'appened," he looked from face to face.

In the darkness of the back room, I froze. I knew what came next. The crowd waited quietly for the story to continue, but Sticks waited in silence for the tension to rise. He sat shaking his head sadly back and forth as if he could not believe what he would tell next.

"A tragedy. A cruel end to such a brave and honorable man!" He reported.

"Who?" the excited crowed asked in unison.

Forgetting the horrible picture he painted of the cruel captain in the earlier part of the story, now he described the captain as the "Crown's officer." He described the captain in his Royal Navy regalia, not as we saw him every day. The captain's excellent sailing record was extolled.

"And to 'ave ended in such a fashion," Sticks sadly shook his head.

"What end?" The crowd begged Sticks to continue.

Sticks drained his cup and pulled his knife from his belt, and laid the sharp blade on the table. The crowd marveled at the carved handle in the shape of a mermaid. Sticks called for someone to bring a bag of feed to the table in front of him. Men came forward with his request, placing a heavy burlap bag on the table before him. Without warning, Sticks plunged his knife into the bag of feed as the crowd shrank back in shock. Sticks ripped the bag down to the bottom and then across from side to side. Corn spilled across the table and onto the rough wooden floor. Sticks reached inside the bag, pulled out a fist full of corn, and threw it against the far wall. The corn rattled and skittered in every direction on the sawdust covered floor. The drinkers shrieked as if it were blood.

Sticks looked around the room with blood-streaked eyes. He mumbled something the men could not hear.

"What?" They shouted in unison.

Sticks eyes rolled up into his head as he collapsed in a drunken daze, his head dropping face first onto the ripped bag of corn.

"What did he say?" They asked to each other. "What was it?"

They lifted his face by the hair of his head from the bag of feed and asked him to repeat his words.

"What happened?" they wanted to know.

Not getting a response, they let Stick's head drop back onto the bag with a thud.

I could see Ben watching me as I quietly went through the back door.

"Gents," the barman said to the crowd, "I think he said," he paused and faced the crowd, "murder."

I ran until I bogged down in wet sand. For all my efforts, the lighthouse did not appear any closer. I followed a little path toward the light until I realized I took the wrong path. The trail to the lighthouse turned off somewhere and went down another spit of land. I was separated from the lighthouse by a small peninsula and a wide expanse of water. I did not want to swim unless necessary so I turned back and searched in the dark for a road nearer the lighthouse. I soon found the cutoff I thought would lead me out to the point. I ran all the way. It did not take long to come to the lighthouse.

Wary of the keeper and his dogs, I stayed well to the left of the lighthouse and worked my way around the rocky beach. The beach held plenty of sand overlaid with large, heavy, slabs of stone. It smelled of fish from the heaps of clam or oyster shells littering the beach. I hid among the boulders to catch my breath and to try to decide what to do next.

I was too far away from the little village to see. I did not know if Sticks regained consciousness or not, or if he identified me as the murderer. The look Ben gave me as I slipped out the back door told me he knew I was involved in some way. When Sticks revived and gave my name, what would Ben do? Would he set the town on me, or would he allow me time to make my escape? Would Ben defend me or would he expose me for the liar and imposter I was? I felt cheap and guilty. But, no matter how badly I felt, I knew I was no killer. I also knew it would be impossible to prove I did not kill the captain. The only one who knew I was innocent was Mawken, and he was lost at sea in the storm – probably drowned. He would probably shift the blame to me anyway.

I felt relatively safe concealed in the rocks. I was out of sight so I knew unless someone saw me crossing the flats no one could see me from the shore. I did not think anyone could see me from the lighthouse either, as upended rocks, standing several times my height, screened my hiding place. If I stayed low, I could not see the lighthouse, so I was sure no one could see me.

After I caught my breath, I decided my best chance would be to swim to the other side. I wished for my barrel to save my leather shoes from the water. The additional buoyancy would also be helpful on the water of the bay. I decided I would tie my shoes together and hang them around my neck so they would not be lost. As I bound up my shoes, I looked out on the bay. I could see lights on the opposite shore. It appeared to be close enough to swim, so long as the waves and wind were not too high. I believed I could make it across in under an hour, and escape Goat Island long before sunrise. I would skirt the town of Galveston and make my way to the ferry landing to be ready to cross the next morning. I searched my pockets for anything that might be useful. I found some coins Ben left on the table after our meal. I did not intend to steal them. I tried to figure out the local money system but got distracted when Sticks came. I thoughtlessly dropped them into my pocket. I did not know how much money it was, but I hoped it was enough.

I could see no way of escaping the island except by swimming. I saw no reason to delay the inevitable, so I rose from my rocky hiding place and went down to the frothy water. I tested the water; it was cold but not icy. Off to my left, I saw a small light bobbing on the surface of the bay. A boat paddled its way around the point toward me. As the light from the lighthouse flashed, I could see it was a small fishing boat, outfitted with outriggers to hold nets. The nets were not out, so the fishermen were either going out or coming in. I allowed the boat to get near and then hailed across the water.

"Hellooooo!"

"Hellooooo!" came back the answer.

"Might you take me to the other side?" I called.

"Who's a askin'?" came the reply.

"Only a poor sheep shearer who has lost his way."

After a pause, I heard, "How poor?"

"Very poor," I volunteered.

"Then we ain't got no time."

I could hear two men laughing. Then one said, "Ya got a nickel?"

"I think so," I offered. "Would a nickel suffice?"

"Suffice?" The laughter grew louder. "Suffice?" They snickered as the boat drew nearer. It was obvious they were drinking; they were having too much fun. "If you mean will it be enough to take you across, then that would suffice – real nice." Their raucous laughter echoed off the rocks so loudly I was afraid it would draw attention. Yes, they must be drinking.

I took the coins from my pocket and looked at them. I counted six coins. Some were brown and looked like a penny I saw on the *Glendora*. "How many pennies are in a nickel?" I hollered.

The question stirred even more laughter. "You must be a sheep shearer if you don't know what a nickel is. Any numb skull knows that five pennies makes a nickel." After a pause he yelled, "Ok! We'll take you across for two cents since you ain't got no nickel! Ya got two cents?"

"Yes," I hollered back.

"Then, swim for it!" came the response. "We'll back-paddle 'til you get here."

"Can't you pull ashore and pick me up?"

"Not for two cents! You got another half-penny?"

"Yes, I'm sure I do."

I could hear them argue in low tones, but finally one called out, "Stay right where you are, ya' Honor. We'll pull to shore and you won't even have to get your dainty feet wet!" Suddenly, the prow of the fishing boat appeared out of the misty darkness and struck the rocks with a loud hollow thump. Again with the noise. It came to barely an arms-length from where I stood. "Hop in, sir!" came the laughing invitation.

I stepped aboard and gave the man in the stern three of my coins. He looked at them in the dim light and handed one back. "Give me one of them," he pointed at the other coins in my hand. I gave it to him and quickly stuffed the remainder in my pocket. He held up one of the coins, "You need to learn how to read money, boy! Ya gonna get cheated if ya don't – 'specially around these parts. You're lucky I'm a good Christian man."

His partner laughed so hard I thought he would fall out of the boat. All he could do was sputter the word, 'Christian' repeatedly, until the other man shouted, "Shut up, Bart!"

He showed me where I could sit, so I sat on the rocking boat and waited. For the next fifteen minutes, I endured an intense interrogation from Bart and Frank as we made our way across the channel. They asked if I were English. I was not so naïve as in the past and answered, "Yes."

"Hear that, Bart? I told you he was an Englishman. I heard them Englishmen talkin' before, so's I know what they sound like! Englishman!" Bart peered at me through the darkness from beneath his yellow slicker hood.

"He seems mighty dark for an Englishman, Frank."

"He's from southern England, Bart! Don't you know nothin'?" They both guffawed at this, although I could not imagine what was so funny.

I decided the less they knew, the better it would be for me. I sat and listened while they made up for themselves the details of who I was, where I was from, what I was doing on a Texas beach in the middle of the night; along with specifics as to my religion, family, personal life, and where I was going. I agreed with everything the man in the stern decided, to his great delight. They were artfully creative. By the time I landed in Galveston, I was an English merchant who had been cheated out of my property and land in London, escaped England before being deported to debtor's prison, and worked my way across America shearing sheep. They were so engrossed in creating my life story they forgot to ask my name. If the crossing took another fifteen minutes, they would have promoted to Duke.

On the other side, I bid my fishing friends a hearty goodbye and struck off walking. I counted myself lucky I did not even get my boots wet. I followed the road signs reading "Ferry"; and just before sunrise, I found myself sitting with a few other groups, waiting for the morning passage to the mainland of Texas. Old sailors had told stories of Texas on the ship; it was a land of cowboys on horses. They all carried guns and wore big wide hats. I wondered if I might meet my first real cowboy.

The ferry was not ashore yet, so I sat near a lanky youth I judged to be near my age. He sat with his back to a post, trying to sleep. He was exactly as my shipmates described a cowboy. He had a horse and a gun, and a big white hat. He tethered his horse to the same post he leaned against, and was in the process of trying to get some sleep. Every time the boy drifted off, the horse would nudge his shoulder or head with a large wet nose. The youth would take his hat and swat at the pony for his insolence. "Dang it, Pete! Let me alone,

155

or I'm going to move over thar and leave you here by ya own dang self!"

I sat nearby and untied my shoes. I tied them so tight earlier I wore a large blister on my heel. "Go soak it in tha bay," the cowboy offered. "Salt water'll do it good. Make sure you dry ya foot off real good 'fore ya put tha boot back on."

I did as he said and hobbled over to soak the blister in the salt water near the ferry landing. The cowboy gave up trying to sleep and moved over to sit near the edge of the water while I soaked my foot. "If ya got somethin' to carry it in, ya can pull up a pot of that water and go heat it up on tha fire over yonder," he pointed. "Warm salt water is even better." He spoke slowly, dragging out every word. I never heard anyone speak in such a slow, lazy manner. Even simple words like "in" and "fire" gained a couple of syllables.

"I don't have a pot," I responded. For some reason my speech slowed considerably as I answered.

"I ain't got none neither." He took off his hat and looked around the ferry landing. "Mebbe you can borry one from that famly over yonder," he pointed again. "You got your foot in tha water," he nodded, "want me to go over and fetch one? I don't mind."

I did not want to draw attention to myself, so I answered, "Thank you, but I think this will be fine. It's not bad, and it already feels much better."

"Well, that's fine then. Glad to hear it's feelin' better. Them thangs can cripple ya' up sometimes." He looked around, wiped his brow with a big red cloth, and put his big hat back on. "Headin' across, huh?" He did not wait for an answer. "Me too. I been punchin' cows down here on tha island for a spell, but now I'm headin' back home – see if I can find me some work up there or somewhere."

"Me too," I mumbled.

"What's that?" he asked. "You lookin' too?"

"Yes."

"As a cowpuncher? Ya shore don't look like one."

"No. I thought maybe I could cook or something somewhere."

"You a cook?" He brightened considerably. "Hells bells! If ya know how to cook, you can work most anywhere! Boss men can't get a cowboy to cook! Most of us thank it is the lowest job on the range, but it ain't. A good cook is an important man on the trail; it's just that no decent cowboy will do tha job as long as he can ride!"

"Good news to me, then. Now if I can find someone who will take me on…"

"Don't ya worry none about that! You go see a man named Dutch in Pine City over there. He's got a wagon train building up right now. I'll bet he needs a cook. Tell him Whistle Britches sent ya. That's what they call me mostly – Whistle Britches. I don't like it much, but most folks don't even know my real name is Donny. I don't like the name Donny neither, so it don't matter much. You go tell Dutch Whistle Britches sent ya and he'll take you on. But one thang!" he pointed a long finger directly at me.

"What is the thing?"

"Ya better be a good cook, or they'll run ya off – or hang ya! And, ya gotta get there before they roll out tomorra. Ya know where Pine City is at?" He looked up as the ferry pulled into the landing.

"No."

"I'll show ya tha road when we get to tha other side. It's about ten mile. Walkin', you should make it in time, but don't dawdle."

I was not sure how far ten mile was, or how to dawdle, but it must be close enough to walk. I had enough money to pay the ferry from the coins I left in my pocket. Leaving the ferry on the other side, Donny led his horse and walked along with me for a couple of miles. He talked a steady stream as we walked. Donny told me of his home west of Austin in a town called Fredericksburg. His people owned a ranch outside of town; but he could not get along with his father, so he struck out on his own. Donny was on his way to see his folks, and to try to find work a little closer. He told me if he found work nearby, he would come to Austin to look me up.

He pointed up a dirt road leading through the pines. "Ya stay on this road and you'll run right into it pretty soon. It ain't far. I'd go with ya, but gotta get up there 'fore the fall roundup."

"How long will it take?"

He mounted his horse, took off his hat, and looked far down the road as he bid me goodbye in his cowboy way.

"Welll…" he drew out as he mopped his brow with his cloth again, "might take me a week. But you, bein' on tha wagon train, now that's gonna take longer – mebbe a month. If it rains you'll be lucky to get thar before October." He stuck out his hand to shake mine, then turned his horse and rode away. He shouted back, "See ya in Austin in about a month! Don't forget me. I'll come and look ya up, ya can count on it! Hey! What's your name?"

Without thinking I shouted, "Maurice!" I slapped my hand across my forehead for my stupidity. He galloping away on Pete.

"See ya, Maw-reece!" Donny shouted over his shoulder as he galloped away.

After Donny out of sight, I turned down the road he pointed out. Countless wagons had cut deep ruts through a thick forest mixed with tall pine trees and low growing fan-shaped palms. It was a jungled, almost impenetrable in places. The smell of wood smoke drifted through the shadowy pines but I could not tell its source. The sun was quickly heating up the sand, but I decided to keep my boots off as long as possible so my blister would heal. After a couple of hours, I ran from one shady spot to another because of the hot sand. I felt like my feet were on fire.

Finally, I decided I should put on my boots so I sat down under a pine tree by a large gray rock. I calculated I was probably half way to Pine City. I hoped it was a small town and not a huge city. I wondered what I would do if Dutch did not hire me, but Whistle Britches sounded so sure he would, I decided to walk now and worry later.

After I tied my boots as tight as I dared, I stood up and walked a few more steps down the road to see how my foot felt. I did not notice any pain, so I decided to continue walking. I was hungry and I knew the sooner I got to Pine City the sooner I might be able to eat. As I passed the rock, I heard someone laugh. I turned and saw someone sitting on top of the rock, scraping a knife against a sharpening stone. It was Mawken – the traitor!

I ignored him; he was no friend of mine. He abandoned me. I kept walking down the road, despite his calls to stop and come back. The last person in the world I wanted to see was Mawken! What was he doing here? Why wasn't he drowned? The tide must have washed him ashore while I was at the sheep ranch. How did he know I would come this way? How could he have known?

"Maurice! Come back. We need to talk. You are in danger! I must warn you! Come back!"

I stopped in my tracks and listened. Should I just keep walking? What danger I did not already know, and for which he was not responsible? All of my problems in this world tied directly to Mawken. I was so mad at him I could not speak. What would I need to do to escape from Mawken? I turned and walked back to the rock, intending to speak harshly. He remained on the rock calmly sharpening his knife. I knew what he was capable of so I kept my distance. I was prepared to run if he jumped from the rock. I looked around for something I could use to defend myself if necessary, but only spotted a few tree branches before he said, "Maurice, we must talk."

"Why would I want to talk to you?" I angrily spit out.

"Because I am your friend," he said softly.

"My friend?" I shouted. "My friend, who abandoned me in my time of need?" I shouted, my face distorted in anger. I felt I might cry. "My friend, who stood by and let them accuse me of murdering the captain? My friend, who led me into a trap at Haji's? Or, my friend who murdered Sofi? What kind of friend are you?" I asked behind clenched teeth!

"The kind of friend who would save you from being murdered by the pirates." He calmly answered. "The kind who would risk his life to recover belongings of your dead mother and father so you would have at least something to remember them by. The kind of friend who would lead you safely over the mountains to escape the hangman who believed you killed your own parents." His voice rose higher and higher as he spoke, "I was the kind of friend who rescued you from human bondage from the Arab traders after Haji sold you. I was even the kind of friend who would take your place and suffer the punishment of a cruel captain, while you slept safely in your snug bunk each night! That is the kind of friend I am!" At this point, he stopped yelling.

I knew he was right, but I was still angry.

"You have no idea," he said in a calmer voice, "the horrors I suffered in your place. You cannot imagine what that captain did to me – what he wanted me to do to him!"

I pointed a shaky finger at him, "You let them think I murdered the captain!" I accused.

"Maurice," his voice softened, "I was the only one who could get you off that boat without you being killed by the crew."

"You are lying again!" I shouted at him. "I escaped the ship on my own after you sided with the crew. You would have let them hang me! I escaped from the ship by pushing the captain's desk through the window."

"Maurice, who do you think turned the ship into the breach after Hognose and Sticks trapped you in the captain's cabin?"

I stopped as the terrible night came crashing back into my mind. *"She's breached in the trough!"* The wind screamed in my ears once again, as thunderous waves pounded the ship. *"Turn 'er into tha wind, damn ya!"*

Mawken's voice penetrated my memory of the horrifying storm. "Who do you think retrieved your keg and hung it on the hook for you to find?"

Emotion and guilt over doubting Mawken quickly flooded my mind. He was a friend after all. However, I was still angry at him. "How did you get here?" I asked.

"Oh, I jumped from the ship as soon as I knew you were in the water. I knew you were smart enough to break through the captain's window. It was your only way out. As soon as I hit the water, I grabbed the desk and held on. The waves were so high, and the wind was so wild, I could not keep sight of you. I wanted to help

161

you, but within minutes, we were separated in the dark. I tied myself to the desk and rode the waves all night. Unlike you, I was without food or water; and once the sun came up, I could see no sight of you anywhere. I rode the desk as long as I could before it broke apart. Then, I bundled the remains into a sort of raft, which helped keep me afloat. After a day or so, I found myself on the shore near a little lighthouse outside a village. I stole some food and took some clothes I found hanging on a line outside a house. I went to the tavern to look for work; I saw you come in with an old man. I was so happy you survived. I knew if you saw me, as angry as you were at the time, you might turn me in for murdering the captain. You would have, too! Do not deny it – it is true. I was in the alley, trying to come up with a plan when they discovered Sticks. It was a stroke of luck he passed out before he could name you as the captain's killer."

"But it was you who killed the captain!"

"No one knows, Maurice – but you. Sticks thought you were the murderer; and you know as well as I do, as soon as he revived, he would name you as the killer. I saw you leave the tavern and run to the lighthouse. I would have followed then, but I had work to do."

"What kind of work?" I asked.

"The work I always do – protecting you."

"What of Ben?"

"Who is Ben?" he asked.

"Ben. The old man with me; does he think I murdered the captain?"

"No. I am quite sure he knows nothing. He thinks it strange you left suddenly, but he never said anything to anyone else. The crowd at asked for you, but he said you must have gone back to the bunkhouse. He left soon after. They did not care anyway. All they wanted was for Sticks to wake up to finish the story. They wanted to find out who killed the captain."

"Did Sticks tell?"

"Sticks was out cold, so they laid him on the back porch, hoping the cool night air would revive him. They went back inside to drink until he recovered."

"Then what?"

"Sticks never woke up. The poor old fellow died in his sleep – probably from all the liquor he drank."

"He did not name me as the killer?"

"He never will," he promised.

I felt a surge of relief. It was as if a huge boulder rolled from my shoulders. I was safe at last. I would not be hunted down as a fugitive after all. No one looked for me. I could not believe my luck. I no longer needed to clear my name.

"How did you find me here?" I wondered.

"I followed you," he answered. "I saw you leave the ferry with the cowboy, so I followed and waited."

"I didn't see you."

"I am not seen if I don't want to be seen, Maurice. I have a talent; you know well enough by now."

I realized it was true. I knew no one else who could keep out of sight better than Mawken. He crept back to my house after the pirates killed my parents. Didn't he break into Haji's compound right in front of a guard?

"What are you going to do?" he asked me.

"I intend to go to the next town. A wagon train may need a cook. Other than that, I have no plans. I believe I'll stay on land awhile and see what comes. I have no great desire to return to the sea."

"I'll join you," he offered.

"Do as you please, but I do not think it is a good idea. I am not even sure I can get a job for myself, much less get one for you. Besides, what if someone else survived the storm; someone from the *Glendora*? I think we will be safer if we split up and go separate ways.

He thought for a long while before he agreed, "I suppose you are right. I will just walk along with you to the village – in case you do not get the job. You may need me then."

I shrugged my shoulders, "Suit yourself." Secretly, I wanted him to come, but I did not want him to know. It would be hard to see him leave for good. I knew that one day we would part if I were ever going to be on my own.

He jumped from the boulder and landed solidly on the road. I watched as he placed the knife in his belt, and my mouth dropped open. The sun glinted from a carved mermaid handle.

Dutch was a huge man with big shoulders and a wide chest. Upright, he appeared to be over six feet tall. His voice was gruff and grainy. A pistol swung from his belt for easy reach. He was clearly not a man one wanted to anger. Before I could say a word, he barked, "Don't hire niggers!" He barely looked at me as he turned to walk away.

I heard of "niggers" on the ship. Some of the sailors called the Africans that, but I did not think of myself as one. The British Army often used the word to indicate Indian peasants, but I had never been to India. A little confused, but I blurted out, "Whistle Britches sent me. He said you needed a cook."

Dutch stopped walking away, but he did not turn around to face me. "Donny?" he asked.

"Yes, sir. He said you might need a cook."

Dutch turned sideways so he could see me better, "You can cook?"

"Yes, sir."

"What I meant to say was, I don't hire niggers for muleskinners." Dutch turned all the way around, tilted his head to one side, and scrutinized me from head to toe. "How do you know Whistle Britches?"

"We came across together on the ferry, sir – from Galveston."

Dutch stood quietly considering things in his mind for a moment. "You don't sound like no nigger. Where you from, boy?"

"Kadan Kyun, sir."

Dutch shook his head, and then put his hands on his hips. He stood with his legs wide apart; he was balanced and ready for

165

anything. It was hard to tell if he was going to draw his gun, knock me down, or just stare at me with a stern look on his face. "Where in the hell is … Kada … Kadu … that?" he asked.

"Malay, sir. In the southeast of Asia."

"Whatever!" Dutch grunted. "What do ya' cook? You don't cook that Chinese shit, do ya? You can cook American?"

I remembered what Ben fixed me for breakfast the day before. "Yes, sir. Eggs, bacon, biscuits, coffee – and beans."

He pointed across the camp, ringed by twenty wagons. "Well, I already said no," he said doubtfully. I was sure he rarely changed his mind after he spoke, but he was trying to make an exception.

"See that last wagon over yonder? That's the chuck wagon. You can drive a team, can't you? Dollar a day, and you get paid when we get to Austin. See that ugly, short, bowlegged sumbitch with the black hat? That's the wagon boss; name's Jake. Ever' thing you want to say to me goes through him! Got it?"

"Yes, sir."

Dutch turned and walked away without looking at me again. He did not say the words, but I decided he hired me, and if I had any questions I should probably ask Jake. I looked around the crowded camp. Men were working hard, loading wagons from a large stockpile of crated goods piled at one end of the camp near the road. As soon as one wagon was loaded and tied down, they would drive it aside while another wagon pulled into position. The air was full of cursing and yelling as the drivers tried to get their wagons into position. Whips cracked over the heads of the poor confused animals hitched to the long, wooden wagons. I noticed the strange looking horses – I had never seen the like those before. Later, I learned they were mules.

I moved toward the area of camp where I last saw Jake, but it was not easy. I kept changing course because he was constantly moving and screaming at the men on the wagons. Even though I caught up with Jake, I struggled to keep up with him as he moved up and down the wagon line. Some of the freight wagons were so large the rear wheels stood as high as my head. I saw the front wheels were smaller, so I thought the bed would be at a slant, but it was as even as any wagon. I noticed the front axle was lower than the rear, making the bed level. The high wooden sides were open at the top. Freight was loaded through a rear gate, which they called a tailgate. Other wagons, including the one Dutch pointed out as the "chuck wagon", were smaller. The axles on these wagons were on the same level and had smaller wheels. Jake moved around from wagon to wagon, shouting orders with me right on his heels.

"What do ya' want?" Jake whirled around on me suddenly. "Didn't Dutch tell you we don't hire no niggers?" he yelled.

"Mr. Dutch already hired me, Mr. Jake," I mumbled.

He stopped in his tracks. "The hell you say? You know how to skin a mule?"

"No, sir! I have never skinned one; but if someone showed me, I would try it. I'm your new cook!"

He laughed so hard he lost his plug of tobacco. The black wad shot out of his mouth and bounced off my chest. He bent over and put his hands on his knees as he laughed.

"It means to drive a mule team, boy. You better not be skinnin' our mules for supper! And what the Sam Hill you doin' follerin' me around for? Get the hell over thar and get ta cookin'! You'll find Grady over thar to help ya. Tell 'em what ya' want, and he'll do it for ya. He won't like it much, but he'll do it! He'll be glad he don't have ta cook no more – and so will we!"

"Yes, sir!" By the time I reached the chuck wagon, Grady was no longer by the fire. I walked around back and peered inside the wagon. I saw a sleeping pallet on the floor crammed in between boxes, barrels, and sacks all piled around. A large flat wooden panel that folded down to form a table was affixed to one side of the wagon folded down revealing a small box with shelves and square holes filled with utensils and jars of spices. I climbed up into the seat in front as a red-faced youth came out of the woods, wiping his hands on his shirt. He wore baggy pants and suspenders like most of the men in the camp.

"Hey, you! Get down off that thar! Who in hell do you thank you are?" He yelled.

"I'm the cook!" I shouted back.

"Tha hell you say!" he responded. "Dutch don't hire no niggers!"

I wondered if these people had any other topic of conversation.

"Well, he hired me. I'm not African, I'm from Malay."

He looked me up and down, as a toothy smile grew across his face. "Well, I'll be John Brown! You sure don't sound like no nigger at all, that's for sure. More like a Englishman. You say he hired you as cook?"

"Yes. I am Maurice."

"Thank, God!" He laughed. "I was startin' to thank I was gonna have ta' cook for this gang all the way to Austin. I sure am glad to see you." He reached up to shake my hand.

"Are you Grady?" I said as I pumped his hand.

"That's me!" He pointed to himself. "I'm your fetcher and your runner. Whatever you need, you tell me, and I make it happen. That's my job, and I sure like it a heap better than bein' a damn cook!"

"What is so bad about being the cook?"

"Oh, nothin' much, I guess. Long as ya' don't mind ever'one in the camp hatin' you, and afraid to say anythang for fear you'll put saltpeter in tha coffee, and gripin' about how bad the chow tastes! Then there's havin' to get up earlier'n anyone else, and going to bed later; havin' to pack up and leave ahead of tha train so ya' can have the fires started and the meal ready by the time we get to tha next camp; talkin' to yourself all day with no one to hear; havin' to stay up late at night cleanin' while ever'one else is sleepin'! It ain't much if ya' don't mind all that!"

"You get used to it." It didn't sound much different to me than cooking on a ship.

"Well, you better get crackin' then. I got the fire built over thar and the pots out. Beans are 'bout done. I was comin' back over here to get a side of beef to put on the coals. Now, you can do that; and I can go back to bein' a driver!"

He showed me where the stored the beef, I pulled a heavy side from the chuck box, and carried it to the fire pit. As I laid it on an iron grate, Grady went over the daily routine. "We leave out tomorra. You gotta get up and fix breakfast before sun-up. I'll get you up. I'll have the fire ready for you like I will ever' mornin'. The way we do it is while you cook, I hitch up your team. As soon as breakfast is finished, you grab somethin' to eat on the way and head out down the road to the next camp. I gather up the pots and truck and come along with the rest of the train. Camps up ahead are marked along the road; you can see alongside where we been stoppin'. There is a map of tha trail in your seat box. You drive 'till you get there, stop and make a

169

fire in the fire pit. It'll look like this one here, except the grate is in the wagon. Use whatever wood you find there for the fire. I'll fill the wood stack back up before we leave next mornin'. By the time we get thar coffee should be made and the dinner almost done. You'll finish cookin' while I take care of your team. If you get thar early, you can break out the dutch oven and fix somethin' sweet. These old boys don't like to wait, so don't be late! They'll bitch about ever'thang, so don't worry none about what any of 'em says. After everyone's fed, you and I will clean up and lay stuff out for breakfast next mornin'. You sleep on a pallet in the wagon here. Then next day, you get up 'fore daylight and do tha same thang ever' day, rain or shine!"

"What about you?"

"Oh, I drive the maintenance wagon back thar. I'm the last wagon in the train. It has all the tools and stuff we might need on the trail, including extra wheels and hubs and stuff like that. I sleep in thar. You'll be mostly on your own, 'cept at night when in camp. What you need, you tell me and I'll tell Jake, who'll pass it on to Dutch. Stores is all laid in for tha trip – you shouldn't need nothing else 'till we get thar. Cook what ya' have and don't waste none. Thar ain't much to spare, so go easy – especially on the molasses and sugar."

After the first meal, and we cleaned and packed the equipment, I arranged the disorderly wagon. After I was finished, everything was in its place. Unfortunately, I had worked into the morning hours and it was not long before Grady called me to get up and cook. I cooked breakfast in the dark dawn while he hooked up my team. After a few days, I settled in to the routine; and just as Grady promised, the daily schedule never varied. The only thing that changed was the weather.

It took me half a day to get the hang of driving the mules, so I was a little late finding the next campsite. Grady fussed at me for not being ready and told me I would have to keep a better pace. I did

170

not get many complaints on the cooking, but after the second day, Grady asked me if I knew how to make skillet bread. I did not, so he showed me how and told me the muleskinners liked to have it every day or so. By the end of the first week, I was making beans Mexican style with little hot peppers in it. The Mexican drivers taught me how to make tortillas on a flat iron. Grady said I was the best cook yet, and he hoped I would stay with the train for a few more trips.

Mawken showed up on the third night. After the entire camp was asleep, I saw him peering at me over the tailgate. What Grady called "a little cold snap" blew in, and the temperature dropped overnight. Mawken climbed in to sleep next to me. By the time Grady called, he was gone. Where he went during the day, or how he kept up with the train, was a mystery I never did figure out. After that night, after the wagons and mules were bedded down, he would appear out of the darkness and climb into my wagon.

One night, before the end of September, something happened that changed all of that forever. I was tired from the long day, and I was sleeping soundly when I heard him softly calling my name. "Maurice," he said in a low voice. We normally slept back to back, but I realized he faced me. I could feel his hot breath on my neck. I shivered and pretended to be asleep, hoping he would turn over and leave me alone.

"Maurice, I know you are awake. Listen, I have something to tell you."

I yawned and stretched, and I felt him move against me. It was uncomfortable and I reached behind me to push him away. He would not move.

"What do you want? Be quiet and go to sleep. I have to get up soon and start breakfast. I need some sleep."

"Maurice. I have something to tell you."

171

"What?" I said irritably.

"I'll move closer so no one can overhear," he whispered.

"You are smothering me now! Just say what you have to say and leave me alone." I could feel the heat of him under the covers. I wanted to move away but he held me by the shoulder as he whispered in my ear.

"Maurice, I have been with you forever it seems. Don't you remember when we were young boys in our forest together? You taught me so many things. I knew nothing. I had no one but you. You taught me everything. Maurice, if you sent me away I would have nothing – no one. You are my only family now."

"You are my only family now, too. Everyone is dead. The old life is gone, and we can never get it back. All we have is each other. Now go to sleep."

"Maurice…"

I was a little irritated. "What?" I whispered.

"Maurice, you know that you mean more to me than anything."

I felt his hand move to my hip. I was instantly awake. I felt my body tighten. "You know I would do anything for you – anything at all."

Chills ran up and down my spine. I felt like a horse when it flinched its muscles. I did not know what to say or what was happening. I was repulsed and sickened. The more he talked the more he sounded soft and feminine. Slowly his hand moved down my hip toward my thigh. I was mortified.

"Maurice. I love you. If you will just let me, I will make you very happy. I know how. I adore you. I worship you, Maurice. You are everything to me. I will never leave you."

I felt the nausea rise in my throat as he groped me in the darkness beneath the blanket. I felt behind me and found he was naked beneath the blanket. I pushed him away from me and kicked out with my feet. He went backwards over the wagon gate onto the ground. I groped around and found his clothes in the dark and threw them at him.

"Get out!" I hissed. "Don't come back! You are disgusting! That is disgusting!"

He was crying and trying to get me to let him back in the wagon, but I refused. "No! Get away from me or I'll call some men to drive you away!"

He went off, sobbing into the forest, carrying his clothes in a bundle under his arm. I was sickened to the point of nausea. I wished never to see Mawken again. He turned my stomach. Was that what he wanted from me all this time? I did not care where he went or what became of him. I never wanted to see him again. I was so upset I got no sleep that night.

We moved on day-by-day through the low, swampy Texas marsh flats. Each day I would rise and cook breakfast and then move on to the next stop on the road to Austin. They were clearly marked, so I had no problem finding them. I thought we were making good progress, and I saw the distance to Austin on the map each day. It seemed to me we would make it before the end of September as planned. I knew nothing of Texas weather.

Although it seemed like it was still summer, changes were in the wind. Nighttime seemed to come a little earlier with each passing day. You could not tell at first; but by the time we were across the Brazos River, the days seemed to grow shorter. I knew something of sailing, and I realized these changes were seasonal and not navigational. Our progress was only a dot on the map compared to how far a ship could travel each day.

I also saw some changes in the leaves of some trees; not the pines though – they remained as green and unchanging as ever. Around the marshes, f water birds flocked daily and grouped into long formations with two trailing legs as they flew off to the south each morning. Sometimes the sounds of them filled the morning again amid the booms of our hunters shooting at them as they flew. The fresh fowl provided a welcomed variety to our daily meals. The sunny days seemed to be fewer and farther between. We would have one sunny, hot, summer day followed by two or three overcast, cooler days.

Grady said we were pushing hard to cross the Brazos before the rains came. After crossed the Brazos River, the focus shifted to the Colorado River to our west. The main question seemed to be whether we should stay on the east bank of the Colorado where the roads were better, or should we cross over to the west bank? The argument went on for days. Grady would keep me up on the progress each day because I would need to know which trail to take to lead to our next stopover. The main consideration was the weather. On the west bank of the Colorado, the roads were rocky with more hills to climb, causing much slower progress than the east side where it was flatter with sandy, loamy road surfaces. If it rained, the road we were on would become muddy and difficult to run; and we would be better off across the river on the hard surfaces. Dutch seemed to be making the decision on crossing the Colorado after talking with Jake each night. It was Dutch's decision to make, but he and Jake had made many runs down this road in the past. While the remainder of the drivers discussed it among themselves around the fire each night, they made sure that Jake and Dutch did not get wind of the talking. No one wanted to cross Dutch.

At first, the plan was to stay on the east bank of the Colorado. Each day, we plodded through the sandy, shady trail leaving deep wagon ruts behind. The one thing you learn about Texas weather is how fast it can change. One morning, we woke earlier than usual to make ready for the trail – a storm was coming. Our instructions that day were for a quick breakfast and a fast break toward the Colorado, some twenty miles away. Dutch wanted to cross.

Overnight, the weather changed suddenly; as if someone turned the page of a book. It was not raining heavily yet, but the raindrops were larger than any I ever saw, and they had a cold, icy feeling. Fingers of frigid air poked at your bones like cold icy steel. The air was much cooler, and the wind blew from the north. Leaves were falling from the trees in great circular swirls of red and yellow. It was hard to tell if the leaves fell because of the season or from the wind velocity. Leaves of all types were fluttering through the air.

We did not bother with a breakfast fire. I laid out some dried beef and biscuits we always carried; as soon as Grady had my team rigged, I moved off to a new location they marked on my map. I stopped at the edge of the Colorado and waited to cross with the remainder of the train. All morning I kept checking my trail map to make sure I was at the right crossing place. The weather grew worse. Huge billowing ominous clouds were ahead, while directly above the gray overcast sky hid the sun.

By mid-morning, a full-blown thunderstorm was underway. Menacing dark clouds covered the sky in a dark blanket. If we had been at sea, we would have lowered the main sheets and hoisted the storm sails. As it was, the canvas cover of my wagon caught the wind so neatly I was afraid it would tip us over. The wagon seat had no overhang, so I sat in the cold rain all day. I would have been soaked through except I found a rubber slicker in the back of the wagon and was able to stay relatively dry, but I had no protection from the gripping wind. The farther I drove, the harder the rain fell until at last, I could barely see the trail ahead. I kept checking the map. Once, the wind tore the map from my freezing fingers; and I stopped the wagon to go running off after it in the brush. Luckily, the map hung up on a low bush not far away; and I was able to retrieve it. It was wet but still readable. I tucked it in an inside pocket under the slicker and kept moving toward the crossing. I knew the train was not more than an hour behind me, and I did not want them to catch up. I was supposed to make coffee at the crossing, but I had no instructions to cook a meal. As soon as the train reached the crossing, we would ford the river before it was too late. I wondered what we would be too late to do. I thought they were talking about the time of day.

I arrived at the marked crossing a little before noon and put the coffee pot on the fire. Few bridges crossed the rivers in this part of the country. I could see old wagon tracks leading into the river, and I could see them coming out of the river on the other side. What I saw in between made me wonder how a wagon could possibly get through that wild torrent of water. Logs and trees were floating downstream amid the brown churning waves of water floated quickly past the crossing. I stuck a tree limb in the mud at the water's edge, and a half hour late the limb was half covered. The water level rose as I watched. I squatted beneath my wagon and watching the rushing river in the driving rain. It was clear to me we would not be crossing our wagons here.

It was not long before the train pulled into the camp. I poured Dutch and Jake a hot cup and crawled under the wagon to sit with Grady out of the rain. Dutch and Jake stood looking at the river and cursing their luck. We were "too damned late." I asked Grady what would happen now. He quietly said, "We'll have to stay on this side 'till we get to Austin. It'll take another week or ten days, I reckon." The two men came back to the chuck wagon and asked for the map. I gave it to them, and they hurried off to their covered wagon to talk. I suppose they were plotting a new course.

After an hour, the two men came out of the wagon. "What the hell did you do to this map?" Jake asked as he flung it back at me.

"It got away from me, but I saved it," I offered.

"Hell! It's all damp and hard to read now. Ya' gotta be more careful! You lose that map, and you get lost, and then we lose another couple a' days trying to find you!"

"Grady!" Jake barked so loud I jumped, "Get everyone together for a meeting at the boss wagon. Now!" Every time he tilted his head, great streams of water ran from the front of his hat. The cold drops hitting the brim of his hat sounded like rain falling on my wagon's canvas cover. This rain was not letting up.

Grady went down the line passing the message to the drivers, while Jake turned his attention back to me. "You get on your wagon and head for the next layover. We've marked it on the map. We ain't crossin'; we're stayin' on this side. It's gonna be longer days now, and you won't reach the camps before dark. You have to watch the road. Don't get that wagon stuck, boy! You get hung up in the mud and there'll be hell to pay. We ain't got no time to be pullin' you out ever' few miles. If you can't handle it, say so now! We'll put Grady up here and you on his wagon."

"I can handle it, sir."

"Alright then. Get on down the road. Keep that map dry! You need to look at it get back in the wagon under cover. You lose that map and we're all in a heap a' mess!"

I drove off down the road toward the next stop as the weather grew steadily wetter and colder. By nightfall, I felt like I would freeze. The temperature stayed above freezing, but I was cold, wet, and tired. I wanted to stop, but I did not want to anger Dutch or Jake. I was so cold I shivered. I knew how Jake dealt with some of the men, and I did not want to take the chance. I was so glad to arrive at the camp and get the fire going. The warm flames felt so good licking around my legs. I rummaged around in the back of the wagon and found a heavy coat. I gratefully wrapped it around my freezing body. I did not have any instructions for the meal; but I realized the men were probably as cold, wet, and tired as I was, so I boiled up some water and threw some lard and vegetables in the pot. By the time the teams arrived, a boiling hot cauldron of soup was ready to eat.

Late that night I was in bed, a familiar visitor peeked over the wagon gate, begging to come in. I sighed. I had calmed down some since I kicked Mawken out, but I made sure he knew the rules before I let him back in the wagon. There was to be no touching, except accidentally as we lay together under the covers. He was to be fully dressed at all times. We would not mention what happened before. What he did on his own time was to be his business, and I did not want to hear about it – ever! If that was what he wanted, he was free to go about it; I wanted nothing to do with it. He promised never to touch me again. Furthermore, once we reached Austin, we would go our separate ways. Mawken readily agreed with all my demands – except for the last one. He begged to stay wherever I was, just in case I needed him. I told Mawken I planned to start a new life and settle down. I might even take a wife and start a family. I knew that could not happen with him around, and I told him so. He seemed hurt and dejected. But, it was either my way or freeze to death, so he finally agreed and climbed into the wagon and under the covers. He mainly stayed in the wagon out of sight until we reached the town limits of Austin. I remember one night in particular. On the third night after Mawken's return, I finally worked up the courage to ask a question I had long wanted to ask. "How did my father die?"

He pretended to be asleep, and yawned and stretched his body, "What?" Mawken asked.

"My father. How did he die?"

"You remember – the pirates. They came ashore and killed my parents, then raided your compound and murdered yours too. Have you forgotten?"

"No, I did not forget. I mean, how – exactly – was my father killed? Was he shot?"

"No. He was struck in the back of the head with an ax from your woodpile."

I froze. My mind immediately flashed a scene of the captain's murder! In my mind, I went whirling back in time. My father never left the ax in the woodpile. He was strict in making sure I kept it properly hung on the barn wall. Father disciplined me many times for not putting the ax away properly. I thought back over the months of our travels. I thought of Sofi and how her head was severed. I thought of the sailor outside Haji's wall, lodged in the tree, his pipe still smoking, and his brains leaking from a huge gash in the back of his head.

For the first time, I felt afraid of Mawken. I managed to whisper, "Thanks," before I pretended to go off to sleep.

It rained all the way to Austin.

We finally reached the outskirts of Austin in mid-October. It was mid-afternoon, and I was certain the wagon train would arrive early. The road dried up, and the rain stopped falling. The last two weeks were muddy and long, and I was happy I did not get my chuck wagon stuck a single time. I could see why the preferred route was west of the river because the Colorado ran east in this section, requiring a trip around Bastrop instead of a direct route to Austin. The Bastrop ferry washed away in the storm, forcing us to take an even longer route around the huge loops of the Colorado. It took most of the day. I reached the designated point on the outskirts of Austin and made camp to wait for the remainder of the train to arrive. Most of the time, over the last leg of the trip, the wagons arrived very late due to the work involved in getting heavy freight through the mud and mire. Texas caliche is an odd substance. It is a mixture of clay, sand, and loam. When dry, it is very hard and the surface can easily support the heaviest wagons hardly leaving a track. When damp, caliche becomes slick and wagon wheels sink in deeper leaving ruts. It is hard to keep the wagons on the road in such conditions as they often slide off to the side especially hills or grades. But when wet, caliche becomes like glue, holding wheels tightly in the muck like a trap. Everyone has to stop to help push the wagon bodily out of the bog. It is dirty, bone aching, heavy work.

Because of the terrible weather, Mawken stayed hidden in the back of the wagon most of the trip. It was time to say goodbye – I told myself to stay strong and not relent. I packed a little food for him to take on his way. He did not take the parting well. He reluctantly walked toward the woods turning to look back at me every so often – I suppose in case I motioned him back. I did not change my mind. I was determined to be done with Mawken, and I wished him well, but it was time for me to make a new life for myself. Besides, I no longer felt safe around him. I knew what he was capable of; and I feared his anger, hostility, rage – or whatever it was that enabled him to kill – might turn toward me one day. Every night I would go to sleep not knowing if I would wake up the next morning. Nothing prevented

Mawken from killing me in my sleep. I was unwilling to subject myself to his strange moods any longer. It was better he left for good.

I would miss him, of course. He was a confidante and a protector. I admired Mawken's confidence and his ability to take decisive action to solve problems. How he solved problems bothered me. I did not feel it was ever proper to take a life unless your own was in danger. Much later, I would learn to feel differently.

As I watched him disappear into the woods, I wished him well in his life. I hoped one day when we were old, we might meet again and share our life stories with each other. We could point to our grandchildren and watch them play. I hoped he would find peace and prosperity and a finally find a happy life he deserved. I hoped he would be able to put anger and violence behind him at last and lead a settled life. I fully intended to try to do the same.

The rest of the wagons arrived an hour behind me to great joy and jubilation among the drivers. Dutch ordered no breakfast that morning, but no one seemed to mind. They were more interested in beer. Great kegs of it were unloaded from one of the wagons, and all the drivers anticipated a huge beer party. Dutch and Jake were saddling fresh horses to ride off to some nearby ranch to spend the night. How nice it would be to sleep in a bed for a change. They left instructions that no matter how late the party lasted everyone was to be ready to roll at daylight.

Before Jake left, he told me to prepare one final breakfast in the morning and which would mark the end my duties this trip. "I can offer you a job for the trip back if ya want it," he said rolling a smoke. "We'll be loaded with cotton headin' for the docks at Galveston – we'll need a cook for the train. The job's yours if you want it." The flame lit his face beneath the wide-brimmed hat. Jake said it might be the last land freight job for a long time because the new railroad would be taking most freight to Houston by rail. "We can't compete," he explained. "The train is faster and cheaper than a wagon train."

I did not think returning to Houston or Galveston was in my best interest. I knew Sticks died before he could turn me in, but I did not know how much Ben figured out from my sudden departure. I thought it best to avoid that part of the country altogether for now. I thanked Jake for the offer as I explained I wanted to try to stay in one place for a while. Either I was on the sea or traveling the roads the past year, all I wanted now was to find a rocking chair and rest for a while. Jake laughed and said he knew how I felt. He thanked me for giving him an answer up front and not holding out until it was too late to find someone else. Jake added I was a welcome addition to their crew; and if I changed my mind later, I could always find a job with any crew he ran. Then he got on his horse and rode away with Dutch.

After breakfast the next morning, I stayed behind for a change to clean and pack away all of the equipment. Cranky drivers nosed their teams out of camp toward the last stop. Grady went ahead with the rest of the team, and I followed after I finished packing the gear one final time.

As I rolled into the wagon yard where bleary-eyed drovers unloaded the wagons, Grady came over to say goodbye. "We're sure gonna miss you, Hoss – wish you'd change your mind and go back with us."

After I gathered my gear and made my final farewells, I walked off in the direction of town. I stopped for a short rest a mile away and looked at my pay. It was more money than I ever saw. I stuffed all of it deep in my pocket and got back on the highway. Austin was only five miles further. It was October 1884; and although it was late in the fall, the weather turned favorable. The rains passed, and the sun came out; it was like spring again. Texas weather was so strange. Because we were on the right side of the river, I would not have to cross the river to get to town. However, the river looped and

182

twisted like a serpent, and many creeks with steep banks joined the riverbed, creating barriers that also had to be crossed. It may have been five miles as the bird flies, but it was ten by the time I followed the road into town.

Austin was a great surprise. This was no Cowtown, nor was it like the small farming communities and villages we passed coming north; Austin was a thriving and busy city. Two railroads ran through Austin, one went north and the other toward Houston. The city contained multiple story buildings, hotels, and wide clean streets. Austin was the capital of Texas, and the state was building a new capitol building. A new university rose on the hill, and even a college for people of color was in town. It was a beautiful town with a river running through it. Many people from many different places in the world lived in Austin. I saw some of the tallest buildings I ever saw.

A local man suggested I might find lodging on the southern end of town, along Pecan Street, near the rail station – where people like me stayed. I thought he meant Malays, but I soon discovered he meant black people.

Guy Town, as that part of Austin was called, was a rough area filled with saloons, gambling halls, and prostitutes. I secured a room with a balcony at the Pearl House and squandered the afternoon away in a rocking chair like I dreaming. I calculated I would have enough money to last me through the winter; then I would see what spring would bring.

Over the next few weeks, I indulged in exploring the city and taking in the sights and amusements. There were many amusements for all. The idle life was pleasurable; but after an accounting one afternoon, I knew at the rate my money was spent I would not have enough to last the entire winter unless I became much more frugal. Once the merchants and saloonkeepers discovered I was not African, they allowed entry into most of the establishments along the Congress Avenue. Now, with my money running low, I resolved to stay out of the saloons along the avenue. Alcohol was not my main problem. In those saloons were temptations beyond my ability to resist, especially when drinking. Not familiar with American customs, I was a prime target for every flimflam deal invented. Word spread fast, and I was heartily welcomed in most of the darkened taverns. I learned a lot in those first weeks, but the cost was heavy.

Resolving not to listen to any more "good deals", I made one last stop at my favorite spot for one last beer. Beer was not my main objective, as I hoped to collect some loans I was owed. I did not see any of my debtors, so I finished my beer and stepped out onto the grand avenue. It was alive with activity. Trollies went up and down the street; horses, carts, and all types of conveyances went in all directions to a great cacophony of noise. I breathed it all in deeply; I loved my new city life.

After a streetcar passed, I crossed over to the east side at 9th Street in front of the opera house. As I turned down Pecan Street, I heard the loud clapping of horse hooves on the brick street and a loud call echoed from the stone buildings.

"Maw-reece!"

It was great to see Donny again. Fall roundup was over and he decided to come to "town." Before they went home to mama, most cowboys went to town after their work was over to let off some steam. Donny was already in a party mood, having already searched for me through several main saloons. I was so happy to see him. Donny climbed down from Pete's back and gave me a bear hug right in the middle of the street. He walked with me as I led him to the Pearl House, his spurs jingling on the hard ground with every step. He got a room right across the hall from mine. After, we took Pete down to the livery stable, which was only a couple of blocks from our hotel. We set Pete up in a nice, clean stable. I realized Donny would be in town for a while when he paid the stableman for a week. Donny said he was beginning to get dry, and he wanted more to drink. He might be a little fellow, but his capacity for alcohol was unmatched by anyone I knew.

For the next two days, we drank every waking moment. Donny seemed willing to spend every cent of his money; and most of the time, he paid the bar bill. Many times, I would have to go behind his back and pay the barkeeper before Donny could. It seemed everyone on the street knew Whistle Britches and loved listening to his wild tales – including me! I was convinced everything he said was the solid truth.

He asked me about my trip on the wagon train one evening. "Did Uncle Dutch treat you well?" He grinned his lopsided smile.

I got my first clue why Dutch agreed to take me on without question after I mentioned Whistle Britches. Neither Donny nor Dutch or anyone else for that matter ever revealed the family link. It was no big secret; it just never came up in the conversation. I found their ways strange, but I learned the ways of these cowboys, who seemed to live a different life than the rest of us. They had their own colorful language, and I was enchanted by their stories. Donny knew the best places in town, and most of them were not on the avenue. Some of the side streets had much better accommodations and attractions. Donny helped me avoid some to the traps and pitfalls, and served as my guardian when hucksters tried to draw me in.

Cowboys love to pick on each other. Sometimes the picking and prodding turned personal and ended in a physical fight. Donny was small like me, but he knew how to handle himself in a difficulty. The morning after the first brawl, we went to a nearby gymnasium and Donny taught me how to defend myself with my fists. "If you're gonna be my pard, ya gotta have my back," he laughed.

He taught me other things as well. "If a deal sounds too good to be true, you can bet your bottom dollar it is! Don't do it!" All the time I was with Donny those few days, everyone seemed to

185

consider me "hands off." No one challenged me a single time for being too dark to enter. No one offered me any of the "sure thang" deals that previously had taken so much of my money. Donny was quick to label me as Malay to everyone around; I suppose to avoid misidentification and misunderstandings. The great American Civil War was over, but Negro people were still undesirable in some sections of town. In other parts of town, like Guy Town, it seemed the streets and neighborhoods were set aside just for them. We often drank in those neighborhoods too.

For four days, Donny and I were inseparable. We went everywhere and did everything together. I was so happy to have a friend in my life. It was the best four days I could remember since my youth. I knew Donny would not be able to stay after his week in town; but I enjoyed Donny's visit so much, I did not think about money. I just thought about having a great time with my best friend. Every night, we would stagger home dead drunk and sleep until ten when we would rise, eat a hearty breakfast, and do it all over again. I thought how wonderful and free life was.

Donny was used to drinking and I was not. So, I usually became drunk a lot quicker than he did, but Donny watched over me and made sure I did not come to any bad end. A couple of nights, I do not remember even going to bed. Each morning, I would awaken and realize I was in my own warm, safe bed – usually fully dressed, boots and all. No matter how late we stayed out Donny was usually rattling my door by ten, fully sober, fully dressed, and ready to go. He would hand me a cup of coffee to ease my aching head and off we would go again. I would have to scramble to catch up. Before I realized it, we would be off on some grand adventure; which usually included shooting, fishing, or riding somewhere.

Donny was determined to make a cowboy out of me. He taught me to shoot and even helped me pick out a gun for myself. It was a shiny blue six-shooter. We ordered a new leather holster for me complete with knife sheath. The leather was stiff and new, and I found it uncomfortable to wear. I usually just put the pistol in my back pocket. I did not have a knife to put into the sheath, and the marlinspike was too long to fit. Oh, how I wished I had the one with the carved mermaid handle. I would have worn the holster every day just to impress Donny. After a full day of cowboy school, we usually ended up at a tavern and another glorious evening of drinking, laughing, and dancing with the bar girls.

On the morning of the fifth day, everything changed. I woke up in my room later than usual. I ached from a large bump on the back of my head. It was quiet in the room, and I was surprised Donny had not appeared with coffee to wake me up. I feared something was wrong, so I crossed the hall, but he was not in his room. Then, I realized it was nearly noon, and I could not remember anything about the night before. I had no idea how I got a bump on my head. Things were not right. It was odd for Donny to go off without me. Maybe I did not hear his call and left without me. All of Donny's belongings were missing. I found no note to indicate why he left town so unexpectedly. I was confused. Donny still had a couple of days before he was supposed to leave for home.

I decided to go to the livery to check to see if Pete was still in the stable. Pete was gone, and his stall was clean. A new horse had taken up residence. I called for the stable master who came out of a stall he was cleaning.

"What can I do you for? The man in the apron asked.

"I – I'm looking for my friend," I stuttered.

"Who might that be, boy?" I noticed since Donny was not with me, he was calling me boy again.

"Donny. His horse was in this stall yesterday," I pointed.

"Oh! Whistle Britches. Yeah … Donny. He's gone."

"Gone?" I repeated.

"Yeah! Gone. He come bustin' in here way 'fore dawn –
woke me up from a dead sleep! Said he had to get out of town. Tore
out of here on Pete like the devil was chasing him and his hair was on
fire! He was white as a sheet – scared to death! I ain't never seen
Whistle Britches so spooked! Told me some sumbitch tried to kill
him!"

Mawken! It had to be him! I just knew it! For some reason it just came to my mind he was responsible. Why would he try to kill Donny? As far as I knew, he never met Donny; and I certainly never mentioned him to Donny in any way. I had not seen Mawken since we said our goodbyes and he walked off into the forest. Where he went until now, I did not know. He was supposed to be gone weeks before Donny even arrived. Why was he back; what did he want? I could not understand, but I knew only one thing – he was back. I do not know why, but I was convinced Mawken was the "sumbitch" who tried to kill Donny.

I could not contain my outrage and resentment. I felt betrayed, angry, disappointed, and afraid all at the same time. Once more, he showed up and interfered in my life. I realized my thoughts were only suspicions. At the moment though, I believed it was true and I hated Mawken. Where was he? I ran from the stable back to the Pearl House. Even the late November sky looked different this morning. Gone were the singing birds and the sunny sky.

Now, the sky was dark and gloomy. It seemed to be getting darker every moment. I barely realized the change in the weather. When I left the hotel, only a half-hour before, it was warm and pleasant. Now, the temperature dropped dramatically, but I was so angry and upset I did not have a sense of being cold. I noticed people on the street huddled beneath blankets and overcoats, but I was still running around in shirtsleeves.

The clouds, especially beyond the new capitol building, were turning a purplish blue color and seemed to be advancing on us as they overtook a slate gray sky above. The wind began to blow extremely hard. People all along the street were taking down their sidewalk signs and advertisements. Restaurants were moving tables back inside. Anything loose and not tied down was blowing into, and sometimes down, the street in the harsh cold wind.

The weather was not important to me at the time; I was determined to find Mawken and to get him out of my life finally. It seemed with every step my rage grew, and I became even more convinced he was at the center of all my problems. I am not a violent man, but I believe had I found him at that moment, I would have killed Mawken without waiting for the lying excuse he was sure to give. Never was I so angry and so willing to take a life. I could not believe I was thinking these thoughts. I never harmed a living thing in my life, and here I was ready to commit murder.

I ran up the steps of the Pearl House and saw the wind had blown the swinging sign from the porch through the dining room window. Employees were busy cleaning up the mess. Hector, the Mexican porter, patched the window as I nearly ran over him on the porch.

"What is wrong, Maurice? The old Devil chasin' you?" he laughed.

It occurred to me it was the second time someone had mentioned the devil this morning. Without answering Hector, I ran up the stairs, burst into my room, and looked around, half expecting to see Mawken lounging in the easy chair by the bed. He was not there. "Where are you?" I shouted at the top of my lungs. No answer. I looked under the bed and behind the wardrobe without finding him. I knew he was hiding somewhere nearby, and I was determined to find Him. I dropped my gun into my pocket and ran into the hallway.

I burst through Donny's door, leaving it standing wide open. Stepping into the room, I called loudly.

"Mawken! I want you! Where are you, damn you?"

There was no answer. I searched Donny's room, under his bed, and behind the furniture. I did not find Mawken. For some reason, not finding him made me even angrier. *"I am not seen if I don't wish to be seen,"* kept running through my mind.

190

"Damn You! Show yourself. I know you are here somewhere!" Mawken neither answered nor appeared. It did not matter. I was convinced he was here somewhere and I would find him. I was so outraged; I was out of my mind. I could not believe I was behaving in such a manner. Somehow, all of the indignation and anger I kept stifled within myself over the past year came rushing out; overcoming me. I was insane with rage. I felt I was losing my mind.

At the time, in my state of mind, it seemed I could force Mawken to respond to me and to show himself. Nothing else would do. It was my will against his, and I was determined to prevail. I fully intended to do him harm if I got the opportunity. I wanted to rid myself of him for the last time – he ruined my life. It was obvious Donny's room was vacant. I walked back into the hall, closing the heavy wooden door behind me. I went down the stairs and saw Hector, the porter, waiting at the bottom. The entire hotel staff was upset, and my yelling and running wild had not helped.

Before I could reach the bottom of the stairs Hector asked, "Maurice! What has got into you? Are you all right, amigo?"

"Hector! Have you seen any strangers around here last night or this morning?"

"Si, Señor Maurice. This is a hotel. We have the strangers every day. What did he look like?"

I was so upset I failed to take care with my answers. "He … He looks like me, Hector. He is the same size and build, maybe a little smaller. But the same skin color as myself, and he talks like I do."

"No, Maurice," Hector slowly shook his head, "there has been no hombre aroun' here that looks like you. Come to think of it, there is no hombre like you in all the town, *señor*."

Still beside myself with anger, I pushed Hector aside and went through the back door into the alley. I searched every place I could imagine, loudly calling, "Where are you hiding? I know you are here! Come out!" In my rage, I flung ash cans across the alley and against walls; kicking them as the contents spilled out and, caught up in the raging wind, blew skyward in great whirling circles. The wind whipped even higher, and I could hear it howling around the corners of the building and under the eaves. The sound of the wind was as if someone laughed at me – Mawken! The same, cruel, hard laugh enraged me. The rage exploded out of me in a way never before. I pulled at my hair, screaming loudly, as I ran in tight little circles in the alley.

After a time, it became clear to me he was not going to show himself. He was not going to answer me. I slumped down with my back against a wall, unsure of what to do next. Why? Why did this have to happen to me? Why would he do this to Donny? Donny was my friend – the only friend I made since I left my home; except for Mawken – and he certainly was no friend. He was a dangerous, sinister, evil killer who would murder anyone in his path – including me. I sank farther down the wall until I was sitting, and put my hands to my face as tears fell. I cried. I realized I had barely shed a tear over all the tragedies I lived though. But now, alone in the alley, I felt the grief overcome me. I cried. I cried for everything that happened to me over the last year. I cried for my mother and father. I cried for Sofi. I even cried for the despicable sea captain. I cried for the loss of what may have been with Ben. I cried huge, wet, cold tears as the winds shrieked and swept down the alley behind the Pearl House. I cried for the loss of my friend, Donny. Why would he attack Donny – my only friend? Then, the thought struck me. Donny was my only true friend. Did Mawken attack Donny because he was too close to me? Was jealousy behind this? In his sick, twisted mind, was he jealous of me? I shivered against the wall and cried some more. I hated Mawken with all of my heart and being. Even so, as I wept, I felt the urge to

192

kill weakening within me. He ruined my life, and I just wanted him away from me forever.

I also cried for me. What was I to do now? What was to become of me? I threw out all the stops during Donny's visit. We had "done the town" every night in celebration of friendship, youth, freedom, and just being alive. I spent far more than I should have, but it did not matter. What was money, except a means to an end? I knew I would need to get a job after Donny left, but in my innocence, it did not seem important to me at the time. I would somehow raise enough to return to the coast and find a berth on the next sailing ship going to sea – it did not matter where. I supposed the time was here. For now, however, all I could manage to do was to sit, out of the wind, and grieve for the loss of my friend.

I heard a soft female voice calling, "Maurice. Maurice, where are you?"

"Here," I whimpered as I wiped tears from my eyes. I could not stop crying.

I blinked my eyes as Mrs. Schmidt, the proprietor of the hotel, knelt before me. "My dear! Whatever is the matter? Here," she offered her apron. "Wipe your face, and tell me what is wrong?"

I had not spoken to a motherly figure in so long. All I could manage to snivel out was, "My mother is dead."

Mrs. Schmidt gathered me into her arms as she caressed my hair. "*Auch du meine güte!* You poor dear. *Es tut mir leid.* I am so sorry." In the warmth of her arms, I realized how cold and lonely I was. She pulled away and spread a warm blanket around my shivering shoulders, "*Mein Gott!* You are cold as an icicle. You will catch your death of cold in this wind." She pulled me to my feet and walked me back toward the door. "*Kommin sie.* Let us go back inside. I have some fresh potato soup to warm you up, you poor dear."

193

The freezing wind still howled, but it no longer laughed, as she led me inside – her arm tight around my shoulders. She sat me at a table in her personal dining room, and ladled a steaming bowl of soup and placed it before me. She broke off a large hunk of bread and handed it to me, along with a spoon. "*Jetzt essen*! Eat now, and get warm. We can talk later. Just now, you need to warm up, *Liebling*. We will talk later about your *mutter* – your ma' ma, I promise."

I sat in a stupor, wondering what came over me. I understood Mrs. Schmidt wanted me to eat, but I was still too distraught. How could I eat? She insisted. As soon as the creamy soup touched my lips, I felt famished. I ate the entire bowl, much to the delight of Mrs. Schmidt. She offered me more, but I was satisfied. The warmth of her rooms made me feel much better, and I found I no longer needed the blanket. She sat across from me at the table after tidying up the kitchen. She looked at me with clear, blue eyes. "What will you do? Must you return to your home?"

I decided to stick with the story of my dead mother, as I would not know how else to explain what was wrong. Besides, it was the something of the truth. "No," I shook my head. "It is too late and too far. She is already gone and buried, and I have no means to go back."

Mrs. Schmidt shook her head in sympathy. She dabbed her eyes with the corner of her apron and turned her head away so I could not see her tears. "What will you do?" she sighed with a catch in her voice.

"I do not know, Mrs. Schmidt. All of my money is gone. I shall have to leave the hotel. I can no longer pay for my room."

"*Nein*!" she asserted. "You will not leave this house. You will stay here for a few days until you are ready. I will not hear of it!"

"But, Mrs. Schmidt …"

"But, Mrs. Schmidt nothing! I am not so heartless as to throw an orphan out on the streets without a place to go! It is freezing out there, and the next week may bring rain and ice. *Nein*! You will stay here! Perhaps you can do something around the hotel to earn your bed and meals. What can you do? What was your last job?"

"I was a cook."

"*Koch*? You know how to cook?" She asked.

"Only simple meals men in the field eat. I am no chef – I have no talent for fancy cooking. Just meat and beans mostly."

Mrs. Schmidt laughed a hearty laugh, as her entire ample body shook. "*Meine Leibste*!" She laughed some more. "You are in Texas! That *is* fancy cooking for these *affen*!"

Mrs. Schmidt said if I would cook the breakfast and the noon meal in the restaurant, I could live at the hotel free of charge, and eat all I wanted. She called it "room and board". I would have to move to the small room off the main kitchen. She would even pay me two dollars a month besides my keep. I learned the current day cook threatened to quit unless Mrs. Schmidt assigned to the evening shift. The current evening cook was such a total disaster, Mrs. Schmidt would be happy to be finished with him.

"Now, you must be ready to start early in the morning – before daylight! Are you sure you can do it?"

"I awaken early – when I am not out in the bars all night," I assured her.

"Now, there will be none of that, *junger mann*! There is no drinking in this house – and no drunks either!"

I agreed. "I no longer have anything to celebrate," I sadly assured her, "except for you, and this chance to make a living."

195

"Very well, then. You start in the morning. Hector!" she called loudly over her shoulder. Hector appeared in the doorway almost immediately. "*Si, señora?*"

"Hector go tell Beulah to move out of the cookhouse into the main building. She will be the new evening cook. Tell Estevan to come and see me right away."

"*Si!*" Hector responded. "But *señora* Schmidt, I was goin' to tell you; but *señor* Estevan, he is gone! He left this place only moments ago. He said he was damn sure not going to pick up all this mess in the *cocina*! He has quit, *señora.*"

"Even better!" Mrs. Schmidt laughed. "Tell Beulah to move as soon as dinner is over. She will need to cook supper for tonight."

"*Al presente, señora*! But, who will cook the breakfast and *la lunche*?"

Mrs. Schmidt pointed directly across the table at me. She told me to go pack my things and move down to the cook's room near the kitchen where I would take up residence. After I packed my few belongings, I went across the hall once more to see if I missed anything in Donny's room. I entered the room as the door slowly closed behind me. I sat on the bed, trying to think. My gaze drifted around the room and there, stuck in the back of the door, was a knife with a handle carved in the shape of a mermaid.

I knew it! It was Mawken! I pulled the knife free from the back of the door and left Donny's room. Far from being elated at being right, I actually felt sad and a little sorry. I hid the knife in my new room and got everything arranged to take over my duties next morning. Lying in bed, I fingered the knife I placed beneath my pillow. I felt safer with the knife beneath my pillow; I felt like it gave me more protection than the marlinspike, in case Mawken came around again.

All through the night, I would reach under my pillow and feel the reassuring, smooth contours of the instrument. The smooth handle complimented the cold sharp steel of the blade. The silky curves and raised features of the mermaid warmed to my touch and seemed to meld into my palm. I would trace the carvings of the hair and breasts with my thumb and rub the scales on the mermaid's torso.

I was no longer angry. In fact, I did not feel any hurt or sense of loss either. I felt nothing at all. The hostility I felt just hours earlier was gone, along with the deep sorrow and disappointment afterward. Now, I felt like an empty shell – as cold as the steel blade laying beneath my pillow. I slid the knife out and rubbed my thumb along the sharp edge of the blade. The steel glinted in the dim light shining through my window, reflecting in a flash in my eyes. I turned the knife slightly and I could see my reflection in the mirror-like blade. My image did not even look like me any longer. My face had become hard and unrecognizable. My eyes were sunken and dark, and my upper lip supported a light growth of hair. It was a pitiful excuse for a mustache – and I felt myself a pitiful excuse for a man.

For a moment, I did not feel I was inside my body – it was as though I were somewhere else – I knew not where. I was just present. Physically, I knew I was still in my room; but somehow, part of me seemed distant and far away. I could not understand why I thought these things, but I did.

197

Everything seemed out of my control. Donny was gone; I lived in fear of my own safety; and, absolutely no one cared for me. Mrs. Schmidt did, I told myself, but she was just a kindly old woman – I had no special place in her heart I thought. She barely knew me. I felt tossed around like the captain's desk on a wildly heaving sea, and the waves of dark water were overwhelming me, with only the mermaids to save me. I actually felt as if I were drowning. Yet, even so, it seemed everything that happened was my fault.

In the dim light of my room, I raised the knife to my face and ran the cool flat of the blade down my neck and across my shoulders. I did not even care if I cut myself accidentally. To prove it to myself, I turned the blade on edge, ran it across my forearm, and sliced through a thin layer of skin. Still, I felt nothing. I only felt empty and devoid of any feeling at all. I sliced deeper into my arm and a trickle of blood ran down my arm before I could feel any pain. I immediately felt better – at least the pain told me I was still alive – at least part of me was alive. I found some control over some part of my life. I felt I could kill myself if I wanted, but I did not want to die – I just did not want to drown beneath the waves of my life. It was hard for me to understand these feelings. I never felt this way before – I just knew how I felt. I took out my father's watch and watched, mesmerized, as drops of my blood dripped on the face and into the hinge of the cover – just as my father's blood must have dripped.

I wrapped a cloth around my cut arm and gradually drifted off to sleep. I dreamt I ran down a long, dark alley. I was not sure what I ran from; but it was important I escape from something – from someone who chased me. I could hear footsteps behind me, and evil laughter. I knew the laugh, but I did not recognize it in my dream. Somehow, I knew if it caught me, I would die. I would die like the captain or Sofi in a violent, brutal way. I was terrified. In my dream I turned several times to see my pursuer but I could see nothing but foggy darkness. The mist twisted and blew in swirling clouds, which obscured everything beyond a curtain of fog. Once, I turned to look back, and I saw my own reflection in a distorted mirror, like those in carnivals that twist your face into an unrecognizable resemblance of a face. It was a horrible image of myself, and I screamed in terror. I screamed so loudly I woke myself. It was time to build the fires and start the meal.

During the days, I led as normal a life as possible – although I kept my sleeves buttoned down. Each night, my feelings of uselessness and terror haunted my dreams. I would reach for the smooth shape of the mermaid, which gave me such painful relief. I would soak my father's watch in my own blood. I did not understand why I did this; but as I cleaned the watch each morning, I felt the same as I did when I cleaned my father's blood from the same watch. After a few days, I felt better and no longer felt the need to cut my arms. Gradually, the sores healed; and by Christmas, I could show my arms again without fear of questions.

I met Mollie for the first time at the butcher shop where we shopped. She took one look at my several bundles compared to her only one, and remarked I must have a large family. We laughed when she learned I worked at a hotel. She worked as a cook for the Hall family who lived not far from the Pearl House. She recently moved to town with her husband Walter. I later discovered Walter was not her husband at all, and she came to town with different man. It became important later, but at the time, I was not concerned with her marriage situation since she was not a love interest for me. We developed a close friendship – often arranging to go shopping at the same time. I met Walter one day, and he seemed moody and suspicious of my relationship with Mollie. I resolved neve to do anything Walter might not like. I missed having someone to talk to, so I was determined keep my friendship with Mollie.

Mollie was fun and outgoing. We would often sit on the bench along the avenue and talk. She said she loved to hear me talk. Mollie's voice had a pleasing, melodic tone. Her speech was slow and silky like honey. I looked forward to seeing her; and on those days she did not come, I missed her companionship. We would watch the mule-drawn streetcar go up and down the avenue on its shiny rails. Neither of us had ever been on a trolley; so we resolved to save our pennies and one day ride the six blocks up to the capitol and walk back. She invited me to go to church with her and Walter on Sunday, and I accepted. I heard the gospel preached for the first time. I heard the Christmas story; and for the first time understood what the upcoming holiday meant. Up until then, I thought it a celebration of decorated trees and exchanging gifts.

One day, Mollie did not appear; but Walter sat on our bench. I reached out my hand to shake and my palm disappeared into his massive paw. I sat down next to him with my hand still trapped tightly in his.

"Whut you wont wif my wife?" He asked right off.

I told Walter I just liked talking to his wife – nothing else. We agreed Mollie was a pleasing companion, and was easy to talk with. He did not seem angry or threatening, but he kept my hand in his powerful grip. I felt my hand was in some trap I could not escape. I did not want to try to pull away for fear of offending him – or upsetting him further. He was a huge man with powerful muscles and big arms. It was clear I was not going to get my right hand back until he was ready. He was not hurting me in any way. I looked Walter in the eye and told him what he wanted to hear – which was the truth. Mollie and I were just friends.

Walter let my hand go, much to my relief, and sat back against the bench. Walter told me a bartender named Brooks who worked over at the Barrel House Saloon on East Pecan Street. I knew the place; and I knew who he mentioned. I had visited the saloon several times. I admitted I knew the man, but I did not like him much. Brooks was a little too pushy for my tastes. This seemed to please Walter, who nodded and told me Mollie and this Brooks fellow were from a town up north called Waco. Walter told me Mollie and Brooks came to Austin together a year earlier, but she and Brooks parted company soon after arriving in Austin. Brooks, so Walter said, still "carried tha torch" for Mollie. Now that Mollie had money, Brooks was coming around again. Walter said he did not want any trouble; but he was not going to stand by while this Brooks fellow, "or *anyone*" – he said looking directly at me – "trifled wif my wife."

I assured Walter he had nothing worry about from me, and I never heard her even mention Mr. Brooks. This seemed to give Walter some comfort. He placed a huge arm around the back of my neck and squeezed my neck.

"That's good, Maurice. I like you Maurice – I don't want nothin' bad to happen to ya. You stay friends wid Mollie; that's ok by me. But if I find that Brooks fella sniffin' around her, I'm gonna break his neck for sure; and it don't matter who ya tell that to." After shaking my hand again, Walter ambled off down the street without a backward glance.

The next day I told Mollie that Walter and I talked. She was not surprised. "He's always doin' that," she laughed. "Ever' man I talk to, he thanks is tryin' to steal me away! He's just a big ole hound dog! He don't mean nuthin' by it. He didn't hurt you none, did he?"

"No. He was just concerned I might have some ambition toward you."

"Do ya?" She asked with her eyes twinkling. I could not tell if she were serious or just teasing me.

I did not know how to answer. I did not, but would it offend her if I said no? I hesitated, not sure how to reply, when she suddenly burst out laughing.

"Maurice! It's ok. I'm just funnin' ya. Do you know what today is?"

I said I did; it was Wednesday, the day before Christmas. She told me they called it Christmas Eve.

"Whut you gonna give me fo Christmas?" She asked, her eyes dancing with excitement. I told her I did not know; I had not thought of giving anything. She pouted her lips.

"Well, I know whut I'm gettin' you! A ride on the streetcar!" She got up and took my hand, "Come on, Maurice! One is leaving right now. We'll ride up to tha Cap'tol and come walkin' back, just like you said."

She paid the trolley man two pennies for each of us. The conductor frowned, but showed us where we were to sit. She sat near the window and looked outside. The seats were nice leather and were soft and comfortable. Because the weather was warm again despite the season, the glass windows were off; and a frilly awning hung over each to provide shade if needed.

After a few moments, the car lurched ahead. Once underway, it was such a smooth ride; I could not believe it. Once we took off, it was as if we were floating on the air. The steel wheels made a harsh screeching noise on the rails, and the car jolted and bumped each time it came to a stop and took off again. In between starts and stops, the car glided down the tracks; not like a carriage ride at all.

After six blocks, we climbed off, laughing and holding hands. Once on the sidewalk, I released her hand and we walked back toward Pecan Street, looking in the shop windows. She admired some women's handkerchiefs in one window, and I secretly decided to come back and buy them for Christmas. I bought a pair for Mrs. Schmidt, too.

I wrapped the gifts in some white tissue paper Hector gave me. On Christmas day, I gave Mrs. Schmidt her gift; she was so pleased she remarked how fine the lace work was, and how neatly stitched and dainty they were. She even gave me a kiss on the cheek.

So I knew Mollie would be pleased when she opened hers the day after Christmas. Of course, Mollie complained I spent far too much money, but I could tell she was not about to give them back. She squealed with joy in her musical laugh and gave me a small kiss on the cheek. It was nice to have a friend again. I received a card she drew and colored herself. I treasure the card today as much as I do my father's watch and my mother's locket.

You can imagine how devastated I was to read, a week later, that she was killed on New Year's Eve.

Not much appeared in the newspaper about Mollie's death, though the neighborhood buzzed with rumors. Some of them were true. Everyone seemed to know details of the murder, but everyone had a different idea about who killed Mollie – even I had my suspicions, but I kept them to myself. What they told seemed horrible – unexplainable. Why would someone want to a kind person like kill Mollie?

I pieced together what must have happened from a variety of stories. Mollie and Walter lived in an apartment behind the Hall house on Pecan Street. It turned out Mollie Smith was not married to Walter Spencer after all, and she had been cooking for the Hall family for only about a month.

On a fairy tale night, laced with glistening snow, Walter Spencer screamed bloody murder. Walter rushed into Tom Chalmers' bedroom in the main house. Tom was Mr. Hall's brother-in-law who was staying at the house while Mr. Hall was in Houston. "Mr. Tom, for God's sake, please help me! Somebody has nearly killed me!"

Spencer bled heavily from several head wounds, and a large gash nearly cut to the bone on his forearm. "Walter, you need to go to the doctor right away. Can you get there on your own?" Walter was clearly dazed by the attack. Tom bound Walter's wounds with towels and held them tight to stop the bleeding. Walter stumbled off to see the doctor who lived around the corner at the end of the block.

"Mr. Tom, Mollie's gone!"

"What do you mean she's gone? Where would she go in this weather – It's freezing outside!"

"She ain't in the house, Mr. Tom. I don't know whur she's gone, but she ain't in the room no more."

"Did she do this to you, Walter?"

"No, sir. He hit her too, Mr. Tom. There's blood ever'where, and it ain't all mine."

After sending Walter on his way to the doctor, Tom dressed, took his shotgun from the corner of the room, and strapped on his six-gun. Tom quietly walked out on the back screened porch and looked across the wide backyard. The dim silver-lined moon did not give much light to the heavily overcast night. Next door, a rooster crowed and was soon rewarded with an answer from a few blocks away. It was dark outside still, so Tom lit a lantern and put on a pot of coffee. It snowed during the night, and it was still freezing cold. Tom felt it was bad enough he was awakened, he certainly was not going to go traipsing around the neighborhood over a servant girl. Everyone said the weather was going to get worse. No one else was in the house at the time; the owner, Walter Hall, was in Galveston conducting business. It would not be long until daylight, so Tom planned to wait until the sun was up to investigate.

Few sounds filtered through the night, and nothing moved in the yard, so Tom sat rocking on the porch and sipping coffee, but every time something bumped in the night, Tom jumped and leveled his shotgun. After assuring himself nothing moved in the darkness, Tom sat back in his rocker and waited. Time went slowly. Walter Spencer had not returned by the time the sky turned gray with streaks of light. A powder of snow covered everything in the yard. Tom sat still in the shadows of the back porch and quietly watched for something to move.

Suddenly, a dark figure emerged from the barn and walked into the yard. Tom raised his shotgun, "Halt! Who's there?"

"It's Albert, Mr. Tom." Albert was the groom who kept the horses and other animals on the Hall property.

"Albert!" Tom shouted, "Hurry and go get the police. We've had some trouble here."

205

"Sure, Mr. Tom. Right away."

When the police officer arrived, Walter Spencer still was not back from the doctor. The policeman took notes sitting in the Hall parlor drinking coffee. Just as he and Tom were about to go outside to investigate the scene, Jackson, the next-door neighbor's yardman, ran through the back door of the Hall house.

"Mr. Tom!" he screamed. "It's Mollie. She's lyin' out back there! Dead!"

The men ran through the back yard and found Mollie Smith lying nearly naked on the grass behind the outhouse. The men saw no trail in the snow, so the killer must have dragged to the rear of the yard before it snowed. She was obviously dead. A gaping hole was in the left side of Mollie's head. From the signs, the men determined Mollie was attacked in the bedroom of the apartment and was hauled outside to the place where she was found. They scuffed the snow away and found a bloody trail across the lawn showing she was severely injured, probably already dead when found. She lay on her back, a pool of her own blood beneath. Her vacant eyes looked skyward until they pulled her eyelids down. Tom told Albert to place a blanket over her nakedness and told Jackson to fetch the Justice of the Peace.

Beneath the snow, a bloody trail led the two men to Mollie's room. Mollie's heels left two clear trails beneath the snow. It did not appear she conscious at the time. Blood lay like a pool beneath the body and splattered the side of the outhouse. It seemed like the killer laid her down, probably to finish the job. It was fifty yards from the little house to the outhouse. Someone wanted her in a dark, secluded place for some purpose.

"Why would someone do that?" Walter pondered.

"Probably so he could do stuff to her without being detected," the detective offered.

"You mean with a dead woman?" Walter asked, obviously shocked and revolted.

"Happens all the time," the officer said as he stooped to inspect something on the lawn.

In the disheveled room, they found broken glass and furniture scattered across the floor. Bloody fingerprints covered the walls, mirror, and the inside of the door. The Justice of the Peace, acting as a coroner, arrived and went outside to examine the body. After declaring Mollie dead, her head was covered, but they left her body in place until they could complete their investigation. A little before nine o'clock, the City Marshall arrived and took charge of the scene. Marshall Lee sent police officers out to arrest Walter Spencer and bring him back to the house for questioning. Some of the wooden furniture showed deep cuts in the wood. Tom looked under the bed and pulled out a bloodstained ax. The ax must have been kicked under the bed during the struggle.

When I heard about the ax, my mind flashed immediately to Mawken. I could see our family ax in the woodpile back home and in Haji's woodpile. I could not stop my mind from seeing the ax blade buried deep into the captain's head. I could imagine the blood and gore spraying across the bedroom. The stories were explicit.

Soon Walter Spencer returned from the doctor, sporting a huge bandage around his head. The officer immediately placed him in handcuffs and sat him in the parlor against Tom's wishes. Once they had Walter chained, the marshal told him Mollie was dead. Walter was heartbroken and said wanted to see her. For the next hour, both men heartlessly peppered Walter with questions what happened and his possible motive. They removed Walter's bandage to inspect his wound. The lawmen questioned Walter about every detail of his relationship with Mollie. A grieving Walter was clearly upset and cried throughout the interview.

The Marshall finally opened the handcuffs; he was not going to arrest Walter. It would be unlikely for Walter to inflict a wound that severe on himself. A mournful Walter knelt behind the outhouse a few minutes and grieved over Mollie's body.

The next day, I stood on the street and saw a loudly protesting Brooks hauled into police headquarters. If Brooks was the killer, maybe it was not Mawken after all. Brooks had to be the murderer. All the pieces of the puzzle fit. Brooks was jealous of Mollie and Walter, so he must have attacked them with the ax out of revenge. Why he waited over a year to carry out his deadly plan, I did not know. No one I talked with seemed to doubt Brook's guilt, until January 2, 1885, when he walked out of the jail a free man. "They got 'hold of the wrong man for sure!" Brooks exclaimed his innocence to everyone who would listen. Brooks gave proof he was several miles away when Mollie was killed; he could not possibly be the murderer.

If it was not Brooks – then who? Once again, my mind snapped back to Mawken. But, why would he kill Mollie? Would he kill her over an innocent friendship with Mollie? Had he attacked Mollie as he had Donny?

For the first time in weeks, I reached beneath my pillow in the night for the warm, smooth mermaid and the cold steel blade seeking the shallow relief it offered. I was drenched in clammy sweat as I ran my hand on the cold sheets beneath the pillow. In a panic, I yanked the pillow onto the floor and gasped in disbelief.

With my heart pounding in my chest, I threw myself on the floor and peered through the gloom beneath the bed. I searched the room frantically to no avail. The mermaid knife was missing. In its place was a pair of starched white women's handkerchiefs.

The missing knife gave me a lot of concern. If Walter and Brooks were innocent, then who would have done such a thing to a harmless person like Mollie? I knew Mawken was capable, but I did not understand why he would kill Mollie. She and I were only friends. Then, I remembered what happened to Donny. Was Mawken still in the dark, watching my every move? Was he making sure no one could get close to me? Would I ever be free of this lurking menace? Had he come back to retrieve his missing knife? I did not know how long the knife was missing, because I stopped using it weeks earlier.

The next afternoon, I finally took Donny's advice and carried the gun with me. It seemed heavy and bulky in my back pocket. I was not a good shot, but if the target was still and I was close enough, I could hit it pretty well. Austin was becoming a dangerous place to live; and before long, almost everyone in town went about armed. The police were trying to keep men from wearing guns in town, but it was a rule largely ignored. The police enforced the order more severely enforced in our area of town. In order to stay out of trouble, most wore their pistols under their clothing or carried them in their pockets. I kept mine in my pocket during the day and never went out without it. At night, I lay in my cot with the pistol clutched in my hand or on the table next to me, and the marlinspike beneath my pillow.

After a few days, all but her closest friends forgot Mollie. Walter moved to a farm outside of town, and Brooks went back to Waco. Many people, especially in my end of town, were saying Brooks slipped out and killed Mollie, but the police were not trying hard enough to find her killer because she was black. It seemed true. Through the spring, we read of numerous reports of attacks at homes in the middle of the night. All of the victims were black servant girls, and all lived within blocks of the Pearl House. Some of the women were struck or shot at, but no further brutal murders of the type occurred. No one was arrested. Things quieted down, and although people were still nervous, gradually things got back to normal.

One afternoon at the market, a cook called Liza and I got into an ugly argument at the dry goods store. Eliza Shelley worked for one of the city leaders who was a doctor and a former legislator, so she thought she had more importance than anyone else did. She was rude and pushed people around, and no one liked her. When I took the last of the baking soda, she attempted to take it from me. She told me her people were important and the hotel would just have to wait or find baking soda somewhere else. The proprietor disagreed and sided with me. He saw me take the baking soda first. This set her off into a tirade against me and the storeowner. She was going to tell her boss who would rain down hell upon the store and get it closed. She was something to see and hear as she went through the store yelling to anyone who would listen. She slammed the door on the way out.

I placed my purchases on the credit book and gathered them in a bag to carry back to the hotel. The owner said to not worry, Eliza was "just like that." He told me Eliza had a temper, and tomorrow she would probably apologize. She thought she was special, and expected everyone else to give in to her. As I went through the door and onto the sidewalk, Eliza came from out of nowhere and pushed me into the street in the path of a passing wagon. Had a passerby not quickly grabbed my arm and pulled me out of the street, I would have been crushed. Eliza laughed, and said, "That should teach you a lesson!"

I watched as she disappeared around a corner as I dusted off my clothes and retrieved my spilled goods. I was angry, but I had an awful dread I hoped would not come true. Somewhere in my mind, something told me this would not be the end of the matter. I felt like something horrible was about to happen, and I tossed and turned all night.

The next morning I woke up, exhausted, only to hear the awful news. Someone shook Eliza's eight year-old son awake during the night in the shack behind the house where she worked. Rough hands covered his mouth before he could cry out and arouse his mother who slept nearby.

The boy reported a man asked, "Where does your mother keep her money?" The boy did not know. The frightened child promised to keep quiet. He could not see the face of the man who held him down against the rough floor. A white rag covered his features. "You cover your head up!" The youth told, "You do not come out until morning. If you come out, I'll kill you!"

The attacker showed the boy the knife, which he described as having a white handle. The child nodded as the killer threw a heavy quilt over his head. He was afraid. He heard terrible noises, but he obediently stayed under the covers, trembling in fear. Soon the struggle ceased, and everything got quiet. It was daylight before he gained the courage to uncover his head. His screams roused the main house, and Mrs. Johnson sent her niece out to see what the matter was. When the niece returned screaming, the family summoned the police.

Eliza lay dead on the floor with a deep wound above her right eye. There was a curious round hole between her eyes, and another just above her left ear. Her pillows and sheets were soaked in blood, and furniture scattered around the room as if someone was looking for something.

She was stabbed the first few times on the bed, but then the killer dragged her body off onto the floor and wrapped her in a bedspread. The police found no weapons in the room. Her throat was cut, and there were various cuts on her abdomen, legs, and arms. The Marshall thought may have been stabbed in the head with a rod or an ice pick. Outside the door, they found a footprint of a barefoot man. There were no other clues recovered.

Later in the day, the police arrested a local black man named Andrew Williams. They found him walking barefoot in the neighborhood. Many believed Williams was innocent. The report of a white-handled knife was enough to convince me to believe Mawken was involved. Once again, the victim was a person who had been involved with me. I was scared. It was only a matter of time before someone told the police that Eliza pushed me into the street, and then they would come to question me. What would I do? I could tell them, but no one would believe me. I would be sent to prison or hung. I waited nervously for days, yet no one ever came to question me.

A week later, the police arrested a man named Ike Plummer and questioned him about the murder. Eliza and Plummer got into a disagreement over money weeks before her death. The disagreement occurred over on Red River Street before she went to work for Dr. Johnson. Someone reported Plummer demand money from Eliza, who refused to give him any. The morning of the murder, a neighbor saw Plummer return home with a hammer or a hatchet in his pocket. They searched his room and recovered a clean hammer. They did not find a knife with a white handle.

Eventually, I knew someone would remember her pushing me into the street and report it to the police. I was nervous, and I worried every time someone I did not know came into the café. I thought about running away. I hated to close my eyes to sleep at night because I knew the fitful nightmares would continue. Once again, a man would chase me through the dark streets of Austin with a white handled knife. I could never see if the knife had a mermaid handle.

In my dreams, I would plunder through the dark night and watch paralyzed and unable to move to scream as another helpless woman was bludgeoned and slaughtered. I would awaken in a cold sweat, and shiver until dawn. I would be haunted in my dreams by an unseen monster with a cruel laugh. I knew that laugh too well by this time. I had been hearing it for the past two years. Mawken!

Two weeks later, the killer struck again. Plummer was clearly not the killer since he was still in the lock up. This time, however, the victim was a woman I did not know named Irene Cross. Like the former cases, the killer attacked Irene during the night or early morning hours using a knife or a hatchet. Left barely alive and bleeding heavily, she stood outside the house where she worked, screaming for help.

A reporter, who was tried to interview the woman before she died, said she looked as if a wild Indian had scalped her. Irene was so badly injured she could not speak. There was a hole in her head. A long gash crossed her forehead, and her right arm was nearly severed. She finally died a few days later, but never told who had attacked her.

There was a description of the killer. Her son had seen the dark man. The description of the man certainly did not sound like Mawken, except in one detail.

"He 'as a big man – a big black man with a brown hat. He wore a brown coat, and carried a long knife with a white handle."

At that time, few people believed one person was committing all of the killings. Murders usually happened in a fit of rage or jealousy by someone the victim knew. Passion gripped the killer in bloody fury. Filled with remorse after an act of violence, the culprit was usually easy to find. These new cases baffled the police. It was easier for the police to blame them on the loose lifestyle of the low living blacks than to admit the city had a serious problem.

I did not tell anyone why I believed only one man was involved. Some people believed a gang of men prowled Guy Town during the night. A few thought it might even be the Ku Klux Klan, but no one saw a mob of men during that time, or any crosses burned.

The police still did not seem overly concerned. Throughout the summer, several more women were attacked at night. Homes were burglarized, rocks were thrown through windows, and property was stolen. Servant girls were shot at, and their rooms were broken into. The Marshal blamed the city government on his failure to stop the crimes. His excuse was the department did not have enough officers to cover the entire city all the time. He needed more men and more equipment. Priorities must be set. It was clear Guy Town was not one of those priorities.

The long hot summer moved slowly past; and despite nightly clashes between drunks and hell raisers, there were no unsolved night murders.

The tension grew daily as the residents on the Southside waited to see who would be the next victim. No one I talked to thought the murder spree was over, though most blamed it on gangs of white men.

The police released Plummer for lack of evidence. I considered going to the Sheriff with my story. I played it out in my head, repeatedly. What would I say? How would I explain Mawken and our relationship? Why would anyone believe it? I was convinced who the killer, was but would anyone else believe me?

I went over each murder. Mollie was killed because she was too close to me. Had Mawken killed Eliza out of revenge because she attacked me? What of Irene? I did not even know her, and the only reason I thought they were connected was a report of the white-handled knife. It did not seem like enough to convince them, so I decided to wait.

Then, in September, another brutal killing and rape occurred in our neighborhood of Guy Town. Another black woman was attacked in the night, and a young child was molested. Again, it was truly someone I did not know.

Rebecca Ramey worked for a family named Weed who lived on East Cedar Street, not far from the other attacks. Mr. Weed owned the stables. Since the killings began, many of the servant girls began sleeping in the main houses where they worked. Rebecca made a pallet on the floor of the kitchen for herself and her eleven-year old daughter, Mary. She believed they would be safer there than in her quarters out back.

During the night, someone entered the Weed kitchen. The intruder held a buckskin bag filled with sand and lead. Rebecca was startled awake seconds before the prowler struck her with the bag, which fractured her skull. The attacker dropped the bag near where Rebecca lay unconscious.

When she regained consciousness, her groans awakened Mr. Weed who found her. She had a crooked jaw, was bleeding from her head, and her skull was fractured. No one knew where young Mary was.

Mr. Weed went outside with his shotgun and roused his neighbor, Mr. Stephen Jacqua. Together the men searched the yard and the tool house. They found Mary on the floor of the outhouse, barely breathing. Blood trickled from her ears as if someone had pushed a sharp object into her ears on one side, and then did the same thing through the other ear. The police did not know what was used, but I believed it was a marlinspike.

I remembered the same thing had happened to Eliza. It was a strange thing to do since the killer had a knife and even an ax. Why would the killer take the time to puncture her brain? Despite her injuries, Mary lived for a short time before bleeding to death in the backyard.

"Well, sir!" Weed reported to the papers, "I woke up in the night to a horrible sound outside – like a dog howling, but more human like. It scared the bejesus out of me! Rebecca and her kid slept in the kitchen, so I went to see what it was and if she heard it too. I found Becka on the floor knocked unconscious and bleeding. Her kid was not on the kitchen pallet. That's when I sent someone for the Sheriff."

Someone called out the dog trackers, and they tried to get a trail on the attacker using the dogs. The police hoped the scene was fresh enough the dogs would be able to follow a fleeing attacker on foot. The dogs made a beeline for the stables three blocks away, where they found and arrested a man named Tom Allen. A mob of angry black men wanted to lynch Allen right on the spot, but the police dissuaded them.

I breathed a small sigh of relief. They found the killer. Maybe it was not Mawken after all. Had all my fears been for nothing?

The entire city seemed to believe the danger had passed. People came out on the street again, and everyone was thankful the police finally captured the fiend who terrorized the city for so long. Everyone was shocked when, three days later, the police released Tom Allen from the city jail.

Allen's doctor swore out a statement proving it was not possible for Allen to have raped the child. No one ever understood why, but the police seemed too eager to agree Allen was innocent. Still, Allen left town as soon as he was freed, probably nervous those lynch mobs might take matters into their own hands.

Within a day, the papers wrote the police were questioning a man named Aleck Mack. They did not arrest Mr. Mack, and the community once again erupted into a state of anger and frustration.

After little Mary's attack, the newspaper turned on the local police with a vengeance, blaming them for allowing the attacks and murders to continue unabated. The shortcomings of the police force splashed across the pages daily. The attacks against the city marshal turned personal and ugly. They accused him of corruption and incompetence. They questioned his ability to run the police force in the rudest terms.

In response, the police turned vicious and vindictive. They rounded up dozens of local black men and beat them like dogs. Stories and rumors of cruel police beatings and torture were whispered throughout the community. The newspaper said it was clear "the crimes are cunningly planned, carefully directed and intelligently consummated." The paper believed that the men arrested did not seem to be involved in the least, and were rounded up primarily because they were black. This created anger among the black people in the neighborhood, most of whom agreed with the paper.

The papers called upon the marshal to resign; and when he did not, they turned to attacking the city government that allowed him to stay in office. "While unbridled ruffians spread terror across the city, Austin's crime rate is second to no place in the civilized world!"

I was glad I had not gone to the police with my story. There is no telling what may have become of me once inside the walls of the city jail. I may have been beaten or tortured like those unfortunates who they arrested. By the end of the week, over three hundred men were detained and hauled into police headquarters – some would not be seen again for days. Of all the people arrested, Mawken was not among them. He remained at large.

A week after little Mary was raped and killed I turned on the lights and lit the fires in the hotel kitchen when something caught my eye. Someone had driven a knife into the chopping block, pinning a note in place.

"Tonight. Midnight." It said, "Alley behind Black Elephant. Be there!"

Someone left the note during the night or surely, Beulah would have brought it to me. Besides, she would never have stuck a knife into a chopping block. It immediately aroused my suspicions. So, this would be how Mawken would reenter my life – in the dark of night behind a saloon. I wondered what he wanted. I did not think he meant to kill me to keep me from telling what I knew; he could have murdered me in my sleep any night.

I intended to go armed. If it were Mawken, I wondered if I had the courage to shoot him. I was not sure I could pull the trigger unless he attacked me first.

A little before the allotted hour, I stepped from the hotel steps and walked west on Pecan Street. The Black Elephant was a known hangout of rough thugs. Some of them would no doubt still be drinking inside the saloon. The gun was nestled inside my right pocket and it clinked against my marlinspike as I walked. Dim yellow light spilled from the windows across the wooden walkway. Music and loud laughter came from the open tavern door as I passed the saloon and calmly walked around the corner to the alley in back. The alley was littered with the usual things: ash cans and a few boxes strewn around. I did not see anyone standing around, so I sat down on a box and waited.

"Anybody foller you here?" A voice I did not recognize came from the darkness alongside the building. It was not Mawken.

"No," I answered. "It's just me. Who are you?"

A tall black man emerged from the shadows and sat on a box facing me.

"You don't know me," he said. "But I know you – I damn sure knows you. My name is Orange. Orange Washington."

"Why did you call me here, sir? What do you want?"

"I seen it," he said.

"You saw what?"

"Damn right! I saw it all. No use denying it. I seen what went on at Mr. Weed's house the night that lil' chile was killed. You know what you done! I seen it."

"No, sir. You are mistaken."

He face contorted in anger and frustration as Orange rose to his feet, his fist barely inches from my face. I flinched anticipating a blow, but he struggled to hold back. The whites of his eyes were yellow and streaked with red. I was afraid. He gradually calmed himself and sat back on his box. I turned sideways to hide my hand sneaking into my pocket.

"No use to go fer that gun! I got one too," he threatened.

"I don't know what you think you saw, but you did not see *me* outside Mr. Weed's house that night."

"One hunert dollars." Orange blurted.

"A hundred dollars? What for?"

"To keep me from goin' to the police. You don't want that do ya? Even if you are innocent, by the time they got through with you, you'd claim to be Abraham Lincoln if they tole ya'. Anyway, by the time they beat your hide off, it won't matter much."

219

"What exactly do you think you saw, Mr. Washington?"

"I seen you outside the fence of Mr. Weed's house where that little girl stay. You was carryin' a sock filled up with sand, and you had a hatchet stuck in your waistband. Just waitin' – waitin' for the lights to go out. You didn't see me – I hid in the shadas and watched. I knowed right away *you* was the killer. I knowed it as soon as I seen you just standin' there – waitin'. Somebody pass by on the walk, and I heard you say, 'Good evening' in that strange soundin' kind of talk you do. I knowed right then it was you – you the cook over to the Pearl House. I wondered what you were doing there, so I stood in the shadas and I watched."

My thoughts went running wild. Orange must have seen Mawken just before the murder. Here was a witness who could place Mawken at the scene of the crime! Orange thought he saw me. I was sure the police would believe him.

I stalled.

"I don't carry that much money around with me. It'll take a few days."

"Two days!" he barked. "You be back here in two nights with that money, or I'm goin' to the sheriff!"

"Tomorrow is Sunday, and on Monday the bank is closed," I bluffed. "I won't be able to get money until Tuesday."

He stood up and demanded, "That night then! You be here at midnight with that money!"

I stood, and he grabbed me by the arms, keeping my hand from getting to the gun. Orange placed his huge fist in my face and panted, his breath smelling of beer.

"You little sumbitch! I should beat your ass good for what you done to that baby. You ain't here with the money in two nights,

I'm going to hunt you down just for the aim of messing you up before I turn you in to the police! Don't you even thank of runnin'."

He pushed me into the dirt of the alley, and by the time I was able to regain my feet, he was gone.

I went back to my room trying to decide what I should do. I did not have the one hundred dollars Orange demanded. I thought my only chance was to leave on the train right away. The train pulled out of Union Station at five in the morning. Running away seemed like my only option. It was a little past one o'clock, so I threw my things in a cloth bag, and sat in the chair to wait. I intended to get to the station just in time to catch the train. I awoke with a start! I looked at my father's watch and saw it was after four o'clock. I was astonished how fast time passed. I was late! I hurried out the back door of the hotel and ran to the train station three blocks away.

Breakfast would be late this morning.

I sat on the hard, wooden bench outside the closed station house, waiting for the train. I would buy my ticket on the train. I could hear the whistle in the distance as the train neared. Suddenly, I heard dogs barking, and two policemen rushed onto the station platform with their guns drawn. One of them stepped up to a couple who were waiting for the train, and the other came directly at me.

"Who are you? And what are you doing here?" he demanded.

I told him my name and admitted I was waiting for the train to Houston.

"Hey! I know you. You are that cook over at the Pearl House."

I admitted it, even though I was afraid he would immediately arrest me. Instead, the lawman seemed to let down his guard.

"Yeah. You're OK," he waved his hand dismissively. "Goin' to Houston, huh? What for?"

"I have family there, and I have to go on family business," I lied. I was clear Mr. Washington had not turned me in yet. "What's happened? Why are the police here?"

"You know that killer is on the loose? An' tonight he hit again, over on San Marcos Street, at Mr. Dunham's house. His servant girl and her man was both killed tonight. Gracie Vance – do you know her?"

I did not.

"Well, it's a pretty bad scene over there. It happened after midnight. We're checking all the usual places; stables, station, and all the roads out of town are blocked. We think he is on foot because he left his horse tied outside. They think Gracie was raped too, and the man had his head nearly sliced in two. Maybe you know him; let's see, what is his name? He had an odd name…" The policeman searched his notes. "Yeah! Here it is. *Orange.* Imagine that? A man named Orange. Orange Washington!" he laughed to himself.

After the police left, I went back to the hotel and lit the stoves. Breakfast would not be late after all.

Gracie Vance dreaded seeing her man come home. She prayed to herself Orange would be on his best behavior tonight in front of her cousins, Lucinda and Patsy, who were spending the night before catching the train the next day.

Orange was a hard man with hard ways, and nothing Gracie could do seemed to satisfy him. He would come home smelling of beer and other women and demand Gracie fix him some food. It did not matter what, it would never be hot enough – sweet enough – good enough. Then he would start beating on her. She tried to keep quiet so it would not disturb Mr. Dunham in the main house; she needed this job and Orange would not work. "*Maybe he won't hit me tonight – not with 'Cinda and Patsy here. Mebbe not tonight*," she hoped to herself.

Many times Gracie wondered if Orange was hurting all those women. He could do it. He was a big man and he had a violent temper. Maybe, she thought, Orange killed those women so he would not have to kill her. Sometimes she thought he didn't like women at all – expect for one thing. Her mind was a whirl of emotions and thoughts, as she sat in the dim light and tried to predict what Orange might want when he got home. Eggs probably. She kept her mind busy by visiting with her cousins.

The two cousins had been teasing Gracie about a man called Doc Woods. He was not a real doctor, but everyone called him Doc. Doc worked on horses sometimes, but no person would ever let Doc treat them for anything worse than a headache. Doc had a crush on Gracie and would often come by in the evening to "check" on her – make sure "ever' thang was all right." Doc had been by earlier that evening; and when he found the cousins visiting, he was eager to come inside the house.

No matter how often he begged Gracie refused to let him in. She lied and told him Orange would be home any minute, hoping he would go away. But, Doc persisted. He talked to the women through

223

the back screen door and told them to leave the window unlatched. He would come in later that night for them after Gracie went to bed. The two cousins giggled and egged him on. Gracie told him to "get gone!" before Orange came home. Doc said he was not afraid of Orange.

"Hell! I'll kill him if you want me to," he bragged.

The two cousins could not see Doc's face; they could only hear his voice. Eventually, he gave up and went away, like he always did. Doc was more talk than do, Gracie figured. But, all the same, she never invited Doc in. Orange would kill her for sure if she did. Patsy and Lucinda wanted to know what Doc looked like. Gracie said he was a funny looking little man. The girls giggled and teased Gracie by saying maybe they would leave the window unlatched after all.

"Them little guys try harder to make up for it," Cinda teased. Gracie knew she would never do such a thing. It was just girl talk. They made so much noise, Mr. Dunham, Gracie's boss, yelled out the back door of his house for them to settle down.

The women sat and talked for a while about the news from home. They were on their way back to their home near Dallas when the train from Houston dropped them off in Austin. They would switch trains and go north in the morning. They told Gracie about Houston and all the things they saw. They were planning on going back and working down there, if their pa would let them. Gracie knew it was just wishful thinking, but she went along with them anyway. It was something to talk about.

She jumped once when she heard a noise outside, but it was nothing. Just some cats going by she reckoned aloud. Patsy laughed at her for being so "spooky." Patsy was unaware of how Gracie lived. The cousins knew nothing of the murderer who crept the streets at night. She and Orange lived in a small shack out back of the Dunham place. It was not much, but it was a bed and a roof overhead. The wind blew through the live oak trees in the back yard, and one limb sometimes scraped the roof of the house in a creepy sort of way. She asked Orange plenty of times to cut that limb down, but of course, he never did it. Every time it scraped against the house, she flinched. "I guess I'll have ta do it myself," she mumbled to herself, only realizing she spoke out loud when Lucinda laughed.

"I don't know why you put up with that lazy bum, Gracie. Why don't you leave Orange, and come on home with us?"

"... Or, let Doc kill him," Patsy chimed in to great peals of laughter. Of course, it was a horrible joke, but they laughed anyway. Gracie changed the subject.

"Oh, I miss my daddy – an' momma, too!" Gracie admitted. "Been so long since I seen 'em. If I wadn't so tied down here, I b'lieve I would go home. Sweet Jesus! Wouldn't they be happy to see me too? We'd have a high ole time, we would. Daddy'd call all the kin – your momma and papa too – and, he'd bring in the homemade wine he fixed up from the wild mustang grapes that grew down on the bottoms. You know Momma would kill some chickens; and Little George would go get some corn and watermelons out of tha fields out yonder. Y'all could bring some plums and strawberries from your truck patch. Sister would pull out the makin's she had been savin' for Christmas and bake us a big ole cake. It'd be so sweet and peaceful, sittin' and rockin' on that big ole porch, while the crickets and frogs sang in the trees. That big old moon would cast shadows on the house while my Daddy and your daddy would play some tunes..." Gracie could almost hear the music as she dreamed of her homecoming.

"Well," she said, as she rose from her chair and went back into the kitchen to make sure the fire was still going, "if wishes was wings, frogs wouldn't bump they ass ever' time they hopped! It don' look like I'm goin' nowhere anytime soon. Wish I could – Lord don't I wish I could." The girls got ready for bed and retired to the back room, leaving Gracie to wait up for Orange. It was clear they did not

225

care much for Gracie's current man. It would be better if they were out of sight when he got home.

"You leave that window latched!" Gracie hollered into the back room, as the cousins giggled and tittered as they settled down for the night.

Gracie felt a little hungry herself.

"Maybe Orange will come home in a good mood, and we can share a little something before we go to bed." She would go ahead and get something ready if she knew when he was coming. But she never knew. "Sometimes, he don't come home at all," she confided in Patsy when she came for her goodnight kiss. "Sometimes he stay out all night – prob'ly with her!"

Maybe tonight would be a night like that; she often wished Orange would not come home at all. But he usually did.

After the cousins were in bed, she decided if Orange did not come home soon, she would turn out the lights and go to bed herself. She wanted to fix the girls breakfast before their train left, and before she went to work over in the Dunham house. Orange would probably wake her up in the middle of the night when he crawled into the bed – "prob'ly wantin' somethin'," she thought. She sat in the dim light and rocked as she thought some more of her family. Finally, she heard his step on the porch. She knew it was Orange from the sound of his walk.

"Gracie!" he barked as soon as he came through the screen, "Fix up some supper!"

Gracie pleaded with Orange to be quiet and not wake the women, but she knew he would not listen. She rose and went into the kitchen and pulled out the iron skillet and the eggs. She laughed as she mumbled under her breath, "She prob'ly done turn him down t'night, so he come home to me. Mebbe her man was home, or she just didn' wanna fool with old Orange tonight. Anyway, here he is. Drunk and hungry – just like always."

She heated the bacon fat in the skillet and cracked two eggs against the edge with one hand. She fixed up a batch for both of them. He wasn't cussing and fussing, so maybe he was in a good mood after all. She smiled and shook her head as she pushed the hot grease over the top of the bubbling eggs. "Over easy," she mused, "That's me. Over easy t'night for sure," she giggled at the joke. She thought the two cousins must have put Orange in a loving mood instead of a hitting one. Something sure made him happy. She turned to face Orange as he came into the kitchen.

"Eggs ready yet?" he demanded.

"Jus' about. Jus' like you like 'em, Orange." She tried to be cheerful, hoping things would stay calm. Orange sat down at the table and pulled something from his pocket. It looked like a train schedule. He put it close to his face as he struggled to make out the writing in the dim light.

"Gracie," he said slowly. "How would you like us to leave this place?" Gracie's heart leaped in her chest. Home!

"Oh, Orange. Can we go home? I been wantin' to go home really bad for a long time. Cain't we go back there and live? Why we could go in the mornin' with Patsy and Cinda! I don't like this town, Orange, and I'm scared from all them women bein' killed…"

"Shut the hell up, woman! Damn! I didn't say nothin' about goin' back ta have to work like a dog fer your ole papa! Hell! I'm talkin' about mebbe goin' to Houston in a few days. Them girls said it was nice down there. We could start over down there. I get my hunert dollars, we're leaving here."

Gracie's heart sank. She wondered where Orange would get a hundred dollars. She hoped the girls had not heard his outburst. She

227

sadly turned back to the stove to finish the eggs, trying not to cry. Suddenly the wind blew and brushed the branch against the roof again. Orange jumped.

"Whut 'us that?" he asked.

Gracie wiped tears from her eyes and said, "That's that branch that keeps brushin' the roof you'us gonna cut down th'other day. It ain't nothin'…"

"Shut up! No, it ain't! Somebody's out there – movin' aroun' in the dark."

Gracie turned to face him, fear building up inside her, gripping her heart and stopping her breathing. "*Oh, God!" she thought, "Don't let it be Doc!* Orange moved closer to the door and peered outside through the rusty screen.

"Them cousins of yours in bed, or are they out there foolin' aroun'?" he asked over his shoulder.

"No, Orange. They went to bed an hour ago. It ain't them."

Orange eased open the back screen and stepped into the yard, gun in hand. She heard his footsteps fade as he walked over to the barn out back. She stood by the stove, afraid to move. "*What if it's that killer?*" she thought. "*What if he's come to kill us all?*" She reached behind her for the hot skillet from the stove and stood ready to use it on whoever came through the back screen that was not Orange. She was afraid, but she knew hot grease would stop any killer in his tracks. After what seemed like an hour, she could hear Orange's footsteps returning from the barn. He stopped outside, and Gracie could hear the splash as he peed against the wall like he did sometimes.

"What was it, Orange?" she asked.

"Nothin', I guess. I could have sworn there'us somebody out there, but I guess not." He came back into the kitchen and stood by the table watching her. He gestured at her with his head and open hands, as if she was stupid for keeping him waiting.

"You ain't got them eggs ready yet?" he demanded.

"They's done," she said. Gracie turned back to the stove and ladled the eggs onto a plate. "I'us jus' waitin' fer you to come back in, Orange."

She shook salt and pepper over the eggs and turned to put them on the table. What she saw froze her in mid-stride as the eggs and plate crashed to the floor.

"Damn it, woman! Is you crazy? What the hell is wrong with you?" Orange roared as Grace cringed back against the hot stove.

Standing quietly behind Orange was a small dark man she did not recognize. Orange did not realize anyone was behind him, and Gracie was so shocked she could not speak. Orange doubled up his fist as if to knock Gracie silly. The strange man did not speak, but he looked right at Gracie and slowly shook his head "no" as if to warn her not to speak.

The stove burned into Gracie's back, but she did not cry out. She fumbled behind her for a grip on the skillet as the sizzling grease splashed across her hand, but still, she did not make a sound. It was as if her voice froze, something was stuck in her throat, and time slowed to a crawl. She could not even scream.

Meanwhile, Orange cursed and yelled at her at the top of his lungs. She heard Lucinda scream behind her, "No! Doc! Don't do it!" Gracie's mind whirled, confused, as she wondered where Doc was, and what he had to do with it. Orange paused with his fist in the air as he tried to understand what Lucinda was yelling. Gracie watched, mesmerized, while the stranger slowly raised an ax over Orange and

229

swiftly brought it down deep into his head. It sank into Orange's head with a solid thud sound, as if it sunk into a wooden log. Blood and brains flew everywhere, including the table and Gracie's new white apron she wore for company.

"Oh, my God! He's going to kill us all!" Lucinda screamed. All Gracie could do was stand, statue-still, as the stranger pushed Lucinda back into the back room. He swung a heavy bag against Lucinda's head, knocking her unconscious. Then he turned on Patsy, giving her a heavy blow with the loaded sock, knocking her off her feet back onto the bed. The stranger threw the bloody ax onto the bed and turned back toward Gracie, who was still standing against the hot stove, unmoving – unbelieving – uncomprehending. She looked vacantly at Orange lying with his brains leaking out all over the kitchen floor. All she could think of was the blood streaked across her new white apron. How was she ever going to get those stains out?

The stranger rushed forward and grabbed Gracie's hair, forcing her to her knees. She was still conscious as he picked Gracie up and threw her through the window into the yard. It was over for Orange and probably the poor girls too. The night was just beginning for Gracie.

The next morning Mr. William Dunham, at his home on San Marcos Street, told his story to the City Marshal and a reporter from the local paper. The men stood in the barn looking down at Gracie's dead body. The Marshal held a lantern close to Gracie's mangled corpse to get a better look. Gracie Vance worked for Mr. Dunham, and she and Orange Washington lived in the shack out back. Orange was a worthless bum, but Gracie supported him. Dunham told the marshal all about the couple, the cousins who were visiting, Patsy Gibson and Lucinda Boddy.

"I woke up sometime after midnight. It seemed like Orange was whippin' Gracie again. It happened a lot – almost every night. I thought maybe he wouldn't do it with company there and all. But, you know them people – how they are.

Anyway, it sounded like he was whippin' her. It sounded like someone slappin' somebody. I figured he came home drunk again and was pushing her around. I was getting' tired of it, so I told the old woman I was gonna get rid of Gracie if it didn't stop. I didn't thank no more about it, and went back to sleep, but not before I heard someone holler 'No, Doc! Don't do it!" Then it got quiet again and I drifted back off.

"Who's Doc?" the marshal asked.

"You know that squatty little nigger man that ever'body calls Doc? He dopes up the horses sometimes, but he ain't no real doctor. I seen him sniffin' around the shack a few times when Orange wadn't home. Doc. You know him – you've seen him around."

"Doc Woods?"

"Yeah! That's the guy. Anyway, as I said I went back to sleep. Then, a little while later, that racket started up again. I was pretty peeved about it. I thought someone had busted out the glass in the winda back there. Sounded like somebody throwed somethin' right through it. They was tearin' up my place, and I knew they didn't have no money to fix it up. So I got up and grabbed my shotgun to put a stop to this nonsense once and for all. I was gonna get stuck with the damage. I was thinkin' of kicking Gracie out right then. This mess was gettin' out of hand, Marshal. I knew Orange was gonna kill her some night for sure, and I damn sure didn't want him to kill her on my place."

"Before I could get to the door, I heard a woman scream. I pulled open the door and saw Lucinda fighting with some man out by the gate in the shadows. Damn, that does it! Now we gotta put up with the kinfolk fighting all night too? The man just hauled off and hit her right in the face! Knocked her to the ground and run off.

Lucinda came crawlin' toward me screaming, "My God! Mr. Dunham! We all dead!" I didn't have no idea what she was talkin' about. She damn sure wadn't dead, and she was screamin' loud enough to wake up the chickens! She grabbed me around the ankles and I couldn't get a shot off before he cleared the fence. Just then, Harry Duff, next door, took a shot at the man running away, but missed him – lost him in the dark. Old lady Hotchkiss yelled a darky was running toward nigger town. Duff here, took off chasin' him with a pistol; but he never caught up with the man. Like I said, he was fast. Seemed like the whole neighborhood was out after this guy. But he just vanished. I don't know who he was – ain't never seen him before."

"Was it Doc Woods?"

"No sir! It kind'a looked like him in the dark. He was small like that, kind of wiry and spindly. Tha boy had some rabbit in him, though. There ain't no way Doc could have moved that fast. Took out of here like a jack and hopped over a fence down at Brady's and was gone!"

"What time was this?"

"Must'a been 'bout three thirty in the mornin'."

"Then what?"

"Well, sir, I took my shotgun and went out back to check on the damage to my property. Sounded like they done tore the whole damn place down. The side winda was completely gone! I went in the front door and there's the other girl, the one named Patsy, sittin' there in a kind of daze – like she wadn't even aware of what was going on. Lucinda was running around in little circles screaming that they were being killed. I seen an ax layin' on the bed. It had blood all over the handle. Over in the kitchen, I saw Orange, lyin' there with his head chopped 'most in two. He was dead for sure. No man can lose that much brains and live. I reckond somebody hit him with that ax –

maybe Gracie. I didn't know. Could be ole Orange came home and found Gracie with this Doc feller, and things went bad. I don't know. But Orange was layin' there with his head split in two, dead as a doornail. I didn't see Gracie nowhere around. I asked Patsy, but it was like talkin' to the wall. She was out of her mind. Whatever she seen, sure messed her up."

"Then what?"

"Old Evers here came over, and said the rascal got away, but his horse was tied up out front. We posted a guard to watch the horse in case the killer came back. Then Evers here saw Orange layin' there, and choked up all over the floor."

"Bill! Damn you! I didn't throw up," Evers interjected from behind the men.

"The hell you didn't!" Dunham guffawed.

"You're a lyin' sack of …" The marshal told them to shut up and tell the story.

"Well, Marshal," Durham drawled, "as I said, we didn't see Gracie nowhere around. But the winda was blown plumb out. Bits of cloth was ripped off, and hanging from the glass. It looked like somebody threw her clean through the winda, then went around and drug her off toward the fence to this Hotchkiss' place. So, me and Evers followed the trail of blood. And that's when we found her on the other side of the fence …," he turned his face away.

Evers picked up the story, as Dunham cleared his throat. "He had, sure 'nuff, throwed her clean through the winda, drug her through the yard, and prob'ly throwed her over a fence too, into the pen out back. It's about 75 yards across to that fence to tha stable, Marshal, and it looked like he drug her all the way. You see her there, Marshal. She's layin' just like that when we found her, 'fore somebody went to fetch you. She was cut up somethin' awful. Her

233

dress was ripped to pieces, and she wasn't wearin' nothing below but that bloody apron hiding her woman parts. Bill covered her up with that feed sack just before you come."

"She wouldn't want to be layin' there like that – exposed," Dunham offered. "Whatever that bastard done to her, she was alive when he done it because you could see where her fingers scratched the ground next to her. She had cuts and scrapes all over her face and backside. It looks like he raped her, then bashed her brains out with that rock there. It was that killer that's been going around rapin' and killin' them negra girls for the past year! How come you ain't locked him up yet?"

The marshal ignored the comment.

"Is that your ax back at the house?"

"No, sir," Dunham shook his head. "it ain't mine. I don't even own a ax. My yard man takes care of that and cuts my wood for me. It ain't his ax neither."

The marshal knelt down next to Gracie, taking care not to get blood on his pants or boots. He closed her eyes with two fingers and looked up at Dunham. "Well, it looks like Gracie and Orange won't be botherin' you folks anymore." The marshal rose and shook his head sadly, as he looked down at the mangled woman.

"You got another feed sack?"

Gone were the boisterous but cheerful party crowds that shopped nightly on Pecan and Congress streets; they were replaced by anxious worried small groups who scuttled from store to store hurriedly completing their shopping before going straight home to lock themselves in their dim houses. Now the public had enough. As word of the double murders swept the neighborhood, the streets filled with colored people, all of them angry. All of them carried guns, knives, or some kind of weapon to protect themselves. Everyone believed the same man was killing black folks, and the police were not even trying to solve the case. The city should do more to keep the town safe. Several families moved out of Austin to other parts of the country. It was mayhem outside the city office. The newspapers were selling faster than ever; most of them carrying bold headlines warning of a murderer stalking the streets of south Austin every night, killing house servants.

The Marshal and most of the city still did not believe in the one killer theory. How could one man have something against all those people? They thought different men were guilty, but the newspapers soon took up the idea of a single killer. They complained of the incompetence of the police and city fathers and wrote that the killer probably lived on the south side around Pecan Street. The city defended its police force and blamed the inability to solve the crimes on the lack of enough policemen to cover the entire city. More men were hired, and the Marshal increased foot patrols along Congress and Pecan Streets every night. But all they ever arrested were more black men who later proved to be innocent. The harsh interrogation methods were cruel. The police did not hesitate to use fear, imprisonment, and physical pain. The beatings would continue until someone confessed. Later, when they discovered the suspect was innocent, they simply released him back to the streets, with no apology or remorse on the part of the police or city.

The story spread all over the country, even as far away as New York City – especially the story of the young girl who was raped. Newspaper reporters from far away roved the streets of Austin each night, hoping to catch a lead. Several of them were staying at the Pearl House. I saw a copy of the Galveston paper someone left in the hotel. "Tragedy in Austin," it said in the headline. "Another one of those horrible murders for which Austin is becoming notorious...." The paper told of how the police tracked down and arrested poor Tom Allen. Austin was getting a bad reputation around the country. The city leaders wanted it stopped.

Because of all of the outside attention and the demands of the public, the police set up a curfew over the city south of the capitol. Anyone caught out between midnight and daylight was arrested and questioned. More police were hired. The local newspaper blasted the incompetent police and city officials daily, and writing such things as "shocking butcheries", while headlines screamed "BLOOD!" in large print. The single killer theory caught on; still, dozens of black men were being brutally arrested and questioned. I knew all along, of course, it was one man, but I could not figure out how to tell without putting myself in jeopardy.

I kept thinking about the saddled horse which was discovered outside the house the night Orange was murdered. Did Mawken have a horse? The owner of the horse, Netherly Overton, was promptly arrested. Mr. Overton said his stepson took the horse to the store in town and hitched it to the rack. When he came out of the store the horse was gone. A lot of people in the neighborhood said he was only released so quickly because he was white. Mr. Overton's stepson was not even questioned. This perceived inequity made the situation even worse.

The police did arrest and question Oliver Townsend and Doc Woods. Doc was wearing a bloody shirt at the time of his arrest. Most of the people in the neighborhood thought Doc and Oliver were guilty because a witness reported he overheard them plotting to kill Gracie. The story spread like fire. The witness also said he heard them plotting earlier to kill Rebecca, the young girl's mother. Frustration and anger swept the city when the two were abruptly released without explanation. The saddled horse had reported stolen hours before the killings, the blood on Doc's shirt was not related to the murder, and the man who reported the plot was discredited. Woods produced an alibi who swore they were together all night. Doc did not mention stopping by Gracie's house that evening before he met up with his friend. At any rate, Doc could prove he was working for a farmer five miles out of town at 4:00 o'clock that morning, just as the murders were occurring. The police did not think it was possible for Doc to walk that far that fast.

Once again, I considered going to the police with my story, until I remember that Orange threatened me just hours before he was killed. That put me in another bad position. What if they thought I was the killer? How would I explain how and why Orange tried to extort money from me?

How could I explain my relationship with Mawken, and why I believed he was guilty? As I read the stories of the brutal killings, I felt I could see them happening in my mind's eye. Even though I was not actually present, I could see the figures move as though through dusty window screens. I could see the broken window. The newspaper printed such clear pictures of the murders that I could see the trails of blood, and the body of poor Gracie lying naked on the ground. I never met her, but I sometimes saw her around shopping for supplies. When I dreamed, her bloody face would stare up at me; and I would awaken horrified and sickened at the sight.

By October, the police admitted the murders were still a mystery and they were at a loss to explain the crimes. In addition to extra police, the city authorized special investigators to track down the killer. One night a man named Aleck Mack was raising cane at a local saloon – he was good at that. He was arrested dozens of times for fighting, theft, and just being drunk and rowdy on the streets. He was the son of Aunt Sallie, a sweet woman everyone loved. Aunt Sallie helped everyone she knew. No one held it against her that her son was one of the biggest troublemakers in the city. Either because the police were tired of dealing with Mack or because maybe they had some evidence to back them up, two policemen, along with two detectives, tracked Aleck down that night to the Black Elephant.

Aleck Mack was not a man to go without a fight. As soon as the policemen came through the door, Aleck recognized them. He did not recognize the two detectives who entered earlier and stood on each side of him at the bar. He watched the two policemen position themselves in the room. By the way they were eyeing him, Aleck sensed he was the target. He did not know what they wanted him for, but he was not going to go down peacefully. Rather than wait for the police to sneak up behind him, Mack decided to press the case. He threw his nearly full beer glass as hard as he could at the nearest policeman. The glass missed the officer but struck a customer standing nearby, knocking him to the floor.

The detectives quickly pinned Mack's hands to his side before he could bring out a gun, and the four men drug Aleck Mack out of the back door into the alley. After beating him nearly senseless, they threw a rope over a nearby limb and placed a heavy noose around Mack's head. One way or another, the police were going to be done with Aleck Mack.

"Why you messin' with me?" Mack pleaded. "I ain't done nothin'!"

"Yeah?" One of the detectives asked, "What about the women you killed, and that little girl you raped?"

Mack spat blood as he denied any knowledge of those horrible crimes. Later, Mack claimed the police made him confess to avoid being hanged. They cut him down and hauled him off to jail. The Marshal denied the reports of misconduct and claimed he had evidence that tied Mack to the murders. If there was evidence, it must have been weak, because nine days later Aleck Mack was released, bloody and bruised, back to the streets of Austin.

It was obvious to everyone the police had no idea of the killer's identity. Every man with a badge had a favorite suspect. All through November, over a dozen more men were arrested in connection with the murders, some of them a second or third time; and all were released within a few hours or a couple of days. The police even arrested poor Walter Spencer again; and this time, the district attorney promised they were going to send him to trial for Mollie's murder. The city was desperate for a solution, and Walter was as good as any.

The news of Walter's arrest did not give the public any relief. Armed men – vigilantes – roamed the streets at night accosting anyone they caught out after dark. A horrible situation became even more dangerous. Doors were barred, and windows were shuttered each night, as people locked themselves inside their homes for safety. Candles and lamps were extinguished early in the evening, or heavy curtains shrouded the windows so no light could be seen from outside. Any unusual event was a cause for panic. As usual, the police were looking for the wrong person. I knew the man they wanted.

By December, Austin was like a smoldering fuse. Terror filled the streets. Even the boldest dreaded going out for fear of being confronted by police, the vigilantes, or even the killer. Christmas was coming, and shopkeepers were complaining no one shopped their stores. The hotel was nearly empty. No one wanted to come to Austin out of fear. I stopped going to market except for two days a week myself. Something must happen soon, or the city would explode.

Christmas Eve was nearly a year since poor Mollie's death, and her killer was still at large. Once again, that night I dreamed I could see Mollie's murder as if I stood there in the dark, watching it happen. In my dream, a shadowy figure knocked poor Walter

239

unconscious with the blunt end of the ax. I could not see who swung, but in my dreams, I knew it was Mawken. Horrified, I watched as he pulled Mollie from the bed. Bright blood streamed from a gaping hole in her head. I could see the naked back of a shirtless man lying on top of her. Suddenly, I realized I could not breathe.

The dream was so real; I felt as though a heavy hand covered my mouth – smothering me. I awoke with a start and struggled, but I could not move! I was pinned helplessly on the bed by strong arms. I realized this was no dream! Someone in the dark was holding me down and suffocating the life out of me!

"Shut up!" Mawken's voice whispered. I immediately knew who it was. He was so close I could feel his breath on my cheek. "What have you done?" he asked. "Have you been talking? Now, we've got to get out of here fast!"

I was still gasping, to the point of passing out, when the hand slid from my mouth. I took huge panting breaths, trying to recover. "If you holler out, I'll cut you, Maurice! I swear to hell I will kill you right here and now."

As frightened as I was, I did not cry out. I knew he would kill me if I resisted.

"What do you mean? I do not have anything to tell anyone," I insisted.

"Well, somebody damn sure knows something!"

He snapped a match in the darkness, and in the light of the flame, I could see Mawken had aged since I saw him last. His eyes were dark and fearful as the smoke from the match curled around his face. He lit the lamp beside the bed and blew out the match.

"Some newspaper man has been hanging around here asking questions about you!"

He pointed directly at me. I slowly swung my legs over the side of the bed and sat up.

"He has already interviewed Ms. Schmidt. That other cook, Beulah, has been blabbing it all over town tonight. It is only a matter of time before they come arrest you – I'm surprised you're not sitting in jail right now!"

It took me a moment to realize the importance of what I heard. Suddenly, I could no longer breathe again. I felt like I might faint.

"They know," he said, looking pitifully down at me.

"How?" I asked.

"You've been talking is my guess," he said.

I had not, but I wondered who else Orange shared his story with before he died. Was someone else in the alley with us that night?

He looked at me with such disgust in his eyes, as though I was a bug or some filthy animal.

"Get dressed!" he ordered. "You're getting out of here tonight. Just take your clothes and whatever money you have and get on the morning train to Houston. Wait for me there."

"You aren't going too?" I asked, feeling stupid and useless.

"They aren't looking for me," he laughed in that cruel way of his that always made me feel so foolish. "They are looking for you! I'll be along in a few days. Get to Houston and lie low. Stay at one of those fleabag hotels along Allen's Landing down on Buffalo Bayou. I'll find you there."

"Why aren't you coming too?" I wearily asked. It made no sense for him to stay behind.

241

"I've got work to do. I will be there in a day or two. You just wait for me; when I come, we'll hire on to the first vessel we can find that will have us."

"What are you going to do?"

"The same thing I always do – clean up your mess!"

I was relieved to understand he was not going to kill me – at least not yet. Surely, the detectives would be closing in on me by morning. Poor Mrs. Schmidt. What would she think of me? I hastily gathered my things; and by daylight, I was riding the rattling passenger train as it rolled toward the big city of Houston. Behind me, in the cold gray dawn, a deeply troubled Austin awoke to more horror. I knew somehow that another murder would be on the books before the sun rose. I wondered who it might be.

I knew by now how up my messes were usually cleaned.

Allen's Landing was located on a point where Buffalo Bayou and White Oak Bayou met. Both bayous were only filthy ditches filled with muddy water. The place did not look like any seaport I ever saw. Someone told me the sea was eighty miles away in Galveston. Every kind of small ship was tied up at the landing. I saw seamen from every part of the world, even a few from Malay. It was an easy place to get lost. Most of the rest of the milling crowd were pickpockets, thieves, or whores – often all three in the same person. Near the docks, I found a dingy room and checked in.

Later, I walked the docks looking for likely ships to use for an escape. It was not going to be hard to find. Ships were leaving daily and were quickly replaced by newly arriving vessels, each disgorging another crew of sea-crazed sailors. At some of the more popular spots, lines of waiting men trailed out of the door and along the streets. It was no secret what they were waiting for. The lines were strictly enforced, and fights broke out when anyone tried to "jump" the line. Anything you wanted could be found at the port: liquor, women, opium, and lots of trouble. Many sailors had to be dragged back to their ships by less drunken shipmates, unwilling to leave their mates behind.

I did not get too close to the boats because every time I did a call of a "Hey! Matey! Lookin' for a berth?" came from the watch decks. Dependable, able-bodied seamen were apparently in short supply despite the huge numbers milling around the streets. Maybe dependable and able-bodied were the characteristics in short supply. Anyway, I was no rookie, and I knew not to get too close. Step on one of those boats and you would wake up in the middle of the ocean. I was not even sure how many of the drunken sailors they dragged aboard were willing – they certainly were not able-bodied. At least not as they were being hauled up the gangplank.

An experienced sailor never signed on to a crew unless he watched the ship come in to dock. You could tell by the attitude of the disembarking crew what kind of a berth it would be. For the price of a beer for those sailors whose thirst outranked their desire, you could learn all you needed to know about the ship and its officers. I did not intend to serve under another abusive and cruel master. They were all cruel, I knew, not all were like my last captain.

I was tempted to sail right away, and I thought hard and long about doing slipping off on one of those ships. Maybe I could accomplish two escapes in one – escape Texas and Mawken at the same time. The more I considered it the less it seemed like a good plan. I knew most of these ships hopped from port to port up the American east coast, and it would be too easy to be overtaken by a faster ship. If Mawken caught me, I believed he would kill me to ensure my silence. If he were going to kill me, he would have killed me in my bed the night before. Since he did not, I supposed he did not intend to murder me – unless I did something to put him at risk.

It was Christmas Eve, but the port did not quiet down as evening approached. No one was Christmas shopping in this town either. Mobs of men in varying degrees of drunkenness were demanding service. I was not tempted by the easy availability of these women – in fact, they disgusted me. I did not like the way they talked, walked, or smelled. I felt finding a mate should be more romantic – cleaner somehow. Like my father and mother – not coupling with some whore in an alley like animals. I saw what indiscriminate relations did to several sailors, and I was determined not to suffer that fate. Besides, I had no desire for those women; so why bother?

I was tempted to take a drink; I thought it might help me sleep. I had not been sleeping well lately. However, I was leery of the traps bar keepers kept for unwary sailors. The bar owners were paid a bounty for enticing men and turning them over to the boat captains. I stayed out of the saloons along the waterfront. You could never be sure what was in those drinks. I did not care much for alcohol anyway, so I satisfied myself with water from a local outdoor café as I ate my meal. It was a clean place, and not crowded because all it offered was food. Food was a commodity not high on the sailor's list. Food they could get later.

After my dinner, I retired to my room to spend Christmas Eve alone. It may have been Christmas, but the town had no respect for the sacred feeling of the holiday – the party raged on through the night. The screams and laughter coming through my windows were not the panicked, horrified screams of my dreams. I leafed through a week's worth of local newspapers and found several articles on the troubles in Austin. I did not find any mention of my name, so I felt a little more at ease. Soon sleep crept up on me, and I drifted off to a restless sleep.

It grew dark on the street, and night sounds of parties and laughter floated on the air and drifted through my open windows. It was a warm night for Christmas, not like the night when Mollie was killed. Poor Mollie. I remembered her smile so well. I felt safe inside my room. In a hazy fog, I dreamed a robber crept into a darkened room and stole a sleeping man's pants. It was neither my room nor my pants. Outside in the hallway, I saw the likeness of a beautiful woman in a long white nightgown. She stood outside her bedroom door in a pool of white moonlight, nearly as bright as day.

In horror, I watched as an arm came from the shadows and grabbed her by the hair, forcing her to the ground. The silhouette of a man came into hazy view as he dragged the woman down a long hallway and outside into the yard, where he bludgeoned her with an ax. The killer was naked. He fractured the woman's skull in two places as blood gushed from both of her ears, matting her hair and staining her white nightgown. I saw the man lay alongside her body for a few moments before he rose, struck her again, and then forced a sharp spike through her ear.

Suddenly, I was running. I realized I was still dreaming, but it felt so real. I could see the bright moon above as I vaulted over the fence into the street. I paused trying to figure out if I anyone followed me. It was a puzzling dream. I did not know why I ran. Was the killer after *me* now? What was I running from? I slowly moved into the moon shadows of a large oak tree and waited for a short time. I felt like the dream was real. I could hear the sounds of alarm coming from behind the house as they discovered the dead woman.

In no hurry now, I calmly walked from beneath the tree and serenely strolled north and east for a few blocks. It seemed to me I was back in Austin again. I recognized the streets. It was as if I knew where I was going, but my conscious mind had no idea. I was still trembling from the horrors I had seen. It was as if I were actually watching that woman be murdered, and unable to stop it. Now, it seemed as if I was moving around as myself. I was baffled. It was as if I was no longer watching – I was doing.

I found myself approaching a darkened house with white shutters. It seemed to me I knew that house, but I had no recollection of the place. I watched myself, appalled, as my hands forced open the back screen door. I quietly stepped up onto the porch. I crossed the wooden decking and tried the door. It was unlocked. Without any hesitation, I entered into a poorly lit kitchen. I saw myself walk calmly down a darkened hall lit by the unnatural moonlight streaming through the windows.

Inside a room, a young man about my age lay on a bed. With one swift swing, I hit the man with the flat of an ax. I had no idea where I got the ax – I had no recollection of bringing it with me or even why I hit him. The young man rolled, unconscious, onto the floor. I looked at the ax. Blood coated the handle, and I recognized it as the same ax used to kill the blonde woman just minutes before. Disgusted, I flung the ax onto the bed and left the room.

The next doorway down the hall opened without resistance, and I eased slowly inside. A beautiful red-haired white woman lay on the bed. She was easily the most beautiful woman I ever saw. She was sleeping with a small child. I shook her awake and held my hand over her mouth so she would not scream. She jumped awake, horrified. I could see the fear in her eyes. In some strange way, it made her appear even more beautiful.

"Quiet. Don't wake the child," I heard myself say. "Don't be afraid. There has been another attack, and a young man of this house has been injured. Come with me and I'll take you. Shussh. Do not wake the child. Leave him here. It is just out back."

"Jimmy? Jimmy is hurt? Is my husband alive?" she cried out in panic.

"He is alive, do not be afraid. Just follow me as quietly as you can."

The woman rose from her bed and obediently followed me down the hall and out the back door. I had no idea where we were going or where I was taking her. I was watching again, but this time I was watching myself with no awareness of being able to control my actions.

"Where? Where is my husband?" she plaintively asked between sobs.

"Just over here. Behind this shed," I beckoned.

The same naked man who murdered the first woman waited in the shadows behind the shed. I turned toward the woman, bewildered. I was as mystified as she was.

"If you scream I will kill you," I heard a rough voice say.

Unashamed, I felt relieved he was not speaking to me. As this horrible scene played out in my dream, I was helplessly watching again as the dark figure knocked the woman to the ground. He pulled up her white nightgown, and twisted it around her neck and drug her further into the darkness. The man raped her before plunging the white-handled knife into her repeatedly. I stood, weak and unable to stop the attack. I wanted to stop it, but I did not know how.

The final time he plunged the blade into her breast, the knife was left standing upright. I watched aghast as he placed lengths of lumber across her body. My eyes were transfixed onto the bloody handle of the knife, which wobbled back and forth on her chest. The knife had a handle carved in the shape of a mermaid. I heard myself scream aloud.

I awoke screaming. I jumped from the cot and looked around, disoriented. I searched through my things and could not find my marlinspike. I could not believe I was still in my room on the Houston waterfront. The dream seemed so real. Outside, in the noisy night, drunks were still carousing and whores were still plying their trade. The screams and loud shouts from outside must have been what I heard in my nightmare. No one was being murdered – not here. There was no bleeding, naked woman at my feet being savaged.

It was all a dream, but a disturbing one even so. Still trembling and badly shaken, I left my room and went to the nearest tavern to get drunk as quickly as possible. I drank until I mercifully passed out into a black void where with no dreams, no murders, and no me.

Harsh daylight streamed through the open window. I tried to open my eyes, but the glare was so intense it was painful, and I shut them tight against the bright sunlight. Beneath my closed eyelids, it seemed the light moved back and forth, as it flickered. My head felt three sizes too big, and I remembered why I did not often drink. I felt like Donny and I had "tied one on," but I remembered Donny was around since that terrible day in Austin. I shielded my head with a pillow and gradually eased my eyes open. I was still dressed.

As my eyes became accustomed to the light, I could see the sun filtered through a tree outside my window. The sun was high in the sky and it was obviously the middle of the day. The leaves fluttered in the sea breeze, and that explained the flickering I saw. I nearly slept through the entire morning. I was so tired lately, and I knew I needed the sleep. I was thankful I passed out and had not dreamed again. I sat on the edge of the bed and looked around the room. I wondered if I had been drugged and robbed but all my things were there, including the marlinspike. I must have misplaced it earlier. I did not recognize it as the room I rented the day before. I wondered where I was. In my drunken state, maybe I could not find my room and rented another in which to sleep.

Rubbing my eyes, I stood and walked out into the street. Nothing was as I remembered it from the day before. The buildings were different – cleaner and better kept. This part of town was much more modern than the run-down village I toured the day before. I decided that in my drunken state, I wandered into a more prosperous part of town. I stopped a man passing by and asked him for directions to the port at Allen's Landing. He looked at me as if I was making some sort of joke.

"Turn around three times, young man, click your heels together twice, and you will be at Allen's Landing."

Thinking he was a local lunatic, I moved further down the street, his cackling laughter in my ears. I had not gone a block before

I saw a sign indicating I was already at Allen's Landing. In fact, I was two blocks over from the wharves. Remembering my original room was near the docks, I walked in that direction. Nothing was as I remembered it. It was as if I were seeing the town for the first time. The buildings, though more run-down and decrepit, were not the same squatty shacks of the day before.

As I walked through the dirty, low part of town along the waterfront, even the docks seemed different and unlike what I saw the day before. There were knots of sailors in the streets, but they behaved better than those before. And, the houses where the women were kept were quieter and more organized. I thought because it was Christmas day things were calmer. As I walked along the piers it seemed even the ships were different from those I remembered earlier.

It was as if someone came in the middle of the night and changed everything around. I searched and searched in vain for the hotel room I rented the previous day. Sailors were still drinking in the bars, but they were less boisterous. Gone were the rowdy mobs and the rampant orgy of sights and sounds I saw before. I did not encounter even one drunken sailor on the street. No one hailed me from the ships; and if there were opium dens, I did not see them.

I saw a hotel where I thought I rented my first room. However, the people at the desk were different and did not recognize me. I rented the same room. I flipped the book to the signature page for the day before, could not find my name. Maybe I was mistaken.

I obtained some bread from a bakery nearby and a long tube of summer sausage from a street vendor and went upstairs to the room to wait for Mawken. For some reason, I still felt incredibly tired, as though I had not slept at all the night before. It did not take long for me to drop off to sleep.

I have no idea how long I napped, but I could tell from the light it was late afternoon. I was not alone. I had not heard Mawken come in. He sat in a chair facing the bed. The partially eaten sausage and bread were lying on the table next to the chair.

Even in the light of day, he looked much older than I remembered. There was no trace of joy or pleasure in his face or his eyes. He was no longer angry or threatening toward me, but he seemed harder and less warm than I remembered. He told me we would be leaving at dawn on a new ship trading along the coast. We would sail on the *Willow* at midnight; it would be bound for points east. There was no question or indication I had any recourse but to follow his plan. It was as if he made the decisions, and I meekly followed. What kind of man was I? I felt I had no will or any life of my own. I may have been meek, but I needed some answers.

"Was it you?" I asked, despite my fears.

"Was what me?" He rose from the chair and moved to the window as if to look outside.

"Was it you who killed those women ... Mollie ... Did you murder my friend Mollie?"

"Who is Mollie?" he said nonchalantly, still looking out the window.

"My friend ... my good friend. All those women who were killed in Austin, are you the killer?"

He did not answer. I was calm until I remembered Donny. I realized he might turn on me in anger, but I did not care any longer. Mollie was dead, and Donny was gone. I needed to know the truth. He did not answer. I lost my temper.

"Why did you try to kill Donny?" I accused him.

When he spoke his voice was calm, but he did not turn away from the window to look at me. I only see the back of his head while he spoke. "I do not know anyone named Donny. I did not kill anyone in Austin."

I knew he was lying – there was the knife! "I found your knife stuck in the back of Donny's door the morning he left claiming someone tried to kill him."

"His name was Donny?" he asked innocently.

"Yes. Donny. Why did you try to kill him?"

He turned to look at me with the most tortured look on his face.

"Maurice, I did not try to kill Donny or anyone else for that matter."

"But it was your knife. I kept it for several months – until it disappeared again."

"Yes, I came into your room when you were not there to take the knife away. You were cutting yourself with it, and I feared you would do yourself harm. I did not try to kill your friends. I lost the knife in a bar the day before your cowboy friend came to town. I suppose someone found it and used it to attack him, but it was not me."

He seemed so sincere, yet I was unsure if I could believe him or not.

"All I have done is try to protect you. I have not killed anyone, but I have worked to keep you safe."

"By killing Mollie?"

"Mollie was killed by her jealous husband," he assured me in convincing tones.

"And the others…?"

He laughed at me in a way that made me feel so insignificant. He walked across the room to stand in front of me.

"No, Maurice. I killed no one. That town has figured out a way to get rid of its undesirables. A stranger, haunting the streets at night and killing innocent women makes a perfect villain to blame for an unexpected death in the family. After all, you believed it."

He sounded so reasonable I could almost believe him. I was not going to fall for his excuses again. I was so confused. I wanted to believe him. Still, I was unsure.

"What about Eliza? The woman who pushed me into the street?"

He went back to the window and stood, staring out at the street.

"Maurice," he said patiently, "do you suppose I have nothing to do but hang about solving your little problems and killing people for you? You kicked me out, remember?"

He turned and sat back in the chair as if annoyed, unable to hide the hurt in his eyes.

"You sent me on my way without a concern for me. So, I went my own way and found a life for myself that did not include you. Yes, I checked on you from time to time – as any true friend would do. But no, I did not kill anyone for you or because of you. I heard of the horrible murders in Austin, and rather than let you take the blame, I had to get you out of there. Just in time too, from what I heard. You were about to be arrested and hung, Maurice."

I thought my dream recent dream. "What of last night? I saw you kill that woman. You made me go inside and bring her out to you. I watched as you drove a sharp spike through her head. I saw you."

With an astonished look on his face, he got out of the chair and clutched the edge of the table. His eyes grew wide and excited.

"Tell me exactly what you saw," he implored.

As I described what I remembered, the more farfetched it seemed, even to me. I could no longer tell what was real or what was a dream. I admitted my uncertainty. When I finished, he rose and walked around the room, stroking his chin, and thinking. He stared out of the window for a long time before he turned back to me.

"Maurice, I think your dreams have been stolen by *Baku*. The woman you saw killed must have been a *Pontianak*."

Along the coast of Mergui south to Singapore, they tell the night tales of witches and monsters that roam the dark, searching for victims. More than just stories, many of my people believe them to be real. I knew many people who had been haunted by such demons – even my own father told me stories of how *Baku* stole his own dreams when he was a boy. *Baku* was a spirit known as the dream eater. It devours the dreams and nightmares of the believer and protects him from evil. *Baku* is a shape shifter who has many forms, and carries his dreamer aloft on his nightly pursuits of the evil *Pontianak*.

The *Pontianak* is a demon, as I well knew. She often appears as a beautiful woman. She also has many forms and shapes, which is why I probably did not recognize her. She can be horrible and witch-like, or she can take on the form of a beautiful woman – like the one I saw in my dream. *Pontianaks* are mainly vicious spirits of women who died in childbirth, and who have come back from the grave to have vengeance on men. I do not know why it did not occur to me at

254

the time, except that the *Baku* was in control of my thoughts; but the only way to defeat a *Pontianak* is to drive a sharp spike or nail into her head. This does not kill the demon or the woman; but once done, it makes the possessed woman an obedient, good wife so long as the nail is in place.

"What of the little girl? The little girl who was killed and brutalized."

"Maurice," he sounded annoyed, "surely have not forgotten the *Tianak*."

Yes, I knew of *Tianak* – the vampire child of *Pontianak*. A vampire, in the form of a child, who deceives with its plaintive infant-like wails and then sucks the blood from those who come to rescue the child. I had been gone so long from my home the stories and legends almost forgot them.

Now, I remembered them all. I recalled the stories of the dark man – the *Orang Minyak* – the "Oily Man" who appears in the night to rape and kill the evil *Pontianak*. His form was of a small, dark man who often did his deeds in the nude. He was a spirit – a *Hantu* – who did the bidding of his master *Baku*. The Oily Man was the assassin I saw in my dream. Once I remembered these legends, I realized I was under the spell of *Baku* who made me watch those awful things. It made sense now. I looked at Mawken with guilt and shame, as I understood at last the source of the fantasies that poisoned my relationship with my only true friend.

Only one thing still bothered me.

"What of your knife you left in the chest of the dead woman?" I asked Him.

He withdrew his knife and waved it at me. "This knife?" he asked, slicing off a piece of summer sausage.

Aboard the *Willow,* we maneuvered through the dirty waters of Buffalo Bayou and passed through the narrow passage at Galveston. From the deck, I could see the lantern on the dock of the ferry landing where I met Donny. Across the channel, I could see the flash from the lighthouse. I wondered about Ben and if he still remembered me. I wished I could have lived with him forever, and Mawken and Sticks had not survived the shipwreck.

I was the new cook on this vessel and had a small cubby off the main kitchen. I was not required to serve or clean, as the crew included a mess steward and his assistant. The mess steward and boy were berthed below decks. Mawken worked in the bowels of the freighter somewhere. Although it was against the rules, on long, lonely nights he would quietly join me in my bunk in the little alcove attached to the kitchen. He behaved and kept his hands to himself, and I must admit it was nice to have some company those first lonely nights. Mawken always left before I woke to begin my duties. We established a pattern, which would last, throughout our passage on the ship. Mawken soon grew weary of my constant questions and, finally, refused to talk about Austin or anything in the past at all.

I dreaded going to sleep at all for fear *Baku* would take me again. For three nights at sea, I had peaceful sleep with no dreams. I soon learned *Baku* only came on those nights were in port.

We reached the Mississippi and sailed upstream to the Port of New Orleans, where we off-loaded our cargo and took on something else bound for further up the eastern coast. I did not know, nor did I have any interest in what our cargo was. Most of the crew went ashore for the two days we lay in the port. Mawken went ashore on his own and did not invite me to go along. I suppose he went with his new friends on the crew.

It was a muddy, filthy place, which held no interest to me at all. I went ashore alone the first day, intending to return to sleep on board rather than bother with the nightlife along the docks. I ate a nice meal at a nearby café and gathered up the local newspapers to take back to the ship.

With no duties to perform since the crew was not aboard, I planned to have a relaxing evening on my own. I sat on the deck in the fading light and unfolded my newspapers. I read with great interest the incredible murders that happened in Austin just a few days earlier on Christmas Eve. Not servant girls this time, the victims were well-known white women in one of the wealthiest neighborhoods in Austin. Most of the residents felt safe there because all of the murders happened in the south part of town. I could not help but think Mawken was right – people of Austin figured out how to get rid of their undesirables by blaming it on a killer who stalked the night. These murders did not fit the mold of those earlier killings.

The newspaper reported Susan Hancock and her husband, Moses, slept while the couple's older children went out to a party. Moses left the doors unlocked for their return. He awoke in the night woke with the feeling something was not right. He felt around for his clothes and discovered his pants were missing. The couple no longer slept together because Moses suffered from loud snoring; or rather, his wife suffered while Moses snored and slept throughout the night. Sensing something was amiss, he went to his wife's bedchamber. Finding it empty, he was greatly concerned. He went to the back door to see if maybe the young folks had returned and Susan was outside in the unseasonably warm evening, quietly visiting with them on the veranda. Maybe she had taken his pants to put in the wash.

In the bright moonlight, he saw a white mound of something lying on the grass. He stepped through the door and slipped on a slippery pool. He fell to his knees trying to catch himself from falling headlong. As he brought his hands up to his face, he was shocked to see them covered in blood. It was not his blood. He rose and ran to the white mound to discover the white-clad body of his injured wife. She was still alive but moaning in pain. Shocked, he picked his wife up and carried her back to the house, yelling loud enough to rouse his neighbor who came to help carry Susan into the parlor. He summoned the doctor, who quickly pronounced her dead. She had a fatal skull fracture, and she was bleeding from her ears.

The police came, and Moses reported it as a robbery. His pants still missing and the neighbor reported seeing two men jump the fence in the back when Moses first came outside. Poor Susan must have heard something and tried to stop them before they brutally killed her.

Before the bloodhounds could strike a trail, more horrified screams filled the early morning air. The police quickly responded and found another murder at the Phillips house a few blocks north.

The elder, James Phillips shared the house with his son Jimmy, and Jimmy's wife Eula. The household awoke before dawn by the shouts of Jimmy calling for his father. Someone had struck Jimmy with a heavy object he thought was an ax. He suffered from a huge bump on his head but lost surprisingly little blood. The ax obviously hit him broadside, or it would have cut him badly. In addition, a bloody ax was found on his bed. The ax was dripping in blood. Since Jimmy barely bled at all, it was obviously not his blood.

Eula had not appeared despite the racket the two men were making in the hallway. Panicked, they ran to the room where Eula slept with her small son. They found the child sitting up in the bed crying softly, but unharmed. Eula was not in the room. Bloody footprints of a barefoot man led down the hallway toward the back door. They found Eula behind a shed by the back fence. She was naked, her nightgown twisted around her neck, and pieces of lumber were stacked across her chest. It appeared the killer used the wood to help hold her down. Her hands were outstretched, and the elder James could not help but compare her appearance to the likeness of the crucified Christ. Blood pooled around her head as she bled from both ears.

I realized how similar these murders sounded to my dream: two murders within a few blocks of each other; the man's pants stolen, and his wife found bludgeoned, raped, and dying. Even the name "Jimmy" sounded familiar. Another woman, sleeping with a small child and taken outside behind a shed where she was brutally raped and killed. The child was left alone and uninjured. I was sickened as I read the final paragraph. A sharp metal object was thrust into the ears of his victims. I trembled as my skin crawled. I knew the reason. I had *seen* the murders in my dream. The *Baku* showed me. That was how you killed a *Pontianak*. The newspaper reported the killer was a "Negro affected by idleness and drink."

Sickened, I burned the papers so no one else could see them and read about what happened in Austin the night after I left. I do not know why the *Baku* took me to see the death of two *pontianaks* – but surely, he had. There were too many similarities for it to be a coincidence. I did not know either woman. I had no reason to be in that proper neighborhood. The spirit world held many mysteries that could not be explained.

Suddenly, I remembered something I had forgotten. I recalled our stop back in Port Royal; and I remembered Aida Wedo, the *Penanggalan* who came aboard to warn us of the coming storm. She had looked me directly in the eye! She infected me with the *Baku*; I was sure of it! That was why she stared so intensely at me. She summoned the spirit world for *Baku* to take me and punish me because of my unfaithfulness. I remembered shivering under her gaze as she opened the doors of my eyes and entered my mind. She intended to kill me if she could – I could feel it. There were too many others around for her to do her evil at the time, so she had put the *Baku* in me instead – and no telling what else. It was clear all of my troubles directly tied to the *Penanggalan* in Port Royal.

It made sense now. I could not wait to tell Maurice when he returned. Maybe there was a way to expel this evil spirit infecting my mind.

The night wore on; as I sat alone on the empty ship, rocking with the waves that slapped against the solid wharf, I gradually fell asleep. After three peaceful nights, the *Baku* chose this night to torture me once more. He swept me up on wings that neither flapped nor fluttered; and together, we glided past the wharves deep into the darkened city. *Baku* took me to the low places where filth and depravity were normal and accepted. What better place for the *Pontianak* do her treacherous deeds?

She lurked in the streets singing her song: *Come with me, and you shall have all you want or desire. It is just here behind this wall, my dear.* She beckoned and lured the unsuspecting sailor to places even darker. And, he went – oh, yes! He went like a sheep to the slaughter. He willingly followed the lure of pleasure as he eagerly descended deeper into depravity. The promise of what she would provide was far more powerful than his fear of the unknown. The alley was lit only by a pale, dry moon now in its waning stages. There was barely enough light to see the small passageway through the wall at the end of the alley. It was a narrow, arched passage with no door – just an opening. He followed, helpless against the powers of lust and desire that drew him onward. Once, in his impatience, he clutched at the woman; but she dodged and assured him he would have all he desired when they were in a safe place – just a few steps more.

He followed her. Like a lamb, he followed. She passed through the arched passage before him; and when he emerged on the other side, she was not there.

Her accomplices were there, and they immediately pounced on him like dogs. *Baku* made me watch from atop the wall as the victim was viciously mauled. The drunken sailor reeled from the blows and fell back against the wall, bleeding from his face. The thieves quickly relieved the old sailor of everything of value he owned and left him bloody and bruised against the wall. The assailants disappeared at the end of the alley, leaving the broken man alone but alive. Slowly, he pulled himself to his feet and tested his legs. He could walk, but just barely. He hobbled back through the arched passage and gradually made his way back to his ship.

He was a broken, disheartened man. He felt himself the fool to have fallen for such an obvious ruse. He not only had to deal with the guilt and shame of his desires and his weakness to resist the temptations, now he must deal with the indignity and humiliation of having been taken advantage of. The worst part was not the treachery of his potential temporary lover or the loss of the money – he was going to give both up willingly in a few hours anyway. The worst of it was the loss of his dignity. He felt crushed – a sucker – a living joke with no friends – somehow less a man without even enough money to ease his shame in drunkenness. Without a backward look, he slowly hobbled up the gangway back onto his ship like a whipped dog.

The assailants quickly ducked into another alley and confidently walked among the trash buckets and stray cats to a red doorway where they knocked. In a few moments, the door opened and she came into the alley with them. She, with the bait, led many to their doom, smiled as though she had done something good. The *Pontianak,* with her charms and deceptive beauty, laughed with the men as they sat together on upturned buckets while the *Baku* and I watched from the dark shadows.

"Did ya' kill him?" she asked, even though she did not care one way or the other.

"Nah," one grunted, "Didn't have'ta. He gave it up easy enough."

"What did we get?"

261

One thief drew a wad of his pocket along with some jingling coins and metal objects. He dropped a penny and reached to pick it up, but she covered the coin with her foot. He shrugged and held the remainder out in one palm, as he fished through the objects, carelessly discarding the worthless items.

"Four dollars, six bits, a few pennies, a jackknife, and a key," he reported. He flipped the key over his head onto the cobbled pavement. The key, useless to all but one, dinged, and bounced, and disappeared into the darkness.

"That's a dollar and two bits for you," he said, as he tossed the money into her lap. "That's more than you'd'ave made lyin' on yer back," he laughed.

"Are we goin' for another?" she asked.

The thieves looked at the other in silence for a few moments before they broke into snickering laughter at the ridiculous question. They rose from their buckets and gallantly swung their arms toward the street at the end of the alley.

"Madam, after you," they said in imitation of proper gentlemen.

Later, she stood alone in her favorite alley as she waited for the next sucker to come along. It did not take long. A dark, small man entered the alley. From the glow of the streetlight, he looked strangely familiar; but he quickly passed into the darkness as he neared the temptress. He leaned closer to her and whispered something I could not hear. She pulled back, repulsed, but was still not willing to give up the fish she had caught.

Come with me, and you shall have all you want or desire. It is just here behind this wall, my dear.

He followed toward the treacherous arched passageway. Again, *Baku* made me watch from atop a wall. As the *Pontianak* passed through, she gasped in disbelief. Her accomplices apparently fell asleep against the wall on the other side. She kicked at one in disgust.

"Wake up, ya stupid idiots! Ya've ruined this take, and scared the mark away!"

The robbers did not rouse. She jostled one sleeping thief with her shoe as he slumped farther down the wall. She jumped back, mouth agape, as his head tumbled from his shoulders onto his lap and lay looking up at her upside-down. Her eyes shifted to the other thief slumped beside him. He sat with a grisly grin, as his vacant eyes stared into hers, blood draining down the front of his shirt from the wide gash in his throat. She screamed and turned back toward the archway, intending to run. There stood the mark she intended to rob – the dark man she lured into the snare that had now become her own trap. I knew him as the *Orang Minyak*, the Oily Man. He stood before her, naked and unafraid. His clothes were in a neat pile, stacked beneath a short ax. She stood paralyzed as a black arm reached out for her from the darkness. Her terrified eyes fixed on his other hand, which held a sharp marlinspike.

Another *Pontianak* would meet her doom.

As the ship pulled away from the New Orleans docks, I could not dismiss the dream or its meaning. I could not wait to tell Mawken what I saw in my dream and what I thought it meant. I had no doubt the morning papers carried an account of a murdered prostitute and two thieves in the alleys of New Orleans.

Later that night at sea, he came to my kitchen nook. I told him everything I remembered of the dream. He seemed unconvinced and said it was a scene that was played out nightly in almost every port city around the world. Prostitutes were known to lure their marks into a trap for their accomplices to rob. This time, he laughed, it sounded like they got their just reward for a life of treachery.

"Still," he mused, "I am unsure how you were able to see it so clearly. Surely, the *Baku* has you under his wings; but how did you get infected?"

I reminded him of Aida Wedo at Port Royal – how she came on board the ship while he was gone and gave me the eye as she warned of the coming storm. Almost immediately, he confirmed my theory.

"*Penanggalan*," we said in unison.

It was clear the only way to free myself from this curse was to go back to Port Royal and confront Aida Wedo. I hoped I could convince her to take back the *Baku*. Who knew how long it might take? My dreams would continue to be stolen and used by the *Baku* until he could be banished from my mind.

It all made sense now. Aida Wedo, the *Penanggalan*, infected me with *Baku* – the Dream Thief. It was well known that *Baku* was the slave of the great *Hantu* who ordered him to find and exterminate the *Pontianak*. *Baku* would steal my dreams to ride with me through the night in search of his quest, with me as an unwilling passenger. *Baku* chased me in my dreams through the streets of

Austin and who forced me to witness the brutal killings that horrified and disgusted me. He killed them just as a *Pontianak* would be killed, with a spike through the head. I was ashamed and I felt guilty for thinking Mawken was the killer. It was clear that Mawken only protected me from harm as he had done since the days of our youth on Kadan Kyun. I was such a fool to suspect the only friend I had, and the only one to watch over me.

If anyone could help me escape the curse of *Baku*, it was Aida Wedo. I would find some way to travel to Port Royal and force the *Penanggalan*, Aida Wedo, to release me from this evil spell. I knew it would not be easy – she might be dangerous. Aida Wedo would kill me if she could. I knew I could count on Mawken to help me. Unfortunately, it might take years for us to find our way to Port Royal on a ship. But we would try even if it meant we must change ships a few times.

As we traveled from port to port along the coast of America, evil, horrible dreams haunted my nights. At every port, a new dream would reveal the extermination of another new *Pontianak,* with me an unwilling eyewitness. At every port, we searched in vain for a ship that might take us back to Port Royal. Strangely enough, at sea, my nights were peaceful and undisturbed. I grew to hate going into port, knowing what the night would bring.

I would try to remain awake as long as possible; but eventually, sleep would overcome me and I would dream I was walking or sometimes floating in some new place I had never seen. Invariably, I would find myself focused on a woman, usually a woman of the night. Finally, the end would come at the hands of the dark, oily man, *Orang Minyak*, who would assassinate the *Pontianak* with his rod that looked oddly like a marlinspike. I did not need to go ashore; I went ashore each night regardless.

We worked our way as far as New York City before we turned back south toward the Bahamas. In each fresh harbor, a new

Pontianak was found and destroyed. I went ashore in none of those towns, yet I knew the slums around those ports as well as I would know my home village. I realized the killings were for the best; the victims were evil and unworthy of life. The *Pontianak* were similar to the vampires the European cultures revile. Like vampires, they also traveled about sucking the blood from helpless victims. The way to kill a vampire was to drive a wooden stake through its heart. That was not much different than driving a spike through a *Pontianak's* head. The difference is that while a vampire does his evil act to survive, the *Pontianak* does her evil deeds for revenge. To make things worse the revenge is extracted from the innocent.

Finally, after more than a year, we learned we would be heading on a course to the islands of the Antilles, including Port Royal. After all the waiting, at last, I was to have an opportunity to meet Aida Wedo again. The thought filled me with fear and apprehension. What would I do? How would I convince her to free me from the *Baku*? What would happen if she refused? What if Aida Wedo tried to kill me? I consulted with Mawken on these questions and we agreed we would approach her together. Maybe together we could offer her a tribute to try to convince her to extract the *Baku* from my mind. "If not," he said ominously, "we will have to try more extreme measures." I shivered at these words, not knowing what might come of Aida's refusal. Did he mean we would try to kill her?

Port Royal was exactly as I remembered it from my first visit. It was as if time stopped for them. Even the workers on the dock appeared to be the same. Again, the royal coach appeared and swept the finely dressed captain off to some official reception. I waited, but Mawken did not appear. When he did not appear in an hour, I went down the gangplank alone.

We were only to be in port for a short time, and I did not want to miss my chance. I did not know if he went ashore ahead of me to find and face Aida Wedo alone, or if he had a change of heart and decided to leave me to do my dreaded task alone. Either way, I only had a short time to find the *Penanggalan* and be freed from this awful curse. I entered the first saloon I came to on the damp and moldy dock. It was named the Ugly Stump, and the sign featured a one-armed man with a bloody, ragged stump for an arm.

Once my eyes adjusted to the dark, I saw the same one-armed man behind the bar serving up drinks. He served well despite only having one arm. It did not seem to bother him. The stump was covered by a leather cup that covered the ugly, ragged tear depicted on the sign. I ordered a beer and looked around the dark tavern to see if Aida Wedo was present. She was not in sight. I sat, sipping my drink, trying to decide if I should go to another place or if I should ask outright for Aida. I decided not to do either. I would wait for a short while to see what would happen. If she did not come by, at least maybe Mawken would catch up with me.

After a time, I gave up on that idea. It was then another idea occurred to me. Sailors are notoriously superstitious and believed they suffered from all sorts of fears, curses, and spells. I decided it would be safe to ask if anyone knew of a local *curandero* they might recommend.

"A *curandero*?" he asked as he looked at me oddly. "What'ja' need one of dem fo'?"

I immediately decided the truth was not a safe path. I thought quickly.

"I have been wondering about my future – uh, if I will be married or have children, and when," I lied.

"Yeah?" He backed away and eyed me with renewed suspicion. It did not seem he believed my story. "Well, we gots plenty of dem aroun' dis place, dat for sho'. Won't be hard ta find one out dere," he said, pointing to the door.

A half-drunken sailor sitting down the bar chimed in. "I know one. A good 'un too. Lives about a mile from here – and a good looker to boot," he smiled a toothy grin.

I brightened at the possibility. "What is her name?"

"What difference do it make?" he asked. Several men in the bar laughed out loud. It was clear others were listening to my conversation.

I lowered my voice and leaned closer to him. "Is it Aida Wedo?" I realized my mistake almost immediately.

"Whut you know about Aida Wedo?" the bartender roughly demanded.

"I … I don't know," I stammered. "I heard the name. That's all."

"Ya heard the name, did ya? Well, dat's nice." His attitude belied his words. He did not seem nice at all.

Suddenly, he became more intimate as he leaned closer to me and spoke in a whisper, "Why di'nt ya say so in the furst place? I knows Aida Wedo – Hell! Everybody know Aida Wedo. She ain't da one dis sot is talkin' about though."

"Can you tell me how to find her?"

He motioned me over to a corner of the bar, where no one sat. "I can tell ya' how to find'er. I'll even draw ya' a map!"

He checked around the tavern to make sure no one was listening, and reached for a pencil and paper and sketched out the streets and alleys around the docks. He drew out a curious, circuitous path to a box he labeled "Aida Wedo's hut." I noticed the course he laid out was not a direct route; but rather, it wound around and through several small streets and back alleys.

When he placed the roughly drawn map before me, I traced my finger across it and asked, "Why don't I just go this way?"

He snatched the map back and eyed me harshly.

"You know dis town? You been here afo'?"

"Only once, a few years ago – but I stayed on the ship."

He slowly slid the map back towards me, eying me closely.

"Din you listen to me, boy. Dis ain't no safe place," he said, looking all around the tavern again. "Deys peoples on dis island that robs and kills boys like you who come off dem ships. You go de way I said, and you be OK. You wander off an' you might not get back to sail away."

I took his word and thanked him for the advice. I made my way back into the sun along the street and studied the map. After a few wrong turns due to errors in the map, I finally found my way to Aida Wedo's hut, a run-down little wooden structure that appeared to be supported by the vines that grew completely over the roof. The leaves were trimmed away around a rough plank door with no handle. There were no windows or any markings on the house to indicate who might live there. Had it not been for the map, I would never have found the place.

An iron gate was ajar on the street that opened onto a rock path leading to the unpainted door. I slowly entered the gate and walked down the path. No porch fronted the house; the threshold was just a small rise nearly even with the ground. The entire house kind of listed to one side like it might topple over. I stepped up to the door and knocked three times. There was no answer. After a suitable time, I knocked again.

"Who dat?" came from behind the door.

"My name is Maurice. I am looking for Aida Wedo. Do I have the right place?" I asked through the closed door.

Slowly the door swung open from inside. No one invited me to enter. I could hear no other sound other than the door swinging on rusty hinges. It was dark beyond the doorway, as dark as the saloon I just left. No one told me to come in or addressed me in any way. There was only an open door, an open invitation. I was afraid, but there was no other way, so in my desperation, I stepped through the darkened portal.

Immediately, a heavy canvas bag descended from somewhere above my head and trapped me inside. It was quickly cinched tight around my waist, trapping my arms and upper body inside the bag. I could see nothing from inside the bag and could not swing my arms to defend myself. The bag smelled of old canvas, and some kind of earthy plant I could not recognize. I could breathe, but it was obvious I was now at the mercy of whoever trapped me in the bag. I heard the door slam shut behind me, and I knew for better or worse I was now in the clutches of the *Penanggalan*.

The sweet odor of some pleasant fragrance overwhelmed me, and I felt my knees grow weak. I felt lifted and carried forth in strong arms, just as I passed into a deep paralyzing sleep. I no longer cared if it was good or bad – it was a black sleep with no dreams.

I do not recall waking up so much, as simply becoming aware I was awake. I was still in the canvas bag, lying on my back on a hard surface, which I assumed to be the floor. I was grateful to be alive. I had no idea how long I was out – in the dark void of the bag, there was no way of telling. It could have been an hour or a day. I did not seem to be injured in any way. It was not cold, and I did not seem to have any difficulty breathing. Whatever she used to dope me did not leave any grogginess or a headache. I simply went to sleep and woke up in much the same condition as I was when I lost consciousness.

I heard no voices or anything moving in the room where I lay. I tried to move my feet and discovered they were tied. I could lift them slightly and could move them side-to-side, but I could not move them apart. Something hard prodded through the bag; and someone mumbled, "He be 'wake now."

I heard a rope slide through a cranky pulley and felt my feet lifted from the ground. I was being hoisted upside down. When I was fully hanging, with no way to give myself any support, I felt the cinch around my waist loosen. The canvas bag slowly slid downwards over my body, until it came to rest on the floor with my head and upper body still inside. I could look at my feet and see the opening of the bag with my legs sticking through. The effect of the drug began to wear away, and I could feel fear. I realized I a helpless prisoner hung upside down. The blood rushed to my head, and I felt dizzy. Were these the robbers Stump warned of, or was I in the clutches of the *Penanggalan*? I hoped it was the robbers. I was not sure, but either way, it was an unsettling feeling as I hung up like meat about to be butchered.

I felt my feet pulled part, as the ropes again squeaked through system pulleys. My shirt slid up around my neck as I hung upside down in a spread-eagle position. Slowly the heavy bag collapsed of its own weight and slid onto the floor exposing my head.

271

I could finally see I was in a room lit by only a few candles. I could raise my head a little and peer between my legs but I saw no one. Lowering my head back toward the floor, I looked around at what I could see of the room from my upside-down position. I could not see anyone operating the ropes, which disappeared into the dark rafters above. My hands were unbound, but I could reach nothing as they rested upon the floor. I could see a bed covered in a patchwork quilt. A table with a flickering candle on top sat next to the bed, along with a cane-backed chair. I looked up and saw my head was only a foot above the floor. The ropes binding my feet passed through the rusty red pulleys I heard squeaking earlier. My shoes were gone, and my bare feet extended into the darkness above the rafters.

I trembled in fear, realizing I was helpless. Any moment I expected someone to come forth to slit my throat. I raised my head again and peered once more between my legs. All I could see was the far, rough-planked wall on the other end of the room. There was no one else in the room. It appeared I left alone to hang in a room – for how long I did not know. Meanwhile, blood pooled in my head; and I felt like I was going to pass out again. I wished I had waited for Mawken. I was convinced this time there would be no rescue.

I heard a door open and felt a breeze sweep across my back before the door closed shut again. I summoned up the strength to raise my head again and I saw Aida Wedo scrutinizing me closely from between my legs.

She was dressed much as I remembered her from our last meeting, except she looked thinner – more drawn in the face. She still wore a flowing dress of many colors over a pure white blouse cut low over her breasts and exposed her shoulders. She had long, dangling earrings extending to her shoulders. A white scarf wound around her head like a turban held together with some sort of jewel. On one side, her gray hair was braided and was laced with colored beads, while the other side was covered by the scarf.

She no longer had the fat jowls I remembered; now her face appeared to be bony and angular rather than round and happy. Her face was still overly large – fully twice the size of mine. Her cheekbones were high and very pronounced; and she was smoking an absurdly large cigar, which was fully as long as my forearm, though not as thick. The smile lines on her cheek curled up perfectly to a crease ran down the side of her nose almost to the tip. I could see a jewel that glittered in the flickering light embedded into her nose.

She looked different, but it was Aido Wedo. There was no mistaking her eyes – the eyes bored as though they could see right through me. Her left eye was slightly slanted under heavy eyelids that sat at a different tilt than the other eye, giving her face a strange uneven look. Her dark pupils lay in a pool of creamy milk-colored whites. I would have recognized her anywhere.

She blew a puff of sweet smelling smoke from her cigar and motioned someone with a gesture of her bony hand. I heard the squeaking of the pulley as they lowered me onto my back with my legs still spread and raised. I was grateful for the relief; it was a more comfortable position even though I was still fully restrained and helpless. She looked at me from between my still suspended legs.

"Why you come to kill Aida Wedo?" she asked.

I was astounded. "I have not come to harm you," I protested. "I only came to have my fortune read," I claimed.

"You lie," she assured me as she expelled another long plume of blue smoke.

"My good lady, I have not come to harm you. I swear." I insisted.

"Dat may be true, but you don' come to have no fortune read; dat's for sho'" Suddenly her eyes widened and her mouth opened to form a perfect lipped circle. "I knows you, chile! I knows

273

you for sho'," she gleefully pointed at me as she triumphantly drew another puff of her huge cigar. From inside a cloud of blue smoke, she nodded and said, "You dat boy from de ship two-tree years ago. Da one what was lost in de storm! I knows you."

"Yes," I admitted. "I was on that ship. I have seen you before. We were lost in the storm just as you foretold. That is why I came to seek you out – not to harm you. I need your help. Please."

She blew another cloud of thick smoke and eyed me carefully, "You power is strong. Stronger den me, mebbe. You survive de storm. I got no way to help you, boy." She turned to walk away.

What power did she think I had strung up like an animal? I had no power.

"Wait, please. Aida Wedo, do not leave yet. Please let me up, and let me talk to you. I said I need your help. Have mercy on me, please," I pleaded.

"I let you go, you be good boy?" she asked. "You don' fight Aida Wedo?"

"I promise. I just need you to help me."

She looked at me through the smoke for a long time before she snapped her fingers. My legs were lowered to the floor.

"Untie youself and come wid me," she said, pointing at a door in the wall behind her. She turned without looking back at me, opened the door, went inside, and closed it behind her.

I gratefully realized I was not going to be butchered. I released my feet from the ropes and stood on wobbly legs for a moment. It was a relief not to be restrained. My feet were asleep from being held upside down for so long, but gradually they came alive and I walked toward the wooden door. I was hesitant to open the door, remembering what happened to me last time I went through an unknown doorway; but I reasoned if she were going to tie me up again she would not have let me go in the first place. I opened the door and stepped inside.

Aida Wedo sat behind a small table that held a large glass globe. The table was draped in a purple cloth that sparkled in the flickering candlelight as though it was wet. On each side of the table and slightly behind her stood two of the largest men I ever saw. They were black and naked to the waist, their muscled arms glistening in the dim light. They wore white, sailcloth pants cut short, and no shoes. Each held a knife like a machete with a sharpened hook on the end. The edge of the blade caught the light and reflected against the walls. I was envious of those blades and could not help but wish for one.

Aida Wedo stubbed out her cigar and left it smoldering in a tray across the room. Now that she was no longer smoking it, the cigar stunk of a rank pungent odor. The black men neither moved nor spoke. Aida Wedo sat in her chair behind the table, her hands folded on the surface. She did not speak or move but watched me with careful eyes. I looked around the dim room. Hanging from the rafters were bones of some animals I could not identify. A large human-sized, grass-filled doll with a painted face dressed in a shirt and pants stood in the corner with a knife protruding from its chest. What looked like blood streaked down the front of his shirt. How could a strawman bleed I wondered? The silence in the room was as heavy as the smoke.

After a time, I realized she was waiting for me to speak. I decided not to accuse her of cursing me with the *Baku*. I would pretend I did not know what was inside me. It would be better if she revealed what she knew to me before I told her what I believed.

"Can you help me?" I asked.

"How I help you, boy?" she asked, her hands palms up before me.

I lowered my head and placed my hands to the side of my face. I did not know how to begin.

"I … uh… I have dreams," I began hesitantly.

"What'ju dream?" she asked.

"Things. Terrible things. Things I could not possibly know or dream on my own."

"Yes," she nodded as if she knew what I meant. I was encouraged.

"I am … I am transported by these dreams to places I have never been or seen before, where terrible deeds are committed. I am forced to watch." I began to cry despite my resolve, "I don't want to see them – I don't want to – but they appear before to me as though they are real. I cannot stop them."

"What kind of tings?" she prodded.

"Horrible, bloody murders. People are tortured and killed. It is ghastly. I cannot stand it anymore. Please take it away from me!" I begged.

"When dis begin, boy? When you start havin' dese dreams?"

I looked at her and trembled as tears fell down my cheeks in streams. She met my eyes as I confessed, "When I met you."

"An you tink I put something inside you – make you see dese dreams?"

"Yes. I think you infected me with *Baku* – the dream thief. Can you take him away, please?"

"Boy, I don' know dis *Baku* you speak of. Dis dream tief. I don' know you spirits, man." She shook her head so emphatically her earrings jingled. "We don' have none of dat here in dese islands. No dream stealers. I don' put nothin' on you dat day."

"But," I protested, "you gave me the evil eye. I saw you looking inside me."

"Yes," she nodded. Her face softened as she looked at me, "I see you. I see the evil aroun' you dat day."

"Can you take it away?" I pleaded.

"Boy," she shook her head, "I don' know dis evil. You have it before you see Aida Wedo. I see it, but I don' know it. Mebbe somebody in another port or somebody on de ship give it to you. I don' know. But not Aida Wedo," she insisted.

"Can't you help me?" I begged.

I hung my head in shame and despair. She reached out a skinny arm and handed me a small packet strung on a rough string to hang around my neck. "I don' know if dis help, but mebbe it give you some ease," she kindly said.

I thanked her and turned to leave, disappointed in myself and disappointed she could not or would not help me.

"Boy," she said before I went out the door. I slowly turned to face her.

"Don' you come back here no mo' see Aida Wedo," she admonished as she wagged her bony finger. She hesitated, "I don' know if de evil be inside you …" she shook her head slowly, "… or if *you* be inside de evil."

I felt as though I was that sailor in New Orleans returning to my ship broken, disappointed, and empty.

I was devoid of hope and the means to find comfort. Aida Wedo had crushed all my hopes – the one thing I needed most in this world. She condemned me to a life of servitude to the evil *Baku*; she sentenced me forever to be an unwilling witness to the garish work of the demons who haunted my mind. She crushed and threw me upon the refuse heap of humanity and I counted for naught. If Aida Wedo could not help me, then who? Not Mawken. He was as powerless in this as was I. Besides, Mawken abandoned me again in my weakness.

Why would Aida Wedo refuse me? Why did *she* fear me? What power could I possibly hold over her? Yet, she said my power may be greater than hers. How could it be? I was weak, scared, and hopeless. The only strength I had was through Mawken. Where was he? He never failed me in my need until now. Why would he abandon me now?

I looked back over the years, and over the troubles of my life. Mawken was the crutch I often leaned on. Through the torments and cruel childish taunts of my schoolmates, he had been there. He comforted me through the death of my parents; even securing for me the only mementos I had of their lives – my father's watch and my mother's locket. He saved me from the gallows by leading me over the mountain to the archipelago of Mergui. He rescued me from the prison Haji planned for me at the hands of the treacherous Sofi, who herself was a helpless victim. He sacrificed himself to save me from a powerful and merciless sea captain. And, even though it seemed he had turned against me by blaming me for the murder of the captain, I could see it was the only way to save me from the vengeful crew, the storm, and the eventual shipwreck. He protected me from exposure by Sticks and the quick justice I would have received there. Mawken warned me I would be accused of the horrible murders of my friend and others. Finally, it was he who realized and informed me of my current affliction and helped me find and confront the evil curandera who infected me with this evil curse.

I did not believe Aida Wedo for a moment. There was no one else who could have placed such a curse on me. For the first time, there was no way out for me – no one could help me this time – not even Mawken. I did not blame him for leaving.

Perhaps that is why he was so conspicuously absent. He was a mighty defender against physical and material threats, but he was as powerless as I against the spiritual. I felt resigned to my fate. I would forever ride the night skies on the silent flapping wings of *Baku* and witness the hideous deeds of the *Orang Minyak* – the oily man.

As the crew stumbled back onto the ship in their usual condition, it became obvious something was amiss. We were not preparing to shove off. Word quickly spread that the captain would address us all at the mid-morning bell. We massed in front of the bridge and waited. I scanned the crowd, but Mawken was still not among us. Gradually, the time passed as we waited and speculated on the news.

After we were all sweating and growing weary of waiting, the Captain appeared on the deck to the whistle of the boson's mate and the shouts for silence from the first mate.

"Men." He surveyed the mob. "This ship, the *Willow* that has been our home these long months, has been summoned back to her home port in England." Great cheers erupted from a majority of the assembled sailors. "We are going home."

The captain spread his arms to silence the jubilant mass of men below him.

"Those of you, who for your own reasons," he pointed to one sailor on the front row amid the good humored laughter of the others, "might rather *not* return to England, may disembark this day

279

before mess. You will report to the first mate to be paid, and go ashore to find berth on some other ship. The rest of you, we sail tomorrow on the noontide."

The captain turned and left the decks to the mostly jubilant crew – most of them British, and left the more detailed instructions for his officers to deliver. Others embraced their mates in goodbyes and went below to gather their gear in preparation to leave the *Willow*. For them, it was payday.

I looked around once more for Mawken – unsure of what course to take. Not finding Mawken, I decided on my own to stay on board and finally see the land I heard about so often in my young life. I wondered if Mrs. Prichard was still alive and would still remember me. It had not been that long ago; maybe I could find her.

The chief steward approached to ask me my intent and seemed pleased to hear I was staying aboard. He told me the captain ordered additional half-rations of food daily and a weekly ration of rum during the trip. The extra rations were intended as an inducement to get as many of the crew to stay aboard as possible. Once in England, the *Willow* would go into dry dock for a few months for maintenance and repairs. The entire crew, except the officers, would be discharged with promises of a berth when the ship was refloated.

To that end, the Quartermaster ordered the laying in of additional stores. He assigned the steward's boy to go ashore to secure and butcher some lambs and a sow for fresh meat on the voyage; we had not had fresh meat in so long. Due to the boy's youth and inexperience, the steward asked if I would go ashore with the boy to teach him of prepare meat. The boy was no butcher. Others of the crew would gather live fowl to keep in the hold until needed. I could already taste roasted duck.

I agreed; and in the warm and muggy afternoon, we went ashore to secure three lambs and a fat sow. We worked beneath a thatched overhang off of a small back room of a local meat shop, where we quickly dispatched, quartered, packed, and sent the lambs back to the ship. The sow needed special preparation and handling. The boy was attentive as I instructed him on the proper methods. He washed the hog thoroughly led calmly it into the killing pit. It was necessary to stun the animal before it was bled. If done properly, the heart muscle would aid in pumping out the blood more efficiently than gravity could. When time was a factor, such as the warm weather we were having now, this was much more preferred than hanging and bleeding the animal. A sharp blow to the head was often all that was necessary to render the animal unconscious. Once out cold, I would sever the jugular. It was preferred I do this without the kicking and thrashing of the legs and torso in the throes of death. You did not want a jerking and kicking animal while working in such close quarters with a sharp knife in your hand.

When the deed was done beneath a darkening sky from an approaching spring storm, the body of the sow was placed upon the cooling board. The hog drained as the blood ran off in rivulets into the catch basin. Thunder rumbled in the clouds above our open shed as we rolled the carcass on its back, limbs askew. Just as the rain began to fall outside our cover, I instructed my charge in the necessary delicate procedures of dressing this type of meat. He watched, growing increasingly nauseous as I made tight circular cuts around the sexual organ and anus of the animal, tying them off tightly. This step was necessary to prevent contamination of the meat when we drew those organs up through the empty body cavity.

A great peal of thunder nearly floored my assistant, who was already weak and trembling. A brilliant flash of white light flooded the small room, making it seem even darker inside once the light faded. I made a shallow incision at the sternum and worked my knife slowly downwards toward the abdomen. I showed the boy how not to cut so deep as to pierce the intestines, which would ruin the meat, but deep enough to free the skin, fat, and muscle from the belly; it was a

281

delicate knack that must be practiced to perfect. Then, making a cross cut to form a flap, we rolled the body onto its side to let the guts fall into the trough, which ran along the table. This was more than the boy could take, and he quickly reached for a bucket. Before the body cavity was empty, so was the boy. I looked into his pale youthful face, as we rolled the carcass onto its back.

Another streak of lightning lit the room in a brilliant burst of white light as I turned and looked down into the dead face and unseeing eyes of Aida Wedo.

Throughout the voyage, I saw little of Mawken. I knew he stayed on the ship with me; from time to time, I would catch sight of him moving along the deck or on the other side of the ship. He never ate in the mess cabin. He preferred to take his meals below decks where I had few chances to go. But, I knew he was there. I felt him.

We were still several days out of London before he finally came to me during the night. Though I was glad to see him, I was furious with Mawken because he had not helped me with Aida Wedo, and he had left me alone in that dangerous place. I told him of my encounter with her, and he seemed totally unconcerned.

"You were not in any danger," he declared.

"Why have you avoided me since then?"

"Maurice, listen to me. I wanted to help you. I swear I did. Aida Wedo would have killed me had I gone with you. She would have seen my power, and she would have destroyed me out of her own fear. She was much more powerful than I was, and she would have completely annihilated me. I would no longer be able to help you."

"What if she killed *me*?" I shouted.

"That did not happen. She had no reason to kill you. You are innocent. But, me? She would have seen the evil in me, and she would have finished me forever."

"What do we do now," I asked.

"Aida Wedo is not your problem any longer. She either could not or would not help you; she is far behind us, and we have no further need of her."

I remembered my vision while I was butchering the sow. I wanted to tell him, but I was afraid of what he might say. It was best not to know.

"When we get to England, I have some ideas," he confided. "I learned a man named Murrell who lives in Essex may help us. His fame has spread far, and he has done some amazing things. I think he may be able to help us. He is a witch doctor. He calls himself "The Devil's Master". Much has been written about him."

I felt a sense of relief and once more, my hope strengthened me. Maybe this man – this witch doctor could help relieve me of the burden of *Baku*. Maybe I could be free of his evil power at last.

"Meanwhile, we must not be seen together," he said. "If we make any stops along the way, you *must* stay on the ship. Do not go ashore under any circumstances. *Baku* still has you under his control, and he will continue to use you if he can."

I listened carefully to his instructions.

"Once we reach London, we will dock at St. Katharine Docks. From there, it is a short walk to a street named Buck's Row. Rent a small apartment that looks out on the street. Try to get a first floor accommodation; but if you must rent on the second floor make sure it has an outside stairway. This is important, Maurice. An outside, staircase. Do you understand?"

I assured Mawken I understood and would follow his directions.

"Talk to no one," he warned. "Tell no one why you are in the city. If anyone asks, just say you will be leaving shortly after your ship is repaired. Hundreds of ships were in the docks undergoing maintenance. Do not give anyone your name or the name of the ship if you can avoid it. And do not tell anyone about me."

Once I assured him again I fully understood, he gave me further instructions.

"I will be nearby, but we will not talk again until I find you in the apartment. Do not worry; you will not be hard to find if you follow my instructions. Stay there until I come. Do not venture out – especially at night. It is a dangerous place, and robberies and murders occur almost every night. It is a lowly place on that end of town, and the docks attract all sorts of immoral and shameful people. You must be careful as you leave the wharf area. I will try to help you if I can."

Then, he was gone. He slipped away into the dark as silently as he had come.

The next day, in the afternoon, we entered the Thames River and stood by waiting for the tide to push us up the river the next morning. St. Katharine Docks consisted of two pools linked together by a lock. We stood at the rail and watched as tugs pulled us into the lower pool. We gasped in disbelief as we saw our ship magically rose five meters to the level of the docking pool. Huge steam engines pumped water into our pit to raise us to the level where we would be towed to the docks.

Large warehouses lined the port streets; and goods were stacked in neat rows along the quayside, waiting to be moved inside. From where I stood, I could see London Bridge and the great Tower of London stood upstream. Because of delays in tying up and putting the ship to "bed", we were not allowed to disembark until nearly sunset. Our belongings were tied up in sheets or duffels and carried to the deck as we waited for the word we could go ashore. At the bottom of the gangplank, a tent was set up containing a table to serve as a pay station. Armed guards stood nearby.

One by one, they called our names, and each sailor called bid his mates goodbye and walked down the ramp to the pay tent. Once his business was completed, he would walk through of the back of the tent, past the wooden warehouses, and strike off for the city. One or two might stop and wave as they passed out of sight, but mostly the British sailors were more interested in trying to get to their homes at last.

As I waited for my name, I walked along the deck to the forward bow of the ship to see what I could of the city. I had no idea which way I should go to find Buck's Row. I asked someone before I left the ship, and was told to simply follow Dock Street to Whitechapel and from there someone would guide me. From the bow of the ship, I could see the darkened streets beyond the warehouses. We were close enough I could make out the sound of the horses on the paved streets and occasionally the shouts and voices of people passing by.

It was fully dark now, and the gas streetlights were lit. When the darkness came on, the other inhabitants of the city came out – the low-life ones who took advantage of the weak. I wondered how I was supposed to get past this assemblage of prostitutes, pickpockets, and thieves. They swarmed like flies over the recently wealthy seamen who came ashore.

When my name was called, I thought I caught a glimpse of Mawken waving at me from a block away. I had not heard the call Mawken's name nor had I seen him leave the ship. I must have been distracted by my thoughts. I moved to the ramp and entered the paymaster's tent. I received an unbelievable amount of cash in British Sterling. I had not realized I accrued two years pay. It was a lot of money. The paymaster told me to take my money to the bank as soon as they opened the next day. I stuffed it in my pocket and made my way out of the backside of the tent.

The street people were waiting, knowing the sailors were easy marks stuffed with money. I walked down the wharf and along Dock Street, hoping to pass unseen. Plenty of other seamen preceded me, so I hoped all of the bandits were too busy with their fresh catch to bother with me. I was not to be that lucky. A rather large man, with huge muscles bulging from a striped shirt, blocked the sidewalk. I reached into my pocket and withdrew the marlinspike. I would only use the gun if the thief pressed the matter. Thankfully, the thief eyed my weapon and stepped aside, but not before he whacked me on the back as I passed.

"Carry on, mate," he laughed. "I got plenty more beyond you what ain't got no puny marlinspike. You prob'ly ain't got much quid nohow."

I moved quickly down the street, keeping close to the curb to not be ambushed from some blind alley. A block down, another group of rough looking men approached me from the other side of Dock Street. From the way they were eyeing me, I knew I was their intended victim.

Suddenly, a commotion occurred across the street that stopped them cold. A screaming woman was thrown sprawling onto the sidewalk from a nearby alley. As a crowd gathered, my potential robbers turned and crossed back over to watch. The woman was screaming for help. A dark man emerged from the alley and shouted she was a conniving whore who cheated him out of his money.

It was Mawken.

The woman leaped like a cat from the sidewalk, and ran at him with her claws extended; but he pushed her away, sending her sprawling again. The crowd laughed and chose up sides. Many of them encouraged the woman, shouting at her to get up and show him what for. The others sided with Mawken and shouted, "Show the tramp a lesson, mate! We've 'nough of her kind, we have!"

Encouraged by the mob, he reached down, snatched the woman from the ground, and shook her violently. With a long sweep of her arm, she scratched his face. He released her and fell back against a wall.

287

"Damn you!" he cursed wiping blood from his cheeks.

She stood ready to fight him off, shoulders hunched as she held her hands in front of her, daring Mawken to come at her again. They circled each other like gamecocks. Keeping his eye on the woman, he turned to the crowd.

"Gents," he said, "this woman robbed me and took my money. What am I to do? She took my money and did not deliver the goods, so to speak. Left me high and dry."

The crowd erupted in hearty laughs and crows. He faced the woman and demanded, "Give me my money, you whore!"

"Ya' din't give me no money! I ain't got your money," she screamed at him. "You lie!"

The crowd howled. No one believed her – no one even cared. It was a fight they wanted to see. It was a scene acted out almost hourly along the lower east end of the city. The crowd was tiring of the conversation and wanted more action. Among the crowd, bets were being offered and accepted over who would prevail.

"Gowan! Get yer money, chap," shouted those who supported Mawken. "She ain't no match for a strappin' lad like you!"

As violent as the scene was, the mob took on a party atmosphere – like gawkers watching a circus.

Mawken quickly stepped forward and pushed her flat against the brick wall, knocking the breath out of her. He reached for her knit bag in which he hoped to find his money, but the strap was looped around her wrist. From across the street, I could hear the bones snap as he twisted her arm and yanked on her purse.

I heard the whistles a block away. Someone shouted,

"Bobbies comin'!"

The crowd made way for two policemen who quickly confronted the scratched and bleeding pair. The "Bobbies" were dressed in black coats with shiny badges on their chest and wore tall woolen hats.

While the crowd was distracted by this spectacle, I took this opportunity to move as far away from the scene as quickly as I could. I could clearly hear Mawken shouting from a block away.

"I want my money, and if I don't get it back I'll kill every whore in London!"

I could not believe it. Was he trying to be arrested? In the commotion, I slipped quietly away.

In a few blocks away, I found Whitechapel, and turned eastward, looking for Buck's Row. This part of town was still shabby and run down, but was more residential than industrial. The neighborhood consisted mostly of low houses and shabby apartments strung along the street. It had a more family feel, and I felt a little safer. I stopped a man who told me Buck's Row was only a few blocks further on. I had escaped the rough crowd along the docks.

I thought I was out of danger, but I was soon to find I was far from safe.

The descriptions of Spitalfields and Whitechapel had not done them justice. I was told they were the most dangerous and filthy slums in the city. Those descriptions were wrong – they were much worse. Hardly a night passed without a vicious murder. Violence and robbery were nightly occurrences and screams often pierced the night. In this part of town, police whistles were rare.

As directed, I found a small upstairs apartment on a dirty alley off Buck's Row near what I heard others speak of as Ducking Pond Lane. Old stories told that the Ducking Pond was a place where husbands would discipline difficult wives by "ducking" them in the pond. The pond itself was gone, eliminated by disuse and the construction of new rail lines.

An outside stairway led to the only door in the apartment. A coal stove provided heat, but it being summer, heating was of no concern. Two large windows overlooked Buck's Row, but no favorable breeze ever entered the openings. The rooms were sparsely furnished. The parlor contained a rickety stiff couch and a settee along one wall. On the opposite wall stood a rough plank wooden table with two wooden ladder-backed chairs. Above the table hung a large ornate mirror. The frame was cracked and broken on the corners, and the glass was chipped and cloudy. A curtain covered a door to the bedroom containing a wooden bed and a table in one corner.

The walls were dingy and covered with black residue I first took for mildew. I later learned it was soot, absorbed from the early morning air. A wardrobe took up much of the bedroom wall, and a small table by the window held a washbasin and a pitcher. Beneath the table was a chamber pot for night use. The room had no plumbing, of course, so the pot needed emptying each morning in the small outhouse behind the stairway. The stench from the cesspool was so great that after the first night, I was tempted to do what everyone else did and just empty it into a stone-lined gutter running down the alley. I felt guilty, but it would hardly have added to the disgusting and nauseating smell of the alley. I found if you emptied your pot into the cesspool early in the morning, before the heat came, it was not so bad – but it was still stunning.

Not a breath of fresh air ever entered my dingy room. After sunset, the air was cooler and I could breathe a little easier, though sleep was out of the question until late at night. Most of the evening, I would sit in one of the wooden chairs and look out onto Buck's Row. I watched nightly but did not see Mawken. It was such an odd place.

My side of the street held low walls, courtyards of tenement houses like mine, and small cottages, which at one time, must have been pleasant places to live. Now the bungalows were rundown and unpainted, and each yard was occupied by up to two or three shabby families camping out on the property. If the owner got up the courage to confront these vagabonds, then something would happen to cause him to wish he had kept quiet. You cannot imagine the lengths these squatters would go to get revenge. The vagrants would not hesitate to burglarize houses, tear down fences, or assault owners if they were affronted. Some homes mysteriously burned down in the middle of the night. The government did nothing to stop these property offenses.

Construction of warehouses and new rail lines displaced thousands of people from their homes. Homeless, and having no place to go, they squatted on any loose real estate they could find. Refugees from the evictions inhabited every available crevice, alley, alcove, and nook. These were the slums of London, and the police had no interest is maintaining order and discipline. It was no wonder crime and violence was so rampant.

The first few nights, I personally witnessed a dozen urinations, several defecations, and countless fornications right under my window. These were in addition to the fights, loud arguments, and other illicit practices occurring in an almost endless chain of human interaction beneath my window. I lost count after the first night. It became apparent these were normal activities of the night along Buck's Row.

As darkness came on, the lamplighters would make their rounds, and the air would grow heavy. Despite the flickering gas lamps, the air would begin to cool as darkness grew. Later in the night, the fog would thicken until I could barely see the brick walls across the street from my windows. These walls were the backs of warehouses stretching all along the north side of Buck's Row. Once the air cooled, I could, at last, get a little sleep. I would often fall asleep in my chair by the window. Before dawn, I would wake, gagging and coughing as the fog turned toxic with coal smoke and fumes coming from the tanning factories along the wharves. I would douse my head with water from the pitcher beside the bed to clear my nasal passages and then lie down to try to get some sleep before the morning before the heat returned. Oh! How I missed the sea.

After three days, Mawken still had not come. During the day, it was far too hot to stay inside the stifling room; so I found a shady spot on the green in sight of the stairs. As the sun climbed the sky, I would move my position gradually to stay in the shade until I would bump up against a sleeping vagrant who would not move. Then, I would have to find another spot or move back toward the stairway. No one "lived" beneath the stairway because of the cesspool; but often, I threaded my way over and around those who perched on almost every step of the stairway. By mid-morning, while it was still in shade, every riser on my own stairs held an occupant. I was careful not to offend any of these vagrants, knowing of the vengeful retaliation they practiced. For the most part, they left me alone; but I kept a close watch on my property.

On the fourth day, I decided to see if I could look up Mrs. Prichard. It was the end of August, and the summer heat was unbearable in the apartment anyway, so I may as well be outside where I might catch a little breeze. I wished so much to see her. She talked of Kensington so often; I thought I might find her – or at least news of her. I kept track of the streets I passed, so I could find my way back. I found Kensington a two-hour walk away, and I even found some Prichards, but none of them knew her.

Kensington was not what I expected. From Mrs. Prichard's glowing recollections, I anticipated a wonderful place, full of quaint charming cottages and mansions of the rich. Kensington certainly did not live up to my expectations. All along the route, I saw the same poverty and destitution that plagued Whitechapel. It was not as bad as Whitechapel; but it was still rundown, crowded, and exceptionally poor.

Everywhere I traveled, the streets were muddy despite no evidence of rain or precipitation other than the fog. I later learned the muck in the streets was not mud, but layers of caked horse manure. The village paid young men to roam the streets behind the vendors each day, armed with shovels. A long line of coal men, booksellers, rag pickers, icemen, sweeps, and even sidewalk doctors crowded the streets in carriages, horse-drawn wagons, and pushcarts. Nature took its course with the horses, and the boys simply scraped up what they could and spread it in the gutters layer by layer.

As the afternoon wore on, I made my way back to Buck's Row, retracing my steps and learning the streets and alleys of the district. I wanted to make sure I returned before dark. I was happy to find my door still locked and my apartment uninhabited by squatters. The might claim residence, and I would have a devil of a time evicting them. I did not have so many valuables to protect; but I did not want to lose my room, especially since I paid three months in advance – not refundable, of course.

I sat in my chair and watched as the fog come in somewhat earlier than usual. I watched it curl and twist beneath my window as I rested from my hike. It seemed as if it might rain. I hoped the rain would cool things down a little more. By the time the lamps were lit, I could hardly see beyond my window sill. A small shower did come, but it was a brief respite. I realized that since my arrival in London, *Baku* had not swept me up in the night. Did no *Pontianaks* live in England?

The deep fog twisted and curled beneath my window, and crept inside my room like a stealthy spirit or a ghost. It lay like a blanket against my far wall and condensed on the surface, glistening in the shadows like an apparition. As the volume increased, the vapor would take on a peculiar greenish tint; and I was afraid to breathe. Occasionally, the fog would briefly part outside, and the warehouse wall would come into view. In seconds, the wall would disappear in a white cloud again.

I do not know how long I slept, but it was fully dark outside the window. I stood, intending to go off to bed. A sharp sound caught my attention. Something, sounding like a pebble, rattled off my shutter. I peered through a fog as thick as water; and in one of those momentary clearings, I saw something moving.

He stood at the foot of the warehouse wall, dressed in black from head to toe. He wore a black peaked hat with wide brim hiding his features, but I knew it was Mawken. He was looking up at my window. I marveled at how much he resembled the *Orang Minyak* – the Oily Man. Then the fog melded together again and I could no longer see him.

I pulled on my boots and rushed down the stairs and around the corner to where I saw him last, but he was gone. Strangely, no one was on the streets for a change. I reasoned the lateness of the hour caused the "festivities of the evening" to lag due to the poor visibility or the unusually cool temperatures. I could hear footsteps off to the south, and just in case it was not Mawken, I followed at a safe distance. The newspapers carried stories of a man, or a gang of men, who were attacking and killing people in the city, mostly prostitutes. I followed these accounts closely because of the threats I heard him make coming from the boat. I worried he might make good on those threats, but most of the murders occurred before we came ashore. Still, I decided to be careful no one saw me with him. This was my first time on the streets of London at night since I left the boat. I hoped the fog would conceal me as I moved as silently as possible.

He would occasionally pause beneath a street lamp, but I could never get a good look at him because he kept his hat low, and his collar turned up against the damp night. Even so, I knew it was Mawken. He would linger in the dim yellow light as if to allow me to catch up. It seemed he wanted me to follow.

A disturbance on Thrall Street broke the silence as a landlord kicked a woman out of his house for not having the money to secure a bed for the night. Cursing and hacking in the night air, she loudly announced to the proprietor she would return shortly with the money. Some swain had given her a new bonnet, and she was sure she would attract a sponsor in a short amount of time. She moved off down the street looking for a paying customer. We followed as she moved from Thrall towards Osborn Street and Whitechapel Road. On the corner, she encountered another woman of the night, and she pranced around bragging about her new hat to the obvious disdain of the other harlot. After they parted, our woman turned down Whitechapel walking slowly, looking for business. In the shadows, Mawken followed along silently behind her; and I followed, equally as shaded by the gloom of night.

She turned down another street, making a half-completed circle. She stopped beneath a dim light at the stable entrance at the head of Buck's Row. She looked back as if she either caught sight of him or heard someone behind her.

"Lo, lovie," she cooed. "You been followin' me for a while. Why don't you come near? I won't bite."

Making they could not see me, I watched as he approached her. I could not hear their conversation. I could not imagine what he wanted of her, except for one thing. I was wrong.

He leaned close to her and spoke something in her ear. Smiling, she backed herself into the archway where it was slightly darker and I could see her slowly hoist her skirts for him. To my great shock, he was upon her in an instant. While her hands were full of her skirts, he grasped her throat with both hands and squeezed.

What was he doing? I raced from my hiding place to the archway. "Stop!" I shouted, but he ignored me.

I beat his back with my fists as hard as I could, but he did not even seem to notice. He was slowly squeezing the life from her. She looked at me over his shoulder, her eyes mixed with fear and pleading, but I could not make him stop. Her face turned red, then purple, and suddenly turned ghastly pale as she slumped within his grasp. Her eyes rolled up so all you could see were the whites as he slowly and carefully lowered her to the ground, his hands still around her throat, taking care to not bump her head on the pavement.

I looked around for something – anything to swing at him, as he placed the woman on her back. I found a stout limb lying on the street, and stuck him across the back. He knocked the limb away from me, as he knelt close to her side. He looked at me with dark angry eyes, as if he did not recognize me. He looked like a ravenous dog protecting his kill. With one swing, he knocked me against the wall of the alley. I fell, unable to catch my breath as I watched in horror as he placed his knife – that knife – against the main artery in her neck. As I regained my breath, I choked out a plea for her life; but it was too late.

I turned my head away as the blood gushed from her neck in a great flood. Clearly, she was only stunned as her heart muscle pumped out her life-sustaining blood. Why was he doing this? She was no *Pontianak*! In terror and revulsion, I watched as he parted her clothing and pushed her legs up at the knees, preparing to butcher the poor woman like an animal. He looked at me and motioned me to go away. Regaining my feet, I ran as fast as I could down Buck's Row toward my rooms. Halfway home, I stopped and retched against the wall until I emptied the contents of my stomach. The awfulness of the attack was beyond anything I ever witnessed – it was even more horrible than the murder of the captain. This poor woman did not deserve the violence and hate Mawken spewed out upon her helpless body.

My mind was a whirl as the past flooded my memory. I thought of all the horrors that plagued me in my life. Were they the work Mawken all this time? He planted the idea of *Baku* in my head in the first place. Was he the night-stalking murderer of Austin? I realized how much he changed since he killed the captain. He never expressed a regret or any guilt over anything. Was it normal for a man to cut out another man's heart and feel nothing? Had he developed such a perverse pleasure at killing he craved it? Was killing the only way he could gratify is suppressed passion? In my fear and panic, it seemed reasonable to believe he may have doped on those dark and terrible nights in Texas, and probably in New Orleans too, as he led me along to witness his unspeakable deeds. To what end?

I realized each time I confronted Mawken, he provided some excuse or an alibi that made him seem innocent of my suspicions – often making himself out to be the victim. Not this time. I saw with my own eyes –not drugged or spirited away by some dream demon. I saw him slit the throat of a perfectly innocent woman who never did any harm to either of us – she never even met us.

What would happen next? Did he want me to witness this attack so he would have a reason to kill me next? Was he finally allowing me to see what he truly was? I trembled at the thought of what he might do. Surely, he intended for me to watch as he sliced the poor woman's throat. He knew I knew.

I decided I should leave London immediately. If I could make it to the docks and find a boat leaving right away; I would be out danger. I stuffed my few belongings into my pockets and a small drawstring bag. Most of my money was in the bank, which would not open until morning. I weighed the option of abandoning my money when a sound outside interrupted my thoughts.

Step by maddening step, I could hear someone climbing the stairs. Was it Mawken? He was in no hurry, and it was maddening to hear him slowly climb one tread higher – one rung closer to my door. It was the only exit. I crouched by my window, determined to leap for my life if necessary. I hoped beyond hope it was the police. Maybe the Bobbies were looking for the killer, and someone reported seeing me hurrying home like a fiend in the night. Please, let it be the police.

The footsteps on the stairs came higher and nearer, climbing the wooden staircase to my room. He was at my door. He took his time. He knew I had no way to run, no place to hide. He knew stronger than I was, and I had no way to defend myself. Did he know I had a gun? I quickly rummaged through my bag and found it as the footsteps thumped in a regular rhythm. I placed the pistol in my pocket and stood in a corner with my back to the wall. I stood bold and defiant knowing I could defend myself. If he came near me in a threatening way, I would not hesitate to shoot.

Maybe it is not Mawken after all – please let it be a policeman. The steps stopped at the top of the stairs, and my door slowly swung open. The green-gray, whirling fog curled behind him as he stood in the dark doorway. I could not make out his face. He was dressed in dark clothes and wore a large brimmed hat. He stepped into the room as I fingered the wooden grip of my pistol.

"Hello, Maurice. I told you I would come for you."

I nervously fingered the gun in my pocket, hoping he would not notice, as I eyed Mawken standing just inside my doorway.

"What is wrong, Maurice?" He removed his hat. "It's me. Don't you recognize me?"

He did not seem agitated or upset in any way. Mawken was cool and calm despite having brutally murdered an innocent woman on the streets less than an hour earlier. He did not seem threatening toward me in the least. Maybe he would not kill me after all. I relaxed a little but kept my hand in my pocket in case it was a trick.

"I … uh … I – I saw you," I stammered, accusing him with my eyes.

"When?"

"Earlier," I hedged. I wanted to see what he would say and how he would react.

"I thought you did." He did not seem overly concerned. "I thought I caught sight of you in your window." *Was he out of his mind? Surely, he knew I saw what he did.* "I would have come up, but there were still too many people around. I thought it best if no one saw us together, so I waited."

Was it possible he did not remember our struggle over the woman? He clearly saw me – had knocked me against a wall. His eyes seemed so strange at the time – had he been in a trance? It was as if he was unaware I saw him commit a murder.

Not eager to set him off into another murderous rage with me as the next victim, I hedged. He was clearly insane. I feared any misstatement of mine could bring on another fit of madness.

"I … I wondered about that," I stalled.

He suddenly grew excited and exclaimed, "Maurice! I have found him!"

"Found whom?"

"Murrell! You know – the witch doctor I told you about. He is the one who can help you banish the terrible curse that possesses you."

"Yes. That *is* good news."

He threw his hat onto the table and removed the overcoat, which he placed across the back of one of the chairs. "Well, I haven't actually seen Murrell yet – his house was empty when I arrived, but I know where he lives. When he returns, I will be waiting."

I slowly removed my hand from my pocket and smiled uneasily. "That is good news," I repeated. "When do we go?"

"When he returns from his travels, I will set up the engagement. Whatever the cost, he must help you. You must stay here while I make the arrangements. We may not have much time, and I must be able to fetch you quickly if agrees to help."

I looked at the floor, unsure if I should tell him what I knew. "I haven't been having those dreams; not since I've been here. Maybe *Baku* has left me – freed me. Why can't we just leave? Go back to the sea? I hate it here! It is so filthy and …," I hesitated to finish, "… so dangerous."

He sat down on the couch and removed his shoes. He wore no socks. "We cannot leave. The *Willow* is still being repaired."

"There are other ships … "

"No!" he shouted, clearly upset. "We must get this spirit cast from your soul. We must get it off before we leave. This witch doctor is the only one who can help. You cannot go on like this. You have a sickness, Maurice, and it must be removed. I do not think you are mad – I think you are possessed," he insisted.

I did not like the direction this conversation turned, or his threatening change of attitude. I thought it best not to provoke him. Mawken was still pretending I was the problem.

"I don' know if de evil be inside you, or if you be inside de evil."

"As you say," I meekly agreed.

"You must stay here and wait. Do no leave. I do not think you know how unwell you are. When it is time, I will leave a message under the brick at the top of your stairs." I knew the brick he meant. It lay at the top of the stairs as a doorstop to hold the door open for the breeze. "It will give you the day and time I will return – a time for you to see Murrell. You must be ready and prepared not to return to this place once we depart."

I nodded my head, showing I understood, even if I did not agree. I fully planned to be gone by the time Mawken returned – Murrell or no Murrell. I feared for my life. Mawken was capable of anything.

"I need a place to sleep for a few hours until morning," he announced. "This divan will do fine." He stood barefoot and spread his coat across the seat.

"May I use the basin in your room to wash?" he asked.

I motioned toward the curtained door and sat in the chair by the window. "Be my guest."

He disappeared behind the curtain into my bedroom. I could hear him splashing water. I thought of bolting for the door to escape, but I realized he would only chase me down, and it would not end well for me. I walked around the room, fidgeting, while he bathed.

After a few minutes, he reappeared and stretched himself out on the couch, using his arm as a pillow.

"You had better get some sleep, too," he yawned. "It is late and I am leaving early."

I wished him goodnight, and went into my room. I realized from behind the curtain, with the lamp out, I could not see him at all. With the streetlamp behind me, I was afraid he could see me. I could not see if he was lying on the couch or preparing to attack me. I stood by the window for a moment trying to decide what I should do. I fully realized the danger of my circumstances. I took the basin, intending to pour the water out of the window, when I noticed it had a reddish tint. Blood! Her blood! He washed his bloody hands in my basin. Red streaks stained the towel where he wiped his bloodstained hands.

I sloshed the water out into the street below and took my bloody towel through the curtain into the parlor.

"There is blood on this towel," I accused.

"I am sorry, Maurice. I should have told you. I borrowed your razor and got a small cut. It is nothing. I thought I cleaned it up."

I looked closely at his face. He did not have any cuts. In fact, he had not shaved. He could lie so easily. He was so convincing.

"Of course. I, uh… I was just worried you injured yourself." I could also lie.

We said our goodnights again, and I went back to my room. I refilled the basin with fresh water from the pitcher and washed my face. I felt so dirty. It seemed as if the revolting fog clung to my skin. At least, this time, the water was not bloody when I finished.

I lay fully clothed in my bed. I was afraid to get undressed in case I needed to escape into the streets. I wondered how many bones would break if I leapt form the window. I resolved to stay awake until he left in the morning. I did not know but he might be waiting for me to go to sleep so he could easily do away with me. I placed the gun beneath the pillow next to the marlinspike, and stared intently at the curtain hanging over the doorway. Each time a stray breeze moved the curtain, I would aim in that direction. When he did not come through the door, I placed the revolver back beneath the pillow, and waited.

I kept my hand on the gun always. If he came through the door, I was resolved to shoot him if I could. I thought back over the times we were together, of all of the blood and killing that happened. I was sure now that Mawken killed Sofi. I saw him kill the captain and that poor woman earlier – those were no dreams! I thought of those women in Austin -- had they been pierced through the head simply to throw me off suspicion? He knew I would think they were *Pontianaks*. He made sure to plant the idea in my mind. But, why? Why would he do that to me? Why would he go to all the trouble, unless … unless he had developed a craving for blood – a desire to kill. He needed someone to blame if the police caught him. As I thought back further in our past, my imagination kicked in. I thought the unthinkable. Had he killed his own parents? I did not actually seen any pirates – I took his word for everything. I had fully trusted him and believed him. Suddenly, I was ice cold despite the heat. Is it possible? Could he have killed my parents to keep me from leaving him? I searched my memory, trying to find some evidence I might be wrong. How long had he been killing?

I jumped at the sound of a vendor calling from the streets below my window. It was fully light. I realized I had fallen asleep despite my best efforts to stay awake. I threw the curtain aside and rushed into the parlor. There was no one on the couch. He was gone, leaving behind only a bloody towel.

I looked around the apartment, but he left nothing behind, except the bloody towel that marked another horrendous murder. Picking up the towel, I threw the wadded cloth into the wastebasket. I would need to get another towel; blood was hard to wash out, especially in the cold and dingy water of Whitechapel.

As a second thought, I decided to retrieve the towel. I folded it neatly before placing it in a wardrobe drawer for safe keeping. Dressing quickly, I left the apartment and found the closest newsboy. Clutching the daily paper, I walked rapidly to a shady park, and finding an empty bench, sat to read the headlines.

There it was, in print and spread out before all of London. The English papers had a much more restrained approach than the cowboy newspapers of Austin. Yet, the report contained a full description of the bloody murder during the night. Her name was Mary Nichols. She lived on Thrawl Street, not five blocks from where I sat. I read the report eagerly, matching the details of the murder with what I remembered. There was no doubt I witnessed Mrs. Nichols' last living moments.

She was a prostitute; found dead in the early morning hours by a cart driver. She was killed at half past three near the gated stable entrance to Buck's Row, the archway I was thrown against. Her throat was slit twice, and a jagged cut stretched down her abdomen. If that were right, he must have completed his hideous work after I ran away in sickness and disgust.

The article said a local roving gang of thugs, who were preying upon prostitutes, committed the crimes. They linked two previous murders to Mary's killing.

No! The newspapers were wrong. A gang did not do this. Gangs may have perpetrated the two earlier murders, but this one – this Mary Nichols – was killed by one extremely insane fiend – Mawken. I was upset they could not see the truth.

I considered going to the police with my information. I would claim I could not sleep and went out for a breath of fresh air when I heard a commotion. No, that story would not hold. The head of Buck's Row was too far from my rooms for me to hear anything. I could say I saw a stranger and followed him, but that did not sound good either. Even if they believed me, how could I tell them where to find Mawken? Even I did not know where he was. They would surely ask if I had any role in the crime. I could deny I was there, but then how else would I know how it happened? Suddenly, I realized why Mawken wanted me to follow last night. He needed a witness, and he knew I would follow. He also knew I could not tell anyone without exposing myself.

Later in the day, in another paper, I read other reporters suspected a single killer was responsible for Mary Nichols' murder and the two earlier ones. Mawken could not have done the two previous deaths because our ship was still at sea at the time. Did anyone know how to report a crime? To my great concern, one of the writers compared the London murders to those in Austin in 1885. The police were out questioning Americans, looking for anyone who might have lived in both places.

The coroner examined the body of poor Mary, and concluded, rightfully so, that the two earlier deaths were unrelated. The idea spread that a single killer was responsible for a recent spate of prostitute murders. Gradually, over the next few days, the reports seemed to center on this single killer theory; but the murders of the two previous women, Elizabeth Smith and Martha Tabrum, continued to be linked by some of the experts.

It was more than a week before I heard from him. On Saturday night, I woke needing to relieve myself in the chamber pot. Once again, a putrid, snot-like fog permeated the atmosphere. As I stood over the pot, I noticed a light flickering outside.

Someone standing by the wall held lit a cigarette and stood smoking it in the darkness outside my window. I could see the red glow brighten with each puff, the white smoke rising and quickly swirling up into the olive-green sludge London called air. I realized the man could probably see me better than I could see him, so I moved away from the open window.

Without warning, a small pebble the size of a grape flew through my window and bounced across the floor. It came to rest against the far wall. I realized it was the sound I heard a week ago on the night Mary was butchered. I took it as a signal Mawken intended me to follow and serve as a witness again.

I trembled in fear at the thought – must I? How would I be able to go, knowing what would happen to some poor soul out on the streets at the wrong time and on the wrong night? I shuddered to think what I would see this night.

Maybe I could stop him somehow. I could convince Mawken to leave London with me tonight. Something evil and horrific had corrupted his mind. Maybe if we left this awful gloomy city, he might recover. Or maybe this witch doctor Murrell might help him instead of me. I grabbed my pants and shoes and left the room without a hat or coat. I needed to talk to him to prevent what I knew would end in tragedy. I had to try.

At the end of the stairs, I circled back and ran towards Buck's Row, but he was no longer standing at the base of the wall. In the darkness filled with swirling fog, it was difficult to know which way he went; but I knew he would leave clues for me to follow. I walked east, straining to catch sight or sound of him. Far ahead, it seemed I saw the faint red glow swirling in the fog, and I saw him step beneath the light for a brief moment, allowing me to see him. He was dressed as he was earlier with the same dark coat and wide-brimmed hat. I could not make out his features clearly, but I knew it was Mawken.

He led me on a circuitous route. The harder I tried to catch up to him, the more he seemed to stay ahead of me. He was playing with me, taunting me with his nearness, and mocking me with his distance. This was a game for him – a sick, horrific, dangerous game. The city had hired additional police; what if they saw us. They would arrest me for being an accomplice of a man they suspected of sick, cruel murders. What would become of me?

By the time I reached the corner streetlamp where he had paused, he was again out of sight. What sort of game was this? Were we to play cat and mouse all night? I picked up his trail again heading north, and I followed as quickly and quietly as I could. After a couple of blocks, he was out of sight. I retraced my steps; and by a mere chance, I saw a faint red glow down a dark alley to my left. He had turned west then and was leading me back towards Buck's Row.

The red glow of his cigarette did not recede as I advanced; and showed he was there in the darkness, watching … waiting for me to arrive. The glow of his fag was steady. It did not brighten with each puff, so I knew he was simply holding it as a sort of beacon for me. Surely, this could not be the same cigarette.

As I grew nearer, I felt some uneasiness. Was this a trap? Was he allowing me to follow down some darkened alley so no witnesses could see him finish me? I feared I would never leave this alley again. I knew too much. I had seen too much for him to let me live.

I stopped and stood beside one of the walls lining the alley, hoping some movement or splash of light might help me see what was ahead, but the alley was as dark as the inside of a cave. I wished I had remembered to bring my gun; but in my haste to catch up, I had left it under the pillow.

I took a few more steps forward and halted again. The red glow stayed where it was when I first saw it. A few more steps and I would be close enough to call out to him. I cautiously stepped toward the faint spot of red light.

Just as I was calling out, someone struck me from behind and knocked me to the ground. I rolled in the filth and muck covering the pavement, coming to a stop against a large waste bin. While I was dazed, somebody heavy sat upon me so I could not move as someone else pulled my pockets out.

"This bloke ain't got nuttin', mate."

I looked up at the mugger who spoke. He was a boney youth in dark clothing. Offsetting the dark ensemble, a bright yellow cap with earflaps folded up sat jauntily on his head.

"Nuts! Another empty beggar," the heavy one snorted. His breath smelled of garlic.

"Whatta we do with 'em, mate?"

The heavy one on my back got off and grunted, "Nothin'. Leave 'em here for the ripper!"

They laughed as yellow hat kicked me in the side before they ran through the entrance of the alley. After I caught my breath, I got to my knees. I could still see the cigarette glowing, still where it was when I first saw it. I grew angry that he would watch while they cruelly robbed me, and not even lift a finger to help me. What if they had tried to kill me – what then? Would he have let them do his dirty work?

"You would not even come to help me?" I shouted.

No answer other than an echo came forth. I was at the end of my patience. In large angry steps, I went to where he stood, and found the cigarette, still glowing red, stuck on a nail in a fence at the bottom of the dead-end alley.

I limped back home, resolved never again to leave my room without the gun, or at least the marlinspike. I slept until mid-morning and woke stiff and sore. I looked in the mirror hanging on the wall above the table. I could see a purple and black bruise ran from my upper ribs to my waist. Yellow Hat must have worn boots. If I only had a hot tub of water to soak in. I remembered a bathhouse on Whitechapel. I knew the hot water would sooth my aches and pains.

On the way to the bathhouse, I remembered I left my weapons again. I could kick myself for being so stupid. However, it being light on the street, I hoped I would not find any trouble. If trouble found me, I could do nothing about it. I bought the morning news from a boy along the way and tucked the paper under my arm. Once I settled in the hot water, I opened the newspaper to read. As I suspected, news of another murdered prostitute filled the front pages.

Anne Chapman's throat was cut wide open. Her body mutilated by removing her intestines, which the killer pulled up over each shoulder. Part of her uterus was missing, presumed taken by the fiend. The coroner believed the killer must have some medical knowledge to have performed such an operation. He estimated the assassin used a knife 15 to 20 centimeters long. The description matched the size of the mermaid knife. I looked in vain for some other description of the knife, but I did not find any, so I imagined the worst.

She was, indeed, a prostitute. Several witnesses reported she worked the streets nightly. She left her room at 2 a.m. in search of the means to pay her rent. The debate grew in the paper over whether the killer had any medical training. Many of those interviewed, or who wrote letters, believed the killer was a doctor or a surgeon. Others disagreed, calling the slayer a lunatic. Still others believed in the gang theory in which roving mobs of local toughs were attacking women who could not defend themselves and could not go to the police, for obvious reasons.

309

I felt it odd, reading the accounts and knowing who was responsible. It seemed nothing could stop Mawken. He was not seen if he did not want to be seen, as Mawken always said. He worked under cover of the darkness and the thick cloaking fog shrouding the streets each night.

And he *was* quite insane.

A few pages back in the newspaper, what I read caused me to sit upright in my tub, sloshing water onto the floor. Two young men were found beaten to death behind a warehouse. The coroner requested any information on the identity of these two. One man was tall, lean, and wore a bright yellow cap with earflaps. The other man was stout and short. Both bodies were slashed in several places after they were dead, the constable reported. Yellow Hat's right leg was broken in four places. If anyone knew any information on the identity of the two, they were requested to report to the local police station in Whitechapel.

The paper did not link the murder of the prostitute with the murder of the two young thugs. Nevertheless, I knew who the killer was. I was sure of it. It was clear who avenged me, but at an awful price. I never desired Mawken to kill anyone for any reason – much less to punish someone on behalf of me – even if they had almost broken my ribs.

I left the bath and returned to my room determined to find some way to report what I knew. I must! It was the only way to stop his manic rampage. Mawken needed help, and the best way I could help him was to see him captured before other innocents lost their lives.

Over the next two days, I composed no less than a score of letters to "Whom it May Concern." None of them turned out right; and despite the heat, I burned them in the stove. I wanted no chance those rough drafts might fall into the wrong hands.

I had mixed feelings over how to deliver the letter: should I take them in person or place them in the post? Should I address the constable, the police, or the newspaper? How would I convince the reader of the truth without revealing my involvement? The message would be anonymous of course, but I must take care the message could not be traced back to me. I shuddered to think how Mawken would react if he learned I betrayed him. People would be reading of my death in the paper next.

Two days later, the police arrested a man named John Pizer. He was an odd fellow who was notorious around the rookery, known as Leather Apron. He had a reputation of terrorizing local prostitutes, and the police were sure they found the killer. From the evidence presented in the paper, I believed that while he may have violated some prostitutes, I knew he had not killed the last two. A witness reported she saw Anne talking to a man near where she was found dead hours later. She could not positively identify Leather Apron as the suspect; and when Pizer's alibis for the latest murders proved true, he was released. Mobs gathered at the police station at the news and loudly protested his discharge. Who else could the killer be? The poor man was harassed so thoroughly, he fled to the countryside in fear for his life.

Though she could not identify Leather Apron as the killer, the witness did provide some useful evidence. She said the man she saw wore dark clothing and a wide-brimmed hat slung low on his head to shield his face. She reported she thought he was a foreigner and he had a dark complexion. He had a "shabby-genteel" appearance. The description matched Mawken perfectly.

Just like in Austin, the rash of killings caused widespread unrest in London – especially in the Whitechapel and Spitalfields rookeries. A mob formed and protested at the Commercial Railroad Station, believing the police were holding the murderer in secret. No one knew how the rumor got started. A Member of Parliament from the Whitechapel district offered a reward of one hundred pounds for information leading to the apprehension and arrest of the true killer.

Other, more vicious rumors circulated. Some believed Jews were responsible. Those who were inclined to distrust the Jews used the gossip as justification for their bigotry. Some even picketed neighborhood tabernacles.

Just as they had in Texas, residents banded together for protection. If the police would not protect them, they vowed to protect themselves. The Whitechapel Vigilance Committee organized, and recruited members to help patrol the rookery each night. They carried clubs and cricket bats along with chains and hooks. This reaction only served to make the neighborhoods even more dangerous. The vigilantes also offered a reward for the capture of the killer and even hired two private investigators on their own.

The police refused to offer a reward, setting off another round of protests and increasing animosity toward the police. The police explained they feared such an inducement would lead to misleading information and false claims by those trying to collect the reward. They insisted any action taken must be made on evidence or eyewitness accounts. This further frustrated the public, who did not believe the police were working hard enough to apprehend the killer despite the appointment of a new commissioner hired to coordinate the investigation with Scotland Yard. The idea of a single murderer in both Austin and London began to pick up interest.

Several suspects were arrested and questioned but later released. Each time a false lead led to another suspect being released, anger and exasperation grew in the districts. Unlike Austin, the police did not respond with mass arrests based on thin air. Protests and pickets were daily sights on the streets, especially outside the police stations, rail depots, and even the houses of government. People were in a panic. The streets became nearly empty at night. Even the criminals were afraid of being accosted by the vigilantes or the roving police.

Meanwhile, fear and distress plagued the inhabitants of the rookery each night. Where would the killer strike next? Who would be slaughtered next on the streets on the streets of London, as the police stood idly by and did nothing? When three weeks passed with no new killing reported, some believed the slayer moved on to butcher elsewhere. Then, one foggy night near the end of September, he struck again. This time, twice in the same night.

These murders also took me by surprise. He did come for me this time. I had taken a severe cold, which developed into a respiratory infection. The revolting putrid fog I breathed each night sickened me. It was killing me. The doctor prescribed a remedy that made me drowsy. On the night of these murders, I went to bed early, slept through the night, and late into the morning. I was shocked to see I had slept some twenty hours straight. If he had come for me, I would have never known. A fire would not have roused me from that deep, groggy stupor. I slept in sweet, dreamless oblivion.

It was already evening, and I sat at my table still groggy from the medicine. I read about double murders – both prostitutes. The first was Elizabeth Stride, and she lived not far from where they found her. Her lifeless body lay inside the gateway of a cart builder named Dutfield. The enclosed yard was completely screened from the street by a high fence. Dutfield had moved some two years earlier, and the property was used as a freight yard. Small businesses operated within the walls and heavy gates and kept the vagrants out. Delivery carts came and went at all hours of the day and night.

The locks were seldom used. The police long ago stopped checking the yard at night because the only thing they ever found was freighters unloading their wagons. A killer would need a dark, abandoned place to do his deeds. However, the yard went for long periods between wagon arrivals. Actually, it was the perfect place for a murderer to lure his victims -- especially those of such low morals who sought out dark and private places to do their commerce.

Elizabeth was found just after midnight. Her throat slashed wide open. Unlike the earlier murders, Elizabeth's body was not mutilated. When she was found, it was estimated she was slain only moments before. The newspaper theorized the killer was interrupted before he could do his hideous disfigurements. However, a disagreement arose in the paper over whether this murder was connected to the others, despite the victim being a prostitute. Elizabeth's killing was the first murder of the type recorded south of Whitechapel. However, her throat was slashed in such a way as to match the earlier deaths.

Making this night even more horrific, another murder was discovered within the hour just a few blocks away. Catherine Eddowes lay a short distance away. The knife used was the same size as the earlier weapon. Her face and abdomen were mutilated, and her intestines were over her shoulders. Some of the viscera were detached and tucked between her left arm and torso. As in the death of Anne Chapman, a good portion of her uterus was missing. These facts set off another round of disputes over whether the killer had any medical training. No one thought to question whether the murderer might be a hunter who field-dressed game – or was, perhaps, a butcher.

Before dawn, a scrap of bloody apron turned up in a doorway not five hundred meters away from where the body of Catherine lay. Terrible, hateful rumors swirled around a chalked inscription reportedly found on a wall above the bloody apron. Rumors said the message accused the Jews of the string of murders plaguing the city. Not wanting a general riot, the police erased the message, but not before some reporter saw it and reported it in the news.

The reporters supposed the killer attacked Elizabeth from behind because she still held a package of cachous in her dead hand.

She did not even have time to drop them and defend herself. A vendor sold her grapes earlier in the evening and reported she was in the company of a smallish, dark stranger with a wide-brimmed hat. That certainly sounded like Mawken. A witness in Mitre Square, near Catherine's scene, also reported seeing this second victim with a small dark man a short time before she was murdered. This suspect was also described as shabbily dressed, wearing a peaked hat. The witness had only a fleeting glimpse of the suspect, but he was sure he could not identify the man if he saw him again.

Finally, the city and the police offered a reward of five hundred pounds. The brought bloodhounds in to detect a scent trail but to no avail. The dogs led the detectives down a dark, dead-end alley where the trail ended. No doors, fences, gates or other exits led the blind alley. At the end stood a sheer warehouse wall nearly five stories high. No one had any idea how the killer got out of the alley without leaving a clue.

Reading these accounts caused a shiver to run down my spine. The police may have thought a double murder was unique to their experience, but it certainly was not exceptional in mine. I recalled a double murder that occurred on my last night in Austin that was the mirror image of these – except for one thing. It occurred to me none of these London victims had a metal spike thrust through their brains. Whatever this cutthroat was doing, he was not killing *Pontianaks*. What was it Yellow Hat called him – a Ripper?

I decided to renew my letter-writing plan. After several more false starts, which I burned in the stove, I hit upon a novel idea. What if I claimed to be the slayer, and mocked the police for their inadequacies? If artfully done, I could leave enough clues to help the authorities find him. Mawken would not be any wiser, and could not blame me for his arrest.

Nevertheless, I felt if I were going to take this step, it was necessary for me go armed at all times – not just when I went out. If

Mawken suspected me of treachery, he would attack and kill me without hesitation. I left my writing on the table and fetched the gun from beneath my pillow.

I dropped the firearm into my pocket and returned to the living room to finish my letter. I pushed the curtain away and fell back heavily against the wall. I grabbed the curtain to keep from falling to the floor and tore it away from one corner of the doorway. Standing there, looking through my writing materials, my most recent effort in his hand stood Mawken.

I felt so faint I thought I might pass out. My mind whirled through a dozen thoughts in a fraction of a second. *What has he seen? Did I burn my last effort?* I could not remember. I needed an excuse quickly.

"Hello, Maurice," he said calmly. "Aren't you happy to see me?"

Happy? "Oh! Yes… yes! I was just surprised that is all. I was startled for a moment. I did not know you were here. There was no note under the brick."

"Oh, yes. The brick. I am sorry. I did not expect to be here tonight. I am sorry you were alarmed. It is only me."

The room felt so warm. May face flushed with the heat. My skin prickled and small bumps rose on my arms and legs. The tension was unbearable. The air inside the room crackled with tension and clung to my dry lips. The shadows held creepy secrets. *What did he read on that paper?*

"Well, I am happy to see you. You are always welcome here." *Smile and try to look normal.*

"Thank you. You are always so kind to me." He fingered the stationary in his hand. *What was on the paper?* "What have you been up to?"

Yes, I burned the last one. I am sure. "Oh, the letters. I have been trying to locate Mrs. Prichard. That is a letter to the editor of the newspaper asking for information. I went to Kensington but could not find her. So, I thought I would expand my search."

"I see," he said looking closely at the page. "Interesting."

"I am not sure she would even remember me, but I thought I would try."

He looked at the stove and touched its warm surface. "Are you burning something? Aren't you warm enough?"

Oh no! What of the hot stove? "Oh, that." I thought fast. "I've … I've been ill -- desperately ill actually. This place, with its damp nights and poor air, has affected my breathing. The doctor gave me some medicine, which makes me feel cold. It also makes me sleep. Yesterday, I slept the entire day."

"What did the doctor give you?"

"It's there," I pointed. "There on the table."

He put down the page read the label on the bottle.

"Yes. I can see how that would make you sleepy." He placed the bottle on the table and turned to me again.

"How are you feeling now?"

"I'm much better, thank you." *Smile and be gracious.*

"I suppose that is why you did not awaken last night."

"I was not aware you were here. Just like tonight, you come and go so softly, I sometimes do not know if you are here or not."

"So as not to disturb you," he offered.

Change the subject. Change the subject quickly. "What of that doctor – witch doctor – that Murrell? Have you located him?"

"Indeed, I have. He is quite dead."

Dead? The news was shocking. I am sure the shock showed on my face, as I blanched. I could not conceal my astonishment. *What happened? Had he refused to cooperate? What could I say?* I finally managed, "Oh! No." My mouth was so dry I thought my tongue was swollen.

"Now, Maurice. Do not despair. We will find another. It seems that our witch doctor died some two years ago."

Died and not killed. I breathed a sigh of relief. I was so thankful he was not murdered.

"Can we leave now – now that this Murrell cannot help us? We can leave on another ship. I do not like it here."

"Not yet," he said as he sank to the couch. "We have more work to do here. Besides, the *Willow* is not ready for us."

"There are other…" I began.

"Now-now, Maurice. We have been over this before. We must get you cured of your affliction. You don't realize how disturbed you are." *He has transferred awareness of his sickness to me.* "I suffer for you in your need. Another medium has come to my attention that may help you. I will go to secure her services."

Her? "A woman?"

"Indeed. Maurice, you do not know this, of course; but women often make the best mediums and spiritualists. This one lives in Leeds; it is quite far away. I there tonight. I shall be gone for at least a week." *He will be gone a week.* "Now, I don't want you to worry if she can't help us. I have not given up on you. If she cannot assist us, I plan to speak to the vicar of a church in Ashford in Kent. If I am unsuccessful with the mystic, we shall speak with the vicar about a ceremony called a demonic exorcism. Do not fear, it is painless I am told. He has been successful in this sort of thing. If you have any evil spirits, they will leave – of this you can be sure."

"When do you leave for Leeds?"

He rose from the couch and brushed his pants.

319

"I'm afraid I must catch my train within the hour. I must be on my way tonight."

"Shall I go with you?"

"No!" Suddenly, his demeanor became stern. After a moment, he caught himself, and smiled.

"No, you are too kind, but I fear you are too ill to travel. You have not recovered sufficiently. Besides, you are much safer if you stay behind while I make the arrangements."

"Can't I at least walk to the station with you? I'm well enough for that."

He agreed, and together we walked to the train station three blocks from the apartment. As we walked, we passed one of the vigilante groups. They eyed us closely but did not stop us for questioning. They were looking for a man who walked alone. Besides, it was still early in the evening. I told him of the terrible murders happening. I remarked how similar the killings were to those in Austin. He assured me he was aware.

"Other than last night, how have you been sleeping? Have the dreams returned?"

"No, not at all. As I reported on your last visit, *Baku* has left me alone. Maybe I am cured. Maybe he will not trouble me again."

"Nonsense!" He stopped and faced me beneath a street lamp on the corner of the station. "Maurice, listen to me. You must understand, and I say this with all the kindness I can offer. Please do not be distressed. You are ill. Something in your mind is not quite right. I no longer believe you were taken by *Baku*. At first, I did – but no longer. Other spirits in this world prey on innocents like you. We will find help for you. If this clairvoyant cannot help you, we will try something else. There is a doctor – a real doctor. His name is

Maudsley, and he is quite famous. He runs an asylum in Herefordshire. If nothing else works, we shall appeal to him."

An asylum? He is going to place me in one of those hellholes. Never! "No! I cannot go to one of those places. They are horrid. The stories that come out of them …"

"Maurice … Maurice! Calm yourself. There is no intention to put you in an asylum. Believe me. We will just talk to the doctor. That is all. Just talk. He will know how to help us. Do not worry. I will be with you."

That said, he climbed onboard the train, promising to return within a week.

I stood on the station platform and watched the train depart. I was even more determined to end this once and for all. I would not survive in one of those places. Mawken must be caught.

I returned to my room resolved to do something – anything to stop this nightmare – even if it meant I might endanger myself. I reached for the ink. I decided to use red, like the blood of those poor innocent women. Hopefully, it will cause the police to increase their watch and catch him at last. In a bold hand, and mimicking the rough language of the local toughs I often heard beneath my window, I paused over the blank page. I rather liked that line Yellow Hat said about the "Ripper".

Dear Boss,

I waited for a reaction to my letter, certain the authorities would soon make an arrest in the case. There was a slight mention of it two days later in the press, but to my great dismay, the article reported on two such letters – both considered hoaxes.

Later, more was written about these discredited letters; mine was even printed in its entirety. Both letters were signed "Jack the Ripper". The shorter message referenced "Saucy Jack" as the killer. Thereafter, the press began to commonly refer to the killer as "Jack the Ripper." It caught the public's fancy; and before long, Jack was the talk of the town.

Most people still believed Jack had some amount of medical knowledge and skill. I wished I had remembered to put something about meat butchers in my "Dear Boss" letter. Now, it was too late unless I wrote another one, which was far too risky. The slightest mistake and I would be caught, or my betrayal might be discovered. I felt some guilt about my treachery, but I reasoned I might be able to save another innocent soul.

It had been a week, and he had still not returned from Leeds. I did not want to go see this woman psychic. It frightened me because surely she would see I was innocent, and the real murderer was Mawken. What would he do when this was revealed to him? Would he attack me in his anger and frustration? Would he kill the poor woman who gave us the news? I worried constantly and dreaded his return.

A few days after the letters were printed in the newspaper, it occurred to me he might already be aware of my treachery. How much of a coincidence could it be for the news agencies to receive two letters endorsed "Jack the Ripper" in the same week? I was sure he must have seen something on my desk, though I do not know how he could have. Maybe he followed me and retrieved the letter from the post, then sent a similar letter to divert the authorities – making them think both letters were a hoax. He left on the train, but the train made many stops between London and Leeds. He could have gotten off anywhere and doubled back to keep an eye on me. The more I thought about it, the surer I was that the author of the second letter was Mawken.

A few days after the letter was printed, another body was found – or at least the torso of an unidentified body. Of all places, the victim was discovered in the basement of the new Scotland Yard building, currently under construction.

It is not easy to cut off a human limb. The operation most often requires a saw and considerable time to make the cut. It is necessary for the victim to be unconscious or dead during the operation. Otherwise, without assistance, it is impossible to hold the victim down. That simply was not Jack's style. He prefers his victims know what is happening. He wants to see the terror in their eyes – hear the horror in their screams. He wants them alive when he slices through the large vein in their necks; to feel the flush and rush of hot blood as it spurts and gurgles from a still-living body. No, Jack is no sawbones – Jack is bloodthirsty. I did not think Mawken committed any of the latest murders. They do not ring true to what I knew was his major motivation.

Neither did the police consider this murder part of Jack's work. It was shameful enough a murder had occurred literally beneath their noses at Scotland Yard. Her severed arms and legs were never recovered, and a positive identification was never made. Jack was a butcher, no doubt, but he never completely dismembered limbs. Mawken was more spurred by the guts and the bloody gore.

Nevertheless, this case opened the floodgates of sensationalism as imposters, lunatics, and fringe fanatics trouped daily to police headquarters with 'inside information' and even confessions.

323

Police officers treated one poor bloke rudely when he appeared before them at headquarters offering to solve the case. He claimed he would solve the mystery using his paranormal powers, which he said were substantial. This was too much for the beleaguered police, who threw him bodily into the street. The paper gave his name as Lees. I tried to search for the poor physic in the area around the police station, but I assumed he left town after the papers labeled him a "fool and a lunatic." I was probably the only person in town who did not consider him crazy.

I was not sure what had become of Mawken. Writing another letter was out of the question. It was too risky. One innocent slip would lead the police right to me – or worse, would reveal my treachery. Besides, any such message would no doubt be cast aside along with the others as a hoax – unless I offered up some evidence.

The newspapers said the "Ripper" had been quiet for some time now, and probably had moved on to other killing grounds. Other killings that occurred throughout the region were not similar to the methods used by Jack. The press, supported by opinions of the police and medical authorities, wrote several men or groups of men copying the murders and blaming them on Jack as a way to cover their own crimes. I read each of these with great interest, and I tended to agree they were imposters.

London became obsessed with the Ripper. It was the topic of the day on every corner and in every bar. Not a day went by without some "news" of the Ripper or new suspicions of who he might be, inspired by each new arrest. Each day, the newspapers sold more copies because of the dramatic coverage of his exploits. The government used the murders as justification to dislodge even more people into the streets from the crime-infested rookeries – increasing the crowding, poverty, and the crimes they sought to reduce. The police were overwhelmed by the reports, false sightings, confessions, and violent protests from the homeless buggers who infested the slums, which the police considered beneath their concern.

There was only one group who truly wanted the murders to stop – the Whitechapel Vigilance Committee. I decided to seek out their leader, Mr. Lusk. If I could gain his confidence and he could see I was not one of the local lunatics, he might listen to me or at least share some information. I found him in his office off Brick Street.

Mr. Lusk was a middle-aged man with a drooping mustache. He was a professional builder who represented local businessmen being hurt by the outbreak of these crimes. He wore a neat suit with a long coat. He looked up from his desk as I entered his office.

"What are you about here, mate? Come to volunteer for the patrols? See the gentleman at the desk up front. He'll get you squared away, right smart."

"I'm sorry, sir. There was no one at the desk in the front office. So I came back here to you. I hope I'm not intruding too awfully bad."

"Nonsense. Nonsense. Have a seat – here by the desk," he said, pointing to a comfortable side chair. "I'm just finishing this appeal to the police for a reward in this bloody ripper case – one of over a dozen I have written in the past few weeks – all to no avail I might add. I want to finish it before the post arrives, if I may…"

"Certainly. Please finish – I shall wait."

Once he finished his memorandum, he stood and extended his hand as we exchanged greetings. Formalities completed, he motioned me to sit again. "How, then, may I help you, sir?"

"I've come about these terrible killings. I think I might be able to help."

"How so?" he asked, eyebrows arched in anticipation.

"Well, I'm not sure. I need a little more information to help me confirm my opinion before I would reveal what I think."

He exploded with a grand laugh that shook his entire body. "How refreshing," said Mr. Lusk. "You don't know how many people come in here with harebrained ideas, so sure they have the only possible answer. They take so much precious time away from our efforts, but we cannot afford to ignore even one of them. One of them might even be old Jack himself. Wouldn't that be something?"

I agreed it certainly would, as I shivered at the thought.

"How can I be of assistance?" he kindly offered. Apparently, I had gotten off to a good start as he did not consider me harebrained.

I turned in my seat as a man suddenly rushed into the room, his pistol drawn and pointing directly at me! Mr. Lusk quickly waved him off.

"There! There! Mr. Bachelor. This chap is all right. He's come to help us."

Mr. Bachelor put his pistol back into his coat. "Sorry, sir," he said backing away. "I didn't know who this man was. He came in while I was distracted for a moment. It's those bloody threatening letters we've been getting in the post – I feared you might be in danger."

"Not in the least, Mr. Bachelor; but thank you for leaping to my aid as it were. Please join us. We were just discussing how this gentleman might help."

"I would, Mr. Lusk, but the postman is coming down the street just now. I heard his bell."

Mr. Lusk extended the letter. "Excellent! Then here, give him this."

Mr. Bachelor took the letter and returned to the outer office to wait for the postman. Mr. Lusk directed his attention back to me.

"Nervous chap, but quite effective. We've had to hire him as a private detective. We've so many clues and leads to explore, it is quite more than one man can handle. He also serves, as you well observed, as protection for the staff and me. We've gotten a few warnings lately. He's quite the chap for it too, I might add."

I agreed he was, for he certainly frightened me. I made a mental note: here was a man more than adequate to confront Mawken if necessary. Perhaps I could gain his assistance if it came to that. Before we could continue our conversation, Mr. Bachelor returned to the office.

"Package for you, sir, along with a letter."

He placed a package wrapped in butcher paper and tied with string, upon Mr. Lusk's desk. Mr. Lusk rose and carefully sliced through the strings. He gingerly opened the flaps on the box and peered inside. With a gasp and a loud curse, Mr. Lusk recoiled into his chair and nearly toppled over backwards.

Immediately, Mr. Bachelor and I rushed to help Mr. Lusk who, with shaking hands, wordlessly pointed to the box. Mr. Bachelor reached inside and withdrew a glass container filled with some sort of yellow liquid. Floating inside the jar was half of a human kidney.

I watched in horror, as the gory organ lay half-suspended in the yellow-tinted, oily liquid. A ragged tear along one side showed the kidney was ripped in two, much as a dog would rip its meat, rather than being neatly sliced. Perhaps it was a cruel joke. Maybe it was just part of a cow's kidney, but who would do such a thing? Who would go to such trouble?

Mr. Lusk's color returned to his face, as Mr. Bachelor dampened a towel from the side table and offered it to him. Gratefully, Mr. Lusk wiped his face, as he slumped in his chair. While he recovered from the shock, Mr. Bachelor and I examined the glass jar closely.

We forgot the letter, which had tumbled to the floor in the confusion. Mr. Lusk reached down and picked it up. Nothing remarkable was on the outside. With trembling fingers, Mr. Lusk handed it over to Mr. Bachelor to read.

"I've had fright enough for one day. Maybe you had better read this."

Mr. Bachelor unfolded the letter and read aloud.

"*From hell,*" Mr. Bachelor read, giving us an exasperated look as he resumed reading. "*Mr. Lusk...*" Mr. Bachelor paused again.

"He addresses me directly?"

"Yes, sir. Here is what else he says: 'Sor', I am supposing that means "sir." Poor penmanship and no punctuation, I might add. He says, 'Sor'," Mr. Bachelor read the letter phonetically, and did not stop until he reached the end of the message.

> "*I send you half the Kidne I took from one woman*
> *prasarved it for you*
> *T other piece I fried and ate*

It was very nise
I may send you the bloody knif that took it out if you only
wate a whil longer
Signed
Catch me when you can Misther Lusk"

Mr. Lusk sat shaking his head no, in shock and disbelief. "Monster! He must be a living monster! He ate it! He must be stopped!" Mr. Lusk babbled.

Mr. Bachelor stretched the letter out toward Mr. Lusk, who was too overwhelmed to take it. I took the letter, intending into pass it on when I saw the unmistakable handwriting. He changed his grammar and punctuation, but he could not change his script. I was positive beyond a doubt the letter was written by Mawken. Even more frightening to me, he wrote it in red ink, copying my "Dear Boss" letter. Is he trying to give me a message he is aware of my treachery?

By now, Mr. Lusk was beside himself with fear. Mr. Bachelor was trying to revive him. Once Mr. Lusk had sufficiently recovered, I excused myself as quickly as I could, with an invitation to return once things settled down a bit.

It was growing late in the day when I returned to my room on Buck's Row. The usual crowd was sitting around on the stairs as I wound my way through them to my door. I saw something white laying beneath the brick and bent to retrieve it. It was a note written in red ink.

"13 Miller's Court   Spitalfields   half past 8 a.m."

It was his hand. For whatever reason, Mawken wanted me at that address the next morning. I turned to confront the step-sitters.

"Who has been here?" I demanded.

"No one," was the universal answer from several. They had been sitting on the stoop all day, and no one had gone up those stairs. Was it possible I had not noticed the note when I left earlier? I was so focused on getting to Mr. Lusk I could not remember checking the brick. Maybe the note was left overnight.

I intended to be at 13 Miller's Court at the appointed time – armed, of course. What else should I do? I considered going to the police with this note, but I still had the problem of trying to convince them the note was authentic. There were so many fraudulent claims going around; they would no doubt count me off as another nut case. I could go back to Mr. Lusk, but he was in such a state I did not think he could stand another shock in the same day.

I waited up all night, nerves on edge, not knowing what to expect. Many things whirled through my mind. Would he appear in the street below? Would he come into my room? Why did Mawken want me to go there? Would he be waiting for me when I left the next morning? Did he intentionally arrange for the box to be delivered while I was with Mr. Lusk? How could that be possible? How could he have known? It was all so confusing to me. As much as I tried, I could not figure it out. The only thing I knew was he wanted me at 33 Miller's Court, Spitalfields, at half past eight the next morning.

Daylight! It would be daylight. I felt a little better when the thought occurred to me – Mawken never killed in the daylight – he always struck at night. At that time of day, the streets would be flooded with sunlight. What was he trying to tell me or get me to do? Was this the address of the psychic he had told me about – the woman who could help me? It seemed reasonable he had given me the address of the paranormal woman who was going to cure me. But, why would he leave a note? Why not just come up and tell me? I did not know, unless he came while I was gone. Nevertheless, I resolved to have the gun with me when I went. I left the marlinspike beneath my pillow. I was resolved to stop this murderous binge once and for all. Mawken may not kill in broad daylight, but I certainly could. I imagined myself the hero of London when this madman was at last eliminated. Everyone would thank me for having the courage to stop Mawken – the infamous Jack the Ripper.

During another sleepless night, I watched the street below and listened intently for footsteps on the stairs until it was time to leave. I was glad to be greeted by a warm sunny morning. The streets dripped from the nightly fog and morning dew, as I found Miller's Court. There were few numbers on the street, but I found the place where I thought the address must be. I found no doorway marked 33.

Miller's Court was the absolute worst rookery in the city. It was so bad policeman would not enter it alone for fear of their own safety. Thugs and villains hung out on every corner, watching people hurry past, and plotting who knows what manner of meanness. Not finding #33, I decided to ask around; but when I approached people on the street, they would hurry by or go inside without even acknowledging me.

A woman sat on the curbing crying into her hands. She looked decent enough, not like the loose women who normally plied the streets. She was quite young with black hair and fair features. As she looked up at me, her deep blue eyes streamed with tears. My heart moved, and I felt so sorry for her.

"Madam, are you injured?" I inquired.

"Deeper than you know, sir. Much deeper," she said, weeping.

"Might I assist you in some way?"

"I'm beyond help, sir. No one can help me now. All is lost." She burst out in renewed tears.

Not knowing what else to do, I sat next to her on the curb. She cried so profusely she could not talk. The only thing I could do was offer her some comfort, so I sat with my arm lightly across her shoulders as she cried out her woes.

She had no money, of course. What she did have was a son whom she could not bear seeing go without food, because she did not have the means to care for him. It was a common tale often told in an attempt to pry money for charitable souls, but this time, it rang true. She had not even looked at me without tears in her eyes. She told her sad story, and my heart suffered for her. She had been left penniless by the death of her husband. She had not eaten in two days, yielding what food she could manage to her son. She could not see any way out. She had been abused, molested, and had even sold herself for money until now no man would have her for a wife. She would rather die than see her son starve to death.

She told me she was going to her room to hang herself. Life was not worth living any longer; and at least in death, she would be freed from her misery and the knowledge she could not save her young child.

I pleaded with her not to do it. She was young. Surely, she could find some way to support herself. I suggested a trade, like sewing or laundry, to make money. She was so distraught she could not think of a place to engage in such enterprise. She had no hope.

I had heard this and similar stories so many times I thought I was properly steeled against such appeals, but, I realized I had come to her; she w not buttonholed me as so many do. Something about her story rang true and sincere. Despite my resolve to not be used in that fashion, I could not resist the urge to help this poor woman. I dug into my pocket and withdrew a pound note.

"Would this help?" I offered.

She looked at me with such a strange look in her eyes.

332

"What do'ya want? Why would you help me? I suppose you want what all the others want – except you are paying far too much for it. You could have it for tanner, ya know. Why not? One more toss before I stick me neck in the noose. It's all anyone's ever wanted from me, anyway." She turned sarcastic and seemed angry and upset I would attempt to take advantage of her in this hour of her great need.

"No, madam. I want nothing from you," I assured her.

"Nothing, then?" She brightened a little. "What're you a minister, or an angel? "Why would you give me a pound without anything in return?"

"Because I can, and because I think it will make a difference for you – maybe deter you from this plan to hang yourself. It would be enough to feed you and your boy for a fortnight."

"And, pay the rent too!" she added as she wiped her eyes on her apron.

I placed the note in her palm and helped her to her feet. Standing up, I could see the wear on her body, her once beautiful hair faded white around her temples, and the strain of misery on her face. However she smiled through her pain as she looked at the money in wonder.

"I … I don't know how to thank you," she stammered. "It has been so long since I received a kindness. I'm afraid I've forgotten how to be grateful."

I accompanied her to her room a few steps away and left her alone in her doorway. A shopkeeper next door, who had watched the entire scene unfold in front of his doorway, snickered as I passed.

"Last time you'll see that quid, mate. She'll be drunk again within the hour. You should 'ave got the prize before you left." He taunted me for my foolishness.

"Perhaps so," I agreed, "but at least she'll be alive."

Not seeing anyone that looked like Mawken around, I walked up and down the neighborhood streets before leaving. Why did Mawken summon me here to this place? Why did he not make his presence known to me? Had he seen me with the woman and turned away, fearing he might be recognized? I did not know.

It was a little after nine, so I walked several blocks to Brick Street and walked past Mr. Lusk's office. I was told by a woman in the front office that he had not arrived yet. She told me Mr. Lusk was quite ill and may not come that morning. I could check back around in the afternoon. Mr. Bachelor was likewise not available.

Arriving at my room, my mind kept turning back to this poor woman. I was tired after having no sleep the night before, so I lay down on my bed and napped for an hour. When I awoke, I was astounded to find my basin half filled with water – pink, bloody water. Mawken had been here in my absence! I hurriedly checked beneath the brick but found nothing more there.

I recalled how the poor woman looked so destitute and forlorn, even as she held my pound note in her frail hands. I recalled how the wind blew her fine black hair across her blue eyes. How she waved at me as I left her there. I remembered how the shopkeeper had sneered at me for my foolishness. He had stood with his hand against the stone wall as he watched me pass. In my mind's eye, I could see his left hand resting beneath a white 33 someone had chalked on the wall.

She lived at 33 Miller's Court! The address I had been given was her apartment!

I hurried back to her street as fast as I could run. When I rounded the corner on Miller's Court, I could see all hell had broken loose. I saw Bobbies and lines of people stretched all up and down

334

the street. There was total chaos on the block. I made my way through the mob and approached the nearest policeman.

"What has happened?" I asked.

"Another poor wretch has been killed," he responded. "Poor woman's been sliced up pretty badly. It looks like the 'Ripper' has struck in broad daylight – or at least someone who works like him."

Just then a woman pointed me out to another policeman.

"That's him! That's the man I saw her with last! That's the man that killed Mary Kelly!"

The entire street erupted into loud shouts and rough pushing of people trying to get closer to see the villainous "Jack the Ripper". The Bobbies at the scene immediately seized me. I was spirited away in a coach to separate me from the angry and curious crowd outside 33 Miller's Court. Half of them wanted to lynch me on the spot, and the other half wanted to just see or touch me.

The police were polite but firm. They even apologized for the inconvenience as they assisted me into the coach. There were several photo flashes as the coach pulled away from the curb, and several of the spectators ran alongside to see where they were taking me. We soon outran them. I was taken to a smallish ground floor room a few blocks away.

We entered a single room furnished with a large table, a couple of desks, a bookshelf, and a large wooden locker. It was some sort of police waystation. It was heavily used, as evidenced by several pairs of caked mud boots standing in the corner, and the slickers hanging from hooks behind the door. The floor was not swept, and piles of reports and folders were stacked on the desk.

Once again, they searched me, with apologies. Of course, the first thing they found was the gun. I was glad I left the marlinspike beneath my pillow. After checking to see if it was loaded, the officer placed it on the table with the rest of my property. I did not have much: the note, my pistol, a room key, an old watch, a locket, and a few coins.

A man, addressed as "Sergeant" came into the room from the street outside. The others stood back as he stood in front of me, eyeing me up and down. He had not spoken to me yet, so I kept my silence. He was tall with a grand mustache and sweeping sideburns.

He addressed the other policemen in the room. "What'is name?"

"Maurice, Sergeant."

The Sergeant scratched his chin and mumbled my name a time or two under his breath as he continued to inspect me.

"What's 'e got?"

He listened as the nearest policeman reported my inventory.

"No knife?" The Sergeant asked.

"No, sir. Only a pistol, there on the table," the officer pointed.

The Sergeant picked up my gun and checked to see if it was loaded. He sniffed the barrel and looked inside. He tossed it back on the table.

"It ain't been fired in some time, has it? Nothin' else?"

"No, Sergeant."

The Sergeant moved back toward the door. "Strip 'em," he ordered as he exited back onto the street.

The policemen were polite as they carefully folded my clothes and placed them on the table beside my other things. By the time the Sergeant returned, every inch of my body had been inspected.

"Anything?" He asked.

"No, sir. Not a speck," my inspector reported.

Finally, the Sergeant looked at me. "Get dressed and sit down over there," he pointed at a chair by the desk.

After I got dressed, I sat in the chair beside his desk. He was reading a file and did not acknowledge me in the slightest. I could sense he was watching me very closely while pretending to read. Finally, he closed the file and looked at me for a long moment. He did not speak; he just looked me right in the eyes.

"Maurice, is that right?" He broke the overly long silence.

"Yes. That is me."

"Do you know this woman – this …" he checked his notes, "…this Mary Jane Kelly?"

"Is that the poor woman who was murdered?"

"Yes. Mary Jane Kelly." He kept his eyes locked on mine.

"Yes, I know her but not by her name. I do not think she ever told me her name."

"They usually don't," another policeman chortled, drawing the icy stare of the Sergeant.

"Were'ya in 'er presence this mornin' a'fore eight o'clock?"

"She was sitting on the curbing this morning at that time, crying. She was distraught and did not know which way to turn, except to hang herself, because she was poor."

"Lots'a people are poor," he commented almost as soon as the words were out of my mouth.

"Indeed, sir. But she had a small boy about who was starving. It was breaking her heart to see him suffer so, and the pain was such that she would rather be dead."

"Did you help 'er out in that?"

"I did, sir. Precisely so."

"Ya 'elped 'er out by killin' 'er?" He asked, open-eyed.

338

"Killing her? No, sir! I gave her some money – a pound."

"Ya want me to b'live you gave a floozy you barely know a whole pound note? What're you, a vicar?'

"No, sir – Yes, sir. I gave her money to help her. It seemed to me that she was going to do away with herself; what would happen to the child, then?"

"What'd she give you in return?"

"Nothing. I wanted nothing."

"Why wuz you in the neighborhood t'begin with?"

"I was summoned, sir. The note is there," I pointed. "There among my things."

He tilted his chin at a nearby officer who brought the note to him. He unfolded the paper and read the words inside.

"You were left this? By who?" The Sergeant asked.

"I do not know, sir. It was left on my door late last night. Nothing else was written but the address and the time. I went there as it instructed but could not find the address."

"You were sittin' right in front of it when you was with 'er," he accused me. More chuckles came from the back of the room. "How could'ya not know?"

"I didn't realize it at the time, sir. I am not familiar with that street. It was only when I looked at the note again later that I remembered the chalk marks on the wall by the shopkeeper."

He rose from his chair and walked back and forth for a while before returning to his desk.

"Here is what we know, young Maurice. A woman, Mary Kelly, 'us murdered this mornin'. The madman nearly sliced 'er in half and disemboweled 'er. There'us blood and guts all over the room: on the walls, the floor, and even the ceiling. You were the last person she was seen with; we've a witness that identified you'us bein' with 'er. You don't deny it. Yet, ya' have no knife and no blood anywhere on yer body. How is that?'

"Because I am not the one who killed her, sir."

The Sergeant placed his head in his hands and rubbed up and down. "Wus 'is clothes damp?" He asked the men who searched me earlier.

"No, sir, an' 'e ain't 'ad no bath, if that's what yer thinkin', sir. Them's the same togs he was wearin' this mornin' accordin' to tha witnesses."

"It's been two 'ours – 'e had time to change."

The door burst open as another policeman escorted another person into the room. It was the shopkeeper I saw this morning.

"What's this?" Sergeant asked.

The new man pointed directly at me, "'At's 'im, guvnor. That's the bloke I saw her with this mornin'."

"Sergeant, this man says she was still alive when this'un left 'er," he pointed at me. "Says 'e left and din't come back until after the killin'."

"Is that right?" Sergeant asked the shopkeeper.

The shopkeeper looked at me again and nodded, "No, sir. This bloke left before she'us killed. I seen 'im give 'er some money, but he din't even gets nothin' for it."

340

"Did anyone else come to see 'er?" Sergeant asked.

"No, she went in 'er room, and that's the last she wus seen."

"What about 'er kid?" Sergeant asked.

"He ain't been there'a week, Sergeant," the shopkeeper said. "Mary'us about half daft; she was. Imagines 'e's still a young lad – she fretted 'bout 'im all the time, even though 'e'us already out on 'is own, 'e was; an' 'e ain't been around fer days, Sergeant."

The Sergeant looked back and forth between the shopkeeper and me.

"D'ya know this man? Ever seen 'im before?" he asked the shopkeeper.

"No, sir! I ain't seen 'im 'til this mornin'. I wouldn't know 'im from Adam."

The sergeant turned and slapped his folder onto his desk in disgust. "Turn 'em loose," he told the policeman. Then to me, he said, "Well, Maurice. You got lucky on this'un, I wager." He pointed to the door. "You can take yer things and go. We know where'ta find ya if we need anythin'."

I hurriedly gathered my belongings and left as they continued to question the shopkeeper. I could not believe my luck. Had it not been for the shopkeeper, I would have been arrested for murder. I watched behind me as I walked. I was not so stupid as to think the police were not following me. They may have let me go, but that did not mean they thought I was innocent. I was being watched – I could sense it. I could see people on the street huddle and point at me as I passed. I could hear their whispers, "There goes the fiend who killed Mary Kelley!"

I took a paper to my room, and the more I read the more disgusted I became. The paper reported the killer sliced Mary Kelly's throat open and removed most of her intestines. They were spread about the room as if flung from her body. Her breasts were cut off, and parts of her body were missing.

It was clear to me I had been set up. Mawken lured me to the exact spot where he planned to kill his next victim. He was probably waiting inside her room for her as we sat on the curb. He was probably laughing at me as I handed her the money. Mawken *wanted* me to be arrested for her murder.

I remembered the bloody water in my room and tossed the newspaper aside as I went through the curtain. In my absence, everything had been cleaned, and the pitcher was refilled with fresh clean water. I hurriedly opened the drawer and found the bloody towel I saved was gone.

He was here now! Panic swept over me in a hot rush. I looked all about the room. I knew Mawken was in with me, although I could not see him.

"I am not seen if I do not wish to be seen."

I expected to be attacked and killed at any moment. I could feel him nearby, and I could almost hear his cruel laugh. I pulled the gun from my pocket and crouched in the corner behind my bed. I sat and wept in fear. I do not know how long I sat in dread and agony.

Nothing happened. No one came. Slowly, I rose from the floor and went to my front door. The brick had been moved slightly, and something fluttered in the breeze, protruding from beneath the brick.

I lifted the brick and found a note: *"Tonight at midnight. Here."*

It was pinned to a bloody pound note.

It was plain to me now. All of it made sense. All this time Mawken was using me. My purpose was to be the sacrifice. He did not intend to kill me; he would not dare harm a hair on my head. I was too valuable to him alive. I was his escape plan. He intended to keep me around to be a sacrifice, like a fatted sow, to be offered up when the time was right.

He never cared for me in the least – he only pretended to protect me. Everything happened because of Mawken. In the beginning, when we were kids, he may have had some fondness for me. Long ago, in school when my mates would annoy me, I remembered how they would mysteriously be injured. That was Mawken.

What had I ever done for him to treat me so? I had only tried to help him – to help improve his life. I knew he was jealous of me. I had all of the comforts he lacked in his wooded hermitage, where he hid from the cruelty of his savage father and drunken mother.

All of this time, everything he did put me in the position to be blamed should anything go wrong. Everything pointed to this. The evil was not in me – it was in him.

What set off this irrational rage toward me? Was it his fury at the savage pirates who murdered his parents?

No – I had not seen any pirates. There were no pirates. He killed his parents himself. In his mind, he feared I was going to leave him. It was true. I *was* going to abandon him. He became a weight to me – an anchor, tying me to a place where I no longer wanted to be. When I went to Rangoon for my father's business, I fully intended to leave Mawken behind. In his insane mind, that was unacceptable.

If there were no pirates, then he killed my mother and father. He murdered them to keep me for himself. He gave me my parent's bloody jewelry so in case we were caught, I would be blamed for their deaths. He killed Sofi with the bloody ax that held my gory palm print on the handle – soaked in Sofi's blood. The captain and Sticks were both killed to throw suspicion toward me.

In my head, I tried to count how many people had died because of his murderous malevolent mind. I may never know the final tally. It made me ill to think how I had been used – how blind I was. Did he think I was so needful, so piteous, that I would allow him to use me this way? Once he tasted blood, he began to crave it – could not refuse it. I set this in motion when I rejected him. When I exiled him from my life in disgust at his perversions, he had to eliminate anyone that came close to me.

Poor Donny – and poor Mollie, they never knew how poisonous my friendship was to them.

All of those innocent women in Austin – and those women here in Whitechapel who crossed his path fed his lust for blood. Mawken killed them all. With each woman he butchered, he found a way to drive me closer to the blame. Now that I had been apprehended and questioned by the police, they would easily be convinced of my guilt. It is only a matter of time before they come to arrest me. When that happens, he will have won.

I knew he would continue killing until he was stopped. His madness was such that he could not help himself. He was unable to see the damage he was causing to innocent lives. Even if he were caught, he would simply accuse me. All the evidence pointed directly at me. He made sure of that. Even if I could prove my innocence, he would be free to continue his quest for the raw blood that slaked his thirst only temporarily. He would not stop. He could not stop. There was no way out for me – except one. The solution rested here in my hand in the form of a loaded weapon. The cold steel of the gun warms to my touch. The handle fits comfortably in the curve of my palm.

He is coming at midnight, so I listen intently for his arrival. He will climb the stairs and walk confidently into my room, and I will pull the trigger before he has a chance to rush me. I must do it quickly. I must not hesitate. I must not give him the chance to dissuade me. The police will think I killed an intruder, and it will all be over. It is the only way out – for Mawken and for me.

There! Yes, it is near midnight. I can hear him on the stairs slowly climbing to my door. It is Mawken.

I stand and fumble for the revolver as he enters the doorway. My hands tremble as he appears in the dim yellow light. Why does it end this way? There is no other way – no other way out.

Mawken closed the door and turned around before seeing me standing in the shadows with my gun pointed directly at him.

He laughs as if amused. I did not expect that. It angers me, and now I want more – more than just his life. I want an apology. I want a confession before I take his life. I want revenge –payment for what he has done to me.

"Ha!" he laughs again. That cruel laugh shrinks me. "What do you plan to do with that?" he mocks me. "You cannot kill me. You do not have it in you to kill. You are a weak, useless, pitiful excuse for a man."

He moved to the table by the window and removes the knife from his belt. He brandishes it at me and laughs as I shrink back from it in fear. I see the carved handle and the glint of light reflecting from the cold steel. Slowly, deliberately, he lays the shiny blade on the table beneath the lamp in the flickering light.

"See? I am not armed; and still, you cannot shoot. You are pathetic. Go ahead! Shoot. Do what you planned, you spineless weakling." He is taunting me – wanting me to shoot. He wants to die.

He spreads his arms wide and exposes his chest to me. I freeze under his brazen accusations, his lack of fear, and his total contempt for me. He sneers at me as my hand trembles; and the gun slowly lowers to my side, as if on its own.

"No, I am not like you. I do not take life so lightly. I only want to know why. Why?" I plead.

"Because you are weak," he snorts. "That is why I had to do all the heavy work all these years – because you did not have the stomach for it. Put the gun down, Maurice, I need some sleep."

I raise the weapon again and aim it at him. "Not this time."

He steps toward me and reaches to take my pistol from my hand. I hurriedly cock the trigger and place the shaking barrel against his forehead.

He stands still and looks at me with those terrible dark eyes – those mocking eyes that make me feel so insignificant. Then he laughs that cruel way that says how pathetic and weak I am. I cannot take his laugh any longer.

"You bastard!" I scream in his face. "You forced me to watch those women be killed. Why? All because you could not have me?" I accused.

He does not move nor does he respond to my indictment. He stands with my gun pressed to his forehead and waits for me to end his life.

"You forced me to watch, all the while shifting the blame to me to protect yourself. You filled my head with gory details I could not possibly have known on my own. You used me. You said you loved me, but you used me in the most horrible ways. You knew I was powerless to do anything to stop you – except this! Why?" I am crying and talking at the same time; but still, he makes no effort to defend himself. Why won't he just take the gun away and kill me?

"Why didn't you just stop?" I plead through my tears. "Why did you have to keep killing and killing and killing?"

Again, I hear that pitiless laugh I hate, the laugh that makes me feel like less a man. Why is he always laughing at me? Why does he hate me so? Slowly his eyes shift to the table beside us where his knife lies. That knife with the handle carved in the shape of a mermaid – there, beneath the mirror.

I press the gun harder against his head. "Don't you try it – you will be dead before you hit the floor," I threaten.

He laughs again at me. I never want to hear that laugh again.

"Go ahead, shoot me. Put me out of my misery. Do you believe that will fix anything? You will still have yourself, Maurice. Every time you look into that mirror, you will see me. Do you think you can go on living, knowing what you know? Look at you! You cannot sleep without dreaming. You have become like me; you cannot think of anything else except killing and blood. You want to murder me to set yourself free, go ahead! Do it!" He is relentless in his criticism.

"You have become just as much a killer as I am! You are a pitiful, sorry excuse for a man! You watched, hiding in safety, as I did what you wished *you* could do. It thrilled you – do not deny it! Go on, look at yourself," he nodded toward the mirror.

I never hated him as much as now. I know his words are the truth. I know what I must do: I must kill myself after I destroy him – the monster.

Keeping my gun pressed tightly to his head, I look over at the table. I stare at the mermaid lying there – the carved smooth handle – the blade so shiny, so clean.

My gaze rises higher to the mirror. I am shocked beyond words at the image reflected back to me. He laughs that gut-wrenching laugh again as I stand helplessly transfixed in the mirror.

"*I am not seen if I do not want to be seen,*" he reminds me.

The image in the mirror reflects the truth. In the reflection, I stand, quivering, holding the gun to *my own head* as the room spins wildly. There is no one here but me.

Am I in Mawken, or is he in me? Maybe there was never any me – there was only …

Him.

The awful realization of the truth floods over me like a bath of hot blood as I close my eyes and squeeze the trigger.

97789269R00197

Made in the USA
San Bernardino, CA
26 November 2018